Knife

Knife

JO NESBØ

Translated from the Norwegian by Neil Smith

RANDOM HOUSE CANADA

PUBLISHED BY RANDOM HOUSE CANADA

Copyright © 2019 Jo Nesbø
English translation copyright © 2019 Neil Smith
Published by arrangement with Salomonsson Agency

www.penguinrandomhouse.ca

Library and Archives Canada Cataloguing in Publication

Title: Knife / Jo Nesbø ; translated from the Norwegian by Neil Smith.
Other titles: Kniv. English
Names: Nesbø, Jo, 1960- author. | Smith, Neil (Neil Andrew), translator.
Series: Nesbø, Jo, 1960- Harry Hole series ; #12.
Description: Series statement: Harry Hole ; 12 | Translation of: Kniv.
Identifiers: Canadiana (print) 2019008961X | Canadiana (ebook)
20190089709 | ISBN 9780735275348 (hardcover) | ISBN 9780735275355
(HTML)
Classification: LCC PT8951.24.E83 K6513 2019 | DDC
839.82/374—dc23

Printed and bound in the USA

10 9 8 7 6 5 4 3 2 1

Part 1

I

A ragged dress was hanging from one branch of a rotting pine tree. It put the old man in mind of a song from his youth, about a dress on a washing line. But this dress wasn't hanging in a southerly breeze like in the song, but in the ice-cold meltwater in a river. It was completely still down at the bottom of the river, and even though it was five o'clock in the afternoon, and it was March, and the sky above the surface of the water was clear, just as the forecast had said, there wasn't a lot of sunlight left after it had been filtered through a layer of ice and four metres of water. Which meant that the pine tree and dress lay in weird, greenish semi-darkness. It was a summer dress, he had concluded, blue with white polka dots. Maybe the dress had once been coloured, he didn't know. It probably depended on how long the dress had been hanging there, snagged on the branch. And now the dress was hanging in a current that never stopped, washing it, stroking it when the river was running slowly, tugging and pulling at it when the river was in full flow, slowly but surely tearing it to pieces. If you looked at it that way, the old man thought, the dress was a bit like him. That dress had once meant something to someone, a girl or woman, to the eyes of another man, or a child's arms. But now, just like him, it was lost, discarded, without any purpose, trapped, constrained, voiceless. It was just a matter of time before the current tore away the last remnants of what it had once been.

"What are you watching?" he heard a voice say from behind the chair he was sitting in. Ignoring the pain in his muscles, he turned his head and looked up. And saw that it was a new customer. The old man was more forgetful than before, but he never forgot the face of someone who had visited Simensen Hunting & Fishing. This customer wasn't after guns or ammunition. With a bit of practice you could tell from the look in their eyes which ones were herbivores, the look you saw in that portion of humanity who had lost the killing instinct, the portion who didn't share the secret shared by the other group: that there's nothing that makes a man feel more alive than putting a bullet in a large, warm-blooded mammal. The old man guessed the customer was after one of the hooks or fishing rods that were hanging on the racks above and below the large television screen on the wall in front of them, or possibly one of the wildlife cameras on the other side of the shop.

"He's looking at the Haglebu River." It was Alf who replied. The old man's son-in-law had come over to them. He stood rocking on his heels with his hands in the deep pockets of the long leather gilet he always wore at work. "We installed an underwater camera there last year with the camera manufacturers. So now we have a twenty-four-hour live stream from just above the salmon ladder round the falls at Norafossen, so we can get a more accurate idea of when the fish start heading upstream."

"Which is when?"

"A few in April and May, but the big rush doesn't start until June. The trout start to spawn before the salmon."

The customer smiled at the old man. "You're pretty early, then? Or have you seen any fish?"

The old man opened his mouth. He had the words in his mind, he hadn't forgotten them. But nothing came out. He closed his mouth again.

"Aphasia," Alf said.

"What?"

"A stroke, he can't talk. Are you after fishing tackle?"

"A wildlife camera," the customer said.

"So you're a hunter?"

"A hunter? No, not at all. I found some droppings outside my cabin up in Sørkedalen that don't look like anything I've seen before, so I took some pictures and put them on Facebook, asking what it was. Got a response from people up in the mountains straight away. Bear. A bear! In the forest just twenty minutes' drive and a three-and-a-half-hour walk from where we are now, right in the centre of the capital of Norway."

"That's fantastic."

"Depends what you mean by 'fantastic.' Like I said, I've got a cabin there. I take my family there. I want someone to shoot it."

"I'm a hunter, so I understand exactly what you mean. But you know, even in Norway, where you don't have to go back very far to a time when we had a *lot* of bears, there have been hardly any fatal bear attacks in the past couple of hundred years."

Eleven, the old man thought. Eleven people since 1800. The last one in 1906. He may have lost the power of speech and movement, but he still had his memory. His mind was still OK. Mostly, anyway. Sometimes he got a bit muddled, and noticed his son-in-law exchange a glance with his daughter Mette, and realised he'd got something wrong. When they first took over the shop he had set up and run for fifty years he had been very useful. But now, since the last stroke, he just sat there. Not that that was so terrible. No, since Olivia died he didn't have many expectations of the rest of his life. Being close to his family was enough, getting a warm meal every day, sitting in his chair in the shop watching a television screen, an endless programme with no sound, where things moved at the same pace as him, where the most dramatic thing that could happen was the first spawning fish making their way up the river.

"On the other hand, that doesn't mean it couldn't happen again." The old man heard Alf's voice. He had gone over to the shelves of wildlife cameras with the customer. "No matter how much it might look like a teddy bear, all carnivores kill. So yes, you should definitely get a camera so you can figure out if it's settled down somewhere near your cabin or if it was just passing through. And now's the time brown bears emerge from hibernation, and they're *starving*. Set up a camera where you found the droppings, or somewhere close to the cabin."

"So the camera's inside that little bird box?"

"The bird box, as you call it, protects the camera from the elements and any animals that get too close. This one's a simple, reasonably priced camera. It's got a Fresnel lens that registers the infrared radiation from the heat animals, humans and everything else give off. When the level deviates from the norm, the camera automatically starts to record."

The old man was half listening to the conversation, but something else had caught his attention. Something that was happening on the television screen. He couldn't see what it was, but the green darkness had taken on a lighter shimmer.

"Recordings are stored on a memory card inside the camera—you can play it back on your PC afterwards."

"Now *that's* fantastic."

"Yes, but you do have to physically go and check the camera to see if it's recorded anything. If you go for this slightly more expensive model, you'll get a text message every time it's recorded anything. Or there's this one, the most advanced model, which still has a memory card but will also send any recordings directly to your phone or email. You can sit inside your cabin and only have to go back to the camera to change the battery every so often."

"What if the bear comes at night?"

"The camera has black-light LEDs as well as white. Invisible light that means the animal doesn't get frightened off."

Light. The old man could see it now. A beam of light coming from upriver, off to the right. It pushed through the green water, found the dress, and for a chilling moment it made him think of a girl coming back to life at last and dancing with joy.

"That's proper science fiction, that is!"

The old man opened his mouth when he saw a spaceship come into the picture. It was lit up from within and was hovering a metre and a half off the riverbed. The current knocked it against a large rock, and, almost in slow motion, it spun round until the light from the front of it swept across the riverbed and for a moment blinded the old man when it hit the camera lens. Then the hovering spaceship was caught by the thick branches of the pine tree and stopped moving. The old man felt his heart thudding in his chest. It was a car. The interior light was on, and he could see that the inside was full of water, almost up to the roof. There was someone in there. Someone half sitting, half standing on the driver's seat as he desperately pressed his head up to the roof, obviously trying to get air. One of the rotten branches holding the car snapped and drifted off in the current.

"You don't get the same clarity and focus as daylight, and it's black and white. But as long as there's no condensation on the lens or anything in the way, you should certainly be able to see your bear."

The old man stamped on the floor in an attempt to attract Alf's attention. The man in the car looked like he was taking a deep breath before ducking under again. His short, bristly hair was swaying, and his cheeks were puffed out. He hit both hands against the side window facing the camera, but the water inside the car leached the force from the blows. The old man had put his hands on the armrests and was trying to get up from his chair, but his muscles wouldn't do what he told them to. He noticed that the middle finger on one of the man's hands was a greyish colour. The man stopped banging and butted the glass with his head. It looked like he was giving up. Another branch snapped and the current tugged and strained to pull the car free, but the pine wasn't ready to let go just yet. The old man stared at the anguished face pressed against the inside of the car window. Bulging blue eyes. A scar in a liver-coloured arc from one corner of his mouth up towards his ear. The old man had managed to get out of his chair and took two unsteady steps towards the shelves of cameras.

"Excuse me," Alf said quietly to the customer. "What is it, Dad?"

The old man gesticulated at the screen behind him.

"Really?" Alf said dubiously, and hurried past the old man towards the screen. "Fish?"

The old man shook his head and turned back to the screen. The car. It was gone. And everything looked the same as before. The riverbed, the dead pine tree, the dress, the green light through the ice. As if nothing had happened. The old man stamped the floor again and pointed at the screen.

"Easy now, Dad," Alf said, giving him a friendly pat on the shoulder. "It *is* very early for spawning, you know." He went back to the customer and the wildlife cameras.

The old man looked at the two men standing with their backs to him, and felt despair and rage wash over him. How was he going to explain what he had just seen? His doctor had told him that when a stroke hits both the front and back parts of the left side of the brain, it wasn't only your speech that was lost, but often the ability to communicate in general, even by writing or through gestures. He tottered back to the chair and sat down again. Looked at the river, which just went on flowing. Imperturbable. Undeterred. Unchanging. And after a couple of minutes he felt his heart start to beat more calmly again. Who knows, maybe it hadn't actually happened after all? Maybe it had just been a glimpse of the next step towards the absolute darkness of old age. Or, in this case, its colourful world of hallucinations. He looked at the dress. For a moment, when he had thought it was lit up by car headlights, it had seemed to him as if Olivia was dancing in it. And behind the windshield, inside the illuminated car, he had glimpsed a face he had seen before. A face he remembered. And the only faces he still remembered were the ones he saw here, in the shop. And he had seen that man in here on two occasions. Those blue eyes, that liver-coloured scar. On both occasions he had bought a wildlife camera. The police had been in asking about him fairly recently. The old man could have told them he was a tall man. And that he had that look in his eyes. The look that said he knew the secret. The look that said he wasn't a herbivore.

2

Svein Finne leaned over the woman and felt her forehead with one hand. It was wet with sweat. The eyes staring up at him were wide with pain. Or fear. Mostly fear, he guessed.

"Are you afraid of me?" he whispered.

She nodded and swallowed. He had always thought her beautiful. When he saw her walk to and from her home, when she was at the gym, when he was sitting on the metro just a few seats away from her, letting her see him. Just so she would know. But he had never seen her look more beautiful than she did right now, lying there helpless, so completely in his power.

"I promise it will be quick, darling," he whispered.

She gulped. So frightened. He wondered if he should kiss her.

"A knife in the stomach," he whispered. "Then it's over."

She screwed her eyes shut, and two glistening tears squeezed through her eyelashes.

Svein Finne laughed quietly. "You knew I'd come. You knew I couldn't let you go. It was a promise, after all."

He ran one finger through the mix of sweat and tears on her cheek. He could see one of her eyes through the big, gaping hole in his hand, in the eagle's wing. The hole was the result of a bullet fired by a policeman, a young officer at the time. They had sentenced Svein Finne to twenty years in prison for eighteen charges of sexual assault, and he hadn't denied the charges in and of themselves, just the description of them as "assault," and the idea that those acts were something that a man like him should be punished for. But the judge and jury evidently believed that Norway's laws were above nature's. Fine, that was their opinion.

Her eye stared at him through the hole.

"Are you ready, darling?"

"Don't call me that," she whimpered. More pleading than commanding. "And stop talking about knives . . ."

Svein Finne sighed. Why were people so frightened of the knife? It was humanity's first tool, they'd had two and a half million years to get used to it, yet some people still didn't appreciate the beauty of what had made it possible for them to descend from the trees. Hunting, shelter, agriculture, food, defense. Just as much as the knife took life, it created it. You couldn't have one without the other. Only those who appreciated that, and accepted the consequences of their humanity, their origins, could love the knife. Fear and love. Again, two sides of the same thing.

Svein Finne looked up. At the knives on the bench beside them, ready for use. Ready to be chosen. The choice of the right knife for the right job was important. These ones were good, purpose-made, top quality. Sure, they lacked what Svein Finne looked for in a knife. Personality. Spirit. Magic. Before that tall young policeman with the short, messy hair had ruined everything, Svein Finne had had a fine collection of twenty-six knives.

The finest of them had been Javanese. Long, thin, asymmetrical, like a curved snake with a handle. Sheer beauty, feminine. Possibly not the most effective to use, but it had the hypnotic qualities of both a snake and a beautiful woman, it made people do exactly what you told them. The most efficient knife in the collection, on the other hand, was a *Rampuri*, the favourite of the Indian mafia. It emanated a sort of chill, as if it were made of ice; it was so ugly that it was mesmerising. The *karambit*, which was shaped like a tiger's claw, combined beauty and efficiency. But it was perhaps a little too calculated, like a whore wearing too much makeup and a dress that was too tight, too low-cut. Svein Finne had never liked it. He preferred them innocent. Virginal. And, ideally, simple. Like his favourite knife in the collection. A Finnish *puukko* knife. It had a worn, brown wooden handle, without any real relation to the blade, which was short with a groove, and the sharp edge curved up to form a point. He had bought the *puukko* in Turku, and two days later he had used it to clarify the situation to a plump eighteen-year-old girl who had been working all alone in a Neste petrol station on the outskirts of Helsinki. Even back then he had—as always when he felt a rush of sexual anticipation—started to stammer slightly. It wasn't a sign that he wasn't in control, but rather the opposite, it was just the dopamine. And confirmation that at the age of almost eighty his urges were undiminished. It had taken him precisely two and a half minutes from the moment he walked through the door—when he pinned her down on the counter, cut her trousers off, inseminated her, took out her ID card, noted Maalin's name and address—until he was out again. Two and a half minutes. How many seconds had the actual insemination taken? Chimpanzees spent an average of eight seconds having intercourse, eight seconds in which both monkeys were defenseless in a world full of predators. A gorilla—who had fewer natural enemies—could stretch out the pleasure to a minute. But a disciplined man in enemy territory often had to sacrifice pleasure for the greater goal: reproduction. So, just as a bank robbery should never take more than four minutes, an act of insemination in a public place should never take more than two and a half minutes. Evolution would prove him right, it was just a matter of time.

But now, here, they were in a safe environment. Besides, there wasn't going to be any insemination. Not that he didn't want to—he did. But this time she was going to be penetrated by a knife instead; there was no point trying to impregnate a woman when there was no chance of it resulting in offspring. So the disciplined man saved his seed.

"I have to be allowed to call you darling, seeing as we're engaged," Svein Finne whispered.

She stared at him with eyes that were black with shock. Black, as if they had already gone out. As if there were no longer any light to shut out.

"Yes, we *are* engaged." He laughed quietly, and pressed his thick lips to hers. He automatically wiped her lips with the sleeve of his flannel shirt so there wouldn't be any traces of saliva. "And this is what I've been promising you . . ." he said, running his hand down between her breasts towards her stomach.

3

Harry woke up. Something was wrong. He knew it wouldn't take long for him to remember what, that these few blessed moments of uncertainty were all he was going to get before reality punched him in the face. He opened his eyes and regretted it at once. It was as if the daylight forcing its way through the filthy, grimy window and lighting up the empty little room carried straight on to a painful spot just behind his eyes. He sought shelter in the darkness behind his eyelids again and realised that he had been dreaming. About Rakel, obviously. And it had started with the same dream he had had so many times before, about that morning many years ago, not long after they had first met. She had been lying with her head on his chest, and he had asked if she was checking to see if what they said was true, that he didn't have a heart. And Rakel had laughed the laugh he loved; he could do the most idiotic things to coax it out of her. Then she had raised her head, looked at him with the warm brown eyes she had inherited from her Austrian mother, and replied that they were right, but that she would give him hers. And she had. And Rakel's heart was so big, it had pumped blood around his body, thawing him out, making him a real human being again. And her husband. And a father to Oleg, the introverted, serious boy that Harry had grown to love as his own son. Harry had been happy. And terrified. Happily unaware of *what* was going to happen, but unhappily aware that *something* was bound to, that he wasn't made to be this happy. And terrified of losing Rakel. Because one half of a heart couldn't beat without the other, he was well aware of that, as was Rakel. So if he couldn't live without her, why had he been running away from her in his dream last night?

He didn't know, couldn't remember, but Rakel had come to claim her half-heart back, had listened out for his already weak heartbeat, found out where he was and rung the doorbell.

Then, at last, the blow that had been coming. Reality.

That he had already lost her.

And not because he had fled from her, but because she had thrown him out.

Harry gasped for air. A sound was boring through his ears, and he realised that the pain wasn't only behind his eyes, but that his whole brain was a source of immense hurt. And that it was that noise that had triggered the dream before he woke up. There really was someone ringing the doorbell. Stupid, painful, irrepressible hope poked its head up.

Without opening his eyes, Harry reached one hand down towards the floor next to the sofa bed, feeling for the whisky bottle. He knocked it over, and realised it was empty from the sound it made as it rolled across the worn parquet floor. He forced his eyes open. Stared at the hand that was dangling above the floor like a greedy claw, at the grey, titanium prosthetic middle finger. The hand was bloody. Shit. He sniffed his fingers and tried to remember what had happened late last night, and if it had involved women. He threw back the covers and glanced down at all 1.92 metres of his lean, naked body. Too little time had passed since he had fallen off the wagon for it to have left any physical trace, but if things followed their usual course, his muscles would start to weaken, week by week, and his already greyish-white skin would turn as white as a sheet, he would turn into a ghost and eventually vanish altogether. Which, of course, was the whole point of drinking—wasn't it?

He pushed himself up into a sitting position. Looked around. He was back where he had been before he became a human being again. Only, one rung further down now. In what could have been an ironic twist of fate, the two-room apartment, all forty square metres of it, that he had borrowed and then gone on to rent from a younger police colleague, lay just one floor below the flat he had lived in before he moved in with Rakel, to her wooden house in Holmenkollen. When he moved into the flat, Harry had bought a sofa bed at IKEA. That, together with the bookcase full of vinyl records behind the sofa, a coffee table, a mirror that was still leaning against the wall, and a wardrobe out in the hall, was the total extent of the furniture. Harry wasn't sure if it was due to a lack of initiative on his part, or if he was trying to convince himself that this was only temporary, that she was going to take him back when she had finished thinking things through.

He wondered if he was going to be sick. Well, that was probably up to him. It was as if his body had got used to the poison after a couple of weeks, had built up a tolerance to the dosage. And demanded that it increase. He stared down at the empty whisky bottle that had come to rest between his feet. Peter Dawson Special. Not that it was particularly good. Jim Beam was good. And it came in square bottles that didn't roll across the floor. But Dawson was cheap, and a thirsty alcoholic with a fixed salary and an empty bank account couldn't afford to be fussy. He looked at the time. Ten to four. He had two hours and ten minutes until the liquor store closed.

He took a deep breath and stood up. His head felt like it was about to burst. He swayed but managed to stay upright. Looked at himself in the mirror. He was a bottom feeder that had been reeled in so quickly that his eyes and innards were trying to get out; so hard that the hook had torn his cheek and left a pink, sickle-shaped scar running from the left side of his mouth up towards his ear. He felt under the covers but couldn't find any underwear, so pulled on the jeans that were lying on the floor and went out into the hall. A dark shape was silhouetted against the patterned glass in the door. It was her, she had come back. But he had thought that the last time the doorbell rang too. And that time it had been a man who said he was from Hafslund Electricity and needed to change the meter and replace it with a modern one that meant they could monitor usage from hour to hour, down to the nearest watt, so all their customers could see exactly what time of day they turned the stove on, or when they switched their reading light off. Harry had explained that he didn't have a stove, and that if he did have one, he wouldn't want anyone to know when he switched it on or off. And with that he had shut the door.

But the silhouette he could see through the glass this time was a woman's. Her height, her outline. How had she got into the stairwell?

He opened the door.

There were two of them. A woman he had never seen before, and a girl who was so short she didn't reach the glass in the door. And when he saw the collection box the girl was holding up in front of him he realised that they must have rung on the door down in the street and one of the neighbours had let them in.

"We're collecting for charity," the woman said. They were both wearing orange vests with the emblem of the Red Cross on top of their coats.

"I thought that was in the autumn," Harry said.

The woman and girl stared at him silently. At first he interpreted this as hostility, as if he had accused them of fraud. Then he realised it was derision, probably because he was half naked and stank of drink at four o'clock in the afternoon. And was evidently entirely unaware of the nationwide, door-to-door charity collection that had been getting loads of TV coverage.

Harry checked to see if he felt any shame. Actually, he did. A little bit. He stuck his hand into the trouser pocket where he usually kept his cash when he was drinking, because he had learned from experience that it wasn't wise to take bank cards with him.

He smiled at the girl, who was staring wide-eyed at his bloody hand as he pushed a folded note into the slot on the sealed collection box. He caught a glimpse of a moustache just before the money disappeared. Edvard Munch's moustache.

"Damn," Harry said, and put his hand back in his pocket. Empty. Like his bank account.

"Sorry?" the woman said.

"I thought it was a two hundred, but I gave you a Munch. A thousand kroner."

"Oh . . ."

"Can I . . . er, have it back?"

The girl and woman looked at him in silence. The girl cautiously lifted the box a little higher so that he could see the plastic seal across the charity logo more clearly.

"I see," Harry whispered. "What about change?"

The woman smiled as though he were trying to be funny, and he smiled back to assure her that she was right, while his brain searched desperately for a solution to the problem. 299 kroner and 90 øre before six o'clock. Or 169.90 for a half-bottle.

"You'll have to console yourself with the fact that the money will go to people who really need it," the woman said, guiding the girl back towards the stairs.

Harry closed the door, went into the kitchen and rinsed the blood off his hand, feeling a sting of pain as he did so. Back in the living room, he looked around and saw that there was a bloody handprint on the duvet cover. He got down on all fours and found his mobile under the sofa. No texts, just three missed calls from last night, one from Bjørn Holm, the forensics officer from Toten, and two from Alexandra from the Forensic Medical Institute lab. She and Harry had become intimately acquainted fairly recently, after he got thrown out, and going by what he knew—and remembered—about her, Alexandra wasn't the sort to use menstruation as grounds to cancel on him. The first night, when she had helped him home and they had both searched his pockets in vain for his keys, she had picked the lock with disconcerting ease and laid him—and herself—down on the sofa bed. And when he had woken up again she was gone, leaving just a note thanking him for services rendered. It could have been her blood.

Harry closed his eyes and tried to focus. The events and chronology of the past few weeks were pretty hazy, but when it came to last night his memory was blank. Completely blank, in fact. He opened his eyes and looked down at his stinging right hand. Three bleeding knuckles, with the skin scraped off and congealed blood around the edges of the wounds. He must have punched someone. And three knuckles meant more than one punch. Then he noticed the blood on his trousers. Too much of it to have come from his knuckles alone. And it was hardly menstrual blood.

Harry pulled the cover off the duvet as he returned the missed call from Bjørn Holm. As it started to ring, he knew that somewhere out there a ringtone in the form of a particular song by Hank Williams had gone off, a song Bjørn was convinced was about a forensics officer like him.

"How's things?" Bjørn asked in his cheery Toten dialect.

"That depends," Harry said, going into the bathroom. "Can you lend me three hundred kroner?"

"It's Sunday, Harry. The liquor store's closed today."

"Sunday?" Harry pulled his trousers off and stuffed both them and the duvet cover into the overflowing washing basket. "Bloody hell."

"Did you want anything else?"

"You were the one who called me, around nine o'clock."

"Yes, but you didn't answer."

"No, looks like my phone's been under the sofa for the past day or so. I was at the Jealousy."

"I thought as much, so I called Øystein and he told me you were there."

"And?"

"So I went over there. You really don't remember any of this?"

"Shit. What happened?"

Harry heard his colleague sigh, and imagined him rolling his slightly protruding eyes, his pale moon of a face framed by a flat cap and the bushiest, reddest beard in Police Headquarters.

"What do you want to know?"

"Only as much as you think I need to know," Harry said as he discovered something in the basket of dirty washing. The neck of a bottle, sticking up from the dirty underpants and T-shirts. He snatched it up. Jim Beam. Empty. Or was it? He unscrewed the top, put it to his lips and tipped his head back.

"OK, the short version," Bjørn said. "When I arrived at the Jealousy Bar at 21:15 you were drunk, and by the time I drove you home at 22:30, you had only spoken coherently about one thing. One single person. Guess who?"

Harry didn't answer, he was squinting cross-eyed at the bottle, following the drop that was trickling down inside it.

"Rakel," Bjørn said. "You passed out in the car and I got you up into your flat, and that was that."

Harry could tell by the speed of the drop that he had plenty of time, and he moved the bottle away from his mouth. "Hm. That was that?"

"That's the short version."

"Did we fight?"

"You and *me*?"

"From the way you stress 'me,' it sounds like I had a fight with someone. Who?"

"The Jealousy's new owner may have taken a bit of a knock."

"A knock? I woke up with three bloody knuckles and blood on my trousers."

"Your first punch hit him on the nose, so there was a lot of blood. But then he ducked and you punched the wall instead. More than once. The wall's probably still got your blood on it."

"But Ringdal didn't fight back?"

"To be honest, you were so fucked that there was no way you were going to hurt anyone, Harry. Øystein and I managed to stop you before you did yourself any more damage."

"Shit. So I'm barred?"

"Oh, Ringdal deserved at least one punch. He'd played the whole of that *White Ladder* album and had just put it on again. Then you started yelling at him for ruining the bar's reputation, which you claimed you, Øystein and Rakel had built up."

"But we had! That bar was a gold mine, Bjørn. He got the whole thing for next to nothing, and I only made one demand. That he should take a stand against all the crap, and only play decent music."

"*Your* music?"

"*Our* music, Bjørn. Yours, mine, Øystein's, Mehmet's . . . Just not . . . just no fucking David Gray!"

"Maybe you should have been more specific . . . Uh-oh, the little lad's started crying, Harry."

"Oh, right, sorry. And thanks. And sorry about last night. Shit, I sound like an idiot. Let's just hang up. Say hi to Katrine."

"She's at work."

The line went dead. And at that moment, in a sudden flash, Harry saw something. It happened so quickly he didn't have time to see what it was, but his heart was suddenly beating so hard that he gasped for breath.

Harry looked at the bottle that he was still holding upside down. The drop had trickled out. He looked down. A brown drop was glinting on a filthy white floor tile.

He sighed. He sank to the floor, naked, feeling the cold tiles under his knees. He stuck his tongue out, took a deep breath and leaned forward, resting his forehead on the floor, as if in prayer.

Harry was striding down Pilestredet. His Dr. Martens boots left a black trail in the thin layer of snow that had fallen overnight. The low spring sun was doing its best to melt it before sinking behind the old four- and five-storey buildings of the city. He listened to the rhythmic scrape of the pavement against the small stones that had caught in the coarse grooves on the soles of his boots as he passed the taller modern buildings on the site of the old Rikshospitalet, where he had been born almost fifty years ago. He looked at the latest street art on the facade of Blitz, the once shabby squat that had been the citadel of punk in Oslo, where Harry had attended obscure gigs in his teens despite never being a punk. He passed the Rex Pub, where he had drunk himself senseless back when it was called something different, when the beer was cheaper, the bouncers more forgiving and it was frequented by the jazz crowd. But he hadn't been one of them either. Or one of the born-again souls talking in tongues in the Pentecostal church on the other side of the street. He passed the Courthouse. How many murderers had he managed to get convicted in there? A lot. Not enough. Because it wasn't the ones you caught that haunted your nightmares, it was the ones who got away, and their victims. Still, he had caught enough to get himself a name, a reputation. For better or worse. The fact that he had been directly or indirectly responsible for the deaths of several colleagues was part of that reputation.

He reached Grønlandsleiret, where, sometime back in the 1970s, mono-ethnic Oslo finally collided with the rest of the world, or the other way round. Restaurants with Arabic names, shops selling imported vegetables and spices from Karachi, Somali women in hijabs going for Sunday walks with pushchairs, their men engaged in lively conversation three steps behind them. But Harry also recognised some of the pubs from back when Oslo still had a white working class and this was their neighbourhood. He passed Grønland Church and carried on towards the glass palace at the top of the park. Before pushing open the heavy metal door with a porthole in it, he turned around. He looked out across Oslo. Ugly and beautiful. Cold and hot. Some days he loved this city, and on others he hated it. But he could never abandon it. He could take a break, get away for a while, sure. But never abandon it for good. Not like she had abandoned him.

The guard let him in and he undid his jacket as he waited in front of the lifts. He felt himself start to sweat anyway. Then the tremble as one of the lift doors in front of him slid open. He realised that it wasn't going to happen today, and turned and took the stairs to the sixth floor.

"Working on a Sunday?" Katrine Bratt said, looking up from her computer as Harry walked into her office unannounced.

"I could say the same about you." Harry sank heavily into the chair in front of her desk.

Their eyes met.

Harry closed his, leaned his head back and stretched out his long legs, which reached all the way to the desk. The desk had come with the job she had taken over from Gunnar Hagen. She had had the walls painted a lighter colour, and the parquet floor had been polished, but apart from that the head of department's office was the same as before. And even if Katrine Bratt was the newly appointed head of Crime Squad as well as a mother now, Harry still saw before him the wild girl who had arrived from the Bergen Police, armed with a plan, emotional baggage, a black fringe and a black leather jacket wrapped round a body that disproved the argument that there were no women in Bergen and that made Harry's colleagues stare at her a little too long. The fact that she only had eyes for Harry had the usual paradoxical explanations. His bad reputation. The fact that he was already taken. And that he had seen her as something more than just a fellow officer.

"I could be mistaken," Harry yawned. "But on the phone it sounded almost as if your little Toten lad was happy on paternity leave."

"He is," Katrine said, tapping at her computer. "How about you? Are you happy with—"

"Marital leave?"

"I was going to ask if you were happy being back in Crime Squad."

Harry opened one eye. "Working on entry-level material?"

Katrine sighed. "It was the best Gunnar and I could get, given the circumstances, Harry. What did you expect?"

Still with one eye closed, Harry surveyed the room as he thought about what he had expected. That Katrine's office would show more of a feminine touch? That they would give Harry the same elbow room he had had before he resigned from his post as a murder detective, started teaching at Police College, married Rakel and tried to live a peaceful, sober life? Of course they couldn't do that. But with Gunnar Hagen's blessing and Bjørn's help, Katrine had literally picked him up from the gutter and given him this as a place to go to, something to think about other than Rakel, a reason not to drink himself to death. The fact that he had agreed to sit and sort out paperwork and go through cold cases merely proved that he had sunk lower than he had believed possible. Still, experience had taught him it was always possible to sink a bit lower. So Harry grunted:

"Can you lend me five hundred kroner?"

"Bloody hell, Harry." Katrine looked at him despairingly. "Is that why you're here? Didn't you have enough yesterday?"

"That's not how it works," Harry said. "Was it you who sent Bjørn out to pick me up?"

"No."

"So how did he find me, then?"

"Everyone knows where you spend your evenings, Harry. Even if plenty of people think it's a bit weird to hang out in the bar you've only just sold."

"They don't usually refuse to serve a former owner."

"Not until yesterday, maybe. According to Bjørn, the last thing the owner said to you was that you're barred for life."

"Really? I don't remember that at all."

"Let me see if I can help you there. You tried to persuade Bjørn to help you report the Jealousy to the police for the music they were playing, and then you wanted him to call Rakel and talk her round. From his phone, seeing as you'd left yours at home and weren't actually sure if she'd answer if she saw it was you calling."

"Bloody hell," Harry said, covering his face with his hands as he massaged his temples.

"I'm not saying this to humiliate you, Harry, just to show you what happens when you drink."

"Thanks a lot." Harry folded his hands over his stomach. He saw that there was a two-hundred-kroner note lying on the edge of the desk in front of him.

"Not enough to get drunk on," Katrine said. "But enough to help you sleep. Because that's what you need. Sleep."

He looked at her. Her gaze had got softer over the years, she was no longer the angry young woman who wanted to take her revenge on the world. Maybe that was thanks to other people, the team in the department, and her nine-month-old son. Sure, that sort of thing could raise awareness and make people gentler. During the vampirist case one and a half years ago, when Rakel had been in hospital and he had fallen off the wagon, Katrine had picked him up and taken him home. She had let him throw up in her otherwise spotless bathroom and granted him a few hours of carefree sleep in the bed she shared with Bjørn.

"No," Harry said. "I don't need sleep, I need a case."

"You've got a case."

"I need the Finne case."

Katrine sighed. "The murders you're referring to aren't called the Finne case, there's nothing to suggest that it's him. And, as I've already told you, I've got the people I need on the case."

"Three murders. Three unsolved murders. And you're telling me you don't need someone who can actually prove what you and I both know—that Finne is the man responsible?"

"You've got your case, Harry. Solve that one, and leave me to run things here."

"My case isn't even a case, it's a domestic murder where the husband has confessed and we've got both a motive and forensic evidence."

"He could suddenly withdraw his confession, so we need a lot more flesh on those bones."

"It's the sort of case you could have given to Wyller or Skarre or one of the juniors. Finne is a sexual predator and serial killer, and I'm the only detective you've got with specialist experience of that type of case, for fuck's sake."

"No, Harry! And that's my final word on the subject."

"But why?"

"Why? Look at yourself! If you were running Crime Squad, would you send a drunk, unstable detective to talk to our already skeptical colleagues in Copenhagen and Stockholm who have pretty much already made up their minds that the same man *isn't* behind the murders in their cities? You see serial killers everywhere because your brain is programmed to see serial killers."

"That may well be true, but it *is* Finne. It's got all the characteristic—"

"Enough! You've got to let go of this obsession, Harry."

"Obsession?"

"Bjørn told me you were babbling about Finne the whole time when you were drinking, saying you have to get him before he gets you."

"When I was *drinking*? Say it like it is: when I was drunk. *Drunk.*" Harry reached for the money and tucked it into his trouser pocket. "Have a good Sunday."

"Where are you going?"

"Somewhere I can properly observe the day of rest."

"You've got stones in your shoes, so pick your feet up properly when you walk across my parquet floor."

Harry hurried down Grønlandsleiret towards Olympen and Pigalle. Not his first choices of watering hole, but they were nearest. There was so little traffic on the main street in Grønland that he was able to cross the road on a red light, checking his mobile at the same time. He wondered if he should return Alexandra's call but decided against it. He didn't have the nerve. He saw from the call log that he had tried to call Rakel six times between six and eight o'clock the previous evening. He shuddered. *Call rejected*, it said. Sometimes technological language could be unnecessarily precise.

As Harry reached the opposite pavement he felt a sudden pain in his chest and his heart started to race, as if it had lost the spring that checked its speed. He had time to think *heart attack*, then it was gone. It wouldn't be the worst way to go. A pain in the chest. Down on his knees. Head hitting the pavement. The End. A few more days of drinking at this rate and it really wouldn't be that unrealistic either. Harry kept walking. He had caught a tiny glimpse. He had seen more now than when it happened earlier that afternoon. But it had slipped away, like a dream once you've woken up.

Harry stopped outside Olympen and looked inside. It had once been one of the roughest bars in Oslo, but had been given such a thorough makeover that Harry hesitated to go in. He checked out the new clientele. A mix of hipsters and smartly dressed couples, as well as families with young children, time-poor but with enough money to shell out for Sunday lunch at a restaurant.

He stuck his hand tentatively into his pocket. Found the two-hundred-kroner note, as well as something else. A key. Not his, but to the scene of the domestic murder. On Borggata in Tøyen. He didn't really know why he'd asked for the key seeing as the case was as good as concluded. But at least he had the scene to himself. Entirely to himself, seeing as the other so-called detective on the case, Truls Berntsen, wasn't going to lift a finger. Truls Berntsen's admittance to Crime Squad owed very little to merit, and a damn sight more to his childhood friendship with Mikael Bellman, one-time Chief of Police and current Minister of Justice. Truls Berntsen was utterly useless, and there was a tacit agreement between Katrine and Truls that he would steer clear of detective work and concentrate on making coffee and other basic office jobs. Which, when it came down to it, meant playing patience and Tetris. The coffee tasted no better than before, but Truls sometimes beat Harry at Tetris now. They made a pretty wretched couple, marooned at the far end of the open-plan office with a one-and-a-half-metre-tall moveable screen separating them.

Harry took another look. There was a free booth next to the families seated just inside the window. The little boy at the table suddenly noticed him, and laughed and pointed. The father, who had his back to Harry, turned round and Harry instinctively took a step back, out into the darkness. And from there he saw his own pale, lined face mirrored in the glass, while at the same time it merged with that of the boy inside. A memory floated up. His grandfather, and him as a boy. The long summer holiday, a family meal in Romsdalen. Him laughing at his grandfather. The worried look on his parents' faces. His grandfather, drunk.

Harry felt the keys again. Borggata. A five- or six-minute walk away.

He got his phone out. Looked at the log. Made a call. Stared at the knuckles of his right hand as he waited. The pain was already fading, so he couldn't have punched very hard. But obviously the virginal nose of a David Gray fan couldn't cope with much before it started to squirt blood.

"Yes, Harry?"

"*Yes, Harry?*"

"I'm in the middle of dinner."

"OK, I'll be quick. Can you come and meet me after dinner?"

"No."

"Wrong answer, try again."

"*Yes?*"

"That's more like it. Borggata 5. Call me when you get there and I'll come down and let you in."

Harry heard a deep sigh from Ståle Aune, his friend of many years' standing and Crime Squad's go-to psychological expert on murder cases. "Does that mean this isn't an invitation to go to a bar where I'll have to pay, and that you're actually sober?"

"Have I *ever* let you pay?" Harry pulled out a packet of Camels.

"You used to pick up the tab, and remember what you'd done. But alcohol is well on its way to eating up your finances as well as your memory. You do know that, don't you?"

"Yes. This is about that domestic murder. With the knife and—"

"Yes, yes, I read about it."

Harry put a cigarette between his lips. "Are you coming?"

He heard another deep sigh. "If it'll keep you away from the bottle for a few hours."

"Great," Harry said, then ended the call and slipped his phone into his jacket pocket. He lit the cigarette. Inhaled deeply. He stood with his back to the restaurant's closed door. He had time to have one beer in there and still be in Borggata in time to meet Aune. The music filtered out. An autotuned declaration of undying love. He held one hand up apologetically towards a car as he lurched out into the road.

The old, working-class facades of Borggata hid newly built flats with bright living rooms, open-plan kitchens, modern bathrooms, and balconies overlooking the inner courtyards. Harry took that as a sign that Tøyen was going to be tarted up as well: rents would go up, the residents moved out, the social status of that part of town adjusted upwards. The immigrants' grocery stores and little cafés would give way to gyms and hipster restaurants.

The psychologist looked uncomfortable as he sat on one of the two flimsy rib-backed chairs Harry had placed in the middle of the pale parquet floor. Harry assumed that was because of the disparity between the chair and Ståle Aune's overweight frame, as well as the fact that his small round glasses were still steamed up after he had reluctantly foregone the lift and walked up the stairs to the third floor with Harry. Or possibly the pool of blood that lay like a congealed, black wax seal between them. One summer holiday when Harry was young, his grandfather had told him that you couldn't eat money. When Harry got to his room he took out the five-kroner coin his grandfather had given him and tried. He remembered the way it had jarred his teeth, the metallic smell and sweet taste. Just like when he licked the blood after cutting himself. Or the smell of crime scenes he would later attend, even if the blood wasn't fresh. The smell of the room they were sitting in now. Money. Blood money.

"A knife," Ståle Aune said, pushing his hands up into his armpits as if he was afraid someone was going to hit them. "There's something about the idea of a knife. Cold steel pushing through skin and into your body. It just freaks me out, as the young folk would say."

Harry didn't reply. He and the Crime Squad Unit had used Aune as a consultant on murder cases for so many years that Harry couldn't actually put his finger on when he had started to think of the psychologist, who was twenty years his senior, as a friend. But he knew Aune well enough to recognise that his pretending not to know that "freak out" was a phrase older than both of them was an affectation. Aune liked to present himself as an old, conservative type, unfettered by the spirit of the times his colleagues chased after so desperately in an effort to appear "relevant." As Aune had once said to the press: *Psychology and religion have one thing in common: to a large extent, they both give people what they want. Out there in the darkness, where the light of science has yet to reach, psychology and religion have free rein. And if they were to stick to what we actually know, there wouldn't be jobs for all these psychologists and priests.*

"So this was where the husband stabbed his wife . . . how many times?"

"Thirteen times," Harry said, looking around. There was a large, framed black-and-white photograph of the Manhattan skyline on the wall facing them. The Chrysler Building in the centre. Probably bought from IKEA. So what? It was a good picture. If it didn't bother you that lots of other people had the same picture, and that some visitors would look down their noses at it, not because it wasn't good, but because it was bought at IKEA, then why not go for it? He had used the same line on Rakel when she said she would have liked a numbered print of a photograph by Torbjørn Rødland—a white stretch limo negotiating a hairpin bend in Hollywood—that cost eighty thousand kroner. Rakel had conceded that Harry was entirely right. He had been so happy that he had bought the stretch limo picture for her. Not that he didn't realise she had tricked him, but because deep down he'd had to admit that it really *was* a much cooler image.

"He was angry," Aune said, undoing the top button of his shirt, where he normally wore a bow tie, usually with a pattern that balanced between serious and amusing, like the blue EU flag with gold stars.

A child started to cry in one of the neighbouring flats.

Harry tapped the ash from his cigarette. "He says he can't remember the details of why he killed her."

"Suppressed memories. They should have let me hypnotise him."

"I didn't know you did that."

"Hypnosis? How do you think I got married?"

"Well, there was no real need here. The forensic evidence shows that she was heading across the living room, away from him, and that he came after her and stabbed her from behind first. The blade penetrated low on her back and hit her kidneys. That probably explains why the neighbours didn't hear any screaming."

"Oh?"

"It's such a painful place to be stabbed that the victim is paralysed, can't even scream, then loses consciousness almost immediately and dies. It also happens to be the favoured method among military professionals for a so-called silent kill."

"Really? What happened to the good old method of sneaking up on someone from behind, putting one hand over their mouth and cutting their throat with the other?"

"Outdated—it was never really that good anyway. It takes too much coordination and precision. You wouldn't believe the number of times soldiers ended up cutting themselves in the hand that was clamped over the victim's mouth."

Aune grimaced. "I'm assuming our husband isn't a former commando or anything like that?"

"The fact that he stabbed her there was probably sheer coincidence. There's nothing to suggest that he intended to conceal the murder."

"Intended? You're saying it was premeditated rather than impulsive?"

Harry nodded slowly. "Their daughter was out jogging. He called the police before she got home so that we were in position outside and were able to stop her before she came in and found her mother."

"Considerate."

"So they say. That he was a considerate man." Harry tapped more ash from his cigarette. It fell onto the pool of dried blood.

"Shouldn't you get an ashtray, Harry?"

"The CSI team are done here, and everything makes sense."

"Yes, but even so."

"You haven't asked about the motive."

"OK. Motive?"

"Classic. The battery in his phone ran out, and he borrowed hers without her knowledge. He saw a text message he thought was suspicious, and checked the thread. The exchange went back six months, and was evidently between her and a lover."

"Did he confront the lover?"

"No, but the report says the phone's been checked, the messages found and the lover contacted. A young man, mid-twenties, twenty-five years younger than her. He's confirmed that they had a relationship."

"Anything else I should know?"

"The husband is a highly educated man with a secure job, no money worries, and had never been in trouble with the police. Family, friends, workmates and neighbours all describe him as friendly and mild-mannered, solidity personified. And, as you said, considerate. 'A man prepared to sacrifice everything for his family,' one of the reports said." Harry drew hard on his cigarette.

"Are you asking me because you don't think the case has been solved?"

Harry let the smoke out through his nostrils. "The case is a no-brainer, the evidence has all been secured, it's impossible to fuck this one up, which is why Katrine has given it to me. And Truls Berntsen." Harry pulled the corners of his mouth into something resembling a smile. The family was well off. But they chose to live in Tøyen, a cheaper part of town with a large migrant population, and bought art from IKEA. Maybe they just liked it here. Harry himself liked Tøyen. And maybe the picture on the wall was the original, now worth a small fortune.

"So you're asking because . . ."

"Because I want to understand," Harry said.

"You want to understand why a man kills his wife because she's been having an affair behind his back?"

"Usually a husband only kills if he thinks other people's opinion of him has been damaged. And when he was questioned, the lover said they had kept the affair strictly secret, and that it was in the process of winding down anyway."

"Maybe she didn't have time to tell her husband that before he stabbed her, then?"

"She did, but he says he didn't believe her, and that she had still betrayed their family."

"There you go. And to a man who has always put his family above everything else, that betrayal would feel even worse. He's a humiliated man, and when that humiliation cuts deeply enough it can make anyone capable of killing."

"Anyone?"

Aune squinted at the bookcases next to the picture of Manhattan. "Fiction."

"Yes, so I saw," Harry said. Aune had a theory that killers didn't read, or, if they did, only non-fiction.

"Have you ever heard of Paul Mattiuzzi?" Aune asked.

"Hmm."

"Psychologist, an expert in violence and murder. He divides murderers into eight main groups. You and I aren't in any of the first seven. But there's room for all of us in the eighth group, which he calls the 'traumatised.' We become murderers as a reaction to a simple but massive assault on our identity. We experience the attack as insulting, literally unbearable. It renders us helpless, impotent, and we would be left without any right to exist, emasculated, if we didn't respond. And obviously being betrayed by your wife can feel like that."

"*Anyone*, though?"

"A traumatised murderer doesn't have defined personality traits like the other seven groups. And it's there—and only there—that you find murderers who read Dickens and Balzac." Aune took a deep breath and tugged at the sleeves of his tweed jacket. "What are you really wondering about, Harry?"

"Really?"

"You know more about murderers than anyone I know. None of what I'm saying about humiliation and categories is new to you."

Harry shrugged. "Maybe I just need to hear someone say it out loud one more time to make me believe it."

"What is it you don't believe?"

Harry scratched his short, stubbornly unruly hair—there were now streaks of grey among the blond. Rakel had said he was starting to look like a hedgehog. "I don't know."

"Maybe it's just your ego, Harry."

"What do you mean?"

"Isn't it obvious? You were given the case after someone else had already solved it. So you want to find something that throws doubt on it. Something that proves Harry Hole can see things no one else has spotted."

"What if I am?" Harry said, studying the glowing tip of his cigarette. "What if I was born with a magnificent talent for detective work and have developed instincts that not even *I'm* capable of analysing?"

"I hope you're joking."

"Barely. I've read the interviews. The husband certainly seemed pretty traumatised from what he said. But then I listened to the recordings." Harry was staring in front of him.

"And?"

"He sounded more frightened than resigned. A confession is a form of resignation. There shouldn't be anything to be frightened of after that."

"Punishment, of course."

"He's already had his punishment. Humiliation. Pain. Seeing his beloved wife dead. Prison is isolation. Calm. Routine. Peace. That can't be anything but a relief. Maybe it's the daughter, him worrying about what's going to happen to her."

"And then there's the fact that he's going to burn in hell."

"He's already there."

Aune sighed. "So, let me repeat, what do you really want?"

"I want you to call Rakel and tell her to take me back."

Ståle Aune's eyes widened.

"*That* was a joke," Harry said. "I've been having palpitations. Anxiety attacks. No, that's not quite right. I've been dreaming . . . something. Something I can't quite see, but it keeps coming back to me."

"Finally, an easy question," Aune said. "Intoxication. Psychology is a science without a lot of solid facts to lean on, but the correlation between the consumption of intoxicants and mental distress is one of the few firm facts. How long has this been going on?"

Harry looked at his watch. "Two and a half hours."

Ståle Aune let out a hollow laugh. "And you wanted to talk to me so you can at least tell yourself that you sought external medical help before you go back to self-medication?"

"It's not the usual stuff," Harry said. "It isn't the ghosts."

"Because they come at night?"

"Yes. And they don't hide. I see them and I recognise them. Victims, dead colleagues. Killers. This was something else."

"Any idea what?"

Harry shook his head. "Someone who's been locked up. He reminded me of . . ." Harry leaned forward and stubbed his cigarette out on the pool of blood.

"Of Svein Finne, 'the Fiancé,'" Aune said.

Harry looked up with one eyebrow raised. "Why do you think that?"

"It's obvious that you think he's out to get you."

"You've spoken to Katrine."

"She's worried about you. She wanted an evaluation."

"And you agreed?"

"I said that as a psychologist I don't have the necessary detachment from you. But that paranoia can also be one aspect of alcohol abuse."

"I'm the one who finally got him locked away, Ståle. He was my first case. He got twenty years for sexual assault and murder."

"You were just doing your job. There's no reason why Finne would take it personally."

"He confessed to the assaults but denied the murder charges, claimed we'd planted evidence. I went to see him in prison the year before last to see if he could help us with the vampirist case, if he knew anything about Valentin Gjertsen. The last thing he did before I left was tell me exactly when he was due to be released, and to ask if my family and I felt safe."

"Did Rakel know about this?"

"Yes. At New Year I found boot prints in the patch of woodland outside the kitchen window, so I set up a camera."

"That could have been anyone, Harry. Someone who just got lost."

"On private property, past a gate and up a steep, icy, fifty-metre driveway?"

"Hang on—didn't you move out at Christmas?"

"More or less." Harry wafted the smoke away.

"But you went back after that, to the patch of trees? Did Rakel know?"

"No, but come on, I haven't turned into a stalker. Rakel was frightened enough as it is, and I just wanted to check that everything was OK. And, as it turns out, it wasn't."

"So she didn't know about the camera either?"

Harry shrugged his shoulders.

"Harry?"

"Hmm?"

"You're *quite* sure that you set that camera up because of Finne?"

"You mean, did I want to find out if my ex was seeing anyone else?"

"Did you?"

"No," Harry said firmly. "If Rakel doesn't want me, she's welcome to try someone else."

"Do you really believe that?"

Harry sighed.

"OK," Aune said. "You said you caught a glimpse of someone who looked like Finne, locked up?"

"No, that's what you said. It wasn't Finne."

"No?"

"No, it was . . . me."

Ståle Aune ran his hand through his thinning hair. "And now you want a diagnosis?"

"Come on. Anxiety?"

"I think your brain is looking for reasons why Rakel would need you. For instance, to protect her from external threats. But you're not locked up, Harry—you've been locked out. Accept it and move on."

"Apart from the 'accept it' stuff, any medication you can prescribe?"

"Sleep. Exercise. And maybe you could try meeting someone who could take your mind off Rakel."

Harry stuck a cigarette in the corner of his mouth and held up his clenched fist with his thumb sticking out. "Sleep. I drink myself senseless every night. Check." His index finger shot up. "Exercise. I get into fights with people in bars I used to own. Check." The grey, titanium finger. "Meet someone. I fuck women, nice ones, nasty ones, and afterwards I have meaningful conversations with some of them. Check."

Aune looked at Harry. Then he let out a deep sigh, stood up and fastened his tweed jacket. "Well, you should be fine, then."

Harry sat there staring out of the window after Aune had gone. Then he got up and walked through the rooms in the flat. The married couple's bedroom was tidy, clean, the bed neatly made. He looked in the cupboards. The wife's wardrobe was spread across four spacious cupboards, while the husband's clothes were squeezed into one. A considerate husband. There were rectangles on the wallpaper in the daughter's room where the colours were brighter. Harry guessed they had been made by teenage posters she had taken down now she was nineteen. There was still one small picture, a young guy with a Rickenbacker electric guitar slung round his neck.

Harry looked through the little collection of records on the shelf by the mirror. Propagandhi. Into It. Over It. My Heart to Joy. Panic! at the Disco. Emo stuff.

So he was surprised when he switched on the record player to listen to the album already on it and heard the gentle, soothing tones of something that sounded like early Byrds. But despite the Roger McGuinn–style twelve-string guitar, he quickly recognised that it was a far more recent production. It didn't matter how many valve amps and old Neumann microphones they used, retro production never fooled anyone. Besides, the vocalist had a distinct Norwegian accent, and you could tell he'd listened to more 1995-vintage Thom Yorke and Radiohead than Gene Clark and David Crosby from 1965. He glanced at the album sleeve lying upside down next to the record player and, sure enough, the names all looked Norwegian. Harry's eyes moved on to a pair of Adidas trainers in front of the wardrobe. They were the same sort as his, he'd tried to buy a new pair a couple of years ago but they had already stopped making them then. He thought back to the interview transcripts, in which both father and daughter had said she left the flat at 20:15 and returned thirty minutes later after a run to the top of the sculpture park in Ekeberg, coming back via the Ekeberg Restaurant. Her running gear was on the bed, and in his mind's eye he could see the police letting the poor girl in and watching as she got changed and packed a bag of clothes. Harry crouched down and picked up the trainers. The leather was soft, the soles clean and shiny, the shoes hadn't been used much at all. Nineteen years. An unused life. His own pair had split. He could buy new ones, obviously, a different type. But he didn't want to, he'd found the only design he wanted from now on. The only design. Maybe they could still be repaired.

Harry went back into the living room. He wiped the cigarette ash from the floor. Checked his phone. No messages. He put his hand in his pocket. Two hundred kroner.

4

"Last orders, then we're closing."

Harry stared down at his drink. He had managed to drag it out. Usually he necked them because it wasn't the taste he liked, but the effect. "Liked" wasn't really the right word, though. *Needed.* No, not *needed* either. *Had to have. Couldn't live without.* Artificial respiration when half your heart had stopped beating.

Those running shoes would just have to be repaired.

He took out his phone again. Harry only had seven people in his contacts, and because they all had names starting with different letters, the list consisted of single letters, not first and last names. He tapped on R and saw her profile picture. That soft, brown gaze that asked to be met. Warm, glowing skin that asked to be stroked. Red lips that asked to be kissed. The women he had got undressed and slept with in the past few months—had there been a single second when he *hadn't* been thinking about Rakel while he was with them, *hadn't* imagined that they were her? Had they realised, had he even told them, that he was being unfaithful to them with his wife even as he fucked them? Had he been that cruel? Almost certainly. Because his half-heart was beating weaker and weaker with each passing day, and he had returned from his temporary life as a real person.

He stared at the phone.

And he thought the same thing he had thought every day as he passed the phone box in Hong Kong so many years ago. That she *was* there. Right then, her and Oleg. Inside the phone. Twelve tapped digits away.

But even that was long after Rakel and Harry met for the first time.

That happened fifteen years ago. Harry had driven up the steep, winding road to her wooden house in Holmenkollen. His car had breathed a sigh of relief when he arrived, and a woman emerged from the house. Harry asked after Sindre Fauke as she locked the front door, and it wasn't until she turned round and came closer that he noticed how pretty she was. Brown hair; pronounced, almost wild eyebrows above brown eyes; high, aristocratic cheekbones. Dressed in a simple, elegant coat. In a voice that was deeper than her appearance suggested, she told him that was her father, that she had inherited the house and he no longer lived there. Rakel Fauke had a confident, relaxed way of speaking, with exaggerated, almost theatrical diction, and she looked him right in the eye. When she walked off, she walked in an absolutely straight line, like a ballet dancer. He had stopped her, asked for help jump-starting his car. Afterwards he gave her a lift. They discovered that they had studied law at the same time. That they had attended the same Raga Rockers concert. He liked the sound of her laughter; it wasn't as deep as her voice, but bright and light, like a trickling stream. She was going to Majorstua.

"It's by no means certain this car's going to make it that far," he had said. And she agreed with him. As if they already had an idea of what hadn't yet begun, what really couldn't happen. When she was about to get out, he had to shove the broken passenger door open for her, breathing in her scent. Only thirty minutes had passed since they'd met, and he wondered what the hell was going on. All he wanted to do was kiss her.

"Maybe see you around," she said.

"Maybe," he replied, then watched as she disappeared down Sporveisgata with a ballerina's steps.

The next time they met was at a party in Police Headquarters. It turned out that Rakel Fauke worked in the foreign section of POT, the Police Surveillance Agency. She was wearing a red dress. They stood talking together, laughing. Then they talked some more. He about his upbringing, his sister Sis who had what she herself described as "a touch of Down's Syndrome," about his mother who died when Harry was young, and that he had had to look after his father. Rakel had told him about studying Russian in the Armed Forces, her time at the Norwegian Embassy in Moscow, and the Russian man she had met, who ended up becoming the father of her son, Oleg. And that when she left Moscow, she had also left her husband, who had alcohol problems. And Harry had told her that he was an alcoholic, something she might already have guessed when she saw him drinking

Coke at a staff party. He didn't mention the fact that his intoxicant that evening was her laughter—clear, spontaneous, bright—and that he was willing to say the most revealing, idiotic things about himself just to hear it. And then, towards the end of the evening, they had danced. Harry had *danced*. To a turgid version of "Let It Be" played on panpipes. That was the proof: he was hopelessly in love.

A few days later he went on a Sunday outing with Oleg and Rakel. At one point, Harry had held Rakel's hand, because it felt natural. After a while she pulled her hand away. And when Oleg was playing Tetris with his mum's new friend, Harry had felt Rakel staring darkly at him and knew what she was thinking. That an alcoholic, possibly similar to the one she had walked away from, was now sitting in her house with her son. And Harry had realised he was going to have to prove himself worthy.

He had done it. Who knows, maybe Rakel and Oleg saved him from drinking himself to death. Obviously things hadn't been one unbroken triumphal march after that, he had fallen flat on his face several times, there had been breaks and separations, but they had always found their way back to each other. Because they had found laughter in each other. Love, with a capital L. Love so exclusive that you should count yourself bloody lucky if you ever get to experience it—and have it reciprocated—just once in your life. And for the past few years they had woken up each morning to a harmony and happiness that was simultaneously so strong and so fragile that it had frightened the life out of him. It made him creep about as if he were walking on thin ice. So why had it cracked anyway? Because he was the man he was, of course. Harry fucking Hole. Or "the demolition man," as Øystein called him.

Could he follow that path again? Drive up the steep, winding, difficult road to Rakel and introduce himself again. Be the man she had never met before. Of course he could try. Yes, he could do that. And now was as good a time as ever. The perfect time, in fact. There were just two problems. Firstly, he didn't have the money for a taxi. But that was easily fixed, it would take him ten minutes to walk home, where his Ford Escort, his third one, was sitting covered in snow in the car park in the backyard.

Secondly, the voice inside him telling him it was a terrible idea.

But that could be stopped. Harry downed his drink. Just like that. He stood up and walked towards the door.

"See you, mate!" the bartender called after him.

Ten minutes later Harry was standing in the backyard on Sofies gate, looking dubiously at the car, which was parked in eternal shadow between the snowboards covering the basement windows. It wasn't as badly covered with snow as he had expected, so he just had to go upstairs, fetch the keys, start it up and put his foot on the gas. He could be at hers in fifteen minutes. Open the front door to the big, open room that served as hall, living room and kitchen, covering most of the ground floor. He would see her standing at the worktop by the window looking out over the terrace. She would give him a wry smile, nod towards the kettle and ask if he still preferred instant coffee over espresso.

Harry gasped at the thought of it. And there it was again, the claw in his chest.

Harry was running. After midnight on a Sunday in Oslo, that meant you had the streets to yourself. His cracked trainers were held together with gaffer tape around the ankles. He was taking the same route the daughter on Borggata had said she had run, according to the report. Along illuminated paths and tracks through the hillside sculpture park—a gift to the city from property tycoon Christian Ringnes, and an homage to women. It was perfectly still, the only sounds were Harry's own breathing and the crunch of the grit beneath his shoes. He ran up to where the park flattened out towards Ekebergsletta, then down again. He stopped at Damien Hirst's *Anatomy of an Angel*, a sculpture in white stone that Rakel had told him was Carrera marble. The graceful, seated figure had made Harry think of the Little Mermaid in Copenhagen, but Rakel—who as usual had read up on what they were going to see—had explained that the inspiration was Alfred Boucher's *L'Hirondelle* from 1920. Maybe, but the difference was that Hirst's angel had been cut open by knives and scalpels so that her innards, muscles, bones and brain were visible. Was that what the sculptor wanted to show, that angels were also people inside? Or that some people are actually angels? Harry tilted his head. He could agree on the latter point. Even after all these years and everything he and Rakel had been through together, and even if he had dissected her as much as she had dissected him, he had found nothing but an angel. Angel and human, all the way through. Her capacity for forgiveness—which had obviously been a precondition for being with someone like Harry—was almost limitless. Almost. But obviously he had managed to find that limit. And then crossed it.

Harry looked at his watch and ran on. Sped up. Felt his heart work harder. He increased his speed a little more. Felt the lactic acid. A bit more. Felt the blood pumping around his body, tugging at the rubbish. Ironing out the past few bad days. Rinsing away the shit. Why did he imagine that running was the opposite of drinking, that it was the antidote, when it merely gave him a different type of rush? But so what? It was a better rush.

He emerged from the forest in front of the Ekeberg Restaurant, the once run-down modernist structure where Harry, Øystein and Tresko had drunk their first beers in their youth, and where the seventeen-year-old Harry was picked up by a woman he remembered as being really old, but who was probably only in her thirties. Either way, she had given him an uncomplicated initiation under her experienced direction, and he probably hadn't been the only one. Occasionally he wondered if the investor who had refurbished the restaurant might have been one of them, and had done it as a gesture of gratitude. Harry could no longer remember what she looked like, just the cooing whisper in his ear afterwards: *Not bad at all, lad. You'll see, you're going to make some women happy. And others unhappy.*

And one woman, both.

Harry stopped on the steps of the closed, dark restaurant.

Hands on his knees, head hanging down. He could feel his gag reflex tickling deep in his throat, and heard his own rasping breath. He counted to twenty as he whispered her name. *Rakel, Rakel.* Then he straightened up and looked down at the city beneath him. Oslo, an autumn city. Now, in spring, she looked like she had woken up reluctantly. But Harry wasn't bothered about the centre of the city, he was looking towards the ridge, towards her house, on the far side of what, in spite of all the lights and febrile human activity, was really nothing but the crater of a dead volcano, cold stone and solidified clay. He cast another glance at the timer on his watch and started to run.

He didn't stop until he was back in Borggata.

There, he stopped his watch and studied the numbers.

He jogged the rest of the way home at an easy pace. As he unlocked the door to his flat he heard the rough sound of grit against wood under his trainers and remembered what Katrine had said about picking his feet up.

He used his phone to play more of his Spotify list. The sound of The Hellacopters streamed from the Sonos Playbar that Oleg had got him for his birthday, which had overnight reduced the record collection on the shelves behind him to a dead monument to thirty years of laborious collecting, where anything that hadn't stood the test of

time had been pulled out like weeds and thrown away. As the chaotic guitar and drum intro to "Carry Me Home" made the speakers
vibrate and he picked the grit from the sculpture park from the soles
of his shoes, he thought about how the nineteen-year-old had will-
ingly retreated into the past with vinyl records, whereas Harry was
unwillingly backing into the future. He put his shoes down, looked
for The Byrds, who weren't on any of his playlists—sixties and early
seventies music were more Bjørn Holm's thing, and his attempts to
convert Harry with Glen Campbell had been futile. He found "Turn!
Turn! Turn!", and moments later Roger McGuinn's Rickenbacker
guitar was echoing around the room. But *she* had been converted.
She had fallen in love with it even though it wasn't her music. There
was something about guitars and girls. Four strings were enough,
and this guy had twelve.

Harry considered the possibility that he might be the one who
was wrong. But the hairs on the back of his neck were rarely wrong,
and they had stood up when he recognised one of the names from
the record sleeve in the interview transcript. And connected it to the
picture of the guy with the Rickenbacker guitar. Harry lit a cigarette and listened to the double guitar solo at the end of "Rainy Days
Revisited." He wondered how long it would be before he fell asleep.
How long he would manage to leave his phone alone before checking
to see if Rakel had replied.

5

"We know you've answered these questions before, Sara," Harry said, looking at the nineteen-year-old girl sitting opposite him in the cramped interview room that felt a bit like a doll's house. Truls Berntsen was sitting in the control room with his arms folded, yawning. It was ten o'clock, they had been going for an hour and Sara was showing signs of impatience as they went through the sequence of events, but no emotion beyond that. Not even when Harry read out loud from the report about the injuries her mother had suffered from the thirteen knife wounds. "But, as I said, Officer Berntsen and I have taken over the investigation, and we'd like to understand everything as clearly as possible. So—did your father usually help with the cooking? I'm asking because he must have been very quick to find the sharpest kitchen knife, and must have known exactly which drawer it was in, and where."

"No, he didn't *help*," Sara said, her displeasure even more apparent now. "He *did* the cooking. And the only person who helped was me. Mum was always out."

"Out?"

"Meeting friends. At the gym. So she said."

"I've seen pictures of her, it looks like she kept herself in shape. Kept herself young."

"Whatever. She died young."

Harry waited. Let the answer hang in the air. Then Sara pulled a face. Harry had seen it in other cases, the way that someone left behind struggled with grief as if it were an enemy, an irritating nuisance that needed to be cajoled and tricked. And one way of doing that was to downplay the loss, to discredit the dead. But he suspected that wasn't actually the case this time. When Harry had suggested Sara might like to bring a lawyer she had dismissed the offer. She just wanted to get it over with, she said, she had other plans. Understandable enough, she was nineteen, alone, but she was adaptable, and life went on. And the case had been solved, which was presumably why she had relaxed. And was showing her true feelings. Or rather her lack of feelings.

"You don't get as much exercise as your mother," Harry said. "Not running, anyway."

"Don't I?" she replied with a half-smile and looked up at Harry. It was the self-assured smile of a young person from a generation in which you were one of the thin ones if you had a body Harry's generation would have thought of as average.

"I've seen your running shoes," Harry said. "They've barely been used. And that isn't because they're new, because they stopped making that sort two years ago. I've got the same ones."

Sara shrugged. "I've got more time to go running now."

"Yes, your father's going to be in prison for twelve years, so you won't have to help him with the cooking for a while."

Harry looked at her and saw that he had hit home. Her mouth was hanging open and her black-painted eyelashes were fluttering up and down as she blinked hard.

"Why are you lying?" Harry asked.

"Wh . . . What?"

"You said you ran from home to the top of the sculpture park, down to the Ekeberg Restaurant, then back home again in thirty minutes. I ran the same distance last night. It took me almost forty-five minutes, and I'm a pretty good runner. I've also spoken to the police officer who stopped you when you got back. He said you weren't sweating or particularly out of breath."

Sara was sitting up straight now on the other side of the little doll's-house table, staring unconsciously at the red light on the microphones that indicated they were recording, when she replied.

"OK, I didn't run all the way to the top."

"How far?"

"To the Marilyn Monroe statue."

"So you must have run along those gritted paths, like me. When I got home I had to pick small stones out of the soles of my shoes, Sara. Eight in total. But the soles of your shoes were completely clean."

Harry had no idea if there had been eight stones or only three. But the more precise he was, the more incontestable his reasoning would seem. And he could see from Sara's face that it was working.

"You didn't go running at all, Sara. You left the flat at the time you told the police, at 20:15, while your father called the police claiming that he'd murdered your mother. Maybe you ran around the block, just long enough for the police to arrive, then you jogged back. Like your father told you to. Isn't that right?"

Sara didn't answer, just went on blinking. Harry noted that her pupils had expanded.

"I've spoken to your mother's lover. Andreas. Professional name Bom-Bom. He may not sing quite as well as he plays his twelve-string guitar."

"Andreas sings . . ." The anger in her eyes faded and she stopped herself.

"He admitted that you and he had met a few times, and said that was how he met your mother." Harry looked down at his notepad. Not because he couldn't remember what was written in it—nothing—but to lower the intensity, to give her a bit of breathing room.

"Andreas and I were in love." There was a faint tremor in Sara's voice.

"Not according to him. He said you'd had a couple of . . ."—Harry pulled his head back slightly to read what wasn't written in his notebook—" 'groupie fucks.' "

Sara twitched.

"But you wouldn't leave him alone, apparently. He said there's a fine line between groupie and stalker, in his experience. That things were simpler with a mature, married woman who accepted things for what they were. A bit of excitement to liven up the daily routine, spice things up a bit. That's how he put it. A way to spice things up."

Harry looked at her.

"It was you who borrowed your mother's phone, not your father. And discovered that she and Andreas had been having an affair."

Harry checked to see how his conscience was doing. Bulldozing a nineteen-year-old with no lawyer, a lovesick teenager who had been betrayed by her mother and a guy she had managed to convince herself belonged to her.

"Your father isn't just self-sacrificing, Sara, he's smart too. He knows that the best lie is one that's as close to the truth as possible. The lie is that your father was at the local shop picking up some things for dinner before going home, borrowing your mother's phone, finding the messages and killing her. The truth is that while he was at the shop, you found the messages, and from that point on I'm guessing that if we swap your and your father's roles in the report, we'd get a fairly accurate description of what happened in the kitchen. You argued, she turned her back on you to walk out, you knew where the knife was, and the rest played out more or less of its own accord. And when your father got home and discovered what had happened, you came up with this plan together."

Harry saw no reaction in her eyes. Just an even, intense, black hatred. And realised that his conscience felt just fine. The authorities gave guns to nineteen-year-olds and ordered them to kill. And this one had killed her mother and was prepared to let her innocent father throw himself under the bus for her. Sara wasn't going to be one of the figures who visited Harry in his nightmares.

"Andreas loves me," she whispered. It sounded like her mouth was full of sand. "But Mum lured him away from me. She seduced him just so I couldn't have him. I hate her. I . . ." She was close to tears. Harry held his breath. They were almost there, the race was on, he just needed a few more words on tape, but crying would cause a delay, and in the delay the avalanche might grind to a halt. Sara raised her voice. "I hate that fucking bitch! I should have stabbed her even more, I should have cut off that smug face she was so fucking proud of!"

"Mm." Harry leaned back in his chair. "You wish you'd killed her more slowly, is that what you're saying?"

"Yes!"

Confession to murder. Touchdown. Harry cast a quick glance through the doll's house window and saw that Truls Berntsen had woken up and was giving him the thumbs up. But Harry felt no joy. On the contrary, the excitement he had felt just a few seconds before had been replaced by a weary sadness, almost disappointment. It wasn't an unfamiliar feeling, it often arose after a long chase where anticipation of solving the case had built up, anticipation of the arrest as a cathartic climax, a hope that it might change something, make the world a slightly better place. Instead, what followed was often a sort of post-case depression with associated alcoholic elements and days or weeks on the bottle. Harry imagined that it resembled a serial killer's frustration when the murder didn't provide any prolonged sense of satisfaction, just a feeling of anti-climax that drove him back out into the chase again. Maybe that's why Harry—for a fleeting moment—felt bitter disappointment, as if he had briefly swapped places with her and was sitting on the other side of the table.

"We sorted that out very nicely," Truls Berntsen said in the lift on the way up to the Crime Squad Unit on the sixth floor.

"*We?*" Harry said drily.

"I pressed the Record button, didn't I?"

"I certainly hope so. Did you check the recording?"

"Did I check it?" Truls Berntsen raised one eyebrow questioningly. Then he grinned. "Relax."

Harry took his eyes off the glowing floor numbers and looked down at Berntsen. And felt that he envied his colleague with the weak chin, protruding brow and the grunting laughter that had earned him the nickname Beavis, which no one dared say out loud, probably because there was something about Truls Berntsen's passive-aggressive demeanour that meant you didn't want to be in his line of fire during a critical situation. Truls was even less popular than Harry Hole in Crime Squad, but that wasn't why Harry envied him. He envied Truls's ability to not give a damn. Mind you, Harry didn't give a damn what his colleagues thought of him either. No, it was Berntsen's ability to shrug off any sense of responsibility, practical as well as moral, for the job he was supposed to do as a police officer. You could say a lot of things about Harry, and he was well aware that plenty of people did, but no one could take away the fact that he was a real police officer. That was one of his few blessings, and probably his greatest curse. Even when Harry was on the skids in his private life, like he had been since Rakel kicked him out, the policeman in him couldn't just give up and tumble headlong into anarchy and nihilism the way Truls Berntsen had. No one would thank Harry for not giving up, but that was fine, he wasn't after gratitude, and he wasn't seeking salvation through good deeds. His tireless, almost compulsive search for the worst offenders in society had been his only reason for getting up each morning until he met Rakel. So he was grateful for that herd instinct or whatever it was, for providing him with an anchor. But part of him longed for total, destructive freedom, cutting the anchor chain and getting crushed by the breakers, or simply disappearing into the deep, dark ocean.

They got out of the lift and walked along the corridor with its red-painted walls that confirmed they had got off at the right floor, past the separate offices towards the open-plan space.

"Hey, Hole!" Skarre called from an open door. He had recently been appointed an inspector and had been given Harry's old office. "The dragon's looking for you."

"Your wife?" Harry asked, not bothering to slow down to wait for Skarre's presumably furious and failed attempt at a retort.

"Nice," Berntsen said with a grin. "Skarre's an idiot."

Harry didn't know if that was meant as an outstretched hand, but he didn't answer. He had no intention of acquiring any more ill-advised friendships.

He turned off left without any word of goodbye and stepped in through the open door to the head-of-department's office. A man was standing with his back to him, leaning over Katrine Bratt's desk, but it wasn't hard to recognise the shiny bald head with its oddly profuse wreath of black hair.

"Hope I'm not disturbing, but I heard I was wanted?"

Katrine Bratt looked up, and the Chief of Police Gunnar Hagen spun around as if he had been caught doing something. They looked at Harry in silence.

He raised an eyebrow. "What? You've already heard?"

Katrine and Hagen exchanged a look. Hagen grinned. "Have *you*?"

"What do you mean?" Harry said. "I was the one who questioned her."

Harry's brain searched and came up with a suggestion that the police lawyer Harry had called after the interview to discuss the father's release must have called Katrine Bratt in turn. But what was the Chief of Police doing here?

"I advised the daughter to bring a lawyer, but she declined," Harry said. "And I repeated the offer before the start of the interview, but she declined again. We've got that on tape. Well, not tape, but on the hard drive."

Neither of them smiled, and Harry could tell that something was wrong. Very wrong.

"Is it the father?" Harry asked. "Has he . . . done something?"

"No," Katrine said. "It's not the father, Harry."

Harry's brain unconsciously noted the details: the fact that Hagen had let Katrine, the one of them who was closer to him, take over. And that she had used his first name when she didn't have to. To soften the blow. In the silence that followed, he felt the clawing at his chest again. And even if Harry didn't have any great belief in telepathy and foresight, it felt as if what was coming was what the claw, the little glimpses, had been trying to tell him all along.

"It's Rakel," Katrine said.

6

Harry held his breath. He had read that it was possible to hold your breath for so long that you died. And that you don't die from too little oxygen, but from too much carbon dioxide. That people can't usually hold their breath for more than a minute or a minute and a half, but that one Danish free diver had held his for over twenty minutes.

Harry had been happy. But happiness is like heroin; once you've tasted it, once you've found out that happiness exists, you will never be entirely happy with an ordinary life without happiness again. Because happiness is something more than mere satisfaction. Happiness isn't natural. Happiness is a trembling, exceptional state; seconds, minutes, days that you know simply can't last. And sorrow at its absence doesn't come afterwards, but at the same time. Because with happiness comes the terrible insight that nothing can be the same again, that you are already missing what you have, you're worrying about the withdrawal pangs, grief at the loss, cursing the awareness of what you are capable of feeling.

Rakel always used to read in bed. Sometimes she read out loud to him, if it was something he liked. Like Kjell Askildsen's short stories. That made him happy. One evening she read a sentence that stuck in his mind. About a young girl who had lived her whole life alone with her parents in a lighthouse, until a married man, Krafft, arrived and she fell in love. And she thought to herself: *Why did you have to come and make me so lonely?*

Katrine cleared her throat, but her voice still sounded muffled. "They've found Rakel, Harry."

He felt like asking how they could have found someone who

wasn't missing. But to do that he would have to breathe. He breathed. "And . . . that means what?"

Katrine was struggling to keep control of her face, but gave up and clapped her hand to her mouth, which was contorted into a grimace.

Gunnar Hagen took over. "The worst, Harry."

"No," Harry heard himself say. Angry. Pleading. "No."

"She—"

"Stop!" Harry held his hands up defensively in front of him. "Don't say it, Gunnar. Not yet. Just let me . . . just wait a bit."

Gunnar Hagen waited. Katrine had covered her face with her hands. She was sobbing silently, but her shaking shoulders gave her away. His eyes found the window. There were still greyish-white islands and small continents of snow on the brown sea of Botsparken. But in the past few days buds had begun to appear on the lime trees that led up to the prison. A month or so from now, those buds would suddenly burst into life, and Harry would wake up and see that Oslo had once again been invaded by the blitzkrieg of spring overnight. And it would be utterly meaningless. He had been alone most of his life. It had been fine. Now it wasn't fine. He wasn't breathing. He was full of carbon dioxide. And he hoped it would take less than twenty minutes.

"OK," he said. "Say it."

"She's dead, Harry."

7

Harry weighed his mobile phone in his hand.

Eight digits away.

Four less than the time he had lived in Chungking Mansions in Hong Kong, those four grey tower blocks that were a small community in themselves, with hostels for guest workers from Africa and the Philippines, restaurants, prayer rooms, tailors, money-changers, maternity rooms and funeral parlours. Harry's room had been on the second floor of C-block. Four square metres of bare concrete with space for a shabby mattress and an ashtray, where a dripping air-conditioning unit had counted the seconds, while he himself lost count of the days and weeks as he slid in and out of an opium haze that decided when he came and went. In the end, Kaja Solness from the Crime Squad Unit had turned up to take him home. But before then he had fallen into a rhythm. And every day, after eating glass noodles at Li Yuan or walking down Nathan Road and Melden Row to buy a lump of opium in a baby's bottle, he had walked back, waited by the lift doors of the Chungking Mansions and looked at the payphone hanging on the wall.

He had been on the run from everything. From his work as a murder detective, because it was eating away at his soul. From himself, because he had become a destructive force that killed everyone near him. But first and foremost from Rakel and Oleg, because he didn't want to hurt them as well. No more than he already had done.

And every day, as he waited for the lift, he had stood there staring at the payphone. Touching the coins in his trouser pocket.

Twelve numbers, and he would be able to hear her voice. Reassure himself that she and Oleg were OK.

But he couldn't know that *until* he called.

Their lives had been in chaos, and anything could have happened since he'd left. It was possible that Rakel and Oleg had been dragged down into the maelstrom left in the Snowman's wake. Rakel was strong, but Harry had seen it happen in other murder cases, where the survivors also ended up as victims.

But as long as he *didn't* call, they were there. In his head, in the payphone, somewhere in the world. As long as he didn't know better—or worse—he could carry on seeing them in front of him, hiking in Nordmarka in October. Where he, Rakel and Oleg had gone walking. The young boy running ahead of them, excitedly trying to catch falling leaves. Rakel's warm, dry hand in Harry's. Her voice, laughing as she asked what he was smiling for, him shaking his head when he realised that he had actually been smiling. So he never touched the payphone. Because as long as Harry resisted pressing those twelve numbers, he could always imagine that it could be like that again.

Harry tapped in the last of the eight digits.

The phone rang three times before he answered.

"Harry?" The first syllable expressed surprise and joy, the second surprise, but mixed with a degree of anxiety. On the rare occasions that Harry and Oleg called each other, it happened in the evening, not in the middle of the working day. And even then, it was to discuss things of a practical nature. Obviously the practical pretext was sometimes rather contrived, but neither Oleg nor Harry were that fond of talking on the phone, so even if they were really only calling to see how the other was, they usually kept things brief. None of that had changed since Oleg and his girlfriend Helga moved up north to Lakselv in Finnmark, where Oleg was doing a year's practical training before his final year at Police College.

"Oleg," Harry said, and heard that his voice sounded choked. Because he was about to pour boiling water over Oleg, and Oleg would bear the scars of the burns he was about to receive for the rest of his life. Harry knew that because he had so many similar scars himself.

"Is something wrong?" Oleg asked.

"It's about your mother," Harry said, then stopped abruptly because he couldn't go on.

"Are you getting back together again?" Oleg's voice sounded hopeful.

Harry closed his eyes.

Oleg had been angry when he found out that his mother had broken up with Harry. And because Oleg had been spared any explanation of the causes, his anger had been directed at Rakel rather than Harry. Not that Harry could see how he had been a good enough dad to warrant anyone taking his side. When Harry had come into their lives he had taken a very low profile, as both a parent and a shoulder to cry on, because it was obvious the boy didn't need a replacement dad. And Harry definitely didn't need a son. But the problem—if that's what it was—was that Harry had taken a liking to the serious, sullen young man. And vice versa. Rakel used to accuse them of being like each other, and perhaps there was something in that. And after a while—when the boy was particularly tired or wasn't concentrating—the word "Dad" would slip out instead of the "Harry" they had agreed on.

"No," Harry said. "We're not getting back together. Oleg, it's bad news."

Silence. Harry could tell Oleg was holding his breath. Harry poured the water.

"She's been reported dead, Oleg."

Two seconds passed.

"Can you say that again?" Oleg said.

Harry didn't know if he could manage that, but he did.

"How do you mean, 'dead'?" Oleg said, and Harry heard all the metallic desperation in his voice.

"She was found in the house this morning. It looks like murder."

"Looks like?"

"I've only just found out myself. The crime team are already there, I'm about to head over."

"How . . . ?"

"I don't know yet."

"But . . ."

Oleg didn't get any further, and Harry knew there was no continuation to that all-encompassing "but." It was just an instinctive objection, a self-sustaining protest, a rejection of the possibility that things could be the way they actually were. An echo of his own "but . . ." in Katrine Bratt's office twenty-five minutes ago.

Harry waited while Oleg struggled to hold back tears. He replied to Oleg's next five questions with the same "I don't know, Oleg."

He heard the hiccough in the boy's voice, and thought that, as long as he's crying, I won't.

Oleg ran out of questions and the line went quiet.

"I'll keep my phone on, and I'll call as soon as I know more," Harry said. "Are there any flights . . . ?"

"There's one that leaves Tromsø at one o'clock." Oleg's heavy, laboured breathing echoed through the phone.

"Good."

"Call as soon as you can, OK?"

"I will."

"And, Dad?"

"Yes?"

"Don't let them . . ."

"No, I won't," Harry said. He didn't know how he knew what Oleg was thinking. It wasn't a rational thought, it just . . . appeared. He cleared his throat. "I promise that no one at the scene will see more than they need to in order to do their job. OK?"

"OK."

"OK."

Silence.

Harry tried to think of some words of comfort, but found nothing that didn't sound meaningless.

"I'll call you," he said.

"OK."

They ended the call.

8

Harry walked slowly up the hill to the black timber house, in the glare of the rotating blue lights of the police cars parked in the drive. The orange and white cordon tape had started down by the gate. Colleagues who didn't know what to say or do stared at him as he passed. It felt like he was walking underwater. Like a dream he hoped he was about to wake up from. Maybe not wake up, actually, because it offered a numbness, a peculiar absence of sensation and sound, just hazy light and the muffled sound of his own steps. As if he had been injected with something.

Harry walked up the three steps to the open door leading into the house he, Rakel and Oleg had shared. Inside, he could hear the chatter of police radios and Bjørn Holm's clipped commands to the other crime-scene investigators. Harry took several trembling breaths.

Then he stepped across the threshold and automatically walked outside the white flags the forensics team had set up.

Investigation, he thought. This is an investigation. I'm dreaming, but I can do an investigation in my sleep. It's just a matter of doing it properly, getting it going, and I won't wake up. As long as I'm not awake, it isn't true. So Harry did it properly, he didn't look directly at the sun, at the body he knew was lying on the floor between the kitchen and living-room areas. The sun—that, even if it hadn't been Rakel—would blind him if he stared straight at it. The sight of a body does something to your senses even if you're an experienced murder detective; it overwhelms them to a greater or lesser extent, numbs them and makes them less sensitive to other, less violent impressions, all the small details of a crime scene that can tell you something.

That can help piece together a coherent, logical narrative. Or the reverse, something that jars, that doesn't belong in the picture. He let his eyes roam across the walls. A single red coat hung from the hooks under the hat rack. Where she used to hang the coat she had used last, unless she knew she wasn't going to wear it next time, in which case she hung it in the wardrobe with her other jackets. He had to pull himself together to stop himself clutching the coat and pressing it to his face to breathe in the smell of her. Of forest. Because no matter what perfume she used, the symphony of smells always had an underlying note of sun-warmed Norwegian forest. He couldn't see the red silk scarf she usually wore with that coat, but her black boots were standing on the shoe rack directly beneath it. Harry looked on towards the living room, but there was nothing different there. It looked just like the room he had walked out of two months, fifteen days and twenty hours ago. None of the pictures were hanging crookedly, none of the rugs were out of place. He looked across to the kitchen. There. There was a knife missing from the pyramid-shaped wooden block on the kitchen worktop. His eyes began to circle towards the body.

He felt a hand on his shoulder.

"Hello, Bjørn," Harry said without turning around, unable to stop his eyes systematically photographing the crime scene.

"Harry," Bjørn said. "I don't know what to say."

"You ought to be telling me I shouldn't be here," Harry said. "You ought to be saying I'm disqualified, that this isn't my case, that I'll just have to wait to see her like any other civilian until I'm called in to formally identify her."

"You know I can't say any of that."

"If you don't, someone else will," Harry said, noting the blood sprayed across the bottom of the bookcase, across the spines of Hamsun's collected works and an old encyclopaedia that Oleg used to like looking at while Harry explained the things that had changed since the encyclopaedia was printed and why. "And I'd rather hear it from you." Only now did Harry look at Bjørn Holm. His eyes were shiny and bulging even more than usual in his pale face, framed by bright red sideburns à la 1970s-era Elvis, a beard and the new cap that had replaced his Rasta hat.

"I'll say it if you want me to, Harry."

Harry's eyes ventured closer to the sun, hit the edge of the pool of blood on the floor. The outline revealed that it was large. He had said "reported dead" to Oleg. As if he didn't quite believe it until he had seen it for himself. Harry cleared his throat. "Tell me what you've got first."

"Knife," Bjørn said. "The forensic medical officer's on the way, but it looks to me like three blows, no more. And one was at the back of the neck, directly below the skull. Which means that she died—"

"Quickly and painlessly," Harry said. "Thanks for that, Bjørn."

Bjørn nodded curtly, and Harry realised that the forensics officer had said it as much for his own sake as Harry's.

He looked back at the wooden block on the kitchen worktop again. The ultra-sharp Tojiro knives that he had bought in Hong Kong, traditional *Santoku*-style, with oak handles, but these had a water-buffalo-horn collar. Rakel had loved them. It looked like the smallest one was missing, an all-purpose knife with a blade between ten and fifteen centimetres long.

"And there's no sign of sexual assault," Bjørn said. "All her clothes are still in place, and intact."

Harry's eyes had reached the sun.

Mustn't wake up.

Rakel was lying curled up with her back to him, facing the kitchen. More tightly curled than when she was asleep. She had no obvious injuries or knife wounds to her back, and her long dark hair was covering her neck. The roaring voices in his head were trying to drown each other out. One was screaming that she was wearing the traditional cardigan he had bought her during a trip to Reykjavik. Another that it wasn't her, that it couldn't be her. A third was saying that if it was the way it looked at first glance, that she had been stabbed from the front at first, and that the perpetrator hadn't been standing between her and the door, so she hadn't made any attempt to escape. The fourth was saying that she was going to get up any moment, walk towards him with a smile and point at the hidden camera.

The hidden camera.

Harry heard someone clear their throat quietly and turned around.

The man standing in the doorway was large and rectangular, with a head that looked like it had been cut from granite and drawn with a ruler. A hairless cranium with a straight chin, straight mouth, straight nose and straight narrow eyes under a pair of straight eyebrows. Blue jeans, a smart jacket and a shirt with no tie. There was no expression in his grey eyes, but his voice and the way he dragged the words out—as if he were enjoying them, had been waiting for the chance to say them—expressed everything his eyes were hiding.

"I'm sorry for your loss, but I'm going to have to ask you to leave the scene, Hole."

Harry met Ole Winter's gaze, noting that Kripos's senior inspector had used an expression directly translated from English, as if Norwegian didn't have a perfectly adequate way of expressing sympathy. And that he hadn't even allowed himself a full stop after his expression of sympathy before throwing Harry out, just a quick comma. Harry didn't answer, merely turned and looked at Rakel again.

"That means now, Hole."

"Mm. As far as I'm aware, the task of Kripos is to assist Oslo Police District, not to issue—"

"And now Kripos is helping to keep the partner of the victim away from the crime scene. You can act like a professional and do as I say, or I can get a couple of uniforms to help you out."

Harry knew Ole Winter wouldn't have any objection to that, letting two officers lead Harry out to a police car in full view of his colleagues, neighbours, and the media vultures who were standing down at the road photographing everything they could. Ole Winter was a couple of years older than Harry and they had worked on either side of the fence as homicide detectives for twenty-five years, Harry with the Oslo Police District and Winter in the specialist national unit, Kripos, which assisted local police departments in serious criminal cases such as murder. And which occasionally, because of its superior resources and competence, took over the investigations altogether. Harry assumed that his own Chief of Police, Gunnar Hagen, had taken the decision to bring Kripos in. A perfectly valid decision, given that the victim's partner was employed in the Crime Squad Unit at Police Headquarters in Oslo. But also a somewhat sensitive decision given that there was always an unspoken rivalry between the two largest murder investigation units in the country. What wasn't unspoken, however, was Ole Winter's opinion that Harry Hole was seriously overrated, that his legendary status owed more to the sensational nature of the cases he had solved than the factual quality of his detective work. And that Ole Winter—even though he was the undisputed star of Kripos—was undervalued, at least outside the inner circle. And that his triumphs never got the same headlines as Hole's, because serious police work rarely did, while an alcoholic loose cannon with one single lucid moment of inspiration always did.

Harry pulled out his packet of Camels, stuck a cigarette between his lips and took out his lighter.

"I'm going, Winter."

He walked past the other man, went down the steps and out onto the drive before needing to steady himself. He stopped, and went to light the cigarette, but was so blinded by tears that he couldn't see either lighter or cigarette.

"Here."

Harry heard Bjørn's voice, blinked quickly several times and sucked in the flame from the lighter Bjørn was holding up to the cigarette. Harry inhaled hard. Coughed, then inhaled again.

"Thanks. Have you been thrown out too?"

"No, my work's as good for Kripos as it is for the Oslo Police District."

"Aren't you supposed to be on paternity leave?"

"Katrine called. The lad's probably sitting on her lap behind her desk running Crime Squad right now." Bjørn Holm's crooked smile vanished as soon as it appeared. "Sorry, Harry, I'm babbling."

"Mm." The wind tugged at the smoke as Harry exhaled. "So, you're finished with the garden?"

Stay in investigation mode, stay sedated.

"Yes," Bjørn Holm said. "There was a frost on Saturday night, so the gravel was harder. If there was anyone here, or any vehicles, they haven't left much evidence."

"*Saturday* night? You're saying that's when it happened?"

"She's cold, and when I bent her arm it felt as if the rigor mortis was already starting to ease."

"At least twenty-four hours, then."

"Yes. But the medical officer should be here anytime. Are you OK, Harry?"

Harry had started to retch, but nodded and swallowed the stinging bile. He would manage. He would manage. Stay asleep.

"The knife wounds, do you have any idea of what sort of knife was used?"

"I'd say a small- to medium-sized blade. No bruising on the side of the wound, so either he didn't stab very deep or the knife doesn't have much of a shaft."

"The blood. He went deep."

"Yes."

Harry sucked desperately at the cigarette, which was already close to the filter. A tall young man in a Burberry jacket and suit was walking up the drive towards them.

"Katrine said it was someone from Rakel's work who called it in," Harry said. "Do you know any more than that?"

"Just that it was her boss," Bjørn said. "Rakel didn't show up for an important meeting, and they couldn't get hold of her. He thought something might be wrong."

"Mm. Is it normal to call the police when one of your staff doesn't show up for a meeting?"

"I don't know, Harry. He said it wasn't like Rakel not to turn up, or at least not to call beforehand. And obviously they knew that she lived alone."

Harry nodded slowly. They knew more than that. They knew she had recently thrown her husband out. A man with a reputation for being unstable. He dropped the cigarette and heard it hiss on the grit as he ground his heel on it.

The young man had reached them. He was in his thirties, thin, upright, with Asian features. The suit looked tailor-made, the shirt chalk-white and freshly ironed, the tie neatly knotted. His thick black hair was cut short, in a style that could have been discreet if it hadn't been so calculatedly classic. Kripos detective Sung-min Larsen smelled vaguely of something Harry assumed was expensive. At Kripos he was apparently known as the Nikkei Index, despite the fact that his first name—Sung-min, which Harry had come across several times when he was in Hong Kong—was Korean rather than Japanese. He had graduated from Police College the first year Harry had been lecturing there, but Harry could still remember him from his lectures on criminal investigation, mostly because of those white shirts and his quiet demeanour, the wry smiles when Harry—still an inexperienced lecturer—felt he was on shaky ground, and also his exam results, which had evidently been the highest grades ever achieved at Police College.

"I'm sorry, Hole," Sung-min Larsen said. "My deepest condolences." He was almost as tall as Harry.

"Thanks, Larsen." Harry nodded to the notepad the Kripos detective was holding. "Been talking to the neighbours?"

"That's right."

"Anything of interest?" Harry looked round. There was plenty of space between the houses up here in fashionable Holmenkollen. Tall hedges and ranks of fir trees.

For a moment, Sung-min Larsen seemed to ponder whether this

was information he could share with the Oslo Police District. Unless the problem was that Harry was the victim's husband.

"Your neighbour, Wenche Angondora Syvertsen, says she didn't hear or see anything unusual on Saturday night. I asked if she sleeps with the window open, and she said she did. But she also said she was able to do that because familiar sounds don't wake her up. Like her husband's car, the neighbours' cars, the dustcart. And she pointed out that Rakel Fauke's house has thick timber walls."

He said this without having to look down at his notes, and Harry got the feeling that Larsen was presenting these minor details as a test, to see if they prompted any sort of reaction.

"Mm," Harry said, a rumbling sound that merely indicated he'd heard what the other person had said.

"So it's her house?" Larsen asked. "Not yours?"

"Separate property," Harry said. "I insisted. Didn't want anyone to think I was marrying her for her money."

"Was she rich?"

"No, that was just a joke." Harry nodded towards the house. "You'll have to pass any information you've managed to get to your boss, Larsen."

"Winter's here?"

"It was certainly cold enough in there."

Sung-min Larsen smiled politely. "In formal terms Winter is leading the tactical investigation, but it looks like I'm going to be in charge of the case. I'm not in the same class as you, Hole, but I promise to do my utmost to catch whoever murdered your wife."

"Thanks," Harry said. He had a feeling the young detective meant every word he said. Apart from the bit about not being in the same class. He watched as Larsen made his way past the police cars towards the house.

"Hidden camera," Harry said.

"Huh?" Bjørn said.

"I set up a wildlife camera on that middle fir tree there." Harry nodded towards the thicket of bushes and trees, a little cluster of raw Norwegian forest in front of the fence to the neighbouring property. "I suppose I'll have to tell Winter about it."

"No," Bjørn said emphatically.

Harry looked at him. It wasn't often he heard him sound so decisive. Bjørn Holm shrugged his shoulders. "If it's recorded anything that can help solve the case, I don't think Winter should get the glory."

"OK?"

"On the other hand, you shouldn't touch anything here either."

"Because I'm a suspect," Harry said.

Bjørn didn't answer.

"That's fine," Harry said. "The ex-husband is always the first suspect."

"Until you've been ruled out," Bjørn said. "I'll get hold of whatever the camera recorded. The middle tree, you said?"

"It's not easy to spot," Harry said. "It's hidden in a sock the same colour as the trunk. Two and a half metres up."

Bjørn looked amiably at Harry. Then the stocky forensics officer began to pad towards the trees with his surprisingly soft and extremely slow gait. Harry's phone rang. The first four digits told him it was from a landline in the offices of *VG*. The vultures scented carrion. And the fact that they were calling him meant that they probably knew the victim's name and had made the connection. He rejected the call and put his phone back in his pocket.

Bjørn was crouching down over by the trees. He looked up and beckoned Harry over to him. "Don't come any closer," Bjørn said, pulling on a fresh pair of white latex gloves. "Someone got here before us."

"What the fuck . . . ?" Harry whispered. The sock had been pulled from the tree and was lying in tatters on the ground. Beside it lay the wreckage of the camera. Someone had stamped it to pieces. Bjørn picked it up. "The memory card is gone," he said.

Harry was breathing hard through his nose.

"Pretty good going to spot the camera with its camouflage sock on," Bjørn said. "You'd pretty much have to be standing here among the trees to see it."

Harry nodded slowly. "Unless . . ." he said, and felt that his brain needed more oxygen than he could give it. "Unless the perpetrator knew the camera was there."

"Sure. So who have you told?"

"No one." Harry's voice was hoarse, and at first he didn't recognise what it was, the pain growing in his chest, trying to get out. Was he waking up? "No one at all," Harry said. "And I set it up in complete darkness in the middle of the night, so no one saw me do it. No one human, anyway." Then Harry realised what it was that was trying to get out. The shrieking of crows. The wailing of a madman. Laughter.

9

It was half past two in the afternoon, and most of the clientele looked up disinterestedly at the door when it swung open.

Schrøder's Restaurant.

"Restaurant" was perhaps something of a misnomer, although the brown café did indeed serve a selection of Norwegian specialities, such as pork chops and dripping, but the main courses were beer and wine. The bar had existed on Waldemar Thranes gate since the mid-fifties, and it had been Harry's regular haunt since the nineties. There had been an interval of a few years after he moved in with Rakel in Holmenkollen. But now he was back.

He sank down onto the bench by the wall at one of the window tables.

The bench was new. But apart from that, the interior had stayed the same for the past twenty years, the same tables and chairs, the same stained-glass ceiling, the same Sigurd Fosnes paintings of Oslo, even the red tablecloths with a white cloth set diagonally on top were the same. The biggest change Harry could remember was when the smoking ban came into force in 2004 and they repainted the bar to get rid of the smell of smoke. The same colour as before. And the smell of smoke never went completely.

He checked his phone, but Oleg hadn't replied to his messages telling him to call him; he was probably in the air.

"It's terrible, Harry," Nina said, removing two half-litre glasses from in front of him. "I just read it online." She wiped her free hand on her apron and looked down at him. "How are you doing?"

"Not great, thanks," Harry said. So the vultures had published her name already. Presumably they had managed to get hold of a picture of Rakel from somewhere. And of Harry, of course. They had plenty of those in their archives, some of them so awful that Rakel had wondered if he couldn't at least try to pose a bit better next time. She never looked bad in photographs, even if she tried. No. *Had* never looked bad. Fuck.

"Coffee?"

"I'm going to have to ask you for beer today, Nina."

"I understand what's going on, but I haven't served you beer for—how many years is it now, Harry?"

"A lot. And I'm grateful for your concern. But I mustn't wake up, you know?"

"Wake up?"

"If I go anywhere that serves strong liquor today, I'll probably drink myself to death."

"You came here because we only have a licence to serve beer?"

"And because I can find my way home from here with my eyes closed."

The plump, stubborn waitress stood there looking at him with a concerned, thoughtful expression. Then she let out a deep sigh. "OK, Harry. But I decide when you've had enough."

"I can never have enough, Nina."

"I know. But I think you came here because you wanted to be served by someone you trust."

"Maybe."

Nina left him and came back with a half-litre of beer that she put down in front of him.

"Slowly," she said. "Slowly."

Some way into the third half-litre the door swung open again.

Harry noted that the customers who had raised their heads hadn't lowered them again, and that their eyes were following the long, leather-clad legs until they reached Harry's table, where she sat down.

"You're not answering your phone," she said, waving Nina away as she approached the table.

"I've turned it off. *VG* and the others have started to call."

"You have no idea. I haven't seen such a scrum at a press conference since the vampirist case. And that's partly because the Chief of Police has decided to suspend you until further notice."

"What? I get that I'm not allowed to work on this case, but suspended from all duties? Really? Because the press are all over a murder investigation?"

"Because you won't be left in peace no matter what you're working on, and we don't need that sort of distraction right now."

"And?"

"And what?"

"Keep going." Harry raised his glass to his lips.

"There isn't anything else."

"Yes, there is. The politics. Let's hear it."

Katrine sighed deeply. "Since Bærum and Asker were moved into Oslo Police District, we're responsible for a fifth of the population of Norway. Two years ago surveys showed that 86 percent of the population had high or very high confidence in us. That figure has now fallen to 65, thanks to a couple of unfortunate individual cases. And that means our beloved Chief of Police, Hagen, has been summoned to see our rather less beloved Minister of Justice, Mikael Bellman. To be blunt: at the present time, Hagen and the Oslo Police District would not find it remotely helpful if the press were to publish an interview with an unhinged officer who was drunk on duty."

"Don't forget paranoid. *Paranoid*, unhinged and drunk." Harry tipped his head back and drained his glass.

"Please, Harry, no more paranoia. I've spoken to Winter at Kripos, and there's no evidence to suggest it's Finne."

"So what *is* there evidence to suggest, then?"

"Nothing."

"There was a dead woman lying there, of course there's evidence." Harry gestured to Nina that he was ready for his next glass.

"OK, this is what we've got from the Forensic Medical Institute," Katrine said. "Rakel died as the result of a knife wound to the back of her neck. The blade penetrated the part of the medulla oblongata that regulates breathing, between the top vertebra and the cranium. She probably died instantly."

"I didn't ask Bjørn about the other two," Harry said.

"The other two what?"

"Knife wounds."

He saw Katrine swallow. He could tell she had been hoping to spare him.

"Her stomach," she said.

"So not necessarily a painless death, then?"

"Harry . . ."

"Go on," Harry said harshly, hunching over. It was as if he could feel the stab wounds himself.

Katrine cleared her throat. "As you know, it's usually extremely difficult to determine the time of death with any degree of accuracy when someone's been dead for over twenty-four hours, as in this case. But as you may have heard, the Forensic Medical Institute and the Criminal Forensics Unit have together developed a new method where they combine measurements of rectal temperature, eye temperature, hypoxanthine levels in the intraocular fluid, and brain temperature . . ."

"Brain temperature?"

"Yes. The cranium protects the brain which means that it's less affected by external factors. They insert a needle-like probe through the nose, into the lamina cribrosa where the base of the skull—"

"You've obviously learned a lot of Latin recently."

Katrine stopped.

"Sorry," Harry said. "I'm . . . I'm not . . ."

"Don't worry about it," Katrine said. "There were a couple of fortuitous external factors. We know that the temperature on the ground floor was constant, because all the radiators are controlled by a central thermostat. And because that temperature was relatively low . . ."

"She used to say she thought better with a woolly jumper and a cold head," Harry said.

". . . the internal organs of the body hadn't yet quite cooled down to the temperature of the room. Which means that we've been able to use this new method to determine that the time of death was somewhere between 22:00 on Saturday and 02:00 on Sunday, 11 March."

"What about the crime-scene investigation, what did that come up with?"

"The front door was unlocked when the first officers arrived, and because it hasn't got a Yale lock, that suggests the perpetrator left via that door. There are no signs of a break-in, which suggests that the front door was unlocked when the killer arrived . . ."

"Rakel always kept that door locked. And all the other doors. That house is a fucking fortress."

". . . or that Rakel let him in."

"Mm." Harry turned and looked impatiently for Nina.

"You're right about it being a fortress. Bjørn was one of the first on the scene, and he says he went through the house from basement to attic, and all the doors were locked from the inside, and all the windows closed with their latches on. So what do you think?"

"I think there must be more evidence."

"Yes," Katrine said with a nod. "There's evidence of someone removing the evidence. Someone who *knows* what evidence he needs to remove."

"OK. And you don't think that Finne knows how to do that?"

"Oh, I do. And obviously Finne is a suspect, he always will be. But we can't say that publicly, we can't point the finger at a specific individual based on nothing but gut feeling."

"Gut feeling? Finne threatened me and my family, I've told you that."

Katrine stayed silent.

Harry looked at her. Then he nodded slowly. "Correction: *claims* the spurned husband of the murder victim."

Katrine leaned over the table. "Listen. The sooner we can rule you out of the case, the less fuss there'll be. Right now Kripos are taking the lead, but we're working with them, so I can push them to prioritise deciding whether or not you're beyond suspicion, then we can issue a press release."

"Press release?"

"You know the papers aren't saying anything explicitly, but their readers aren't stupid. And they're not wrong, because the probability that the husband is the killer in cases like this is around . . ."

"Eighty percent," Harry said loudly and slowly.

"Sorry," Katrine said, turning red. "We just need to stop that in its tracks as soon as possible."

"I get it," Harry mumbled, wondering if he ought to try calling for Nina. "I'm just a bit sensitive today."

Katrine reached her hand across the table and put it on his. "I can't even begin to imagine what it must be like, Harry. Losing the love of your life like that."

Harry looked at her hand. "Nor me," he said. "And that's why I'm planning to be as far away as possible while it eventually sinks in. Nina!"

"They can't interview you if you're drunk, so you won't be ruled out of the case until you sober up."

"It's only beer, I'll be sober again in a few hours if they call. The maternal role suits you, by the way, have I told you?"

Katrine smiled briefly and stood up. "I need to get back. Kripos have asked to use our interview facilities. Look after yourself, Harry."

"I'll do my best. Go and get him."

"Harry . . ."

"If you don't, I will. Nina!"

Dagny Jensen was walking along the spring-damp path between the gravestones in the Vår Frelsers Cemetery. There was a smell of scorched metal from some roadworks on Ullevålsveien, as well as decaying flowers and wet earth. And dog shit. This was what spring was like in Oslo just after the snow melted, but she couldn't help wondering who they were, these dog owners who made use of the usually deserted cemetery, where they could walk away from their dogs' excrement without any witnesses. Dagny had been visiting her mother's grave, like she did every Monday after her last class at the Cathedral School, only three or four minutes' walk away, where Dagny worked as an English teacher. She missed her mother, missed their daily conversations about everything and nothing. Her mother had been such a real, vital part of Dagny's life that when they called from the old people's home to say her mother was dead, at first she hadn't believed it. Not even when she saw the body, which looked like a wax doll, a fake. That's to say, her brain knew, of course, but her body refused. Her body demanded to have actually witnessed her mother's death in order to accept it. Sometimes Dagny still dreamed that someone was banging on her door up on Thorvald Meyers gate, and that her mother was standing outside, like it was the most natural thing in the world. And why not? Soon they'd be able to send people to Mars, and who could know *for certain* that it was medically impossible to breathe life back into a dead body? During the funeral the priest, a young woman, had said that no one knew what lay on the other side of the threshold of death, that all we knew was that those who crossed it never came back. That had upset Dagny. Not that the so-called church of the people had become so feeble that it had surrendered its only real function: to give absolute and comforting answers about what happened after death. No, it was the "never" that the priest had uttered with such confidence. If people needed hope, a fixed belief that their loved ones would one day rise from the dead, why take that away from them? And if what the priest's faith claimed was true, that it had happened before, then surely it could happen again? Dagny would be forty in two years, she had never been married or engaged, she hadn't had any children, she hadn't travelled to Micronesia, she hadn't realised her dream of starting an orphanage in Eritrea or finished that poetry collection. And she hoped that she would never again hear anyone say the word "never."

Dagny was heading up the path at the end of the cemetery closest to Ullevålsveien when she caught sight of the back view of a man. Or rather she noticed the long, thick, black plait that hung down his back, as well as the fact that he wasn't wearing a jacket over his checked flannel shirt. He was standing in front of a headstone that Dagny had noticed before, when it had been covered by snow in winter, and she had thought it belonged to someone who had left no one behind, or at least no one who had cared for him or her.

Dagny had the type of appearance that's easy to forget. A thin, small woman who so far had managed to creep quietly through life. It was already rush hour on Ullevålsveien—though it wasn't even three o'clock—because the working week had shrunk so much in Norway over the past forty years, to a level that either irritated or impressed foreigners. So she was surprised when the man evidently heard her approaching. And, when he turned around, that he was an old man. His leathery face had furrows so sharp and deep that they seemed cut to the bone. His body looked slender, muscular and young beneath the flannel shirt, but his face and the yellowish whites around his pin-sized pupils and brown irises declared that he must be at least seventy. He was wearing a red bandana, like a Native American, and had a moustache around his thick lips.

"Good afternoon," he said loudly to drown out the traffic.

"How nice to see someone at this grave," Dagny replied with a smile. She wasn't usually so talkative with strangers, but today she was in a good mood, almost a little excited, because she had been asked out for a drink by Gunnar, a new teacher who also taught English.

The man smiled back.

"It's my son's," he said in a deep, rough voice.

"I'm sorry to hear that." She saw that what was sticking out of the ground in front of the headstone wasn't a flower, but a feather.

"In the Cherokee tribe they used to lay eagles' feathers in the coffins of their dead," the man said, as if he had read her thoughts. "This isn't an eagle's, but a buzzard's."

"Really? Where did you find it?"

"The buzzard feather? Oslo's surrounded by wilderness on all sides, didn't you know?" The man smiled.

"Well, it seems fairly civilised. But the feather is a nice thought, perhaps it will carry your son's soul to heaven."

The man shook his head. "Wilderness, no civilisation. My son was murdered by a policeman. Now, my son probably won't get to heaven no matter how many feathers I give him, but he's not in a hell as fiery as the one that policeman is going to." There was no hatred in his voice, just sorrow, as if he felt for the policeman. "And who are you visiting?"

"My mother," Dagny said, looking at the son's gravestone. Valentin Gjertsen. There was something vaguely familiar about the name.

"Not a widow, then. Because a b-beautiful woman like you must have married young and have children?"

"Thanks, but neither of those." She laughed, and a thought ran through her head: a child with her fair curls and Gunnar's confident smile. That made her smile even wider. "That's lovely," she said, pointing at the beautiful, artistic metal object stuck in the ground in front of the headstone. "What does it symbolise?"

He pulled it up and held it out to her. It looked like a slithering snake and ended in a sharp point. "It symbolises death. Is there any m-madness in your family?"

"Er . . . not that I know of."

He tugged at one sleeve of his shirt, revealing a wristwatch.

"Quarter past two," Dagny said.

He smiled as if it were an unnecessary observation, pressed a button on the side of the watch, looked up and added: "Two and a half m-minutes."

Was he going to time something?

Suddenly he had taken two long strides and was standing right in front of her. He smelled of bonfires.

And as if he could read her thoughts, he said: "I can smell you too. I smelled you when you were walking this way." His lips were wet now, they curled like eels in a trap when he spoke. "You're ov-ovulating."

Dagny regretted stopping. But still she stood there, as if pinned to the spot by his stare.

"If you don't struggle, it will soon be over," he whispered.

It was as if she finally managed to pull free, and she spun around to run. But a quick hand had reached under her short jacket, grabbed hold of the belt of her trousers and tugged her back. She let out a short cry and glanced across the deserted cemetery before she was thrown against—and pushed into—the hedge that grew in front of the railings facing Ullevålsveien. Two powerful arms wrapped around her chest, holding her in a vise-like grip. She managed to take a deep breath to scream, but it was as if that was what he had been waiting for, because when she started to make a noise by letting the air out, the arms tightened the vise a bit more and emptied her lungs of air. She saw that he was still holding the curved metal snake in one hand. The other moved to her neck and squeezed. Her vision was already starting to blur, and even though one arm around her chest suddenly let go, she felt her body turn limp and heavy.

This isn't happening, she thought as the other hand forced its way between her thighs from behind. She felt something sharp against her stomach just below her waistband and heard the tearing sound as the sharp object split her trousers from the belt in the front all the way to the belt loop at the back. *This doesn't happen, not in a cemetery in the middle of the day in the middle of Oslo. It doesn't happen to me, anyway!*

Then the hand around her neck let go, and inside Dagny's head it sounded like when Mum blew air into the old inflatable mattress, as she desperately inhaled a mixture of Oslo's spring air and the exhaust fumes of rush hour into her aching lungs. At the same time she felt something sharp pressed against her throat. She caught a glimpse of the curved knife at the bottom of her field of vision and heard his whispering, rough voice close to her ear:

"The first was a boa constrictor. This is a poisonous snake. One little bite and you die. So just stay perfectly still and don't make a sound. That's right. Just like that. Are you standing c-comfortably?"

Dagny Jensen felt tears running down her cheeks.

"There, there, everything's going to be fine. Do you want to make me a happy man and marry me?"

Dagny felt the point of the knife press harder against her throat.

"Do you?"

She nodded cautiously.

"Then we're engaged, my darling." She felt his lips against the back of her neck. Right in front of her, on the other side of the hedge and railings, she could hear footsteps on the pavement, two people walking past, engaged in lively conversation.

"And now to consummate our engagement. I told you the snake pressed to your neck symbolises d-death. But this symbolises life . . ."

Dagny felt it and screwed her eyes tight shut.

"Our life. A life that we shall create now . . ."

He thrust forward, and she clenched her teeth to stop herself crying out.

"For each son I lose, I shall bring f-five more into the world," he hissed into her ear as he thrust again. "And you wouldn't dare destroy what we have created, would you? Because a child is the Lord's work."

He thrust a third time and ejaculated with a drawn-out groan.

He removed the knife and let go of her. Dagny loosened her grip and saw that the palms of her hands were bleeding from where she had grabbed the thorny hedge. But she didn't move, stayed bent over with her back to him.

"Turn around," the man commanded.

She didn't want to, but she did as he said.

He was holding her purse, and had pulled out a bill.

"Dagny Jensen," he read. "Thorvald Meyers gate. Nice street. I'll be calling in from time to time." He handed her the purse, tilted his head and looked at her. "Remember, this is our secret, Dagny. From now on I'm going to watch over and protect you, like an eagle you can never see, but one you know is always up there and it can see you. Nothing can help you, because I am a spirit that no one can catch. But no harm will come to you either, because we're engaged now, and my hand rests upon you."

He held up one hand, and only now did she see that what she had thought was a nasty scar on the back of his hand was actually an open hole that went right through.

He left, and Dagny Jensen sank weakly onto the dirty snow by the railings with a stifled sob. Through her tears she saw the man's back, and the plait of hair, as he walked calmly through the cemetery towards the northern gate. There was a bleeping, pulsating sound, and the man stopped, pulled up his sleeve and pressed his wrist. The bleeping stopped.

Harry opened his eyes. He was lying on something soft, staring up at the ceiling, at the small but beautiful crystal chandelier Rakel had brought home with her when she moved back after her years at the embassy in Moscow. Seen from below, the crystals formed the letter S, he had never noticed that before. A woman's voice said his name. He rolled over but couldn't see anyone. "Harry," the voice repeated. He was dreaming. Was this waking up? He opened his eyes. He was still sitting upright. He was still in Schrøder's.

"Harry?" It was Nina's voice. "You've got a visitor."

He looked up. Right into Rakel's worried eyes. The face had

Rakel's mouth, Rakel's faintly glowing skin. But the father's smooth Russian hair. No, he was still dreaming.

"Oleg," Harry said in a thick voice, made an attempt to get up and give his stepson a hug, but had to give up. "I didn't think you'd get here until later."

"I arrived in Oslo an hour ago." The tall young man sank onto the chair where Katrine had sat earlier. He pulled a face as if he'd sat on a drawing pin.

Harry looked out of the window and discovered to his amazement that it had gotten dark.

"And how did you know . . ."

"Bjørn Holm tipped me off. I've spoken to a funeral director and have arranged a meeting for tomorrow morning. Will you come with me?"

Harry let his head fall forward. Groaned. "Of course I'll come with you, Oleg. Christ, here I am, drunk when you arrive, and now you're doing what ought to be my job."

"Sorry, but it's easier to keep busy. Keep my head working on practical things. I've started to think about what we should do with the house when . . ." He stopped, raised one hand in front of his face and pressed his thumb and middle finger to his temples. "That's sick, right? Mum's barely even cold, and . . ." His fingers massaged his temples, and his Adam's apple bobbed up and down.

"It's not sick," Harry said. "Your brain is trying to find a way to avoid the pain. I've found my own way, but I wouldn't recommend it." He moved the empty glass that was between them. "You can fool the pain for a while, but it will always catch up with you. When you relax a little, let your guard down, when you stick your head up out of the trench. Until then, it's fine not to feel too much."

"Numb," Oleg said. "I just feel numb. I realised earlier that I hadn't eaten anything today, so I bought a chili hotdog. I smothered it with the strongest mustard they had, just so I could *feel* something. And you know what?"

"Yes," Harry said. "I know. Nothing."

"Nothing," Oleg repeated, blinking something out of his eyes.

"The pain will come," Harry said. "You don't have to look for it. It will find you. You, and all the chinks in your armour."

"Has it found you?"

"I'm still asleep," Harry said. "I'm trying not to wake up." He looked at his hands. He would have given anything to take some of

Oleg's pain on himself. What could he say? That nothing will ever be so painful as the first time you lose someone you really love? He no longer even knew if that was true. He cleared his throat.

"The house is shut off until the crime-scene team are finished. Are you staying at mine?"

"I'm staying with Helga's parents."

"OK. How's Helga taking it?"

"Badly. She and Rakel had become good friends."

Harry nodded. "Do you want to talk about what happened?"

Oleg shook his head. "I had a long talk with Bjørn, he told me what we know. And don't know."

We. Harry noted that just a few months into the practical year of his training, Oleg found it perfectly natural to use the pronoun "we" about the police in general. The same "we" that he himself had never used even after twenty-five years in the force. But experience had taught him that it was more deeply imprinted in him than he was aware of. Because it was a home. For better or worse. And when you've lost everything else, mostly for better. He hoped that Oleg and Helga would cling tight to each other.

"I've been called in for an interview first thing tomorrow morning," Oleg said. "Kripos."

"Right."

"Will they ask about you?"

"If they're doing their job, they will."

"What shall I say?"

Harry shrugged. "The truth. Unvarnished, the way you see it."

"OK." Oleg closed his eyes again and took a deep breath. "Are you going to get me a beer?"

Harry sighed. "I am, as you can see, not much of a man, but at least I'm the sort of man who has trouble breaking promises. That's why I never promised your mother much. But I promised her this: because your father has the same bad gene as me, I swore that I would never, ever buy you a drink."

"Mum did, though."

"That promise was my idea, Oleg. I'm not going to get you into anything."

Oleg turned around and raised one finger. Nina nodded.

"How long are you going to sleep?" Oleg asked.

"As long as I can."

The beer arrived, and Oleg drank it slowly in small sips. He put the glass down between them each time, as if it was something they were sharing. They didn't speak. They didn't need to. Couldn't. Their silent sobbing was deafening.

When the glass was empty, Oleg took out his phone and looked at it. "It's Helga's brother, he's picking me up in the car, he's outside. Can we give you a lift home?"

Harry shook his head. "Thanks, but I need the walk."

"I'll text you the address of the funeral director."

"Great."

They stood up at the same time. Harry noted that Oleg was still a couple of centimetres short of his own 1.92 metres. Then he remembered that the race was over, and that Oleg was a full-grown man.

They embraced, holding each other hard. Chins on each other's shoulders. And didn't let go.

"Dad?"

"Mm?"

"When you called and said it was about Mum, and I asked if you were getting back together . . . That was because I asked her two days ago if she couldn't give it another chance."

Harry felt something catch in his chest. "What?"

"She said she'd think about it over the weekend. But I know she wanted it. She wanted you back."

Harry closed his eyes and clenched his jaw so tightly it felt like the muscles would burst. *Why did you have to come and make me so lonely?* There wasn't enough alcohol in the world to fend off this pain.

10

Rakel had wanted him back.

Did that make things better or just even worse?

Harry dug his phone out of his pocket to switch it off. He saw that Oleg had sent a text about a couple of the practical questions the funeral directors had asked. Three missed calls that he guessed were newspapers, as well as one call from a number he recognised as belonging to Alexandra at the Forensic Medical Institute. Did she want to pass on her condolences? Or to have sex? She could have sent a text if she wanted to convey her condolences. Both, maybe. The young technician had said several times that strong emotions turned her on, whether they were good or bad. Rage, joy, hate, pain. But grief? Hm. Lust and shame. The shocking, titillating idea of fucking someone in mourning—there were probably worse things. Wasn't it, for instance, worse that he was sitting here thinking about Alexandra's possible sexual fantasies just hours after Rakel had been found dead? What the hell was that about?

Harry held the Off button until the screen turned black, then slipped his phone back into his trouser pocket. He looked at the microphone on the table in front of him in the cramped doll's house room. The little red light indicated that it was recording. Then he fixed his gaze on the person on the other side of the table.

"Shall we begin?"

Sung-min Larsen nodded. Rather than hang his Burberry jacket on the hook on the wall next to Harry's peacoat, he had hung it over the back of the only free chair.

Larsen cleared his throat before he began.

"Today is 13 March, the time is 15:50, and we're in interview room 3 in Police Headquarters in Oslo. The interviewer is Detective Inspector Sung-min Larsen of Kripos, the interviewee Harry Hole . . .”

Harry listened as Larsen continued, his language so distinct and correct that it sounded like someone in an old radio play. Larsen held his gaze as he gave Harry’s ID number and address without checking the notes in front of him. Perhaps he’d memorised them to impress his hitherto more-esteemed colleague. Unless it was just his standard scare tactic to demonstrate intellectual superiority, so that the interviewee would give up any idea of manipulating and lying to hide the truth. And of course there was a third possibility: that Sung-min Larsen simply had a good memory.

“As a police officer I assume you’re aware of your rights,” Larsen said. “And you’ve declined the option of having a lawyer present.”

“Am I a suspect?” Harry asked, looking past the curtains to the control room, where Police Inspector Winter was sitting with his arms folded as he watched them.

“This is a routine interview, you’re not under suspicion of anything,” Larsen said. He was following the rulebook. He went on to inform Harry that the interview was being recorded. “Can you tell me about your relationship to the deceased, Rakel Fauke?”

“She’s . . . she *was* my wife.”

“You’re separated?”

“No. Well, yes, she’s dead.”

Sung-min Larsen looked up at Harry as if he wondered if that was meant as a challenge. “Not separated, then?”

“No, we hadn’t got that far. But I’d moved out.”

“I understand from other people we’ve spoken to that she was the one who wanted to split up. What was the cause of the break-up?”

She had wanted him back. “Disagreements. Can we skip to the bit where you ask if I’ve got an alibi for the time of the murder?”

“I appreciate that this is painful, but . . .”

“Thanks for letting me know how you feel, Larsen, and your guess hits the nail on the head, it is painful, but the reason for my request is that I don’t have much time.”

“Oh? I understood that you’ve been suspended until further notice.”

“I have. But I’ve got a lot of drinking to do.”

“And that’s urgent?”

“Yes.”

“I’d still like to know what sort of contact you and Rakel Fauke had during the time before her murder. Your stepson Oleg says he felt he never got a good explanation either from you or his mother for why you split up. But that it probably didn't help that you were spending more and more of your free time while you were a lecturer at Police College trying to track down Svein Finne, who had just been released from prison."

"When I said 'request,' that was a nice way of saying no."

"So you're refusing to explain your relationship with the deceased?"

"I'm *declining* the option to tell you about personal details and *offering* to give you my alibi so that we can both save time. So that you and Winter can concentrate on finding the culprit. I assume you remember from your lectures that if murder cases aren't solved within the first forty-eight hours, the witnesses' memories and any physical evidence deteriorate to the point where the chances of solving the case are reduced by half. Shall we get to the night of the murder, Larsen?"

The Kripos detective stared at a point on Harry's forehead as he tapped the end of a pen on the table. Harry could see he would have liked to glance across at Winter to get some indication of where to go from here: press on, or do as Harry wanted.

"OK," Larsen said. "Let's do that."

"Great," Harry said. "So tell me."

"Sorry?"

"Tell me where I was on the night of the murder."

Sung-min Larsen smiled. "You want *me* to tell you?"

"You've chosen to interview other people before me, to make sure you're as prepared as you can be. Which is what I would have done in your place, Larsen. That means you've spoken to Bjørn Holm and know I was at the Jealousy Bar, where he came to find me that night, and took me home and put me to bed. I was drunk as hell, don't remember a thing, and have absolutely no idea what time any of this happened. So I'm in no position to give you any times that can either confirm or contradict what he told you. But with a bit of luck you've spoken to the bar's owner and maybe a few other witnesses who've been able to confirm what Holm said. And seeing as I don't know what time my wife died, it's pretty much down to you to tell me if I've got an alibi or not, Larsen."

Larsen clicked his pen several times as he studied Harry, like a poker player toying with his chips before deciding whether to risk them or not. "OK," he said, putting the pen down. "We've checked the base stations in the area around the crime scene for the time in question, and none of them picked up any signal from your mobile."

"OK. I've been out of the game, but is it still the case that all mobile phones automatically send a signal to the nearest base station every thirty minutes?"

Larsen didn't answer.

"So either I left my phone at home, or I went there and back within half an hour. So I'll ask again: have I got an alibi?"

This time Larsen couldn't help it, he glanced over at the control room and Winter. From the corner of his eye Harry saw Winter rub his hand over his granite head before giving the detective a slight nod.

"Bjørn Holm says the two of you left the Jealousy Bar at half past ten, and the owner has confirmed that. Holm says he helped you into your flat and put you to bed. On his way out, Holm met your neighbour, Gule, who was coming home from his shift on the trams. I understand that Gule lives on the floor below you, and he says he was up until three o'clock that night, that the walls are thin and that he would have heard if you'd gone out again before then."

"Mm. And when does the medical officer say the victim died?"

Larsen looked down at his notebook as if he needed to check it, but Harry knew the young detective had all the facts firmly fixed in his memory, and just wanted time to figure out how much he could tell his interviewee—or how much he wanted to. Harry also noted that Larsen didn't look at Winter before making his decision.

"Forensics are basing their findings on body temperature versus room temperature, seeing as the body wasn't moved. It's still hard to specify an exact time given that she'd probably been lying there for a day and a half, but sometime between ten o'clock in the evening and two o'clock in the morning seems most likely."

"Which means that I'm officially ruled out?"

The suited detective nodded slowly. Harry noted that Winter was sitting up in his chair outside, as if he wanted to protest, and that Larsen was ignoring him.

"Mm. And now you're wondering if I wanted to get rid of her, but that as a homicide detective I knew I'd inevitably be one of the suspects, so did I sort out a hitman and an alibi? Is that why I'm still here?"

Larsen ran his hand over his tie clip, which Harry noticed had the British Airways logo on it. "Not really. But we're aware of how important the first forty-eight hours are, so we wanted to get this out of the way before asking you what *you* think happened."

"Me?"

"You're no longer a suspect. But you're still . . ." Larsen let this hang in the air for a moment before he said the name with his almost exaggerated pronunciation: "Harry Hole."

Harry looked across at Winter. Was that why he had let his detective reveal what they knew? They were stuck. They needed help. Or was this Sung-min Larsen's own initiative? Winter looked oddly stiff as he sat out there.

"So it's true, then?" Harry said. "The perpetrator didn't leave a single piece of forensic evidence at the scene?"

Harry took Larsen's expressionless face as confirmation.

"I've got no idea what happened," Harry said.

"Bjørn Holm said you'd found some unidentified boot marks on the property."

"Yes. But they could just have been from someone who got lost, that sort of thing does happen."

"Really? There's no sign of a break-in, and Forensics have confirmed that your . . . that the victim was killed where she was found. Which suggests that the killer was invited in. Would the victim have let a man she didn't know into the house?"

"Mm. Did you notice the bars on the windows?"

"Wrought-iron bars over all twelve windows, but not the four basement windows," Larsen said without hesitation.

"That wasn't paranoia, but a consequence of being married to a murder detective with a rather too-high profile."

Larsen made a note. "Let's assume the murderer was someone she knew. The presumed reconstruction suggests that they were standing face to face. The killer closer to the kitchen, the victim nearer the door, when he first stabbed her twice in the stomach."

Harry took a deep breath. The stomach. Rakel had been in pain before the blow to the back of her neck. The blow that put her out of her misery.

"The fact that the killer was closer to the kitchen," Larsen went on. "That made me think that the killer had moved into a more intimate part of the home, that he felt at home there. Do you agree, Hole?"

"That's one possibility. Another is that he walked round her to grab the knife that's missing from the block."

"How do you know—"

"I managed to take a quick look at the scene before your boss threw me out."

Larsen tilted his head slightly and looked at Harry. As if he were evaluating him. "I see. Well, the business with the kitchen made us think of a third possibility. That it was a woman."

"Oh?"

"I know it doesn't often happen, but I've just read that a woman has confessed to the Borggata stabbing. The daughter. Heard of that one?"

"I might have."

"A woman would be less suspicious of opening the door and letting another woman in, even if they didn't know each other well. And for some reason or other, I find it easier to imagine a woman going straight into another woman's kitchen than a man. OK, maybe that's stretching things a bit."

"I agree," Harry said, without specifying if he meant the first, second or both ideas. Or that he agreed in general, that he had thought the same when he was at the scene.

"Are there any women who could have had a motive to harm Rakel Fauke?" Larsen asked. "Jealousy, anything like that?"

Harry shook his head. Obviously he could have mentioned Silje Gravseng, but there was no reason to do that now. A few years ago she had been one of his students at Police College, and the closest thing Harry had had to a female stalker. She had visited him in his office one evening and tried to seduce him. Harry had rejected her advances, and she had reacted by accusing him of rape. But her story had been so full of holes that her own lawyer, Johan Krohn, had stopped her, and the whole thing ended with Silje having to leave Police College. After that she paid a visit to Rakel at the house, not to harm or threaten her, but to apologise. All the same, Harry had run a quick check on Silje yesterday. Perhaps because he remembered the hatred in her eyes when she'd realised he didn't want her. Perhaps because the lack of physical evidence suggested the killer knew a thing or two about detection methods. Perhaps because he wanted to rule out all other possibilities before reaching a final verdict. And enacting a final sentence. It hadn't taken long to find out that Silje Gravseng was working as a security guard up in Tromsø, where she had been on duty on Saturday night, 1,700 kilometres from Oslo.

"Going back to the knife," Larsen said when he got no response. "The knives in the block belong to a Japanese set, and the size and shape of the one that's missing matches the knife wounds. If we assume that was the murder weapon, that suggests that the murder was spontaneous rather than planned. Agreed?"

"That's one possibility. Another is that the killer knew about the block of knives before he arrived. A third is that the killer used his own knife, but decided to remove a knife from the scene in an attempt to confuse you, as well as getting rid of the forensic evidence."

Larsen made some more notes. Harry looked at the time and cleared his throat.

"Finally, Hole. You say you're not aware of any women who might have wanted to kill Rakel Fauke. What about men?"

Harry shook his head slowly.

"What about this Svein Finne?"

He shrugged his shoulders. "You'd have to ask him."

"We don't know where he is."

Harry stood up and took his peacoat from the hook on the wall. "If I run into him, I'll be sure to let him know you're looking for him, Larsen."

He turned towards the window, gave a two-fingered salute to Winter. He got a sour smile and one finger in return.

Larsen stood up and held his hand out to Harry. "Thanks for your help, Hole. Obviously you can find your own way."

"The big question is whether or not you lot can." Harry gave Larsen a brief smile, an even briefer handshake, then left.

At the lift he pressed the button and leaned his forehead against the shiny metal beside the door.

She wanted you back.

So, did that make things better or worse?

All these pointless what-ifs. All the self-flagellating I-should-haves. But something else as well, the pathetic hope people cling to about there being a place where those who love each other, those who have Old Tjikko's roots, will meet again, because the thought of that not being the case is unbearable.

The lift doors slid open. Empty. Just a claustrophobic, constricting coffin inviting him in to carry him down. Down to what? To all-encompassing darkness?

Anyway, Harry rarely used lifts, he couldn't stand them.

He hesitated. Then stepped inside.

II

Harry woke with a start and stared out at the room. The echo of his own scream was still bouncing between the walls. He looked at the time. Ten o'clock. In the evening. He pieced together the previous thirty-six hours. He had been drunk for pretty much all of them, absolutely nothing had happened, but despite that he had still managed to come up with a workable timeline with no holes in it. He was usually able to do that. But Saturday evening at the Jealousy stood out as a long, complete blackout. Probably the long-term effects of alcohol abuse finally catching up with him.

Harry swung his legs off the sofa as he tried to remember what had made him cry out this time. Then immediately regretted doing so. He had been holding Rakel's face in his hands, her shattered eyes had been staring, not *at* him, but *through* him, like he wasn't there. She had a thin layer of blood on her chin, as if she'd coughed and a bubble of blood had burst on her lips.

Harry grabbed the bottle of Jim Beam from the coffee table and took a swig. It no longer seemed to work. He took another. The odd thing was that even though he hadn't seen her face, and didn't want to see it before the funeral on Friday, it had been so real in the dream.

He looked at his phone, which lay black and dead beside the bottle on the table. It had been switched off since before the interview the previous morning. He ought to turn it on. Oleg was bound to have called. Things needed to be arranged. He needed to pull himself together. He picked up the cork of the bottle of Jim Beam from the end of the table. Sniffed it. It didn't smell of anything. He threw the cork at the bare wall and closed his fist round the neck of the bottle in a tight stranglehold.

12

At three o'clock in the afternoon Harry stopped drinking. There was nothing special that happened, no particular resolution that stopped him from drinking until four o'clock, or five, or the rest of the evening. His body simply couldn't take any more. He switched his phone on, ignored the missed calls and text messages, and called Oleg.

"Have you surfaced?"

"More like finished drowning," Harry said. "You?"

"Keeping afloat."

"Good. Beat me up first? Then talk about practical stuff?"

"OK. Ready?"

"Go for it."

Dagny Jensen looked at the time. It was only nine, and they had only just finished the main course. Gunnar had been responsible for most of the conversation, but Dagny still felt she couldn't handle any more. She explained that she had a headache, and Gunnar was very understanding, thank goodness. They skipped dessert, and he insisted on seeing her home even though she assured him that wasn't necessary.

"I know Oslo's safe," he said. "I just like walking."

He had talked about entertaining, harmless things, and she had done her best to pay attention and laugh in the right places, even though she was in complete meltdown inside. But as they passed Ringen Cinema and started the climb up Thorvald Meyers gate to the block where she lived, a silence arose. And then he said it, at last.

"You've seemed a little out of sorts in the past few days. It's none of my business, but is anything wrong, Dagny?"

She knew she'd been waiting for it. Hoping for it. That someone would ask. That it might prompt her to dare. Unlike all the rape victims who kept quiet about it, who covered their silence with shame, impotence, fear of not being believed. She had thought that she'd never react like that. And sure enough, she felt none of those things. So why was she behaving like this? Was that why, after she got home from the cemetery, she had cried for two hours non-stop before calling the police, then, while she was waiting to be transferred to the Vice Squad or wherever it was they wanted her to report her rape, she had suddenly cracked and hung up? Then fell asleep on the sofa and woke up in the middle of the night, when her first thought was that the rape was just something she'd dreamed. And she had felt an immense relief. Until she remembered. But she had also caught a glimpse of the idea that it could have been a bad dream. And that if she decided that was the case, it could go on being a dream, as long as she didn't tell a single soul about it.

"Dagny?"

She took a trembling breath and managed to say: "No, there's nothing wrong. This is where I live. Thanks for walking me home, Gunnar. See you tomorrow."

"Hope you're feeling better then."

"Thanks."

He must have noticed that she shrank away when he hugged her, because he let go of her quickly. She walked towards stairwell D as she took her key out of her bag, and when she looked up again she saw that someone had stepped out of the darkness into the light shining from the lamp above the door. A broad-shouldered, slim man in a brown suede jacket and a red bandana around his long black hair. She stopped abruptly with a gasp.

"Don't be scared, Dagny, I'm not going to hurt you." His eyes were glowing like embers in his furrowed face. "I'm just here to check up on you and our child. Because I keep my promises." His voice was low, barely more than a whisper, but he didn't have to speak loudly for her to hear him. "Because you do remember my promise, don't you? We're engaged, Dagny. Until death do us part."

Dagny tried to breathe, but it was as if her lungs were paralysed.

"To seal our union, let's repeat our promise with God as our witness, Dagny. Let's meet in the Catholic church in Vika on Sunday evening, when we'll have it to ourselves. Nine o'clock? Don't leave me standing at the altar." He let out a short laugh. "Until then, sleep well. Both of you."

He stepped aside, out into the darkness again, and the light from the stairwell momentarily blinded her. By the time she had raised her hand to her eyes, he was gone.

Dagny stood there in silence as warm tears trickled down her cheeks. She looked at the hand holding the key until it stopped shaking. Then she unlocked the door and went inside.

13

The altocumulus clouds lay like a crocheted cloth across the sky above Voksen Church.

"My condolences," Mikael Bellman said in a heartfelt voice, with a well-practised facial expression. The former young Chief of Police, now an equally young Minister of Justice, shook Harry's hand with his right as he placed his left hand on top of the handshake as if to seal it. As if to express that he really meant it. Or to assure himself that Harry wasn't going to snatch his hand away before the assembled press photographers—who hadn't been given permission to take pictures inside the church—had done their thing. Once Bellman had ticked off *Minister of Justice takes time to attend funeral of former police colleague's spouse*, he disappeared towards the waiting black SUV. He had probably checked in advance that Harry wasn't a suspect.

Harry and Oleg went on shaking hands and nodding at the faces in front of them, most of them Rakel's friends and colleagues. A few neighbours. Apart from Oleg, Rakel didn't have any close relatives still alive, but the large church had still been well over half full. The funeral director had said that if they'd delayed the funeral until the following week, even more people would have been able to rearrange their schedules. Harry was pleased Oleg hadn't announced any gathering after the funeral. Neither of them knew Rakel's colleagues particularly well or felt like chatting to the neighbours. What needed saying about Rakel had been said by Oleg, Harry and a couple of her childhood friends inside the church, and that would have to do. Even the priest had to confine himself to the hymns, prayers and prescribed phrases.

"Fuck." It was Øystein Eikeland, one of Harry's own two childhood friends. With tears in his eyes he placed his hands on Harry's shoulders and breathed fresh alcohol into his face. Maybe it was just his appearance that made Harry think of Øystein whenever anyone trotted out jokes about Keith Richards. *For every cigarette you smoke, God takes an hour away from you . . . and gives it to Keith Richards.* Harry saw that his friend was thinking hard before he finally opened his mouth to reveal his brown stumps and repeated, with a little more intensity: "Fuck."

"Thanks," Harry said.

"Tresko couldn't make it," Øystein said without letting go of Harry. "That's to say, he gets panic attacks in groups of more than . . . well, more than two people. But he sends his best wishes, and says . . ." Øystein screwed his eyes up against the morning sunlight. "Fuck."

"A few of us are meeting at Schrøder's."

"Free bar?"

"Max three."

"OK."

"Roar Bohr, I was Rakel's chief." Harry looked into the slate-grey eyes of a man who was fifteen centimetres shorter than him, but who still seemed just as tall. And there was something about his posture, and also the slightly archaic "chief," that put Harry in mind of an officer in the military. His handshake was firm and his gaze steady and direct, but there was also a soreness, possibly even vulnerability there. But perhaps that was because of the circumstances. "Rakel was my best co-worker, and a wonderful person. It's a huge loss to the NHRI and all of us who work there, and especially for me, because I worked so closely with her."

"Thanks," Harry said, believing him. But perhaps that was just the warmth of his handshake. The warm hand of a man who worked in human rights. Harry watched Roar Bohr as he walked over to two women standing a short distance away, and noted that Bohr looked down at where he was putting his feet. Like someone who automatically looks for landmines. Then he noticed that there was something familiar about one of the women, although she had her back to him. Bohr said something, evidently quietly, because the woman had to lean over, and Bohr put one hand gently on the base of her spine.

And then the condolences were finished. The hearse had driven away with the coffin, and a few people had already gone off to meetings and other everyday concerns. Harry saw Truls Berntsen walking off on his own to catch the bus back to the office, presumably to play more solitaire. Some of the others were standing in little groups outside the church talking. Police Chief Gunnar Hagen and Anders Wyller, the young detective Harry was renting his flat from, were standing with Katrine and Bjørn, who had brought the baby with them. Some people probably found the sound of a baby crying something of a comfort at a funeral, a reminder that life did actually go on. To anyone who *wanted* life to go on, anyway. Harry announced to everyone who was still there that there was going to be a small gathering at Schrøder's. Sis, his sister, who had travelled up from Kristiansand with her partner, came over, gave Harry and Oleg each a long, hard hug, then said they needed to be getting back. Harry nodded and said that was a shame but that he understood, even though he was actually relieved. Apart from Oleg, Sis was the only person with the potential to make him cry in public.

Helga drove to Schrøder's with Harry and Oleg. Nina had laid a long table for them.

A dozen people showed up, and Harry was sitting hunched over his coffee listening to the sound of the others talking when someone put a hand on his back. It was Bjørn.

"I don't suppose people usually give presents at funerals." He handed Harry a flat, rectangular parcel. "But this has helped me through some rough times."

"Thanks, Bjørn." Harry turned the present over. It wasn't hard to guess what it was. "By the way, there's something I meant to ask you."

"Oh?"

"Sung-min Larsen didn't ask me about the wildlife camera when he interviewed me. Which means you didn't mention it when they spoke to you."

"He didn't ask. And I thought it was up to you to mention it if you thought it was relevant."

"Mm. Really?"

"If you didn't tell them about it either, then it strikes me that it can't be that relevant."

"You didn't say anything because you've figured out that I'm planning to go after Finne without Kripos or anyone else getting involved?"

"I didn't hear that, and if I did, I wouldn't have a clue what you were talking about."

"Thanks, Bjørn. One more thing: what do you know about Roar Bohr?"

"Bohr? Only that he's the guy in charge where Rakel worked. Something to do with human rights, isn't it?"

"The National Human Rights Institution."

"That's it. It was Bohr who called to say they were worried when Rakel didn't show up for work."

"Mm." Harry glanced over at the door when it swung open. And instantly forgot whatever follow-up question he had been thinking of asking Bjørn. It was her, the woman who had been talking to Bohr with her back to Harry. She stopped and looked around tentatively. She hadn't changed much. That face with its high cheekbones, prominent, jet-black eyebrows above almost childishly large green eyes, her honey-brown hair, full lips and slightly wide mouth.

Her gaze finally found Harry and she lit up.

"Kaja!" he heard Gunnar Hagen exclaim. "Come and sit down!"

The Police Chief pulled out a chair.

The woman by the door smiled at Hagen and indicated that she wanted to say hello to Harry first.

The skin of her hand felt just as soft as he remembered.

"My condolences. I really do feel for you, Harry."

Her voice too.

"Thanks. This is Oleg. And his girlfriend, Helga. This is Kaja Solness, an old colleague."

They all shook hands.

"So you're back," Harry said.

"Not for long."

"Mm." He tried to think of something to say. Found nothing.

She put a feather-light hand on his arm. "You carry on, and I'll go and talk to Gunnar and the others."

Harry nodded and watched as her long legs wove their way between the chairs to the other end of the table.

Oleg leaned closer to him. "Who's she? Apart from an old colleague?"

"Long story."

"So I saw. What's the short version?"

Harry took a sip of coffee. "That I once let her go in favour of your mother."

It was three o'clock when the first of the final three guests, Øystein, stood up, misquoted a Bob Dylan lyric in parting and left.

One of the two remaining guests moved to the chair next to Harry's.

"Haven't you got a job to go to?" Kaja asked.

"Not tomorrow either. Suspended until further notice. You?"

"I'm on standby for the Red Cross. I mean, I'm getting paid, but right now I'm just waiting at home for shit to kick off somewhere in the world."

"Which it will, of course?"

"Which it will. When you look at it like that, it's a bit like working in Crime Squad. You go around almost hoping that something terrible is going to happen."

"Mm. The Red Cross. That's a bit of a leap from Crime Squad."

"Yes and no. I'm in charge of security. My last deployment was two years in Afghanistan."

"And before that?"

"Another two years. In Afghanistan." She smiled, revealing her small, pointed teeth, the imperfect feature that made her face interesting.

"What's so good about Afghanistan?"

She shrugged her shoulders. "To start with it was probably just the fact that you were confronted with problems so big that your own personal problems seemed small. And that you could be useful. And then you get to like the people you meet and work with."

"Like Roar Bohr?"

"Yes. Did he tell you he was in Afghanistan?"

"No, but he looked like a soldier who doesn't want to step on any mines. Was he in Special Forces?"

Kaja looked at him thoughtfully. The pupils in the centre of those green irises were large. They didn't waste energy on the lighting in Schrøder's.

"Confidential?" Harry asked.

She shrugged again. "Yes, Bohr was a lieutenant colonel in the Special Operations Forces. He was one of the team sent to Kabul with a list of Taliban terrorists that the ISAF wanted taken out."

"Mm. A desk jockey, or did he shoot the jihadists himself?"

"We both took part in security meetings at the Norwegian Embassy, but I was never told any details. All I know is that Roar and his sister were both shooting champions in Vest-Agder."

"And he dealt with the list?"

"I assume so. You're pretty similar, you and Bohr. You don't give up until you've got the people you're after."

"If Bohr was so good at the job, why did he leave and start working with human rights?"

She raised an eyebrow. As if to ask why he was so interested in

Bohr. But she seemed to conclude that he just needed to talk about something different—anything, as long as it wasn't Rakel, himself, the current situation.

"ISAF was replaced by Resolute Support, which meant a transition from so-called peacekeeping to non-combat operations. So they were no longer allowed to shoot. Besides, his wife wanted him home. She couldn't handle being left on her own with two children any longer. A Norwegian officer with ambitions to become a general needs to have completed at least one tour in Afghanistan, so when Roar requested a transfer, he knew he was effectively ruling himself out of a senior position. And it probably just wasn't as enjoyable anymore. Besides, people with his leadership experience are highly sought-after in other branches."

"But to go from shooting people to *human rights*?"

"What do you think he was fighting for in Afghanistan?"

"Mm. An idealist and a family man, then."

"Roar is a man who believes in things. And who's prepared to make sacrifices for the people he loves. Like you did." She pulled a face. A fleeting, painful smile. She buttoned her coat. "That's worth respect, Harry."

"Mm. You think I sacrificed something back then?"

"We like to think we're rational, but we always follow the diktat of our hearts, don't we?" She pulled out a business card from her bag and laid it down on the table in front of him. "I still live in the same place. If you need someone to talk to, I know a bit about loss and longing."

The sun had slipped down behind the ridge, colouring the sky orange, when Harry let himself into the wooden house. Oleg was on his way back to Lakselv and had given him the keys so that he could let an estate agent in once a week. Harry had asked Oleg to think about whether he really wanted to sell the house, if it wouldn't be useful to come back to when he'd completed his year on placement. Somewhere for him and Helga, possibly. Oleg promised to think it through carefully, but it sounded like he'd made his mind up.

The crime-scene investigators had finished their work, and had cleaned up after themselves. That's to say: the pool of blood was gone, but not the classic chalk outline showing where the body had been lying. Harry could imagine the estate agent anxiously trying to find a tactful way to suggest that the chalk should be removed before the first viewing.

Harry went over to the kitchen window and watched the sky grow pale as the glow disappeared. Darkness took over. He had been sober for twenty-eight hours, and Rakel had been dead for at least 141.

He walked across the floor and stood above the outline. He knelt down. Ran his fingertips over the rough wooden floor. He lay on the floor, crawled inside the lines, and curled up into the same fetal position, trying to stay within the white lines. And then, at last, he started to cry. But there were no tears at first, just hoarse wails that started in his chest, grew and forced their way out through his too-narrow throat before finally filling the room, sounding like a man who was struggling to stay alive. When he stopped screaming, he rolled onto his back to catch his breath. And then the tears came. And through the tears, swimming forward as if in a dream, he saw the crystal chandelier directly above him. And saw that the crystals formed the letter S.

14

The birds were singing with joy in Lyder Sagens gate.

Possibly because it was nine o'clock in the morning and nothing had spoiled the day yet. Possibly because the sun was shining and it looked like it was going to be the perfect start to what was forecast to be a warm weekend. Or possibly because the birds in Lyder Sagens gate were happier than in the rest of the world. Because even in a country that regularly topped the statistics of the happiest countries in the world, this not particularly striking street named after a teacher from Bergen was a particular high point: 470 metres of happiness, free not only from financial worries, but also from exaggerated materialism, with solid, unfussy villas and large but not excessively neat gardens, where children's toys lay scattered with a charm that left no doubt as to the families' priorities. Bohemian, but with a new Audi, though not one of the flashy ones, in a garage full of old, heavy and delightfully impractical garden furniture made of well-seasoned wood. Lyder Sagens gate may have been one of the most expensive streets in the country, but its ideal resident seemed to be an artist who had inherited the house from their grandmother. Either way, the residents largely appeared to be good social democrats who believed in sustainable development and had values as solid as the outsized wooden beams that jutted out here and there from their old-fashioned houses.

Harry pushed the gate open and the creak sounded like an echo from the past. Everything seemed the same as before. The creak of the steps that led up to the door. The bell with no nameplate. The man's shoes, size forty-six, that Kaja Solness left outside to deter burglars and other unwelcome visitors.

Kaja opened the door, brushed a sun-bleached strand of hair from her face and folded her arms.

Even the woolly cardigan that was too big for her and the shabby felt slippers were the same.

"Harry," she stated.

"You live within walking distance of my flat, so I thought I'd try calling round instead of ringing."

"What?" She tilted her head to one side.

"That's what I said the first time I rang your doorbell."

"How can you remember that?"

Because I spent a very long time thinking about what to say and practising it, Harry thought, and smiled. "Memory like an elephant. Can I come in?"

He saw a hint of hesitation in her eyes, and it struck him that it hadn't even occurred to him that she might have someone. A partner. A lover. Or some other reason to keep him on the other side of the threshold.

"If I'm not disturbing you, I mean?"

"Er, no, it . . . it's just a bit of a surprise."

"I could come back another time."

"No. No, goodness, I said you could come anytime." She stepped aside.

Kaja put a cup of steaming tea on the coffee table in front of Harry and sat down on the sofa, tucking her long legs beneath her. Harry looked at the book that lay open, spine up. Charlotte Brontë's *Jane Eyre*. He remembered something about a young woman who fell in love with a gloomy loner who was separated but who turned out to have his wife locked up in the attic.

"They're not letting me investigate the murder," he said. "Even though I've been ruled out as a suspect."

"That's standard procedure in cases like this, isn't it?"

"I don't know if there's a set procedure for murder detectives whose wives have been murdered. And I know who did it."

"You *know*?"

"I'm pretty certain."

"Evidence?"

"Gut feeling."

"Like everyone else who has ever worked with you, I have the greatest respect for your gut feeling, Harry, but are you sure it's reliable when it comes to your own wife?"

"It isn't just my gut. I've ruled out the other possibilities."

"All of them?" Kaja was holding her cup without drinking it, as if she had made the tea mostly to warm her hands up. "I seem to remember having a mentor called Harry who told me that there are always other possibilities, that conclusions based on deduction have an undeserved good reputation."

"Rakel had no enemies apart from this one. Who wasn't actually hers, he's my enemy. His name is Svein Finne. Also known as the Fiancé."

"Who's he?"

"A rapist and murderer. He's called the Fiancé because he impregnates his victims and kills them if they don't give birth to his child. I was a young murder detective, and I worked day and night to catch him. He was my first. And I laughed with joy when I put the cuffs on him." Harry looked down at his hands. "That was probably the last time I felt so happy when I arrested someone."

"Oh? Why?"

Harry's eyes wandered across the beautiful, old, floral-patterned wallpaper.

"There are probably several reasons, and my self-awareness is pretty limited. But one reason is that as soon as Finne had finished his sentence, he raped a nineteen-year-old girl and threatened to kill her if she had an abortion. She had one anyway. A week later she was found lying on her stomach on a forest track in Linnerud. Blood everywhere, they were sure she was dead. But when they turned her over they heard a sound, a babyish voice saying 'mama.' They got her to hospital, and she survived. It wasn't the girl talking. Finne had cut her open, inserted a battery-operated talking doll, and sewn her up again."

Kaja gasped for breath. "Sorry," she said. "I'm a bit out of practice."

Harry nodded. "So I caught him again. I set a trap and caught him with his trousers down. Literally. There's a photograph. Bright flash, slightly overexposed. Apart from the humiliation, I have personally been responsible for the fact that Svein Finne, the Fiancé, has spent twenty of his seventy-plus years behind bars. Among other things, for a murder he says he didn't commit. So there's the motive. That's the reason for my gut feeling. Can we go out onto the terrace for a cigarette?"

They got their coats and sat down on the large, covered terrace that looked out onto a garden full of bare apple trees. Harry glanced up at the windows of the first floor in the neighbouring house on Lyder Sagens gate. There were no lights on in any of them.

"Your neighbour," Harry said as he took out his cigarette packet. "Has he stopped watching over you?"

"Greger turned ninety a couple of years ago. He died last year," Kaja sighed.

"So now you have to take care of yourself?"

She shrugged. There was a rhythm in the movement, like a dance. "I have a feeling someone's always watching over me."

"Have you got religious?"

"No. Can I have a cigarette?"

Harry looked at her. She was sitting on her hands. The way he remembered her doing because she got cold so quickly.

"You know we sat right here doing this years ago? Seven years? Eight?"

"Yes," she said. "I remember." She pulled one hand out from beneath her. Held the cigarette between her index and middle fingers as she let Harry light it. She inhaled and breathed out grey smoke. She handled the cigarette just as clumsily as she had last time.

Harry felt the sweet aftertaste of the memories. They had talked about all the smoking in the film *Now, Voyager*, about material monism, free will, John Fante and the pleasures of stealing little things. Then, as punishment for those pain-free moments, he started at the sound of her name and the knife was twisted again.

"You sound so certain when you say that Rakel had no enemies apart from this Finne guy, Harry. But what makes you think you know all the details of her life? People can live together, share a bed, share everything, but that doesn't necessarily mean that they share each other's secrets."

Harry cleared his throat. "I knew her, Kaja. She knew me. We knew each other. We didn't have any sec—" He heard the tremble in his own voice and broke off.

"That's great, Harry, but I don't know what you want me to be here. Comforter or professional?"

"Professional."

"OK." Kaja put her cigarette down on the edge of the wooden table. "Then I'll give you another possibility, just as an example. Rakel had embarked on a relationship with another man. It might be impossible for you to imagine that she would have gone behind your back, but believe me, women are better at hiding things like that than men, especially if they think there's good reason to. Or, to be more accurate: men are worse at uncovering infidelity than women."

Harry closed his eyes. "That sounds like a big—"

"Generalisation. Of course it is. Here's another one. Women are unfaithful for different reasons than men. Maybe Rakel knew she needed to get away from you, but needed a catalyst, something to give her a push. Like a short-term fling. Then, once the fling had served its purpose and she was free from you, she finished with the other man as well. And bingo, you've got an infatuated, humiliated man with a motive for murder."

"OK," Harry said. "But do you believe that yourself?"

"No, but it just shows that there *could* be other possibilities. I certainly don't believe the motive you're trying to ascribe to Finne."

"No?"

"The idea that he killed Rakel just because you were doing your job as a police officer? That he hates you, had made threats against you, fine. But men like Finne are driven by sexual lust, not revenge. No more than other criminals, anyway. And I've never felt threatened by anyone I sent to jail, no matter how loud-mouthed they were. There's a long way between firing off a cheap threat and taking the risk of actually committing murder. I think Finne would have needed a far stronger motive to risk twelve years, possibly the rest of his life, in prison."

Harry sucked hard, angrily, on his cigarette. Angrily because he could feel every fibre of his being fighting against what she had said. Angrily because he knew she was right. "So what sort of revenge motive would you consider strong enough?"

Once again, the dancing, almost childish shrug of the shoulders. "I don't know. Something personal. Something that fits with what he's done to you."

"But that's what I've done. I took his freedom from him, the life he loved. So he's taken what I loved most away from me."

"Rakel." Kaja pushed her bottom lip out and nodded. "To make you live with the pain."

"Exactly." Harry noticed that he had smoked the cigarette down to the filter. "You see things, Kaja. That's really why I came."

"What do you mean?"

"You can tell I'm not really functioning." Harry tried to smile. "I've become my own worst example of an emotion-led detective who starts with a conclusion and then looks for questions whose answers he hopes will confirm it. And that's why I need you, Kaja."

"I don't follow."

"I've been suspended and am no longer allowed to work with any-one in the department. As detectives, we all need someone to bounce ideas off. Someone to offer a bit of resistance. New ideas. You used to be a murder detective, and you haven't got anything to fill your days."

"No. No, Harry."

"Hear me out, Kaja." Harry leaned forward. "I know you don't owe me anything, I know I walked away from you that time. The fact that my heart was broken may have been the explanation, but that was still no excuse for me to break yours. I knew what I was doing, and I'd do the same thing again. Because I had to, because I loved Rakel. I know it's a lot to ask, but I'm asking anyway. Because I'm going mad, Kaja. I've got to *do* something, and the only thing I can do is investigate murders. And drink. I can drink myself to death if I have to."

Harry saw Kaja flinch again.

"I'm just saying it like it is," he said. "You don't have to reply now, all I'm asking is that you think about it. You've got my number. And now I'm going to leave you in peace."

Harry stood up.

He pulled his boots on, walked out of the door, down to Suhms gate, down past Norabakken and Fagerborg Church, success-fully passed two open pubs with their own congregations crowded around the bar, saw the entrance to Bislett Stadium, which had once had its own congregation but now seemed more like a prison, and looked up at the pointlessly clear sky above him, where he caught a glimpse of an S twinkling in the sunlight as he crossed the street. There was a shriek as a tram braked hard, echoing his own scream when he got up from the floor and one of his boots slipped on blood.

Truls Berntsen was sitting in front of his PC watching the third episode of the first season of *The Shield*. He had watched the whole series twice already, and had started again. Television series were like porn films: the old, classic ones were the best. Besides, Truls *was* Vic Mackey. OK, not entirely, but Vic was the man Truls Berntsen would *like* to be: corrupt through and through, but with a moral code that made it all right. That was what was so cool. That you could be so *bad*, but only because of how you looked at it. From which angle. The Nazis and Communists had made their own war films, after all, and got people to cheer on their own bastards. Nothing was entirely true, and nothing was absolutely false. Point of view. That was everything. Point of view.

The phone rang.

That was disconcerting.

It was Hagen who had insisted that the Crime Squad Unit should be staffed at weekends too. With just the one officer, but that suited Truls fine, he was happy to take other people's shifts too. To start with, he had nothing better to be doing, and he needed the money and time owing for his trip to Pattaya in the autumn. And there was absolutely nothing to do, seeing as the duty officer fielded all the calls. He wasn't entirely sure that they knew there was anyone sitting in Crime Squad at the weekend, but he had no intention of telling them.

Which was why this call was disconcerting, seeing as the screen said it was the duty officer.

After five rings, Truls swore quietly, turned the volume of *The Shield* down but left it playing, and picked up the receiver.

"Yes?" he said, managing to make that single, positive syllable sound like a rejection.

"Duty officer here. We've got a lady who needs assistance. She wants to see pictures of rapists, in connection with a rape."

"That's the Vice Squad's job."

"You've got the same pictures, and they don't have anyone there at the weekend."

"Better if she comes back on Monday."

"Better if she sees the pictures while she remembers the face. Are you open at weekends or not?"

"Fine," Truls Berntsen grunted. "Bring her up, then."

"We're pretty busy down here, so how about you come down and get her?"

"I'm busy too." Truls waited, but got no response. "OK, I'll come down," he sighed.

"Good. And listen, it's been a while since it was called the Vice Squad. It's called the Sexual Offences Unit these days."

"Fuck you too," Truls muttered, almost too quietly to be heard, then hung up and pressed Pause, making *The Shield* freeze just before one of Truls Berntsen's favourite scenes, the one where Vic liquidates his police colleague Terry with a bullet just below his left eye.

.   .   .

"So we're not talking about a rape that you were subjected to, but one you're saying you witnessed?" Truls Berntsen said, pulling an extra chair over to his desk. "You're sure it was rape?"

"No," the woman said. She had introduced herself as Dagny Jensen. "But if I recognise any of the rapists in your archive, I'd be pretty sure."

Truls scratched his protruding Frankenstein's-monster forehead. "So you don't want to file a report until you've recognised the perpetrator?"

"That's right."

"That's not the way we usually do things," Truls said. "But let's say I run a ten-minute slideshow here and now, and if we find the guy, you can go back to the duty officer to file the report and explain. I'm on my own up here and I've got my hands full. Deal?"

"OK."

"Let's get going. Estimated age of the rapist?"

Just three minutes later, Dagny Jensen pointed at one of the pictures on the screen.

"Who's that?" He noted that she was trying to suppress a tremble in her voice.

"The one and only Svein Finne," Truls said. "Was it him you saw?"

"What's he done?"

"What *hasn't* he done? Let's see."

Truls typed, pressed Enter and a detailed criminal record appeared.

He saw Dagny Jensen's eyes move down the page, and the growing horror on her face as the monster materialised in dry police language.

"He's murdered women he got pregnant," she whispered.

"Mutilation and murder," Truls corrected. "He's served his time, but if there's one man we'd be happy to receive a new report about, it's Finne."

"Are you . . . are you completely certain you'd be able to catch him, then?"

"Oh, we'd get hold of him if we issued a warrant for his arrest," Truls said. "Obviously, whether or not we'd get a conviction in a rape trial is an entirely different matter. It's always one person's word against another's in cases like that, and we'd probably just have to let him go again. But obviously with a witness like you, it would be two against one. With a bit of luck."

Dagny Jensen swallowed several times.

Truls yawned and looked at the time. "Now you've seen the picture, you can make your way back down to the duty officer and get the paperwork started, OK?"

"Yes," the woman said, staring at the screen. "Yes, of course."

15

Harry was sitting on the sofa staring at the wall. He hadn't turned the lights on, and the falling darkness had slowly erased the contours and colours and settled like a cool cloth on his forehead. He wished it could erase him too. When you actually thought about it, life didn't have to be that complicated. It could basically be reduced to The Clash's binary question: *should I stay or should I go?* Drink? Not drink? He wanted to drown. Disappear. But he couldn't, not quite yet.

Harry opened the present Bjørn had given him. As he had assumed, it was a vinyl album. *Road to Ruin.* Of the three albums Øystein resolutely claimed were the Ramones' only really good work (here he would usually refer to Lou Reed describing the Ramones' music as "shit"), Bjørn had managed to buy the only one Harry *didn't* have. On the shelves behind him—between The Rainmakers' first album and Rank and File's debut—he had both *Ramones* and his favourite, *Rocket to Russia.*

Harry pulled the black vinyl disc out and put *Road to Ruin* on the turntable.

He spotted one track he recognised and placed the needle at the start of "I Wanna Be Sedated."

Guitar riffs filled the room. It sounded more heavily produced and mainstream than their debut album. He liked the minimalist guitar solo, but wasn't so sure about the modulation afterwards; it sounded suspiciously like Status Quo–style boogie at its most imbecilic. But it was performed with swaggering confidence. Like his favourite track "Rockaway Beach," where they stood just as confidently on the shoulders of The Beach Boys, like car thieves cruising down the main street with the windows down.

While Harry was trying to work out if he actually liked "I Wanna Be Sedated" or not, and whether or not he should go to the bar, the room was lit up by the phone on the coffee table.

He peered down at the screen. Sighed. Wondered whether to answer.

"Hi, Alexandra."

"Hi, Harry. I've been trying to get hold of you. You need to change the message on your voicemail."

"You think?"

"It doesn't even say your name. *'Leave a message if you must.'* Just six words that sound more like a warning, followed by a bleep."

"Sounds like it works the way it should."

"I've called you a *lot* of times."

"I saw, but I haven't been . . . in the mood."

"I heard." She let out a deep sigh, and her voice suddenly sounded pained, sympathetic. "It's just terrible."

"Yes."

A pause followed, like a silent intermezzo marking the transition between two acts. Because when Alexandra went on, it wasn't in either her deep, playful voice or the pained, sympathetic one. It was her professional voice.

"I've found something for you."

Harry ran his hand over his face. "OK, I'm all ears."

It had been so long since he first contacted Alexandra Sturdza that he had given up any hope of getting anything from her. More than six months had passed since he'd gone up to the Forensic Medical Institute at Rikshospitalet, where he had been met by a young woman who had come straight from the lab, with a hard, pockmarked face, bright eyes and an almost imperceptible accent. She had taken him into her office and hung up her white lab coat as Harry asked if she could help him, kind of off the record, to compare Svein Finne's DNA against old cases of murder and rape.

"So, Harry Hole, you want me to jump the queue for you?"

After Parliament abolished the statute of limitations for murder and rape in 2014, naturally there had been a rush of requests to apply new DNA-analysis technology to older cases, and waiting times had shot up.

Harry had considered rephrasing his request, but he could see from the look in her eyes that there was no point. "Yes."

"Interesting. In exchange for what?"

"Exchange? Hm. What would you like?"

"A beer with Harry Hole would be a start."

Under her coat Alexandra Sturdza was wearing black, figure-hugging clothes that emphasised a muscular body that made Harry think of cats and sports cars. But he had never really been that interested in cars, and was more of a dog person.

"If that's what it'll take, I'll get you a beer. But I don't drink. And I'm married."

"We'll see," she said with a hoarse laugh. She looked like she laughed a lot, but it was strangely difficult to guess her age, she could have been anywhere from ten to twenty years younger than him. She tilted her head and looked at him. "Meet me at Revolver at eight o'clock tomorrow, and we'll see what I've got for you, OK?"

She hadn't had much. Not then, and not much since. Just enough to invite herself for a beer every now and then. But he had maintained a professional distance and made sure their meetings were short and to the point. Until Rakel threw him out and the dam had burst, carrying everything away with it, including any principles about professional distance.

Harry saw that the wall had turned another shade greyer.

"I haven't got an exact match from a case," Alexandra began.

Harry yawned; it was the same old story.

"But then I realised that I could compare Svein Finne's DNA profile against all the others in the database. And I found a partial match to a murderer."

"What does that mean?"

"It means that if Svein Finne isn't a convicted murderer, then he's the father of one, at least."

"Oh, shit." Something dawned on Harry. A foreboding. "What's the murderer's name?"

"Valentin Gjertsen."

A cold shiver ran down Harry's spine. Valentin Gjertsen. Not that Harry had more faith in genes than environment, but there was a sort of logic to the fact that Svein Finne's seed, his genes, had helped create a son who had become one of the worst killers in Norwegian criminal history.

"You sound less surprised than I thought you'd be," Alexandra said.

"I'm less surprised than *I* thought I'd be," Harry replied, rubbing his neck.

"Is that helpful?"

"Yes," Harry said. "Yes, it's very helpful. Thanks, Alexandra."

"What are you going to do now?"

"Mm. Good question."

"Do you want to come around to mine?"

"Like I said, I'm not really in the—"

"We don't have to do anything. Maybe we could both do with someone to lie next to for a while. You remember where I live?"

Harry closed his eyes. There had been a number of beds, doorways and courtyards since the dam burst, and alcohol had laid a veil over faces, names, addresses. And right now, the image of Valentin Gjertsen was blocking out pretty much everything else from his memory.

"What the hell, Harry? You were drunk, but couldn't you at least *pretend* you remember?"

"Grünerløkka," Harry said. "Seilduksgata."

"Clever boy. An hour from now?"

As Harry hung up and called Kaja Solness, a thought struck him. The fact that he had remembered Seilduksgata regardless of how drunk he had been . . . he always remembered something, his memory was never *completely* blank. Maybe it wasn't the long-term effects of drinking that meant he couldn't remember that evening at the Jealousy Bar, maybe there was something he didn't *want* to remember.

"Hello, you've reached Kaja's voicemail."

"I've got the motive you were asking about," Harry said after the bleep. "His name is Valentin Gjertsen, and it turns out that he was Svein Finne's son. Valentin Gjertsen is dead. He was killed. By me."

16

Alexandra Sturdza let out a long sound as she stretched her arms over her head so that her fingers and bare feet touched the brass bedstead at either end of the mattress. Then she rolled onto her side, pushed the duvet between her thighs and put one of the big white pillows under her head. She was grinning so much that her dark eyes almost disappeared into her hard face.

"I'm glad you came," she said, putting one hand on Harry's chest.

"Mm." Harry was lying on his back staring into the bright light from the ceiling lamp. She had been wearing a long silk dressing gown when she opened the door for him, then took him by the hand and led him straight into the bedroom.

"Are you feeling guilty?" she asked.

"Always," Harry said.

"For being here, I mean."

"Not particularly. It just fits into the scale of indicators."

"Indicators of what?"

"That I'm a bad man."

"If you're already feeling guilty, you might as well get undressed."

"So there's no doubt that Valentin Gjertsen was Svein Finne's son?" Harry folded his hands behind his head.

"No."

"Christ, it really is an absurd chain of events. Think about it. Valentin Gjertsen was probably the product of a rape."

"Who isn't?" She rubbed her crotch against his thigh.

"Did you know that Valentin Gjertsen raped the prison dentist during an appointment? Afterwards he pulled her nylon tights over her head and set light to them."

"Shut up, Harry, I want you. There are condoms in the drawer of the bedside table."

"No thanks."

"No? You don't want another kid, do you?"

"I didn't mean the condoms." Harry put one hand on the two of hers that had started to undo his belt.

"What the hell?" she snapped. "What's the point of you if you don't want to fuck?"

"Good question."

"Why don't you want to?"

"Low testosterone levels, at a guess."

With an angry sniff Alexandra rolled onto her back. "She isn't just your ex-wife, Harry, she's *dead*. When are you going to accept that?"

"You think five days of celibacy is excessive?"

She looked at him. "Funny. But you're not dealing with it as well as you're pretending to, are you?"

"Pretending is half the job," Harry said, raising his hips and pulling his cigarettes from his pocket. "Research shows that you end up in a better mood if you exercise your smile muscles. If you want to cry, laugh. I sleep. What's the smoking policy in your bedroom?"

"Everything's allowed. But when people smoke in front of me, my policy is to read what it says on the packet. Tobacco kills, my friend."

"Mm. That bit about 'my friend' is nice."

"It's to make you recognise that it isn't just something you're doing to yourself, but to everyone who cares for you."

"I got that. So, at the risk of cancer and feeling even more guilty, I am hereby lighting a cigarette." Harry inhaled and blew the smoke up at the ceiling lamp. "You like lights," he said.

"I grew up in Timisoara."

"Oh?"

"The first town in Europe to have electric streetlamps. Only New York beat us to it."

"And that's why you like lights?"

"No, but you like fun facts."

"Do I?"

"Yes. Such as the fact that Finne had a rapist for a son."

"That's a bit more than a fun fact."

"Why?"

Harry took a drag on the cigarette, but it tasted of nothing. "Because the son gives Finne a strong enough motive for revenge.

I hunted down his son in connection with several murder investigations. And it ended with me shooting him."

"You . . ."

"Valentin Gjertsen was unarmed, but provoked me to shoot by pretending he was reaching for a gun. Unfortunately I was the only witness, and Internal Investigations found it problematic that I had fired three shots. But I was cleared. They couldn't, as they put it, prove that I hadn't acted in self-defense."

"And Finne found out about this? And you think he killed your ex-wife as a result?"

Harry nodded slowly. "An eye for an eye, a tooth for a tooth."

"Logically, he ought to have killed Oleg."

Harry raised an eyebrow. "So you know his name?"

"You talk a lot when you're drunk, Harry. And far too much about your ex-wife and the boy."

"Oleg isn't mine, he's from Rakel's first marriage."

"You told me that too, but isn't that just biology?"

Harry shook his head. "Not for Svein Finne. He didn't love Valentin Gjertsen as a person, he hardly even knew him. He loved Valentin simply because he was carrying his genes. Finne's driving force is to spread his seed and father children. Biology is everything to him. It's his way of gaining eternal life."

"That's sick."

"Is it?" Harry looked at his cigarette. Wondered where lung cancer was in the list of things queuing up to kill him. "Maybe we're more tightly bound by biology than we like to think. Maybe we're all born bloodline chauvinists, racists and nationalists, with an instinctive desire for global domination for our own family. And then we learn to ignore it, to a greater or lesser extent. Most of us, anyway."

"We still want to know where we come from, in purely biological terms. Did you know that over the past twenty years at the Forensic Medical Institute we've seen a 300 percent increase in the number of DNA tests from people who want to know who their father is, or if their child really is theirs?"

"Fun fact."

"That tells us something about how our identity is bound up with our genetic inheritance."

"You think?"

"Yes." She picked up the glass of wine she'd left on the bedside table. "If I didn't, I wouldn't be here."

"In bed with me?"

"In Norway. I came here to find my father. My mother never liked talking about him, all I knew was that he was from Norway. When she died, I bought a ticket and came to look for him. That first year I had three different jobs. All I knew about my father was that he was probably intelligent, because my mother was pretty average but I always got top grades in Romania, and it only took me six months to learn Norwegian fluently. But I couldn't find my father. So I got a grant to study chemistry at NTNU, then got a job at the Forensic Medical Institute, working on DNA analysis."

"Where you could carry on looking."

"Yes."

"And?"

"I found him."

"Really? You must have had luck on your side, because as far as I know, you lot delete DNA profiles taken in paternity cases after one year."

"In paternity cases, yes."

Then the penny dropped for Harry. "You found your father in the police database. He had a criminal record?"

"Yes."

"Mm. What had he—"

Harry's trouser pocket vibrated. He looked at the number. Pressed Answer.

"Hi, Kaja. Did you get my message?"

"Yes." Her voice was soft against his ear.

"And?"

"And I agree, I think you've found Finne's motive."

"Does that mean you're going to help me?"

"I don't know." In the pause that followed he could hear Kaja's breathing in one ear, Alexandra's in the other. "It sounds like you're lying down, Harry. Are you at home?"

"No, he's at Alexandra's." Alexandra's voice cut into Harry's ear.

"Who's that?" Kaja asked.

"That . . ." Harry said, "was Alexandra."

"In that case I won't disturb you. Goodnight."

"You're not disturbing . . ."

Kaja had already hung up.

Harry looked at his phone. Put it back in his pocket. He stubbed the cigarette out on the cube light on the bedside table and swung his legs off the bed.

"Where are you going?"

"Home," Harry said, then bent over and kissed her on the forehead.

Harry was walking west quickly as his brain worked things through.

He took out his phone and called Bjørn Holm.

"Harry?"

"It was Finne."

"We'll wake the baby, Harry," Bjørn said. "Can we do this tomorrow?"

"Svein Finne is Valentin Gjertsen's father."

"Oh, shit."

"The motive's blood vengeance. I'm certain of it. You need to put out an alert for Finne, and once you've got his address, you need to get a search warrant. If you find the knife, it's case closed . . ."

"I hear you, Harry. But Gert is finally asleep, and I need to get some rest as well. And I'm not so sure we'd get a search warrant on those grounds. They'll probably want something more concrete."

"But this *is* blood vengeance, Bjørn. It's in our nature. Wouldn't you happily do the same if someone had killed Gert?"

"That's one hell of a question."

"Think about it."

"Oh, I don't know, Harry."

"You don't *know*?"

"Tomorrow. OK?"

"Of course." Harry closed his eyes tightly and swore silently to himself. "Sorry if I'm behaving like an idiot, Bjørn, I just can't bear to—"

"It's fine, Harry. Let's talk about it tomorrow. And while you're suspended, it would probably be best if you don't tell anyone we're talking about the case."

"Of course. Get some sleep, mate."

Harry opened his eyes and slipped his phone back into his pocket. Saturday night. Ahead of him on the pavement stood a drunk, sobbing girl with her head pressed against the wall. A guy was standing behind her with his head bowed; he had one hand consolingly on her back. "He's fucking other women!" the girl cried. "He doesn't care about me! No one cares about me!"

"*I* do," the guy said quietly.

"*You*, yeah," she sniffed derisively, and went on sobbing. Harry caught the guy's eye as he passed them.

Saturday night. There was a bar on this side of the street one hundred metres ahead. Maybe he ought to cross the road to avoid it. There wasn't much traffic, just a few taxis. Actually, there were a lot of taxis. And they formed a wall of black vehicles that made it impossible to cross the road. Bloody hell.

Truls Berntsen was watching the seventh and final season of *The Shield*. He wondered about taking a quick look at Pornhub, then decided against it: someone in IT probably kept a log of what staff had gone surfing for on the Internet. Did people still say "surfing"? Truls looked at the time again. The Internet was slower at home, and it was time he got to bed anyway. He pulled on his jacket, zipped it up. But something was bothering him. He didn't know what it could be, because he had spent the day at taxpayers' expense without having to do anything useful, a day when he could go to bed secure in the knowledge that the balance sheet was once again in his favour.

Truls Berntsen looked at the phone.

It was stupid, but if it stopped him thinking about it, great.

"Duty officer."

"This is Truls Berntsen. That woman you sent up here, did she file a report against Svein Finne when she got back down to you?"

"She never came back."

"She just left?"

"Must have done."

Truls Berntsen hung up. Thought for a moment. He tapped at the phone again. Waited.

"Harry."

Truls could only just make out his colleague's voice over the music and shouting in the background. "Are you at a party?"

"Bar."

"They're playing Motörhead," Truls said.

"And that's the only positive thing worth saying about the place. What do you want?"

"Svein Finne. You've been trying to keep an eye on him."

"And?"

Truls told him about his visitor earlier in the day.

"Mm. Have you got the woman's name and phone number?"

"Dagny something. Jensen, maybe. You can ask the duty officer if they took any other details, but I doubt it."

"Why?"

"I think she's frightened Finne will find out she was here."

"OK. I can't call the duty officer, I'm suspended. Can you do it for me?"

"I was about to go home."

Truls listened to the silence at the other end. Lemmy was singing "Killed by Death."

"OK," Truls grunted.

"One more thing. My ID card's been deactivated, so I can't get into the office anymore. Can you bring my service pistol from my bottom drawer and meet me outside Olympen in twenty minutes?"

"Your pistol? What do you want that for?"

"To protect myself against the evils of the world."

"Your drawers are locked."

"But you've got a copy of the key."

"What? What makes you think that?"

"I've noticed you moving things about in there. And on one occasion you used it to store a lump of hash that Narcotics had seized, according to the bag it was in. So it wouldn't be found in *your* drawers if they started looking for it."

Truls didn't answer.

"Well?"

"Fifteen minutes," Truls grunted. "On the dot. I'm not going to stand there freezing."

Kaja Solness was standing with her arms folded, staring out of the living-room window. She was freezing. She was always cold. In Kabul, where the temperature veered from minus five to well over thirty, her nocturnal shivers were just as likely to strike in July as they were in December, and there'd been little she could do but wait for morning, when the desert sun would warm her up again. Her brother had been the same, and once she had asked him if he thought they were born cold-blooded, that they were incapable of regulating their own body temperature and were reliant on external heat to stop them seizing up and freezing to death like reptiles. For a long time she had thought that was true. That she wasn't in control. That she was helplessly dependent on her surroundings. Dependent on others.

She stared out into the darkness. Let her gaze slip along the garden fence.

Was he standing out there somewhere?

It was impossible to know. The blackness was impenetrable, and a man like him knew perfectly well how to keep himself hidden.

She was shivering, but she wasn't afraid. Because now she knew she didn't need other people. She could shape her own life.

She thought about the sound of the other woman's voice.

No, he's at Alexandra's.

Her own life. And other people's.

17

Dagny Jensen stopped abruptly. She had gone for her usual Sunday walk along the banks of the Akerselva. Feeding the ducks. Smiling at families with small children and dogs. Looking for the first snowdrops. Anything to stop herself thinking. Because she had been thinking all night, and all she wanted to do now was forget.

But he wouldn't let her. She stared at the figure standing outside the door to her building. He was stamping his feet on the ground, as if he was trying to keep warm. As if he had been waiting a long time. She was about to turn and walk away when she realised it wasn't him. This man was taller than Finne.

Dagny walked closer.

He didn't have long hair either, but scruffy, fair hair. She walked a bit closer.

"Dagny Jensen?" the man said.

"Yes?"

"Harry Hole. Oslo Police."

The words sounded like he was grinding them out.

"What's this about?"

"You wanted to report a rape yesterday."

"I changed my mind."

"So I understand. You're frightened."

Dagny looked at him. He was unshaven, his eyes were bloodshot, and he had a liver-coloured scar running across one side of his face like a no-entry sign. But even if his face had something of the same brutality as Svein Finne, there was something that softened it, something that made it almost handsome.

"Am I?" she asked.

"Yes. And I'm here to ask for your help to catch the man who raped you."

Dagny flinched. "*Me?* You've misunderstood, Hole. I'm not the person who was raped. If it was actually a rape at all."

Hole didn't answer. Just held her gaze. Now he was the one looking hard at her.

"He was trying to get you pregnant," the police officer said. "And now that he's hoping you're carrying his child, he's keeping watch over you. Has he been?"

Dagny blinked twice. "How do you know . . ."

"That's his thing. Has he threatened you with what will happen if you have an abortion?"

Dagny Jensen swallowed. She was about to ask him to leave, but found herself hesitating. She didn't know if she could trust what he said about catching Finne, there wasn't much to go on. But this policeman had something the others hadn't had. Resoluteness. There was determination in him. Maybe it's a bit like with priests, Dagny thought; we trust them because we're so desperate to believe what they say is true.

Dagny poured coffee into the cups on her small, folded-out kitchen table.

The tall policeman had squeezed himself onto the chair between the worktop and the table. "So Finne wants you to meet him at the Catholic church in Vika this evening? At nine o'clock?" He hadn't interrupted her while she was talking, hadn't taken any notes, but his bloodshot eyes had stayed on her, giving her the feeling that he was taking in every word, that he was seeing it in his mind's eye the way she did, frame by frame of the short horror film that kept replaying inside her head.

"Yes," she said.

"OK. Well, obviously we could pick him up there. Question him."

"But you haven't got any evidence."

"No. Without evidence we'd have to let him go, and because he'd realise it was you who told us . . ."

". . . I'd be in even more danger than I am now."

The policeman nodded.

"That was why I didn't report him," Dagny said. "It's like shooting a bear, isn't it? If you don't bring it down with your first shot, you won't have time to reload before it gets you. In which case it's better not to have fired the first shot."

"Mm. On the other hand, even the largest bear can be brought down by a single, well-aimed shot."

"How, though?"

The policeman put one hand around his coffee cup. "There are several ways. One is to use you as bait. Fitted with a hidden microphone. Get him to talk about the rape."

He looked down at the table.

"Go on," she said.

He raised his head. The blue of his irises looked washed-out. "You'd have to ask him about the consequences if you don't do as he says. That way we'd have the threats. If we have those and a conversation in which he indirectly confirms the rape, we'd have enough on tape to get him convicted."

"You still use tape?"

The policeman raised his coffee to his lips.

"Sorry," Dagny said. "I'm just so . . ."

"Of course," the policeman said. "And I'd understand completely if you said no."

"You said there were several ways?"

"Yes." He said no more, just sipped from the cup.

"But?"

The policeman shrugged. "In many ways, a church is perfect. There's no noise, nothing to stop us getting a good-quality recording. And you'd be in a public place where he couldn't attack you . . ."

"We were in a public place last time."

". . . and we could be there to monitor the situation."

Dagny looked at him. There was something in his eyes she recognised. And now she realised what it was. It was the same thing she'd seen in her own eyes, and at first had thought was a flaw in the mirror. A defect. Something broken. And something about his voice put her in mind of pupils with unsteady voices serving up fake explanations of why they hadn't done their homework. She went over to the stove, put the coffee pot down and looked out of the window. Down below she could see people out for Sunday walks, but she couldn't see him. Life, going on around her, had become an unnatural, strained idyll. Dagny had never thought about it like that before, she had just thought that was the way it was supposed to be.

She walked back and sat down on the kitchen chair.

"If I do this, I need to be certain he won't turn up again. Do you understand that, Hole?"

"Yes, I understand. And you have my word that you'll never see Svein Finne again. Ever. OK?"

Never. She knew that wasn't true. Just as she had known that what the female priest said wasn't true when she spoke of salvation. That it was meant as a comfort. But it worked. Even if we saw through "never" and "salvation," they were passwords that opened the door to the heart, and the heart believed what it wanted to believe. Dagny could feel herself breathing easier already. She half closed her eyes. And when she looked at him like that, with the daylight coming through the window forming a halo around his head, she could no longer see the hurt in the policeman's eyes, could no longer hear the false note in his voice.

"OK," she said. "Tell me how we do this."

Harry stopped in the street outside Kaja Solness's house and called her number for the third time. Same result again. *"The person you are calling has their phone switched off, or is . . ."*

He opened the creaking wrought-iron gate and walked towards the house.

It was crazy. Of course it was crazy. But what else could he do?

He rang the doorbell. Waited. Rang again.

Put his eye to the large peephole in the door and saw her coat, the one she had been wearing at the funeral, hanging on a hook. And her tall black boots were standing on the shoe rack below.

He walked around the house. There were still patches of snow on the withered, flattened grass in the shade of the north side.

He looked up at the window of what had been her bedroom, although obviously she could have moved her bed into one of the other rooms. When he bent down to gather enough snow to make a snowball, he saw it. A footprint in the snow. From a boot. His brain began to search its databases. Found what it was looking for. A boot print in the snow outside the house in Holmenkollen.

His hand reached inside his jacket. Obviously, it could be a completely different print. Obviously, she could have left the house. He clasped the butt of his pistol, a Heckler & Koch P30L, hunched up and walked with long, silent strides back to the front steps. He shifted his grip on the pistol, holding it by the barrel so that he could break the glass in the peephole, but tried the door first.

It was open.

He stepped inside. Listened. Silence. He sniffed. Could only detect a faint smell of perfume—Kaja's—probably from the scarf hanging from a hook next to her coat.

He walked along the hallway with his pistol in front of him.

The door to the kitchen was open, and the button on the coffee machine was glowing red. Harry tightened his grip on the butt, put his finger on the trigger. He moved farther into the house. The living-room door was ajar. A buzzing sound. Like flies. Harry nudged the door open cautiously with his foot, still holding the pistol in front of him.

She was lying on the floor. Her eyes were closed, and her arms were folded across her chest in that wool cardigan that was too big for her. Her body and pale face were bathed in the daylight streaming through the window.

Harry let the air out of his lungs with a groan. He lowered the pistol and crouched down. He held his thumb and forefinger around her worn slipper and pinched her big toe.

Kaja started, screamed and pulled her headphones off. "Bloody hell, Harry!"

"Sorry, I did try to get hold of you." He sat down on the rug beside her. "I need help."

Kaja closed her eyes, put one hand to her chest, still breathless. "So you said."

What had previously been just a buzzing sound from the headphones was now clearly audible as familiar hard rock, played at loud volume.

"And you called me because you wanted me to persuade you to say yes," he said, pulling out his cigarettes.

"I'm not the type who lets themselves be persuaded, Harry."

He nodded towards the headphones. "You let yourself be persuaded to listen to Deep Purple."

Did he see a hint of a blush on her cheeks? "Only because you said they were the best group in the 'unintentionally ridiculous but still good' category."

"Mm." Harry put an unlit cigarette to his lips. "Seeing as this plan belongs to the same category, I'm counting on it being of interest and—"

"Harry . . ."

"And bear in mind that by helping me put a notorious rapist behind bars, you'd be helping all the women of this city. You'd be helping Oleg by getting the man who murdered his mother punished. And you'd be helping me—"

"Stop, Harry."

". . . to get out of a situation I've only got myself to blame for."

She raised one of her dark eyebrows. "Oh?"

"I've recruited one of Svein Finne's rape victims to act as bait, in order to catch him red-handed. I've persuaded an innocent woman to wear a microphone and record him in the belief that it's part of a police operation, whereas it's actually a solo performance directed by a suspended police officer. Plus his accomplice, a former colleague. You."

Kaja stared at him. "You're kidding."

"No," Harry said. "It turns out that I have no moral boundaries when it comes to how far I'm willing to go to catch Svein Finne."

"Those are precisely the words I was going to use."

"I need you, Kaja. Are you with me?"

"Why on earth would I do that? This is utter madness."

"How many times did we know who the culprit was, but couldn't do anything about it because we had to follow the rules? Well, you're not in the police, you don't have to follow any rules."

"But you do, even if you are suspended. You're not just risking your job, but your liberty. You're the one they'll end up putting away."

"I won't be losing anything, Kaja. I've got nothing left to lose."

"What about your sleep? You know what you're exposing this woman to?"

"Not my sleep either. Dagny Jensen knows this isn't by the book, she's seen through me."

"Did she say that?"

"No. And we're keeping it that way. So afterwards she can claim she thought it was a legitimate police operation, so she won't be risking anything. She's just as keen as I am to see that Svein Finne is eliminated."

Kaja rolled onto her stomach and pushed herself up on her elbows. The sleeves of her cardigan slid down her long, thin lower arms. "*Eliminated.* What exactly do you mean by that?"

Harry shrugged. "Taken out of the game. Removed."

"Removed from . . . ?"

"The streets. Public life."

"Put in prison, then?"

Harry looked at her as he sucked on the unlit cigarette. Nodded. "For instance."

Kaja shook her head. "I don't know if I dare, Harry. You're . . . different. You always pushed the boundaries, but this isn't you. This isn't *us*. This is . . ." She shook her head.

"Just say it," Harry said.

"This is hatred. This is a horrible mixture of hatred and grief."

"You're right," Harry said. He took the cigarette from his mouth and put it back in the packet. "And I was wrong. I *haven't* lost everything. I've still got the hatred."

He stood up and walked out of the living room, hearing the buzzing sound as Ian Gillan shrieked in a shrill vibrato that he was going to make it hard for you, that you'd . . . The sentence remained unfinished, Ritchie Blackmore's guitar took over before Gillan launched into the conclusion: *into the fire* . . . Harry walked out of the house, onto the steps, out into the blinding daylight.

Pia Bohr knocked on the door of her daughter's bedroom.

Waited. There was no answer.

She pushed the door open.

He was sitting on the bed with his back to her. He was still wearing his camouflage uniform. On the bedspread lay the pistol, the sheathed dagger and his NVGs—night-vision goggles.

"You need to stop," she said. "Do you hear me, Roar? This can't go on."

He turned towards her.

His bloodshot eyes and streaked face showed he'd been crying. And that he probably hadn't slept.

"Where were you last night? Roar? You can tell me."

Her husband, or the man who had once been her husband, turned back to the window again. Pia Bohr sighed. He never said where he'd been, but the mud on the floor suggested he could have been out in the forest. Or a field. Or a rubbish dump.

She sat down on the opposite side of the bed. She needed the distance. The distance you'd want to maintain towards a stranger.

"What have you done?" she asked. "What have you done, Roar?"

She waited fearfully for what he was going to say in reply. And when he hadn't answered after five seconds, she got up and quickly walked out. Almost relieved. Regardless of whatever he might have done, she was innocent. She had asked three times. What more could anyone demand?

18

Dagny looked at her watch under the light above the entrance to the Catholic church. Nine. What if Finne didn't come? The traffic was rumbling on Drammensveien and Munkedamsveien, but when she stared along the narrow street leading to Slottsparken she couldn't see any cars or people. Nor in the direction of Aker Brygge and the fjord either. The eye of the storm, the city's blind spot. The church was squeezed between two office blocks, and there was little to show that it was a house of God. The building got thinner towards the top, and there was a spire, but there was no cross on the facade, no Jesus or Mary, no Latin quotes. The carvings on the solid wooden door—which was wide, tall and unlocked—may perhaps have led your thoughts in a religious direction, but apart from that, for all Dagny knew, it could have been the entrance to a synagogue, mosque or temple for some other small congregation. But if you went closer, you could read on a poster in a glass-fronted cabinet beside the door that there had been masses since early morning that Sunday. In Norwegian, English, Polish and Vietnamese. The last one—in Polish—had ended just half an hour ago. The noise never stopped, but this street remained quiet. How alone was she? Dagny hadn't asked Harry Hole how many colleagues he had positioned to keep an eye on her, if any of them were out here, or if they were all inside the church. Possibly because she didn't want to know, because she might then give herself away. She looked along the windows and doorways on the other side of the street, hopefully. But also hopelessly. Because deep down she had a feeling it was just Hole. Him and her. That was what Hole had tried to tell her with that look. And after he had left, she had checked on the Internet and found confirmation of what she thought she'd read in the papers. That Harry Hole was a famous police officer and the husband of the poor woman who had recently been murdered. With a knife. That explained the look in his eyes, of something broken, the cracked mirror. But it was too late now. She had set this in motion herself, and she could have stopped it. But she hadn't been able to. No, she probably wasn't lying to herself any less than Hole had done. She had seen his pistol.

She was freezing, she should have worn warmer clothes. Dagny looked at the time again.

"Is it me you're waiting for?"

Her heart stopped.

How in all the world had he managed to sneak right up on her without her seeing him coming?

She nodded.

"Are we alone?"

Dagny nodded again.

"Really? No one else has come to celebrate our marital covenant?"

Dagny opened her mouth to speak but nothing came out.

Svein Finne smiled. His thick, wet lips curled against his yellow teeth. "You need to breathe, darling. We don't want our child to suffer brain damage from lack of oxygen, do we?"

Dagny did as he said. Breathed. "We need to talk," she said in a shaky voice. "I think I'm pregnant."

"Of course you are."

Dagny only just managed to stop herself from pulling back when he raised his arm—and for a moment she saw the light from the lamp above the church door shine through the hole in his hand before he held it, warm and dry, against her cheek. She remembered to breathe, and swallowed. "We need to talk about practical matters. Can we go in?"

"In?"

"Inside the church. It's cold out here."

"Of course. We're getting married, after all. No time to lose." He ran his hand down the side of her neck. She had taped the tiny microphone onto her bra, between the cups, inside her thin sweater and coat. Hole had said they couldn't be sure of getting a decent recording until she got him into the church, where they would be free of the background noise of the city, and where she would also have a reason to take off the sound-muffling coat. He wouldn't be able to escape in there, and they would grab Finne as soon as they had enough evidence to get him charged.

"Shall we go in, then?" Dagny said, pulling away from his hand. She put her hands in her coat pockets and managed to summon up a visible shiver.

Finne didn't move. He closed his eyes, leaned his head back and sniffed. "I smell something," he said.

"Smell?"

He opened his eyes and looked at her again.

"I smell sorrow, Dagny. Desperation. Pain."

This time Dagny didn't have to pretend to shiver.

"You didn't smell like that last time," he said. "Have you had a visit?"

"A visit?" She tried to laugh, but all that emerged was a coughing sound. "Who from?"

"I don't know. But there's something familiar about that smell. Let me search my memory . . ." He put his finger under his chin. Frowned. Studied her. "Dagny, don't tell me you've . . . You haven't . . . have you, Dagny?"

"Have I what?" She tried to fend off the panic that was creeping up on her.

He shook his head sadly. "Do you read the Bible, Dagny? You know the parable of the sower? His seed is the word. The promise. And if the seed doesn't take root, Satan will come and devour it. Satan will take away faith. Will take our child, Dagny. Because I am the sower. The question is, have you met Satan?"

Dagny swallowed, moved her head, wasn't sure if she was nodding or shaking it.

Svein Finne sighed. "You and I, we conceived a child together in a precious moment of love. But perhaps you regret that now, perhaps you just don't want a child. But you can't go through with the cold-blooded murder of it as long as you know that it's a real love-child, so you're trying to find something that would make it possible for you to get rid of it." He was talking loudly, and his soft lips were forming the words very clearly. Like an actor on stage, she thought. Using volume and diction so that every word was audible, even in the back row. "So you're lying to your own conscience, Dagny. You tell yourself that that wasn't what happened, that I didn't want it, he forced himself on me. And you tell yourself that you can get the police to believe that. Because that man, that Satan, has told you that I have served time for other supposed rapes."

"You're wrong," Dagny said, giving up any attempt to control the tremor in her voice. "Aren't we going inside?" She could hear herself pleading.

Finne tilted his head to one side. Like a bird looking at its prey before it strikes. Almost contemplatively, as if it hasn't quite decided whether or not to let its prey live. "A marital vow is a serious thing, Dagny. I don't want you to enter into it lightly or act too hastily. And you seem . . . uncertain. Perhaps we should wait a little?"

"Can't we talk about it? Inside?"

"Whenever I'm not sure," Finne said, "I let my father decide."

"Your father?"

"Yes. Fate." He felt in his trouser pocket and pulled something out between his thumb and forefinger. Blue-grey metal. It was a dice.

"That's your father?"

"Fate is the father of us all, Dagny. A one or a two means we get married today. Three or four that we wait until another day. Five or six means . . ." He leaned forward and whispered in her ear. "That you've betrayed me, and I'll have to slit your throat here and now. And you'll stand there dumb and obedient like the sacrificial lamb you are, and just let it happen. Hold out your hand."

Finne straightened up. Dagny stared at him. There was no emotion in his eyes, or at least none that she recognised: no anger, no sympathy, no excitement, no nervousness, no amusement, no hate, no love. All she saw was will. His will. A hypnotic, commanding force that required neither reason nor logic. She wanted to scream. She wanted to run. Instead she held out her hand.

Finne shook the dice in his cupped hands. Then he quickly turned the lower hand and put it over Dagny's palm. She felt his warm, dry, raw skin against hers and shuddered.

He took his hand away. Looked down at hers. His mouth stretched into a broad smile.

Dagny had stopped breathing again. She pulled her hand back. The dice was showing three black dots.

"See you soon, my darling," Finne said, looking up. "My promise still holds."

Dagny looked automatically at the sky, where the lights of the city were colouring the clouds yellow. When she looked down again Finne was gone. She heard a noise from one of the archways on the other side of the street.

She nudged the door behind her open and went inside. It was as if the organ notes from the last mass were still lingering in the large nave. She walked over to one of the two confessionals against one of the back walls and sat inside it. Pulled the curtain.

"He left," she said.

"Where?" the voice behind the grille said.

"Don't know. It's too late, anyway."

"Smell?" Harry said, and heard the word echo around the church. And even if he was sure they were alone in there, sitting in the back row, he lowered his voice. "He said he could *smell* it? And threw a dice?"

Dagny nodded and pointed at the recording device she had placed on the bench between them. "It's all on there."

"And he didn't confess anything?"

"No. He just called himself a sower. You can hear for yourself."

Harry managed to stop himself swearing and leaned back so hard against the back of the bench that the whole thing wobbled momentarily.

"What do we do now?" Dagny said.

Harry rubbed his face. How could Finne have known? Apart from him and Dagny, Kaja and Truls were the only people who knew about the plan. Maybe he had just read it from Dagny's face and body language? That was obviously possible; fear acts as an amplifier. Either way, what they were going to do now was a bloody good question.

"I need to see him die," Dagny said.

Harry nodded. "Finne's old, and a lot of things can happen. I'll let you know when he's dead."

Dagny shook her head. "You don't understand. I need to be watching *when* he dies. If I don't, my body won't accept that he's gone, and he'll haunt me in my dreams. Like my mother."

A single buzz announced the arrival of a text message, and Dagny pulled a shiny silver phone from her pocket.

It struck Harry that Rakel hadn't haunted his dreams after he'd seen her dead. Not yet, at least not that he could remember when he woke up. Why not? He had dreamed that he'd seen her face, lifeless, dead, after all. And then it hit him that he wanted, he *really* wanted her to haunt him; sooner a death mask and maggots crawling from her mouth than this cold, empty nothingness.

"Dear God . . ." Dagny whispered.

Her face was lit up by the screen. Her mouth was open, her eyes wide.

The phone fell to the floor with a clatter and lay there, screen upwards. Harry bent over. The video had stopped playing, and was showing the final image, a watch with luminous red numbers. Harry pressed Play, and the clip started again. There was no sound, it was grainy and the camera was moving, but he could see that it was a close-up of a white stomach with blood pumping out of a wound. A hairy hand with a grey watch strap came into shot. It happened so fast. The hand vanished inside the wound, all the way to the screen of the watch, which activated and lit up as more blood pumped out. The camera zoomed in on the watch, then the picture froze. The clip was over. Harry tried to swallow his nausea.

"What . . . what was that?" Dagny stammered.

"I don't know," Harry said, staring at the final image of the watch. "I don't know," he repeated.

"I can't . . ." Dagny began. "He's going to kill me too, and you won't be able to stop him on your own. Because you are on your own, aren't you?"

"Yes," Harry said. "I'm on my own."

"Then I'm going to have to look for help somewhere else. I have to think of myself."

"Do that," Harry said. He couldn't tear his eyes from the frozen image. The picture quality was too poor for the stomach or hand to be used to identify anyone. But the watch was clear enough. And the time. And the date.

03:00. The night Rakel was murdered.

19

The strip of sunlight from the window was making the white papers on Katrine Bratt's desk glow.

"Dagny Jensen says in her statement that you persuaded her to lure Svein Finne into a trap," she said.

She looked up from the document, found the long legs that began in front of her desk and led to the man who was half lying in the chair before her. His bright blue eyes were shaded by a pair of Ray-Ban sunglasses with black gaffer tape on one arm. He had been drinking. Because it wasn't just the acrid smell of stale alcohol coming from his clothes and body, reminding her of an amalgam, old people's homes and rotten blackberries. It was the smell of fresh alcohol on his breath, refreshing, cleansing. In short, the man sitting in front of her was an alcoholic who was partly recovering, and partly on his way towards renewed drunkenness.

"Is that right, Harry?"

"Yes," the man said, and coughed without covering his mouth. She saw a fleck of saliva glint in the sunlight on the arm of his chair. "Have you found who sent the video?"

"Yes," Katrine said. "A burner phone. Which is now dead and impossible to trace."

"Svein Finne. He sent it. He's the one filming, and it's him sticking his hand inside her stomach."

"Shame he didn't use the hand with the hole in. Then we'd have definite identification."

"It *is* him. You saw the time and date on the watch?"

"Yes. And obviously it's suspicious that the date is the same as the night of the murder. But the time is an hour later than the interval in which Forensics think Rakel died."

"The keyword there is 'think,'" Harry said. "You know as well as I do that they can't get it spot-on."

"Can you identify the stomach as Rakel's?"

"Come on, it's a grainy image taken with a moving camera."

"So it could be anyone. For all we know, it could be something Finne found online and sent to scare Dagny Jensen."

"Let's say that, then," Harry said, putting his hands on the armrests and starting to get up.

"Sit down!" Katrine barked.

Harry sank back into the chair.

She sighed deeply. "Dagny has police protection."

"Round the clock?"

"Yes."

"Good. Anything else?"

"Yes. I've just been informed by the Forensic Medical Institute that Valentin Gjertsen was Svein Finne's biological son. And that you've known about that for a while."

Katrine looked for some sort of reaction, but saw nothing except her own reflection in those blue mirrored sunglasses.

"So," she said. "You've decided that Svein Finne killed Rakel to avenge himself on you. You've ignored all protocols for police work and put another person, a rape victim, in danger in order to achieve something you're after personally. That isn't just gross misconduct in service, Harry, that's a criminal offence."

Katrine stopped. What was he looking at behind those damn sunglasses? Her? The picture hanging on the wall behind her? His own boots?

"You're already suspended, Harry. I haven't got many other sanctions available apart from dismissing you altogether. Or reporting you. Which would also lead to dismissal if you were found guilty. Do you understand?"

"Yes."

"Yes?"

"Yes, it isn't exactly complicated. Can I go now?"

"No! Do you know what I said to Dagny Jensen when she asked for police protection? I told her she'd get it, but that the police officers who are going to protect her are only human, and they quickly lose their enthusiasm if they know that the person they're protecting has filed a complaint against a police colleague for being overzealous. I put pressure on her, Harry, an innocent victim. For your sake! What have you got to say about that?"

Harry nodded slowly. "Well. What about: Can I go now?"

"*Go?*" Katrine threw her hands up. "Really? That's all you have to say?"

"No, but it would be better if I left before I say it."

Katrine groaned. She put her elbows on her desk, clasped her hands together and leaned her forehead against them. "Fine. GO."

Harry closed his eyes. He could feel the thick birch trunk against his back and the sharp spring sun warming his face. In front of him was a simple, brown wooden cross. It had Rakel's name on it, but nothing else, no date. The woman at the funeral parlour had called it a "temporary marker," something they usually erected while they were waiting for the headstone to be ready, but Harry couldn't help putting his own interpretation on it: it was only temporary because she was waiting for him.

"I'm still asleep," Harry said. "I hope that's OK. Because if I wake up, I'll fall apart and then I won't be able to catch him. And I'm going to get him, I swear. Do you remember how frightened you were of the flesh-eating zombies in *Night of the Living Dead*? Well . . ." Harry raised his hip flask. "Now I'm one of them."

Harry took a large swig. Possibly because he was already so tranquillised that the alcohol didn't seem to offer any further relief, he slid down the trunk until he was sitting against it, feeling the snow beneath his backside and thighs.

"By the way, there's a rumour that you wanted me back . . . Was that Old Tjikko? You don't have to answer."

He put the flask to his lips again. Removed it. Opened his eyes.

"It's lonely," he said. "Before I met you I was alone a lot, but I was never lonely. Loneliness is new, loneliness is . . . interesting. You weren't filling any sort of vacuum when we got together, but you left a huge, gaping hole when you went. There's probably an argument that love is a process of loss. What do you think?"

He closed his eyes again. Listened.

The light beyond his eyelids grew weaker and the temperature dropped. Harry knew it must be a cloud passing in front of the sun, and waited for the warmth to come back as he drifted off to sleep. Until something made him stiffen. Hold his breath. Because he could hear someone else breathing. It wasn't a cloud; someone or something was standing over him. And Harry hadn't heard anyone coming, even though there was snow all around him. He opened his eyes.

The sunlight spread out like a halo from the silhouette in front of him.

Harry's right hand felt inside his jacket.

"I've been looking for you," the silhouette said quietly.

Harry stopped.

"You've found me," Harry said. "What now?"

The silhouette moved aside, and for a moment Harry was blinded by the sun.

"Now we go back to mine," Kaja Solness said.

"Thanks, but do I really need it?" Harry asked, grimacing as he smelled the tea in the bowl Kaja had handed him.

"I don't know." Kaja smiled. "How was the shower?"

"Lukewarm."

"Because you were in there for three-quarters of an hour."

"Was I?" Harry sat back on the sofa with his hands around the bowl. "Sorry."

"It's fine. Do the clothes fit?"

Harry looked down at the trousers and sweater.

"My brother was a bit smaller than you." She smiled again.

"So you've changed your mind and want to help me after all?" Harry tasted the tea. It was bitter, and reminded him of the rosehip tea he used to be given as a child when he had a cold. He could never stand it, but his mum said it strengthened the immune system, and that one cup contained more vitamin C than forty oranges. Maybe those overdoses were the reason why he had hardly ever caught a cold since. And why he never ate oranges.

"Yes, I want to help *you*," she said, sitting down on the chair opposite him. "But not with your investigation."

"Oh?"

"Do you know, you're showing all the classic signs of PTSD?"

Harry stared at her.

"Post-traumatic stress disorder," Kaja said.

"I know what it is."

"Great. But do you know what the symptoms are?"

Harry shrugged his shoulders. "Repeated experience of the trauma. Dreams, flashbacks. Limited emotional response. You become a zombie. You *feel* like a zombie, an outsider on happy pills, flat and with no desire to live any longer than necessary. The world feels unreal, your sensation of time changes. As a defense mechanism you fragment the trauma, only remember specific details, but keep them apart so the whole experience and context remain in the dark."

Kaja nodded. "Don't forget hyperactivity. Anxiety, depression. Irritability and aggressiveness. Problems sleeping. How come you know so much about it?"

"Our resident psychologist has talked me through it."

"Ståle Aune? And he thought you *didn't* have PTSD?"

"Well, he didn't rule it out. But on the other hand, I've had those symptoms since I was a teenager. And because I can't remember it ever being different, he said it might just be my personality. Or that it started when I was a boy, when my mum died. Apparently grief can easily be confused with PTSD."

Kaja shook her head firmly. "I've had my share, Harry, and I know what grief is. And you remind me far too much of the soldiers I've seen leave Afghanistan with full-blown PTSD. Some of them were invalided out, some of them took their own lives. But you know what? The worst were the ones who came back. Who managed to slip beneath the psychologists' radar and were left as unexploded bombs, a danger to both themselves and their fellow soldiers."

"I haven't been to war, I've just lost someone."

"You *have* been to war, Harry. And you've been there for far too long. You're one of the few police officers who've had to kill several people in the course of their duty. And if there's one thing we learned in Afghanistan, it's what killing someone can do to a person."

"And I've seen what it *doesn't* do to a person. People who shake it off as if it was nothing. Or who just wait for the next opportunity."

"Obviously you're right, in that we react very differently to the experience of killing someone. But for vaguely normal people, the reason why they had to kill matters too. One study by RAND shows that at least 20, probably more like 30 percent of American soldiers who served in Afghanistan or Iraq had PTSD. The same goes for American soldiers in Vietnam. The equivalent figure for Allied soldiers in the Second World War seems to have been only half that. Psychologists believe that's because the soldiers didn't *understand* the wars in Vietnam, Iraq and Afghanistan. Whereas everyone understood why Hitler had to be fought. The soldiers who'd been in Vietnam, Iraq and Afghanistan came home to a society that didn't organise parades, and looked at them with suspicion. And the soldiers weren't able to fit their actions into a comprehensive narrative that justified them. That's why it's easier to kill for Israel. The PTSD rate there is down at 8 percent. Not because the violence is any less grotesque, but because the soldiers can tell themselves that they're defending a small country surrounded by enemies, and because they have broad support among their own population. That gives them a simple, ethically justifiable reason for killing. What they do is necessary, meaningful."

"Mm. You're saying I'm traumatised, but the people I've killed, I've killed out of necessity. Yes, they come to me at night, but I still pull the trigger without hesitation. Time after time."

"You belong to the 8 percent who get PTSD even though they have every possibility of justifying their actions," Kaja said. "The ones who don't do that. Who are unconsciously but actively looking for a way to blame themselves. The way you're now trying to take the blame for—"

"OK, let's say that, then," Harry interrupted.

". . . Rakel's death."

Silence fell in the living room. Harry stared out into space. Blinked over and over again.

Kaja swallowed. "I'm sorry, I didn't mean it like that. At least, I didn't mean to *say* it like that."

"You're right," Harry said. "Apart from the business of *looking* for blame. It is my fault, that's a fact. If I hadn't killed Svein Finne's son . . ."

"You were doing your job."

". . . Rakel would still be alive."

"I know people who specialise in PTSD. You need help, Harry."

"Yes. Help to catch Finne."

"That's not your biggest problem."

"Yes, it is."

Kaja sighed. "How long did you have to look for his son before you found him?"

"Who's counting? I found him."

"No one catches Finne, he's like a ghost."

Harry looked up.

"I worked in Vice within the Crime Squad Unit," Kaja said. "I've read the reports about Svein Finne, they were on the syllabus."

"A ghost," Harry said.

"What?"

"That's what we're all looking for." He got to his feet. "Thanks for the hot water. And the tip-off."

"Tip-off?"

The old man was staring at the blue dress that was swaying and drifting in the current of the river. Life as a dance performed by mayflies. You stand in a room full of testosterone and perfume, moving your feet in time to the music and smiling at the prettiest one because you think she's meant for you. Until you ask her to dance and she says no and looks over your shoulder at the other guy, the guy who isn't you. Then, once you've patched up your broken heart, you adjust your expectations and ask the next prettiest to dance. Then the third. Until you get to the one who says yes. And if you're lucky, and you dance well together, you ask her for the next dance as well. And the next. Until the evening is over and you ask if she wants to spend eternity with you.

"Yes, darling, but we're mayflies," she says, and dies.

And then comes night, real night, and the only thing you've got is a memory, a blue dress waving enticingly, and the promise that it won't be more than a day until you can follow her. The blue dress is the only thing that makes it possible to dream that you will one day dance again.

"I'd like a wildlife camera."

The deep, hoarse voice came from the other side of the counter.

The old man turned round. It was a tall man. Broad-shouldered but thin.

"We've got several different types . . ." Alf said.

"I know, I bought one here a while back. I'd like the fancy sort this time. The one that sends messages to your phone when someone's there. The sort that can be hidden."

"I get you. Let me just get one I think would do the job."

The old man's son-in-law went off to the shelves of wildlife cameras and the tall man turned and met the old man's gaze. The old man remembered the face, not only because he had seen it in the shop before, but because he hadn't been able to figure out if it belonged to a herbivore or a carnivore. Odd, because there was no doubt now. The man was a carnivore. But there was something else familiar about that look. The old man strained his eyes. Alf came back, and the tall man turned back towards the counter.

"When this camera detects movement in front of the lens, it takes an image and sends it directly to the phone number you install . . ."

"Thanks, I'll take it."

When the tall man had left the shop, the old man looked back at the television screen. One day all the blue dresses would be torn to pieces and drift away, the memories would let go and disappear. He saw the scars of loss and resignation in his own eyes in the mirror every day. That was what he had recognised in the tall man's expression. Loss. But not resignation. Not yet.

Harry heard the gravel crunch beneath his boots and thought that this was what happened when you got old, you spent more and more time in cemeteries. Got to know your future neighbours in the place you'd be spending eternity. He stopped in front of the small, black stone. Crouched down, dug a hole in the snow and put the vase of white lilies in it. He packed the snow around it and arranged the stems. He stepped back to make sure it looked right. He looked up and surveyed the ranks of headstones. If the rule was that you were buried in the cemetery closest to your home, Harry would end up here somewhere, not next to Rakel, who lay in Voksen Cemetery. It had taken him seven minutes to get here from his flat—three and a half if he hurried, but he had taken his time. Burial plots were only left alone for twenty years; after that new coffins could be buried in the same plot, alongside the ones that were already there. So if fate was so inclined, they *could* be reunited in death. Harry shivered in his coat as a cold shudder ran through his body. He looked at the time. Then hurried towards the exit.

"How are you doing?"

"Fine," Oleg said.

"Fine?"

"Up and down."

"Mm." Harry pressed the phone closer to his ear, as if to reduce the distance between them, between a flat on Sofies gate where Bruce Springsteen was singing "Stray Bullet" in the evening darkness, and the house two thousand kilometres farther north where Oleg had a view of the Air Force base and Porsanger Fjord. "I'm calling to tell you to be careful."

"Careful?"

Harry told him about Svein Finne. "If Finne is out for revenge for me killing his son, that means you could be in danger too."

"I'm coming to Oslo," Oleg said firmly.

"No!"

"No? If he killed Mum, am I supposed to just sit here and—"

"Firstly, Crime Squad wouldn't let you anywhere near the investigation. Just think what a defense lawyer could do to a case in which you, the victim's son, had taken part. And secondly, it's likely that he picked your mother rather than you because you're well outside his normal territory."

"I'm coming."

"Listen! If he comes after you, I want you up there for two reasons. He won't drive two thousand kilometres by car, so he'd have to fly. To a small airport where you'll be able to give them pictures of him. Svein Finne isn't the sort of person it's easy to ignore in a small place. With you where you are, we're increasing the chances of catching him. OK?"

"But—"

"Reason number two. Imagine that you're *not* there when he arrives. And finds Helga at home on her own."

Silence. Just Springsteen and a piano.

Oleg cleared his throat. "You'll keep me orientated as things progress?"

"Orientated. OK?"

After they hung up, Harry sat and stared at the phone where he'd put it down on the coffee table. The Boss was in the middle of another track that hadn't made it onto *The River* album, "The Man Who Got Away."

Like hell. Not this time.

The phone lay cold and dead on the table.

When it was half past eleven, he couldn't sit still any longer.

He put his boots on, grabbed his phone and went out into the hallway. His car keys weren't on the dresser where he usually kept them, so he hunted through all his trouser and jacket pockets until he found them in the bloody jeans he'd tossed in the laundry basket. He went down to his Ford Escort, got in, adjusted the seat, turned the key in the ignition and reached automatically for the radio, but changed his mind. He had it tuned to Stone Hard FM because they didn't talk and played nothing but brain-dead, pain-numbing hard rock twenty-four hours a day, but he didn't need anything pain-numbing right now. He needed pain. So he drove in silence through the drowsy streets of Oslo city centre, and up into the hills that wound past Sjømannsskolen to Nordstrand. He pulled over to the side of the road, took his flashlight from the glove compartment, got out and looked down at the Oslo Fjord as it lay bathed in moonlight, black and copper-smooth towards the south, towards Denmark and the open sea. He opened the boot and took out the crowbar. He stood and looked at it for a moment. There was something that wasn't right, something he hadn't thought of, but it was so small, like a fragment floating across his retina, and now he'd forgotten it. He tried biting his false finger, and shivered when his teeth came into contact with the titanium. But it didn't help, it was gone, like a dream slipping helplessly out of mind.

Harry waded through the snow to the edge of the hill, to the old bunkers where he, Øystein and Tresko used to come and drink themselves stupid while their contemporaries were celebrating graduation, National Day, Midsummer and whatever the fuck else they used to celebrate.

The council had padlocked the doors after a series of articles in one of the city's papers. It wasn't that they hadn't known that the bunkers were used by drug addicts and prostitutes, and there had been pictures published before. Pictures of young people injecting heroin into arms covered in scars, and foreign women in slutty outfits lying on filthy mattresses. What made them react this time was one single picture. It wasn't even particularly brutal. A young man sitting on a mattress with a user's accessories beside him. He was staring into the camera with puppy-dog eyes. The shock factor was that he looked like an ordinary Norwegian youth: blue-eyed, with a traditional sweater and short, neat hair. You could have imagined it was taken one Easter holiday at his family's cabin. The next day the council had put locks on all the doors, and set up signs warning about trespassing and saying the bunkers were regularly patrolled. Harry knew that was an empty threat—the Chief of Police didn't even have enough money and people to investigate break-ins where things were actually *stolen*.

He inserted the crowbar into the crack in the door.

He had to use the whole of his weight before the lock gave way.

Harry stepped inside. The only sound breaking the silence was the echo of dripping from deep inside the darkness, which made Harry think of the sonar pulse from a submarine. Tresko had said he'd downloaded a soundtrack of sonar pulses from the net, put it on a loop and used it to get to sleep. Said the feeling of being underwater made him calm.

Harry could only identify three ingredients in the stench: piss, petrol and wet concrete. He switched the flashlight on and walked farther in. The beam found a wooden bench that looked like it had been stolen from the surrounding parkland, and a mattress that was black with damp and mould. Planks had been nailed over the horizontal firing slits facing the fjord.

It was—as he had thought—the perfect place.

And he couldn't help himself.

He turned the flashlight off.

Closed his eyes. He wanted to try out the feeling now, in advance. He tried to see it in front of him, but the images wouldn't come.

Why not? Maybe he needed to feed the hate.

He thought about Rakel. Rakel on the stone floor. Svein Finne over her. Feed the hate.

And then it came.

Harry screamed out loud into the darkness and opened his eyes.

What the hell was going on, why was his brain storing these images of himself covered in blood?

Svein Finne woke up at the sound of a branch snapping.

He was wide awake in an instant, staring up into the darkness and the roof of his two-man tent.

Had they found him? Here, so far from the nearest buildings, in dense pine forest in such rough terrain that even dogs would have trouble getting through it?

He listened. Tried to identify what it could be from the sounds. A snort. Not human. Heavy steps on the forest floor. So heavy that he could feel a slight vibration through the ground. A large animal. An elk, perhaps. When he was young, Svein Finne had often gone off into the forest, taking his tent with him, and would spend the night in Maridalen or Sørkedalen. The Oslo forests were vast, and provided freedom and refuge for a young lad who often got in trouble, didn't fit in, who people tended either to avoid or wanted to bully. People often reacted like that when there was something they were afraid of. Svein Finne hadn't been able to understand how they knew. He kept it hidden from them, after all. He only revealed who he was to a very few people. And he could understand that they got scared. He felt more at home out here in the forest with the animals than in the city that lay just a couple of hours' walk away. And there were more animals here, right on their doorstep, than most of the people in Oslo knew. Deer, hares, pine martens. Foxes, of course; they thrived on human waste. The occasional red deer. One moonlit night he'd watched a lynx sneak past on the other side of a lake. And birds. Ospreys. Tawny owls and boreal owls. He hadn't seen any of the goshawks and sparrowhawks that had been common here when he was growing up. But a buzzard had drifted past between the trees above him.

The elk had come closer. It had stopped breaking branches now. Elk break branches. A snout pressed against the tent, sniffed up and down. A snout that was sniffing for food. In the middle of the night. It wasn't an elk.

Finne rolled over in his sleeping bag, grabbed his flashlight and hit the snout with it. It disappeared and he heard a deep sniff outside. Then the snout was back, and this time it pressed so hard against the tent that when Finne switched his flashlight quickly on and off again, he was able to see what it was. He had seen the outline of the big head and jaw. There was a scratching sound of claws tearing at the fabric of the tent. Finne was as quick as lightning, grabbing the handle of the knife he always kept by the side of the underlay, pulled the zip down and rolled out of the tent, making sure he didn't have his back to the animal. He had set up camp on a few square metres of snow-free ground on a slope, in front of a large rock that divided the meltwater so that it ran down either side of the tent, and now he tumbled naked down the slope. He felt no pain as twigs and stones cut into his skin, just heard the cracking of the undergrowth as the bear came after him. It had noticed his flight, and its hunting instincts had kicked in, and Svein Finne knew that no one could outrun a bear, not on this terrain. But he had no intention of trying to do that. Nor of lying down and pretending to be dead, the way some people say is a good strategy if you run into a bear. A bear that had just emerged from hibernation is desperate from starvation and would be more than happy to eat even a corpse. Fucking idiots. Finne reached the bottom of the slope, found his feet, pressed his back against a thick tree trunk and straightened up. He switched the flashlight on and aimed it at the noises coming towards him.

The animal stopped abruptly when the light shone in its eyes. Blinded, it stood up on its hind legs and flailed at the air with its paws. It was a brown bear. About two metres tall. Could have been bigger, Finne thought, as he gripped the sheath between his teeth and drew the *puukko* knife. Grandfather Finne had said the last bear to be caught in the forests around Oslo—in 1882, by forest ranger

Kjelsås, next to a fallen tree in Grønnvollia below Opkuven—had been almost two and a half metres tall.

The bear fell onto all fours. Its skin was hanging loose around it. It was panting hard, swinging its head from side to side, looking alternately into the forest and towards the light, as if it couldn't decide.

Finne held the knife up in front of him. "Don't want to work for your food, Bruin? Feeling a bit weak tonight?"

The bear roared, as if in frustration, and Finne laughed so loud that it echoed off the rock face above them. "My grandfather was one of the men who ate your grandfather back in 1882," Finne called. "He said it tasted terrible, even with plenty of seasoning. But I could imagine taking a bite of you all the same, Bruin, so come on! Come on, you stupid bastard!"

Finne took a step towards the bear, which backed away slightly, shifting its weight from side to side. It looked confused, almost cowed.

"I know how it feels," Finne said. "You've been shut up for ages, then suddenly you get out, and there's too much light, too little food, and you're all alone. Not because you've been cast out—because you're not like them, you're not a herding animal, you're the one who's cast them out." Finne took another step closer. "But that doesn't mean you don't feel lonely, does it? Spread your seed, Bruin, make others who are like you, who understand you. Who understand how to honour their father! Hah! Hah! Get lost, because there are no females in Sørkedalen. Get lost, this is my territory, you poor, starving bastard! All you'll find here is loneliness."

The bear pressed down on its front paws, as if it was about to stand up again but couldn't manage it.

Finne saw it now. The bear was old. Maybe sick. And Finne detected an unmistakable smell. The smell of fear. It wasn't the far smaller, two-legged creature in front of it that was making it frightened, but the fact that this creature wasn't emitting the same smell. It was fearless. Crazy. Capable of anything.

"Well, old Bruin?"

The bear snarled, revealing a set of yellow teeth.

Then it turned and padded away until it was swallowed up by the darkness.

Svein Finne stood and listened to the sound of twigs snapping farther and farther away.

The bear would be back. Either when it was even hungrier, or when it had eaten and felt strong enough to conquer the territory.

Tomorrow he would have to start looking for somewhere that was even less accessible, possibly somewhere with walls that could keep a bear out. But first he had to go into the city and buy a trap. And visit the grave. The herd.

Katrine couldn't sleep. But her son was asleep in his crib over by the window, that was the important thing.

She rolled over in bed and looked directly into Bjørn's pale face. His eyes were closed but he wasn't snoring. And that meant he wasn't asleep either. She studied him. His thin, reddish eyelids with their visible veins, his pale eyebrows, white skin. It was as if he'd swallowed a lit lightbulb. Inflated and illuminated from within. Plenty of people had been surprised when they got together. No one had asked straight out, obviously, but she had seen the question on their faces: what makes a beautiful, self-sufficient woman choose a less than averagely attractive man with no money? A female MP on the Justice Committee had taken her aside at a networking cocktail party for "women in important positions" and told her she thought it was great that Katrine had married a male colleague whose status was lower than hers. Katrine had replied that Bjørn was bloody good in bed, and asked the politician if she felt ashamed of having a high-status husband who earned more than her, and what did she think the chances were that her next husband would be lower-status? Katrine had no idea who the woman's husband was, but from the look on her face she could tell that she had got pretty close to the mark. She hated those "influential women" gatherings anyway. Not because she didn't support the cause, not because she didn't think that true equality was something worth fighting for, but because she couldn't summon up the forced sisterly solidarity and emotional rhetoric. Occasionally she felt like telling them to shut up and stick to asking for equal opportunities and equal pay for equal work. Sure, a change was long overdue, and not only when it came to direct sexual harassment, but also the indirect and often intangible sexual-control tactics men used. But that mustn't be allowed to rise to the top of the agenda and draw attention away from what equality was really about. Women would only harm themselves yet again if they prioritised hurt feelings over the size of their pay packets. Because only better wages, more economic power, would make them invulnerable.

Perhaps she would have felt differently if she'd been the most vulnerable person in the bedroom. She had sought out Bjørn when she was at her weakest, her most fragile, when she needed someone who would love her unconditionally. And the slightly plump but kind and charming forensic specialist had hardly been able to believe his luck, and responded by proclaiming her his queen, almost to the point of self-negation. She had told herself that she wouldn't exploit that, that she had seen too many people—women and men alike—turn into monsters simply because their partner invited it. And she had tried. She really had.

She had been tested before, but when the real test came along—the third person, the baby—the survival instinct that got you through the day took over and consideration for your partner had to give way.

The third person. The one you loved more than your partner.

But in Katrine's case, the third person had been there all along.

Once. Just once she had lain like this, in this very bed with him, the third person. Listened to him breathing while an autumn storm made the windows rattle, the walls creak, and her world collapse. He belonged to someone else, she was only borrowing him, but if that was all she could get, she'd take it. Did she regret that attack of madness? Yes. Yes, of course she did. Was it the happiest moment of her life? No. It was despair and a peculiar numbness. Could the whole thing have been avoided? Definitely not.

"What are you thinking about?" Bjørn whispered.

What if she said it? What if she told him everything?

"The case," she said.

"Oh?"

"How can you lot have absolutely nothing?"

"Like we've said, the perpetrator cleaned up after himself. Are you really thinking about the case, or . . . something else?"

Katrine couldn't see the expression in his eyes in the darkness, but she could hear it in his voice. He had always known about the third person. Bjørn Holm was the person she had confided in back when he was just a friend and she had only just moved to Police Headquarters, when she had a hopeless, silly infatuation with Harry. It was so long ago. But she had never told him about that night.

"A married couple who live in Holmenkollen were driving home on the night of the murder," Katrine said. "They saw an adult male walking down Holmenkollveien at quarter to midnight."

"Which fits the presumed time of the murder, between 22:00 and 02:00," Bjørn said.

"Sober adults in Holmenkollen drive cars. The last bus had gone, and we've checked the security cameras at Holmenkollen metro station. A tram arrived at twenty-five minutes to midnight, but the only person who got off was a woman. What's a pedestrian doing out that late at night? If he was walking all the way home from a bar in the city, he'd have been walking uphill, and if he was heading back into the city, he'd have gone to the metro station, don't you think? Unless he wanted to avoid any security cameras."

"A man, out walking. It's a bit thin, isn't it? Did they give a description?"

"Just the usual. Average height, between twenty-five and sixty, unknown ethnicity, but rather dark-skinned."

"So the reason you've got hung up on this is . . ."

". . . that it's the only lead of any value at all."

"So you didn't get anything useful from the neighbour?"

"Mrs. Syvertsen? Her bedroom is at the back of the house, and the window was open. But she says she slept like a baby all night."

Like an ironic response, a tentative whimpering sound came from the crib. They looked at each other and almost started to laugh.

Katrine turned away from them and pressed her ear down into the pillow, but couldn't shut out two further whines, then the usual pause before the siren started. She felt the mattress move as Bjørn rolled out of bed.

She wasn't thinking about the baby. She wasn't thinking about Harry. And she wasn't thinking about the case. She was thinking about sleep. A mammal's deep sleep, the sort with both sides of the brain switched off.

Kaja ran her hand over the rough, hard grip of the pistol. She had switched off all sources of noise in the living room and was listening to the silence. He was out there, she had heard him. She had got hold of the pistol after what happened to Hala in Kabul.

Hala and Kaja had been two of the nine women in the group of twenty-three people who shared the same living quarters, most of them employed by the Red Crescent or Red Cross, but a few held civilian positions in the peacekeeping forces. Hala was an unusual person with an unusual background, but what really set her apart from the others in the building was that she wasn't foreign but Afghan. The building wasn't far from the Kabul Serena Hotel and Afghan Presidential Palace. The Taliban attack on the Serena had demonstrated that nowhere in Kabul was completely safe, but everything was relative, and they had felt protected by the security guard behind the tall railings. In the afternoons, Hala and Kaja would go up onto the flat roof and fly the kite they had bought at the Strand Bazaar for a dollar or two. Kaja had assumed it was just a romantic cliché from a best-selling book—the idea that the kites in the skies above Kabul were a symbol that the city was free from the Taliban regime, which had banned kite-flying in the nineties because it took people's time and attention away from prayer. But at the weekends now there were hundreds, thousands of kites in the air. And according to Hala, the colours of the kites were even brighter than they were before the Taliban, because of the new ink that had come onto the market. Hala had known just how they had to work together when they flew the kite—one steering it, the other watching the line—otherwise they wouldn't stay clear of other kites that were looking for a fight, trying to cut their line or kite with their own lines, which had slivers of glass attached to them. It wasn't hard to see the parallels with the West's self-imposed mission in Afghanistan, but it was still a game. If they lost a kite, they just sent up another one. And even more beautiful than the kites in the sky was the glow in Hala's beautiful eyes when she looked up at them.

It was past midnight, and Kaja had heard sirens and seen blue police lights from the living-room window. She was already worried because Hala hadn't come home, so she got dressed and went outside. The police cars were parked by an alley. There was no cordon, and a crowd of onlookers had already gathered. Young Afghan men in leather jackets, copies of Gucci and Armani, were pretty much the only people on the streets at that time of night. How many crime scenes had Kaja attended as a detective in the Crime Squad Unit? Even so, she still woke up from nightmares about that night. The knife had cut large flaps in Hala's *shalwar kameez*, baring the skin beneath, and her head was bent back at an impossible angle, as if her neck was broken, making the wound in her neck gape open, and Kaja could see right into the pink, already-dry innards. When she crouched over the body, a swarm of sandflies had emerged from the wound, like an evil spirit emerging from a lamp, and Kaja had flailed her arms about her.

The post-mortem revealed that Hala had had intercourse right before the murder, and even if the physical evidence couldn't rule out the possibility that it had been voluntary, they all assumed—given the circumstances and the fact that she was a single young woman who followed the strict rules of the Hazaras—that it was rape. The police never found the perpetrator or perpetrators. People said that the risk of being raped in the street in Kabul was a fraction of the risk of being blown up by an IED. And even if the number of rapes had risen since the fall of the Taliban, the police had a theory that the Taliban were behind the attack, to show what would happen to Afghan women who worked for ISAF, Resolute Force and other Western organisations. Despite that, the rape and murder in Kabul had frightened the other women in the group. Kaja had taught them how to handle a gun. And in a strange way, this pistol—which was passed around like a baton whenever one of them had to go out after dark—brought them together as a team. A kite team.

Kaja felt the weight of the pistol. When she was in the police, holding a loaded pistol had always filled her with a mixture of fear and security. In Afghanistan she had started to think of it as a necessary tool, something you valued having. Like the knife. It was Anton who had taught her to use it. Who had taught her that even in the Red Cross—at least, in his Red Cross—you defended your own life if necessary by killing. She remembered that the first time she met Anton she had thought that the refined, almost jovial, tall blond Swiss man—who was far too handsome—wasn't for her. She had been wrong. And right. But when it came to Hala's murder, she wasn't wrong, only right.

It wasn't the Taliban who had been behind it.

She knew who it was, but had no evidence.

Kaja squeezed her hand tightly round the handle. Listened. Breathed. Waited. Numb. That was what was so strange: her heart was pounding as if she were on the brink of panic, but at the same time she felt completely indifferent. Scared of dying, but not particularly interested in living. Even so, she had got through the debriefing with the psychologist when they stopped in Tallinn on the way home. And sailed under the radar.

20

Harry woke up, and everything was the same. A few seconds passed before he remembered, realised it wasn't a nightmare, and the clenched fist hit him in the guts. He rolled onto his side and stared at the picture on the table. Rakel, Oleg and himself, smiling, sitting on a boulder surrounded by autumn leaves, on one of those *hikes* Rakel was so keen on, and which Harry suspected that he had rather started to enjoy. And for the first time he thought the thought: if this was the start of a day that was only going to get worse, how many more days could he handle? He was in the process of giving himself an answer when he realised he hadn't been woken by the alarm clock. His phone, lying next to the picture, was vibrating almost silently, like the buzz of a hummingbird. He grabbed it.

It was a text message containing a picture.

Harry's heart began to beat faster.

He tapped the screen twice with his finger, and it felt as if his heart had stopped.

Svein Finne, "the Fiancé," was standing with his head bowed, facing the camera, his eyes focused a little way above it. The sky above his head had a reddish glow.

Harry leapt out of bed, picked up his trousers from the floor and pulled them on. Yanked on a T-shirt on his way to the door, pulled on his coat and boots and rushed out into the stairwell. He stuck his hands in his pockets to check that everything he had put in them the previous evening was still there: car keys, handcuffs and the Heckler & Koch pistol.

He burst out of the door, breathed in the cold morning air and jumped in the Escort that was parked on the edge of the pavement.

Three and a half minutes if he ran. But he needed the car for part two. Harry quietly cursed the starter motor when it failed to work the first time. It would be game over at the next MOT. He turned the key again and pressed the accelerator. *There!* Harry skidded up the wet cobbles of Stensberggata, almost deserted so early in the morning. How long did people stand at graves? He cut across the beginnings of the morning rush on Ullevålsveien and parked on the pavement on Akersbakken right in front of the north gate to Vår Frelsers Cemetery. He left the car unlocked with its police badge clearly visible on the dashboard.

He ran, but stopped when he reached the gate. From where he was standing, at the top of the sloping cemetery, he immediately caught sight of the lonely figure standing in front of the grave. His head was bowed, and a long, thick Native American plait was hanging down his back.

Harry clasped the butt of the pistol in his coat pocket and started walking. Not fast, not slow. He stopped when he was three metres from the man's back.

"What do you want?"

The sound of the man's voice made Harry shiver. The last time he had heard Svein Finne's gravelly, resounding priest's voice they had been sitting in a cell in Ila Prison, when Harry was trying to get help to catch the man who was now lying in the grave in front of them. Back then Harry had had no idea that Valentin Gjertsen was Svein Finne's son. In hindsight, he couldn't help thinking he should have suspected something. Should have realised that such sick, violent fantasies must have come from the same source, one way or another.

"Svein Finne," Harry said, and heard his voice shake. "You're under arrest."

He didn't hear Finne laugh, just saw his shoulders move. "That seems to be your standard line whenever you see me, Hole."

"Put your hands behind your back."

Finne let out a deep sigh. He put his hands behind his back with a nonchalant gesture, as if it made his posture more comfortable.

"I'm going to put handcuffs on you. And before you think of doing anything stupid, you should know that I've got a pistol aimed at the base of your spine."

"You'd shoot me in the base of the *spine*, Hole?" Finne turned his head and grinned. Those brown eyes. The thick, wet lips. Harry breathed through his nose. Cold. He needed to stay cold now, not think about her. Think about what he was going to do, nothing else. Simple, practical things.

"Because you think I'm more frightened of being paralysed than of dying?"

Harry took a deep breath in an attempt to stop himself trembling. "Because I want a confession *before* you die."

"Like you got from my boy? And then you shot him?"

"I had to shoot him because he was resisting arrest."

"Yes, I daresay that's how you choose to remember it. That's probably how you remember shooting me too."

Harry saw the hole in Svein Finne's palm, like Torghatten, the mountain with a hole you can see daylight through. From a bullet fired during an arrest early in Harry's police career. But it was the other hand that caught his attention. The grey watchstrap around his wrist. Without lowering the pistol, he grabbed Finne's wrist with his free hand and turned it over. Pressed the face of the watch. Red numbers indicating the time and date lit up.

The click of the handcuffs sounded like a damp kiss in the empty cemetery.

Harry turned the ignition key counterclockwise, and the engine died.

"A beautiful morning," Finne said, looking through the Escort's windshield down at the fjord below them. "But why aren't we at Police Headquarters?"

"I was thinking of giving you a choice," Harry said. "You can give me a confession here and now, and we can drive back down for breakfast and a warm cell in Police Headquarters. Or you can deny it, and you and I can take a little walk into that wartime bunker."

"Ha! I like you, Hole. I really do. I hate you as a person, but I like your personality." Finne moistened his lips. "And I confess, obviously. She—"

"Wait until I start recording," Harry said, fishing his phone out of his coat pocket.

". . . was a willing participant." Finne shrugged his shoulders. "I think she might even have enjoyed it more than me."

Harry swallowed. Closed his eyes for a moment. "*Enjoyed* having a knife stuck in her stomach?"

"A knife?" Finne turned in his seat and looked at Harry. "I took her by the railings, right behind where you arrested me. Of course I know it's against the law to fuck in a cemetery, but given the way she insisted on getting more, I think it's only reasonable for her to pay most of the fine. Has she really filed a complaint? I suppose she regretted her ungodly behaviour. Yes, that wouldn't surprise me. Unless perhaps she actually believes what she's saying. Shame can make us distort anything. Do you know, there was a psychologist in prison who tried to tell me about Nathanson's Compass of Shame. That I was so ashamed at having killed the girl, like you claimed I had, that I had to flee the shame altogether by denying it had ever happened. That's what's going on here. Dagny feels so ashamed of how much she enjoyed what happened in the cemetery that her memory has turned it into rape. Does that sound familiar, Hole?"

Harry was about to answer when a wave of nausea rose up inside him. Shame. Repression.

The handcuffs rattled as Finne leaned forward in his seat. "Either way, you know what it's like with rape cases, where it's one person's word against another's, with no witnesses or forensic evidence. I'll get off, Hole. Is that what this is about? You know the only way you can get me locked up for rape is by forcing a confession out of me? Sorry, Hole. But, like I said, I confess to fucking in a public place, so at least you've got something you can pin on me. Are you still offering breakfast?"

"Did I say something wrong?" Finne laughed as he stumbled through the muddy snow. He fell to his knees, and Harry pulled him up and shoved him towards the bunkers.

Harry was crouched down in front of the wooden bench. On the floor in front of him was everything he had found when he searched Svein Finne. A dice made of blue-grey metal. A couple of hundred-kroner notes and some coins, but no bus or tram tickets. A knife in a sheath. The knife had a brown wooden shaft, a short blade. Sharp. Could that be the murder weapon? There were no traces of blood on it. Harry looked up. He had removed one of the planks covering the gun slits to let some light into the bunker. Joggers occasionally ran past along the path just outside, but there wouldn't be any until the snow had gone completely. No one would hear Svein Finne's screams.

"Nice knife," Harry said.

"I collect knives," Finne said. "I had twenty-six that you seized from me, do you remember? I never got them back." The light of the low morning sun was striking Svein Finne's face and muscular upper body. Not the pumped-up version jailbirds get from repetitive weightlifting in a cramped gym, but the wiry, fit sort. A ballet dancer's body, Harry thought. Or Iggy Pop's. Clean. Finne was sitting on the bench with his hands cuffed round the backrest. Harry had removed his shoes as well, but had let him keep his trousers.

"I remember the knives," Harry said. "What's the dice for?"

"To make the difficult decisions in life."

"Luke Rhinehart," Harry said. "So you've read *The Dice Man*."

"I don't read, Hole. But you can keep the dice, a gift from me to you. Let fate decide when you don't know what to do. You'll find it very liberating, believe me."

"So fate is more liberating than deciding for yourself?"

"Of course. Imagine that you feel like killing someone, but can't make yourself do it. So you need help. From fate. And if the dice tells you to kill, fate bears the responsibility; it *liberates* you and your free will. Do you see? All it takes is a throw of the dice."

Harry checked the recording was working before he put the phone down on the bench. He took a deep breath. "Did you throw the dice before you murdered Rakel Fauke?"

"Who's Rakel Fauke?"

"My wife," Harry said. "The murder took place in the kitchen of our home in Holmenkollen ten days ago." He saw something begin to dance in Finne's eyes.

"My condolences."

"Shut up and talk."

"Or else?" Finne sighed as if he were bored. "Are you going to get the car battery and use it on my testicles?"

"Using car batteries to torture someone is a myth," Harry said. "They don't have enough power."

"How do you know that?"

"I read up about torture methods online last night," Harry said, running the sharp edge of the knife against the skin of his thumb. "Apparently it isn't the pain itself that makes people confess, but the *fear* of pain. But obviously the fear needs to be well founded—the torturer has to convince the victim that the pain he is willing to inflict is only limited by the torturer's imagination. And if there's one thing I've got right now, Finne, it's imagination."

Svein Finne moistened his thick lips. "I see. You want the details?"

"All of them."

"The only detail I have for you is that I didn't do it."

Harry clenched his fist around the handle of the knife and punched. He felt the cartilage in the other man's nose break, felt the blow in his own knuckles and the warm blood on the back of his hand. Finne's eyes filled with tears of pain and his lips parted. Revealed his big, yellow teeth in a broad grin. "Everybody kills, Hole." His priest's voice had a different, more nasal tone now. "You, your colleagues, your neighbour. Just not me. I create new life, I repair what you destroy. I populate the world with myself, with people who want good." He tilted his head. "I don't understand why people make the effort to raise something that isn't theirs. Like you and your bastard son. Oleg, that's his name, isn't it? Is that because your sperm's too weak, Hole? Or didn't you fuck Rakel well enough for her to want to give birth to your children?"

Harry punched again. Hit the same place. He wondered if the crisp crunching sound came from Finne's nose or was just in his own head. Finne leaned his head back and grinned up at the roof. "More!"

Harry was sitting on the floor with his back against the concrete wall, listening to the sound of his own deep breathing and the wheezing sound from the bench. He had wound Finne's shirt around his hand, but the pain told him that the skin on at least one of his knuckles was broken. How long had they been at it? How long was it going to take? On the website about torture it had said that no one, absolutely no one, could hold out against torture in the long run, that they would tell you what you want, or possibly what they *think* you want. Svein Finne had merely repeated the same word: *more*. And had got what he asked for.

"Knives." The voice was no longer recognisable as Finne's. And when Harry looked up, he didn't recognise the man either. The swelling on his face had made his eyes close, and the blood was hanging off him like a dripping red beard. "People use knives."

"Knives?" Harry repeated in a whisper.

"People have been sticking knives in each other since the Stone Age, Hole. Fear of them is embedded in our genes. The thought that something can penetrate your skin, get inside, destroy what's inside you, that which *is* you. Show them a knife and they'll do whatever you want."

"Who does what you want?"

Finne cleared his throat and spat red saliva on the floor between them. "Everyone. Women, men. You. Me. In Rwanda, the Tutsis were offered the chance to buy bullets so they could be shot rather than hacked to death with machetes. And you know what? They paid up."

"OK, I've got a knife," Harry said, nodding towards the knife on the floor between them.

"And where are you going to stick it?"

"I was thinking the same place you stabbed my wife. In the stomach."

"A bad bluff, Hole. If you stab me in the stomach I won't be able to talk, and I'd bleed to death before you got your confession."

Harry didn't answer.

"Actually, hang on," Finne said, straightening his bloody head. "Could it be that you, who have done your research into torture, are conducting this ineffective boxing match because deep down you don't really want a confession?" He sniffed the air. "Yes, that's it. You don't want me to confess, so you have an excuse to kill me. In fact, you'd *have* to kill me in order to get justice. You just needed a precursor to the killing. So you can tell yourself you tried, that this wasn't what you wanted. That you're not like the murderers who do it just because they like it." Finne's laughter turned into a gurgling cough. "Yes, I lied. I am a murderer, me too. Because killing someone *is* fantastic, isn't it, Hole? Seeing a child come into the world, knowing that it's your own creation, can only be outshone by one thing: removing someone from the world. Terminating a life, assuming the role of fate, being someone's dice. Then you're God, Hole, and you can deny it as much as you like, but that's precisely the feeling you've got right now. It's good, isn't it?"

Harry stood up.

"So I'm sorry to have to spoil this execution, Hole, but I hereby declare: *mea culpa*, Hole. I murdered your wife, Rakel Fauke."

Harry froze. Finne looked up at the roof.

"With a knife," he whispered. "But not the one you're holding in your hand. She was screaming when she died. She was screaming your name. *Haarr-y. Haarr-yy . . .*"

Harry felt a different type of rage hit him. The cold sort, the sort that made him calm. And crazy. Which he had feared might come, and which *mustn't* be allowed to take over.

"Why?" Harry asked. His voice was suddenly relaxed. His breathing normal.

"Why?"

"The motive?"

"That's obvious, surely? The same as yours now, Hole. Revenge. We're engaged in a classic blood feud. You killed my son, I kill your wife. That's what we do, that's what separates us from the animals: we take *revenge*. It's rational, but we don't even have to think about whether it makes sense, we just know that it feels good. Isn't that what it feels like for you right now, Hole? You're making your own pain into someone else's. Someone you can convince yourself is responsible for the fact that you're in pain."

"Prove it."

"Prove what?"

"That you killed her. Tell me something you couldn't have known about the murder or crime scene."

"*To Harri*. With an 'i.'"

Harry blinked.

"*From Oleg*," Finne went on. "Branded into a breadboard hanging on the wall between the top cupboards and the coffee machine."

The only sound in the silence that followed was the metronome-like dripping.

"There's your confession," Finne said, coughing and spitting again. "That gives you two options. You can take me into custody and get me convicted under Norwegian law. That's what a policeman would do. Or you can do what us murderers do."

Harry nodded. Crouched down again. Picked up the dice. He cupped his hands and shook it before letting it roll across the concrete floor. He looked at it thoughtfully. Put the dice in his pocket, grasped the knife and stood up. The sunlight shining in between the planks glinted off the blade. He stopped behind Finne, put his left arm around his forehead and locked his head to his chest.

"Hole?" The voice was slightly higher now. "Hole, don't . . ." Finne jerked at the cuffs, and Harry could feel his body trembling.

Finally, a sign of angst in the face of death.

Harry breathed out and dropped the knife into his coat pocket. Still holding Finne's head tight, he pulled a handkerchief from his trouser pocket and wiped Finne's face with it. He wiped the blood from around his nose, mouth and chin. Finne sniffed and cursed, but didn't try to struggle. Harry tore two strips off the handkerchief and stuck them in his nostrils. Then he put the handkerchief back in his pocket, walked around the bench and looked at the result. Finne was panting as if he'd just run the 400 metres. Because Harry had mostly had Finne's T-shirt wrapped round his fist when he hit him, there were no cuts, just swelling and the nosebleed.

Harry went outside and put some snow in the T-shirt, then went back inside and held it to Finne's face.

"Trying to make me presentable so you can claim this never happened?" Finne said. He had already calmed down.

"It's probably too late for that," Harry said. "But whatever punishment they give me will be based on the amount of damage, so let's call it damage limitation. And you provoked me because you wanted me to hit you."

"I did, did I?"

"Of course. You wanted to get some physical evidence to prove to your lawyer that you were assaulted when the police were questioning you. Because any judge would refuse to allow the police to present evidence acquired using unlawful means. That's why you confessed. Because you assumed the confession would get you out of here but still wouldn't cost you anything later."

"Maybe. At least you're not thinking of killing me."

"No?"

"You'd already have done it by now. Maybe I'm wrong, maybe you haven't got it in you after all."

"You're suggesting I should?"

"Like you said yourself, it's too late now, an ice pack isn't going to fix this. I'll end up walking free."

Harry picked his phone up from the bench. Switched the recording off and called Bjørn Holm.

"Hello?"

"It's Harry. I've got Svein Finne. He's just confessed to me that he murdered Rakel, and I've got it recorded."

Harry heard a baby crying in the pause that followed.

"Really?" Bjørn said slowly.

"Really. I want you to come and arrest him."

"What? Didn't you say you've already arrested him?"

"Not arrested, no," Harry said, and looked at Finne. "I'm suspended, aren't I, so right now I'm just a private citizen holding another private citizen here against his will. Finne can always file a complaint, but I'm pretty sure I'd be treated fairly leniently given the fact he murdered my wife. The important thing now is that he's arrested and questioned properly by the police."

"I get it. Where are you?"

"The German bunkers above Sjømannsskolen. Finne's sitting cuffed to a bench in here."

"I see. What about you?"

"Mm."

"No, Harry."

"No what?"

"I don't want to have to carry you out of some bar later tonight."

"I'll send the audio file to your email address."

Mona Daa stopped in the doorway of her editor's office. He was talking on the phone.

"They've arrested someone for Rakel Fauke's murder," she said loudly.

"I've got to go," the editor said, then hung up without waiting for a response and looked up. "Are you on it, Daa?"

"It's already written," Mona said.

"Get it out there! Has anyone else published it yet?"

"We got notification five minutes ago, there's a press conference at four o'clock. What I wanted to talk to you about is whether or not we should name the suspect."

"Did they give his name in the announcement?"

"Of course not."

"So how have you got it?"

"Because I'm one of your best reporters."

"In *five* minutes?"

"OK, *the* best."

"So who is it?"

"Svein Finne. Previous convictions for assault and rape, and a criminal record as long as a plague year. Do we publish his name?"

The editor ran his hand over his thinning hair. "Hm. Tricky."

Mona was well aware of the dilemma. Under paragraph 4.7 of the Ethical Code of Practice for the Norwegian Press, the press agreed to deal sensitively with the publication of names in criminal cases, especially during the early stages of an investigation. Any identification had to be justifiable on grounds of public interest. On the other hand, her paper, *VG*, had published the name of a professor whose offense was that he had sent inappropriate text messages to women. Everyone had agreed that the man was a pig, but as far as they were aware no laws had been broken, and it was hard to claim that the public *needed* to know the professor's name. In Finne's case they could obviously justify publication of his name by saying the public needed to know who they should be looking out for. On the other hand, was there any possibility of what the code called "imminent danger of offenses against innocent people, with serious and repeated criminal acts," as long as Finne was in custody?

"We'll hold back his name," the editor said. "But include his criminal record and say that *VG* knows who he is. Then at least we'll get a gold star from the Press Association."

"That's how I've already written it, so it's ready to go. We've also managed to get hold of a new, previously unpublished picture of Rakel as well."

"Fantastic."

Her editor wasn't wrong. After a week and a half of intense press coverage of the murder, their choice of pictures was getting pretty repetitive.

"But maybe run a picture of the husband, the policeman, under the headline."

Mona blinked. "You mean Harry Hole, right under *Suspect Arrested for Rakel's Murder*? Isn't that a bit misleading?"

The editor shrugged. "They'll find out soon enough when they read the article."

Mona nodded slowly. The shock effect of Harry Hole's familiar, ruggedly attractive face below that sort of headline would obviously get more clicks than another picture of Rakel. And their readers would forgive them the ostensibly unintentional misunderstanding; they always did. Nobody wanted to be properly deceived, but people had nothing against being misled in an entertaining way. So why did Mona dislike this part of the job so much, when she loved the rest of it?

"Mona?"

"Will do," she said, pushing herself off the door frame. "This is going to be big."

21

Katrine Bratt stifled a yawn and hoped that none of the three other people around the table in the Chief of Police's office had noticed. Yesterday had been a very long day, after the press conference about the arrest in Rakel's case. And when she finally got home and went to bed, her son had kept her up most of the night.

But there was a chance that today wasn't going to turn into a marathon. Because Svein Finne's name hadn't been made public in the media, a vacuum had arisen, the eye of the storm in which—for the moment, at least—things really were calm. But it was still too early in the morning to say what the day would bring.

"Thanks for agreeing to see us at such short notice," Johan Krohn said.

"No problem," Police Chief Gunnar Hagen said with a nod.

"Great. Then I'll get straight to the point."

The standard phrase of a man who feels at home "getting to the point," Katrine thought. Because even if Krohn evidently enjoyed the limelight, he was first and foremost a nerd. A now-renowned defense lawyer, almost fifty years old, who still looked like a boy, someone who used to be bullied and now wore his professional reputation and freshly won confidence like a suit of armour. Katrine had read about the bullying in a magazine interview. It hadn't been the same getting-beaten-up-in-every-break that Katrine had experienced growing up, but low-level teasing and withheld invitations to birthday parties and games, the sort of bullying that every celebrity now claimed to have suffered, to be applauded for their openness. Krohn had said he had come forward to make it easier for other smart kids suffering the same thing. Katrine found it odd that the sought-after lawyer's desire for justice was balanced by his lack of empathy.

OK, Katrine knew she was being unfair. They were—as they were now—on opposite sides of the table, and it wasn't Krohn's job to feel empathy for the victims. Perhaps it was a prerequisite for the judicial system that defense lawyers had the capacity to switch off their sympathy for the victim and only focus on what was best for their clients. The way it had been a prerequisite for Krohn's personal success. That was probably why it bothered her. That, and the fact that she had lost too many cases against him.

Krohn glanced at the Patek Philippe watch on his left wrist as he held his right hand out to the young woman sitting beside him wearing a discreet but ridiculously expensive Hermès outfit and presumably equipped with top grades from law school. Katrine realised that the dry Danish pastries she'd salvaged from a meeting yesterday weren't going to be eaten today either.

As if it was a carefully practised move, like a nurse passing a surgeon a scalpel, the young woman placed a yellow folder in Krohn's hand.

"This case has obviously attracted a lot of media attention," Krohn said. "Something that does no favours either to you or my client."

But it does favour you, Katrine thought, wondering if she was expected to pour coffee for the visitors and the Chief of Police.

"So I assume it's in everyone's interests for us to come to an agreement as quickly as possible." Krohn opened the folder, but didn't look down at it. Katrine didn't know if it was true or just a myth that Krohn had a perfect photographic memory, and that his party trick at law school had been to ask fellow students to give him a page number between 1 and 3,760, and then he would proceed to recite the entire contents of that page of Norwegian law. Nerd parties. The only type of party Katrine had been invited to when she was a student. Because she was pretty but still an outsider, with her leather clothes and punk hair. She didn't hang out with punks, and she didn't hang out with straight, well-dressed students. So the staring-at-their-shoes gang had invited her into the warm. But she had turned them down, she didn't want to fulfill the classic "pretty girl teams up with attractive but socially inadequate nerds" role. Katrine Bratt had had enough to deal with. *More* than enough. She had been bombarded with psychiatric diagnoses. But somehow she had coped.

"In the wake of my client being arrested on suspicion of the murder of Rakel Fauke, three accusations of rape have come to light," Krohn said. "One of these is from a heroin addict who has already received rape victim's compensation twice before on, frankly, very thin grounds, and without any conviction on either of those occasions. The second has, as I understand it, today asked to withdraw her accusation. The third, Dagny Jensen, has no case as long as there is no forensic evidence, and my client's explanation is that intercourse was entirely consensual. Even a man with a previous conviction must have the right to a sex life without being an open target for the police and any woman who feels guilty afterwards?"

Katrine looked for signs of a reaction from the young woman next to Krohn, but saw nothing.

"We know how much of the police's resources get swallowed up by such ambiguous rape cases, and here we have three of them," Krohn went on, with his eyes focused on a point in front of him, as if an invisible script was hanging in the air. "Now it isn't my job to defend the interests of society, but in this specific instance I believe that our interests might coincide. My client has declared himself willing to confess to murder, if no rape charges are brought. And this is a murder investigation in which I understand that all you have is"—Krohn looked down at his papers as if he needed to check that what he was about to say really was true—"a breadboard, a confession acquired under torture, and a video clip that could be of anyone, possibly taken from a film." Krohn looked up again with a questioning expression.

Gunnar Hagen looked at Katrine.

Katrine cleared her throat. "Coffee?"

"No, thanks." Krohn scratched—or perhaps smoothed—one eyebrow carefully with his forefinger. "My client would also—assuming we can reach an agreement—consider withdrawing his charge against Inspector Harry Hole for unlawful imprisonment and physical assault."

"The title of inspector is irrelevant under current circumstances," Hagen muttered. "Harry Hole was acting as a private citizen. If any of our officers broke Norwegian law while on duty, I would report them myself."

"Of course," Krohn replied. "I certainly don't mean to call the integrity of the police into question, I merely wish to suggest that it looks unseemly."

"Then you're no doubt also aware that it isn't normal practice for the Norwegian police to engage in the sort of horse-trading you're suggesting. Negotiations for a reduced sentence, of course. But writing off the accusation of rape . . ."

"I appreciate that you might have objections, but can I remind you that my client is well over seventy years old, and that in the event of a guilty verdict the likelihood is that he would die in prison. I can't honestly see that it makes a great deal of difference if at that point he is in there for murder or rape. So instead of clinging to principles that don't benefit anyone, how about asking the people who have accused my client of rape what they would prefer: that Svein Finne dies in a cell sometime within the next twelve years, or that they see him on the street again in four years? As far as compensation for the rape victims is concerned, I'm sure my client and the supposed victims could reach a suitable settlement outside of the legal process."

Krohn passed the folder back to the female solicitor, and Katrine saw her glance up at him with a mixture of fear and infatuation. She was fairly certain the pair of them had made use of the law firm's dark leather furniture after office hours.

"Thank you," Hagen said, standing up and holding his hand across the table. "You'll be hearing from us soon."

Katrine stood up and shook Krohn's surprisingly clammy and soft hand. "And how is your client taking it?"

Krohn looked at her seriously. "Naturally, he's taking it very hard."

Katrine knew she shouldn't, but couldn't help herself. "Perhaps you could take him one of these pastries, to cheer him up? They'll only be thrown away otherwise."

Krohn looked at her for a moment before turning back towards the Chief of Police. "Well, I hope to hear from you later today."

Katrine noted that Krohn's female appendage was wearing such a tight skirt that she had to take at least three steps for each of his as they walked out of the Police Chief's office. She briefly considered the possible consequences of throwing the Danish pastries at them out of the sixth-floor window as they left Police Headquarters.

"Well?" Gunnar Hagen said when the door had closed behind the visitors.

"Why are defense lawyers always presented as the lone defenders of justice?"

Hagen murmured, "They're the necessary counterweight to the police, Katrine, and objectivity has never been your strong suit. Or self-control."

"Self-control?"

"Cheer him up?"

Katrine shrugged. "What do you think about his proposal?"

Hagen rubbed his chin. "It's problematic. But of course the pressure in the Rakel Fauke case is growing by the day, and if we failed to get Finne convicted it would be the defeat of the decade. But on the other hand, there's all the reports of rapists going free over the past few years, and we'd be dropping three cases . . . What do you think, Katrine?"

"I hate the guy, but his proposal makes sense. I think we should be pragmatic and look at the bigger picture. Let me talk to the women who have reported him."

"OK." Hagen cleared his throat tentatively. "Talking about objectivity . . ."

"Yes?"

"Your attitude isn't in any way affected by the fact that it would mean Harry going free as well?"

"What?"

"You've worked closely together, and . . ."

"And?"

"And I'm not blind, Katrine."

Katrine walked over to the window and looked down at the path that led away from Police Headquarters, through Botsparken, where the snow was finally in full retreat, and down towards the sluggish traffic at Grønlandsleiret.

"Have you ever done anything you regretted, Gunnar? I mean, *really* regretted?"

"Hm. Are we still talking professionally?"

"Not necessarily."

"Is there something you want to tell me?"

Katrine thought about how liberating it would be to tell someone. That *someone* knew. She had thought that the burden, the secret, would become easier to bear with time, but it was the other way around, it felt heavier with each passing day.

"I understand him," she said quietly.

"Krohn?"

"No, Svein Finne. I understand that he wants to confess."

22

Dagny Jensen put her palms down on the cold desk and looked at the dark-haired police officer sitting at the school desk in front of her. It was break time, and in the playground outside the windows she could hear the pupils shouting and laughing. "I appreciate that this isn't an easy decision," the woman said. She had introduced herself as Katrine Bratt, head of the Crime Squad Unit of the Oslo Police District.

"It sounds like the decision has already been made for me," Dagny said.

"Naturally we can't force you to retract an accusation," Bratt said.

"But that's exactly what you're doing in practice," Dagny said. "You're handing the responsibility for him being convicted of murder over to me."

The police officer looked down at the desk.

"Do you know what the main purpose of the Norwegian education system is?" Dagny said. "To teach the pupils to become responsible citizens. That it's a responsibility as much as a privilege. Of course I'll retract the accusation if it means Svein Finne can be locked up for the rest of his life."

"When it comes to rape victims' compensation . . ."

"I don't want any money. I just want to forget it." Dagny looked at her watch. Four minutes until the next lesson started. She was happy. Yes, she was—even after ten years teaching she was still happy, happy to be able to give young people something she genuinely thought would help them to have a better future. It felt meaningful, in a relatively straightforward way. And that was basically all she wanted. That, and to forget. "Can you promise me that you'll get him convicted?"

"I promise," the police officer said, and stood up.

"Harry Hole," Dagny said. "What's going to happen to him?"

"I don't know, but hopefully Finne's lawyer will drop the charge of kidnapping."

"Hopefully?"

"What he did was obviously unlawful, and not how a police officer is supposed to act," Katrine said. "But he sacrificed himself to make sure Finne was caught."

"Like he sacrificed me, so he could get his own personal vengeance?"

"As I said, I can't defend Harry Hole's behaviour in this matter, but the fact remains that without him Svein Finne would probably have been able to go on terrorising you and other women."

Dagny nodded slowly.

"I need to get back and prepare for an interview. Thank you for agreeing to help us. I promise you won't regret it."

23

"No, you're not disturbing me at all, Mrs. Bratt," Johan Krohn said, holding the phone between his ear and shoulder as he buttoned his shirt. "So all three accusations have been dropped?"

"How soon can you and Finne be ready for questioning?"

Johan Krohn enjoyed hearing her rolling Bergen "r"s. Bratt's accent wasn't strong, but there was still a trace of it there. Like a skirt that was long but not too long. He liked Katrine Bratt. She was pretty, smart and she offered some resistance. The fact that she had a wedding ring on her finger didn't have to mean that much. He himself was living proof of that. And he found it rather exciting that she sounded so nervous. The same nervousness a buyer feels after he hands over the money and is waiting for the dealer to give him the bag of dope. Krohn went over to the window, put his thumb and forefinger between the slats of the blind, opened up a gap and looked down at Rozenkrantz' gate, six floors below the law firm's offices. It was only just after three o'clock, but in Oslo that meant rush hour. Unless you worked in law. Krohn sometimes wondered what would happen when the oil ran out and the Norwegian people had to face up to the demands of the real world again. The optimist in him said things would be fine, that people adapt to new situations quicker than you think, you just had to look at countries that had been at war. The realist in him said that in a country without any tradition of innovation and advanced thinking, there would be a slippery slope straight back to where Norway had come from: the bottom division of European economies.

"We can be there in two hours," Krohn said.

"Great," Bratt said.

"See you then, Mrs. Bratt."

Krohn ended the call and stood for a moment, uncertain where to put his mobile.

"Here," a voice said from the darkness over by the Chesterfield sofa. He walked over to her and took his trousers.

"Well?"

"They've taken the bait," Krohn said, checking there were no stains on his trousers before putting them on.

"Is it bait? As in, they're on the hook?"

"Don't ask me, I'm just following my client's instructions for the time being."

"But you think there's a hook there?"

Krohn shrugged his shoulders and looked around for his shoes. "From yourself shall you know others, I suppose."

He sat down at the sturdy desk made of *Quercus velutina*, black oak, that he had inherited from his father. Called one of the numbers he had on speed dial.

"Mona Daa." The energetic voice of *VG*'s crime reporter crackled across the room from the speaker.

"Good afternoon, Miss Daa. This is Johan Krohn. Ordinarily you call me, but I thought I'd be a bit proactive this time. I've got something I think might warrant an article in your paper."

"Is it about Svein Finne?"

"Yes. I've just received confirmation from the Oslo Police that they're dropping their investigation into the baseless accusations of rape that have been tossed about in the chaos surrounding the accusation of murder."

"And I can quote you on that?"

"You can quote me as confirming the rumours that have spread about it, which I presume are the reason you've called me."

A pause.

"I understand, but I can't write that, Krohn."

"Then say that I've made it public to preempt the rumours. Whether or not you've heard the rumours is irrelevant."

Another pause.

"Fine," Daa said. "Can you give me any details about—"

"No!" Krohn interrupted. "You can have more this evening. And hold off publishing anything until after five o'clock today."

"Cards on the table, Krohn. If I can have an exclusive on this—"

"This is all yours, my dear. Speak later."

"Just one last thing. How did you get my number? It's not available anywhere."

"Like I said, you've called my mobile before, so your number appeared on the screen."

"So you stored it?"

"Yes, I suppose I must have." He ended the call and turned towards the leather sofa. "Alise, my little friend, if you could put your blouse back on, we've got some work to do."

Bjørn Holm was standing on the pavement outside the Jealousy Bar in Grünerløkka. He opened the door and could tell by the music streaming out that he was probably going to find him here. He pulled the pram behind him into the almost empty bar. It was a medium-sized English-style pub with simple wooden tables in front of a long bar, with booths along the walls. It was only five o'clock; it would get busier later in the evening. During the brief period that Øystein Eikeland and Harry had run the bar, they had managed to achieve something rare: a pub where people came to listen to the music being played on the sound system. There was no fancy DJ, just track after track, chosen according to the themed evenings announced on the weekly list on the door. Bjørn had been allowed to act as a consultant on the country evenings and Elvis evenings. And—most memorably—when they were putting together the playlist of "songs that were at least forty years old by artists and bands from American states beginning with M."

Harry was sitting at the bar with his head bowed, his back to Bjørn. Behind the bar, Øystein Eikeland raised a half-litre glass towards the new arrival. That didn't bode well. But Harry was at least sitting upright.

"Minimum age is twenty, mate!" Øystein called above the music: "Good Time Charlie's Got The Blues," early seventies, Danny O'Keefe's only real hit. Not typical Harry music, but a typical track for Harry to brush the dust off and play at the Jealousy Bar.

"Even when accompanied by an adult?" Bjørn asked, parking the pram in front of one of the booths.

"Since when have you been an adult, Holm?" Øystein put his glass down.

Bjørn smiled. "You become an adult the moment you see your kid for the first time and realise he's utterly helpless. And is going to need a fuckload of adult help. Same as this guy." Bjørn put his hand on Harry's shoulder. He noticed that Harry was sitting with his head bowed, reading on his mobile.

"Have you seen *VG*'s headline about the arrest?" Harry asked, picking up a cup in front of him. Coffee, Bjørn noted.

"Yes. They've used a picture of you."

"I don't give a damn about that. Look at what they've just published." Harry held his phone up for Bjørn to read.

"They're saying we've done a deal," Bjørn said. "Murder in exchange for rape. OK, it's not common, but it does happen."

"But it doesn't usually appear in the press," Harry said. "And, if it does, not until after the bear has been shot."

"You don't think it's been shot?"

"If you do a deal with the devil, you need to ask yourself why the devil thinks it's a good deal."

"Aren't you being a bit paranoid now?"

"I'm just hoping we get a confession in a proper police interview. The things I recorded in the bunker would be torn apart by a defense lawyer like Krohn."

"Now that the press have published this, he'll have to confess. If not, we'll charge him for the rape. Katrine's interviewing him right now."

"Mm." Harry tapped at his phone and raised it to his ear. "I need to update Oleg. What are you doing here, anyway?"

"I . . . er . . . promised Katrine that I'd check to make sure everything was OK with you. You weren't at home and you weren't at Schrøder's. To be honest, I thought you were barred from here for life after last time . . ."

"Yes, but that idiot's not working until this evening." Harry nodded towards the pram. "Can I take a look?"

"He tends to notice people and wake up."

"OK." Harry lowered his phone. "Engaged. Any suggestions for next Thursday's playlist?"

"Theme?"

"Cover versions that are better than the original."

"Joe Cocker and 'A Little—' "

"Already on it. What about Francis and the Lights' version of 'Can't Tell Me Nothing?' "

"Kanye West? Are you ill, Harry?"

"OK. A Hank Williams song, then?"

"Are you mad? *No one* does Hank better than Hank."

"What about Beck's version of 'Your Cheatin' Heart'?"

"Do you want me to punch you?"

Harry and Øystein laughed, and Bjørn realised they were teasing him.

Harry put his arm round Bjørn's shoulders. "I miss you. Can't the two of us solve a really gruesome murder together soon?"

Bjørn nodded as he looked at Harry's smiling face in astonishment. The unnaturally intense glow in his eyes. Maybe he really had snapped? Maybe grief had finally tipped him over the edge. Then it was as if Harry's smile suddenly shattered, like the morning ice in October, and Bjørn found himself looking into the black depths of desperate pain again. As if Harry had merely wanted to taste happiness. And had spat it out again.

"Yes," Bjørn said quietly. "I'm sure we can manage that."

Katrine stared at the red light above the microphone that indicated that recording was under way. She knew that if she raised her eyes she would see those of Svein Finne, "the Fiancé." And she didn't want to do that—not because it might influence her, but because it might influence him. They had discussed whether to use a male interviewer, given Finne's warped attitude to women. But when they read through the transcripts of previous interviews with Finne, he seemed to open up more for female interviewers. She didn't know if that had been with or without eye contact.

She had put on a blouse that shouldn't seem provocative, or give the impression that she was afraid of him looking at her. She glanced over at the control room, where an officer was taking care of the recording equipment. In there with him were Magnus Skarre from the investigative team, and Johan Krohn, who somewhat reluctantly had left the interview room after Finne himself had asked to talk to Katrine alone.

Katrine gave a brief nod to the officer, who nodded back. She read out the case number, her own and Finne's names, the location, date and time. It was a hangover from the time when audio tapes could go astray, but it also served as a reminder that the formal part of the interview had begun.

"Yes," Finne replied with a slight smile and exaggeratedly clear diction when Katrine asked if he had been made aware of his rights, and the fact that the interview was being recorded.

"Let's begin with the evening of the tenth of March and early morning of the eleventh of March," Katrine said. "Hereafter referred to as the night of the murder. What happened?"

"I'd taken some pills," Finne said.

Katrine looked down as she took notes.

"Valium. Stesolid. Or Rohypnol. Maybe a bit of everything."

His voice made her think of the sound of the wheels of her grandfather's tractor driving along a gravel track out in Sotra.

"So things might be a little unclear for me," Finne said.

Katrine stopped writing. *Unclear?* She detected something metallic at the back of her throat, the taste of panic. Was he planning to withdraw his confession?

"Unless perhaps it's just because I always get a bit confused when I get horny."

Katrine looked up. Svein Finne caught her gaze. It felt like something was drilling into her head.

He moistened his lips. Smiled. Lowered his voice. "But I always remember the most important things. That's why we do it, isn't it? For the memories we can take away and use in lonely moments?"

Katrine caught sight of his right hand painting the picture for her as it moved up and down before she looked back at her notes again.

Skarre had argued that they should cuff Finne, but Katrine had objected. She said it would give him a mental advantage if he thought they were that frightened of him. That it might tempt him to toy with them. And now, one minute into the interview, that was precisely what he was doing.

Katrine leafed through the files in front of her. "If your memory isn't great, perhaps we could talk about the three rape files I've got here instead. With witness statements that might help prompt your memory."

"Touché," Finne said, and without looking up she knew he was still smiling. "Like I said, I remember the most important details."

"Let's hear them."

"I arrived at about nine o'clock in the evening. She had a stomach ache and was rather pale."

"Hang on. How did you get in?"

"The door was open, so I went straight in. She screamed and screamed. She was so frightened. So I h-held her."

"A stranglehold? Or by locking her arms to her sides?"

"I don't remember."

She knew they were proceeding too quickly, that she needed more details, but this was first and foremost about getting a confession out of him before he changed his mind. "Then what?"

"She was in so much pain. Blood was pouring out of her. I used a kn-knife . . ."

"Your own?"

"No, a sharper one, from a knife block."

"Where on her body did you use it?"

"H-here."

"The interviewee is pointing at his stomach," Katrine said.

"Her belly button," Finne said in an affected, childlike voice. "Her belly button."

"Her belly button," Katrine repeated, swallowing a surge of nausea. Swallowing the feeling of triumph. They had the confession. The rest was all icing on the cake.

"Can you describe Rakel Fauke? And the kitchen?"

"Rakel? Beautiful. Like you, K-Katrine. You're very similar."

"What was she wearing?"

"I don't remember. Has anyone ever told you how similar you are? Like s-sisters."

"Describe the kitchen."

"A prison. Bars over the windows. You'd almost think they were frightened of something." Finne laughed. "Shall we call it a day, Katrine?"

"What?"

"I've got th-things to do."

Katrine felt a slight sense of panic. "But we've only just begun."

"Headache. It's tough, going through such traumatic things as this, I'm sure you can understand that."

"Just tell me—"

"That wasn't actually a question, my dear. I'm done here. If you want more, you'll have to come down to my cell and visit me this evening. I'm fr-free then."

"The video recording that Dagny Jensen received. Did you send it, and is it of the victim?"

"Yes." Finne stood up.

From the corner of her eye Katrine saw that Skarre was already on his way. She held one hand up towards the window. She looked down at her folder of questions. Tried to think. She could press on. And risk the possibility that Krohn could invalidate the confession by citing unnecessarily harsh interview methods as the reason. Or she could make do with what she'd got, which was more than enough to get the prosecutor to press charges. They could get the details later, before the trial. She looked at the watch Bjørn had given her on their first anniversary.

"Interview concluded at 17:31," she said.

When she looked up she discovered that a red-faced Gunnar Hagen had walked into the control room and was talking to Johan Krohn. Skarre came into the interview room and put cuffs on Finne to lead him back to the detention cells in the custody unit. Katrine saw Krohn shrug his shoulders as he said something, and Hagen turned even redder.

"See you, Mrs. Bratt."

The words were spoken so close to her ear that she could feel the thin spray of saliva that accompanied them. Then Finne and Skarre were gone. She saw Krohn set off after them.

Katrine wiped her face with a tissue before going in to Hagen.

"Krohn has told *VG* about our horse-trading. It's already up on their website."

"And what did he have to say in his defense?"

"That neither party had given any sort of promise to keep it secret. Then he asked if I thought we'd entered into an agreement that didn't hold up in daylight. Because he prefers to avoid that sort of agreement, apparently."

"Hypocritical bastard. He just wants to show what he can do."

"Let's hope so."

"What do you mean?"

"Krohn is a smart, devious defense lawyer. But there's someone even more devious than him."

Katrine looked at Hagen. Bit her bottom lip. "His client, you mean?"

Hagen nodded, and they both turned and looked through the open door into the corridor. They saw Finne, Skarre and Krohn waiting for the lift.

"You *never* call at a bad time, Krohn," Mona Daa said, adjusting her earphone as she studied herself in the mirrored wall of the gym. "You'll have seen that I've been trying to get hold of you too. Along with every other journalist in Norway, I daresay."

"It's a bit like that, yes. I'll get straight to the point. We're about to issue a press statement about the confession in which we're considering attaching a picture of Finne that was taken just a couple of weeks ago."

"Good, the pictures we've got of him must be ten years old."

"Twenty, in fact. Finne's condition for sending this private picture is that you make it your lead story."

"Sorry?"

"Don't ask me why, that's just how he wants it."

"I'm not in a position to be able to make that sort of promise, as you're no doubt aware."

"Of course I'm aware of journalistic integrity, just as I'm sure you're aware of the value of such a picture."

Mona tilted her head and studied her body. The wide belt she used when she was lifting weights made her penguin-shaped body (the association was possibly more the fault of her rolling gait, itself the result of a hip injury from birth) look briefly as if it was shaped like an hourglass. Occasionally, Mona suspected that the belt, which would never be used for anything except pointless weight training, was the real reason she spent so many hours on pointless weight training. Just like personal acknowledgment was a more important driving force in her work than being the watchdog of society, defending free speech, journalistic curiosity and all the other crap they trotted out each year when the Press Awards were handed out. Not that she didn't believe in those things, but they came in second place, *after* standing in the spotlight, seeing your byline and measuring up against yourself. When you looked at it like that, Finne was being no more or less perverse in wanting a large picture of himself in the paper, even if it was as a serial rapist and murderer. That was what Finne had spent his life doing, after all, so perhaps it was understandable that he wanted to be a famous killer, at the very least. If people can't be loved, it's well known that a popular alternative is to be feared.

"That's a hypothetical dilemma, anyway," Mona said. "If the picture is good quality, then obviously we'd want to blow it up to a decent size. Especially if you let us have it an hour before you send it to the other papers, OK?"

Roar Bohr held his rifle, a Blaser R8 Professional, up to the window frame and peered through the Swarovski X5i sight. Their house lay on a hillside on the west side of Ring 3, just below the Smestad junction, and from the open cellar window he had a view of the residential area on the other side of the motorway as well as Smestaddammen, a small, artificial lake of shallow water that was built in the 1800s to provide the more bourgeois inhabitants of the city with ice.

The red dot in the viewfinder found and stopped on a large white swan that was gliding effortlessly across the surface of the water, as if being blown by the wind. It was between four and five hundred metres away, almost half a kilometre, well above what their American allies in the coalition forces called "maximum point-blank range." He had the red dot on the swan's head now. Bohr lowered the sight until the red dot lay on the water just above the swan. He focused on his breathing. Increased the pressure on the trigger. Even the greenest recruits at Rena understood that bullets flew in an arc because even the fastest bullet is affected by gravity, so obviously you have to aim higher the farther away the target is. They also knew that if the target is higher in the terrain, you have to aim even higher, because the bullet has to travel "uphill." But they usually protested when they were told that even when the target is lower than you, you still have to aim higher—not lower—than on flat terrain.

Roar Bohr could see from the trees outside that there was no wind. The temperature was about ten degrees. The swan was moving at about one metre per second. He imagined the bullet blasting through its little head. The neck losing its tension and crumpling like a snake on top of that chalk-white swan body. It would be a demanding shot even for a sniper in the Special Forces. But no more than he and his colleagues would expect of Roar Bohr. He let the air out of his lungs and moved the sight to the small island by the bridge. That was where the female swan and her cygnets were. He scanned the island, then the rest of the lake, but saw nothing. He sighed, leaned the rifle against the wall and walked over to the chattering, hardworking printer where the end of a sheet of A4 was emerging. He had taken a screengrab of the picture that had just been published on *VG*'s website, and now he studied the almost-complete face that lay before him. A wide, flat nose. Thick lips with a trace of a sneer. Hair pulled back tightly, presumably gathered in a plait at the back of his neck; that was probably what gave Svein Finne those narrow eyes and an impression of hostility.

The printer squeezed out the last of the sheet with a final drawn-out groan, as if it wanted to push this terrible man away from it. A man who had just, with what seemed to be arrogant pride, confessed to the murder of Rakel Fauke. Just like the Taliban when they accepted responsibility for every bomb that went off in Afghanistan, or at least if the attack had been successful. *Claimed* responsibility, the way some of the troops in Afghanistan could do if the opportunity arose to steal a kill. Sometimes it was little short of grave-robbing. After chaotic engagements, Roar had witnessed soldiers claiming kills that their superior officer—after checking the footage on the helmet-cams of their own dead—then revealed to have been made by fallen soldiers.

Roar Bohr snatched the sheet of paper and went over to the other end of the large, open cellar room. He fastened it to one of the targets hanging in front of the metal box that caught the bullets. Walked back. The distance was ten and a half metres. He closed the window, which he'd had fitted with three layers of soundproof glass, and put his ear defenders on. Then he picked up the pistol, a High Standard HD 22, from next to the computer, didn't give himself more time to aim than he could expect in a pressured situation, pointed the gun at the target and fired. Once. Twice. Three times.

Bohr removed the ear defenders, picked up the silencer and began to screw it onto the barrel of the High Standard. A silencer changed the balance, it was like training with two different weapons.

He heard the clatter of steps on the cellar stairs.

"Damn," he muttered, closing his eyes.

He opened them again and saw Pia's pale, tense, furious face.

"You frightened the life out of me! I thought I was alone in the house!"

"I'm sorry, Pia, I thought the same."

"That doesn't help, Roar! You promised there wouldn't be any more shooting inside the house! I get back from the shops and am quietly going about my business and then . . . Anyway, why aren't you at work? And why are you naked? And what's that you've got on your face?"

Roar Bohr looked down. Oh yes, he was naked. He ran one finger over his face. Looked at his fingertip. Special Forces black camouflage paint.

He put his pistol down on the desk and tapped the keyboard randomly with his finger.

"Working from home."

It was eight o'clock in the evening, and the investigative team had gathered at the Justice, the Crime Squad Unit's regular watering hole in good times and bad. It had been Skarre's idea to celebrate the conclusion of the case, and Katrine hadn't managed to come up with a good argument against it. Or any explanation as to why she had gone with them. It was a tradition to celebrate victories, it bound them together as a team, and she as head of the Crime Squad Unit ought to have been the first to announce a trip to the Justice after they'd got Finne's confession. The fact that they had snatched the solution to the case from under Kripos's nose didn't exactly make the victory less sweet. That had led to a half-hour phone conversation with Winter, who said that Kripos should have been responsible for questioning Finne, as the principal unit investigating the case. He had reluctantly accepted her explanation that the case was bound up with three rape accusations that fell under the remit of Oslo Police District, and that only Oslo Police District could have done the deal. It's hard to argue against success.

So why was there something nagging at her? Everything made sense, but there was still something, what Harry used to call the single false note in a symphony orchestra. You can hear it, but you can't figure out where it's coming from.

"Fallen asleep, boss?"

Katrine started, and raised her beer glass towards the row of glasses held aloft by her colleagues along the table.

Everyone was there. Apart from Harry, who hadn't answered her call. As if in response to the thought, she felt her mobile start to vibrate and eagerly pulled it out. She saw from the screen that it was Bjørn. And for a fleeting moment the heretical thought was there. That she could pretend not to have seen it. Explain later—and truthfully—that she had been inundated with calls after they issued the press release about the confession, and that she hadn't spotted his name in the list of missed calls until later. But then, of course, her wretched mother's instinct kicked in. She stood up, walked away from the noisy group towards the toilets and pressed Answer.

"Anything wrong?"

"No, nothing," Bjørn said. "He's asleep. Just wanted . . ."

"Just wanted?"

"To check how late you thought you'd be?"

"No later than necessary. I can't just leave, though."

"No, of course not, I get that. Who else is there?"

"Who? The team who worked on the case, of course."

"Just them? No . . . outsiders?"

Katrine straightened up. Bjørn was a kind and cautious man. A man who was liked by everyone because he also had charm and a quiet, solid air of confidence. But even if it wasn't something she and

Bjørn Holm ever talked about, she was in no doubt that he asked himself at regular intervals how on earth he had ended up with a girl half the men—and a few of the women—in Crime Squad had their eye on, at least until she became their boss. One of the reasons why he had never raised the subject was probably that he knew there were few things as unsexy as an insecure and chronically jealous partner. And he had managed to hide it, even when she had dumped him eighteen months ago and they spent a short time apart before getting back together again. But it was hard to maintain the pretense in the long run, and she had begun to notice that something had changed between them over the past few months. Maybe it was because he was at home with the baby, maybe it was simply lack of sleep. Or maybe she was just a bit oversensitive after everything she'd had to deal with in the previous six months.

"Just us," she said. "I'll be home before ten."

"Stay longer, I just wanted to check."

"Before ten," she repeated, and looked over towards the door. At the tall man who was standing among the other clientele, looking around him.

She ended the call.

He was trying to appear relaxed, but she could see the tension in his body, the hunted look in his eyes. Then he caught sight of her, and she saw the way his shoulders relaxed.

"Harry!" she said. "You came." She gave him a hug. Used the short embrace to breathe in the smell that was simultaneously so familiar and so strange. And she was struck once again that the best thing about Harry Hole was that he smelled so good. Not good like perfume or meadows and woodland. Sometimes he smelled of stale drink, and occasionally she detected an acrid note of sweat. But taken as a whole, he smelled *good*, in some indefinable way. It was the smell of *him*. Surely that wasn't something she needed to feel guilty for thinking, was it?

Magnus Skarre came over to them, slightly glassy-eyed and with a blissful grin on his face.

"They reckon it's my round." He put one hand on each of their shoulders. "Beer, Harry? I heard you were the one who managed to get Finne. Yeah! Ha!"

"Just Coke," Harry said, discreetly shrugging off Skarre's hand.

Skarre went off to the bar.

"So you're back on the wagon again," Katrine said.

Harry nodded. "For a while."

"Why do you think he confessed?"

"Finne?"

"Obviously I know it's because he gets a reduced sentence by confessing, and he realised we had a solid case against him with that video clip he sent. And of course he avoided being charged with rape, but is that *all*?"

"How do you mean?"

"Don't you think it could also be what we all want, what we feel a *need* for—to confess our sins?"

Harry looked at her. Moistened his lips. "No," he said.

Katrine noticed a man in a smart jacket and blue shirt leaning over their table, and someone pointed towards her and Harry. The man nodded and set off towards them.

"Journalist alert," Katrine sighed.

"Jon Morten Melhus," the man said. "I've been trying to contact you all evening, Bratt."

Katrine looked at him more closely. Journalists weren't usually this polite.

"In the end I got hold of someone else at Police Headquarters, explained why I was calling, and was told that I would probably find you here."

No one at Police Headquarters would tell a random caller where she was.

"I'm a surgeon at Ullevål Hospital. I called because we had a rather dramatic occurrence a while back. Complications arose during a birth and we had to perform an emergency caesarean. The mother had a man with her who said he was the child's father, something the woman confirmed. And at first it looked as though he was going to be useful. When the mother found out that we needed to perform the caesarean she was extremely worried, and the man sat with her, stroking her forehead, comforting her and promising that it would all be very quick. And it's true, it doesn't usually take more than five minutes to get the baby out. But I remember it because I overheard him saying: 'A knife in your stomach. Then it's all over.' Not an inaccurate description, but a somewhat unusual choice of words. I didn't think any more about it at the time, seeing as he kissed her immediately afterwards. What was more unusual was that he wiped her lips after kissing her. And that he filmed as we performed the caesarean. But what was most unusual was that he suddenly pushed his way to the woman and wanted to remove the baby himself. When we tried to stop him, he inserted his hand right into the incision we had made."

Katrine grimaced.

"Damn," Harry said quietly. "Damn, damn."

Katrine looked at him. Something was slowly dawning on her, but first and foremost she was confused.

"We managed to drag him away and perform the remainder of the operation," Melhus said. "Fortunately there were no signs of infection in the mother."

"Svein Finne. It was Svein Finne."

Melhus looked at Harry and slowly nodded. "But he gave us a different name."

"Of course," Harry said. "But you saw the picture of him that *VG* published this afternoon."

"Yes, and I've no doubt at all that it was the same man. Especially not after I noticed the painting on the wall in the background. The photograph was taken in the waiting room of our maternity unit."

"So why so late reporting the incident, and why to me personally?" Katrine asked.

Melhus looked momentarily confused. "I'm not reporting it."

"No?"

"No. It isn't unusual for people to behave in unpredictable ways under the mental and physical stress of a complicated birth. And he definitely didn't give the impression that he wanted to harm the mother, he was just entirely focused on the child. It all calmed down and everything was fine, like I said. He even cut the umbilical cord."

"With a knife," Harry said.

"That's right."

Katrine frowned. "What is it, Harry? What have you realised that I haven't quite got my head around yet?"

"The date and time," Harry said, still looking at Melhus. "You've read about the murder, and you've come to tell us that Svein Finne has an alibi. He was in the maternity unit that night."

"We're in something of a grey area here when it comes to the Hippocratic Oath, which is why I wanted to talk to you in person, Bratt." Melhus looked at Katrine with the professionally sympathetic expression of someone who has been trained to pass on bad news. "I've spoken to the midwife, and she says this man was present from the time the mother was admitted around 21:30, until the birth was over at five the following morning."

Katrine put one hand over her face.

From the table came the sound of happy laughter, followed by the clink of beer glasses. Someone must just have told a well-received joke.

Part 2

24

It was just before midnight when *VG* published the news that the police had released Svein Finne, "the Fiancé."

Johan Krohn declared to the same paper that his client's confession still stood, but that the police had, of their own volition, concluded that in all likelihood it did not relate to Rakel Fauke, but to another offence in which his client may have harmed a mother in childbirth and her baby. There were witnesses, and even video evidence, but no report had been filed about the incident. But the confession had been provided, his client had kept his side of the deal, and Krohn warned the police of the consequences if they didn't keep their side and drop the charges in relation to the vague and groundless accusations of rape.

Harry's heart wouldn't stop hammering.

He was standing with water halfway up his ankles, panting for breath. He had been running. Running through the streets of the city until there were no streets left, and then he had run out here.

That wasn't why his heart was so out of control. That had started when he left the Justice. The paralysing cold crept up his legs, over his knees, towards his crotch.

Harry was standing in the plaza in front of the Opera House. Below him, the white marble slid into the fjord like a melting ice cap, a warning of impending disaster.

. . .

Bjørn Holm woke up. He lay still in bed, listening.

It wasn't the baby. It wasn't Katrine, who had come to bed and lain down behind him without wanting to talk. He opened his eyes. Saw faint light on the white bedroom ceiling. He reached out to the bedside table and saw who was calling on the screen of his mobile. Hesitated. Then he crept quietly out of bed and into the hallway. Pressed Answer.

"It's the middle of the night," he whispered.

"Thanks, I wasn't sure," Harry said drily.

"Don't mention it. Goodnight."

"Don't hang up. I can't access the files in Rakel's case. Looks like my access code's been blocked."

"You'd have to talk to Katrine about that."

"Katrine's the boss, she has to go by the book, we both know that. But I've got your code, and I suppose I might be able to guess your password. Obviously you couldn't *give* it to me, because that would be against regulations."

Pause.

"But?" Bjørn sighed.

"But you could always give me a clue."

"Harry . . ."

"I need this, Bjørn. I need it so fucking bad. The fact that it isn't Finne just means that it's someone else. Come on, Katrine needs this too, because I know that neither you nor Kripos have got a damn thing."

"So why you, then?"

"You know why."

"Do I?"

"Because in a world full of blind people, I've got the only eye."

Another pause.

"Two letters, four numbers," Bjørn said. "If I had to choose, I'd like to die like him. In a car, right at the start of the new year."

He hung up.

25

"According to Professor Paul Mattiuzzi, most murderers fit into one of eight categories," Harry said. "One: chronically aggressive individuals. People with poor impulse control who get easily frustrated, who resent authority, who convince themselves that violence is a legitimate response, and who deep down enjoy finding a way to express their anger. This is the type where you can see it coming."

Harry put a cigarette between his lips.

"Two: controlled hostility. People who rarely give in to anger, who are emotionally rigid and appear polite and serious. They abide by rules and see themselves as upholders of justice. They can be kind in a way that people take advantage of. They're simmering pressure cookers where you can't see anything coming until they explode. The sort where the neighbours say he always seemed such a nice guy."

Harry sparked his lighter, held it to his cigarette and inhaled.

"Three: the resentful. People who feel that others walk all over them, that they never get what they deserve, that it's other people's fault that they haven't succeeded in life. They bear grudges, especially against people who have criticised or reprimanded them. They assume the role of victim, they're psychologically impotent, and when they resort to violence because they can't find other ways to control their violence, it's usually directed towards people they hold grudges against. Four: the traumatised."

Harry blew smoke from his mouth and nose.

"The murder is a response to a single assault on the killer's identity that is so offensive and unbearable that it strips them of all sense of personal power. The murder is necessary if they are to protect the essence of the trauma victim's existence or masculinity. If you're aware of the circumstances, this type of murder can usually be both foreseen and prevented."

Harry held the cigarette between the second knuckles of his index and middle fingers as he stood reflected in the small, half-dried-up puddle framed by brown earth and grey gravel.

"Then there are the rest. Five: obsessive and immature narcissists. Six: paranoid and jealous individuals on the verge of insanity. Seven: people well past the verge of insanity."

Harry put the cigarette back between his lips and looked up. Let his eyes slide across the timber building. The crime scene. The morning sun was glinting off the windows. Nothing about the house looked different, just the degree of abandonment. It had been the same inside. A sort of paleness, as if the stillness had sucked the colour from the walls and curtains, the faces out of the photographs, the memories out of the books. He hadn't seen anything he hadn't seen last time, hadn't thought anything he hadn't thought then, they were back where they had ended up last night: back at the start, with the smoking ruins of buildings and hotels behind them.

"And the eighth category?" Kaja asked, wrapping her coat more tightly around her and stamping on the gravel.

"Professor Mattiuzzi calls them the 'just plain bad and angry.' Which is a combination of the seven others."

"And you think the killer you're looking for is in one of eight categories invented by some American psychologist?"

"Mm."

"And that Svein Finne is innocent?"

"No. But of Rakel's murder, yes."

Harry took a deep drag on his Camel. So deep that he felt the heat of the smoke in his throat. Oddly, it hadn't come as a shock that Finne's confession was fake. He had had a feeling that something wasn't right, ever since they were sitting in the bunker. That Finne had been a bit too happy with the situation. He had deliberately provoked physical violence so that, regardless of what he confessed about the murder or rapes, it could never be used in court. Had he known all along that Rakel's murder had taken place the same night he was in the maternity unit? Had he been aware that the video clip could be misinterpreted? Or was it only later, before his interview in Police Headquarters, that he realised this irony of fate, that the circumstances were set for a tragicomedy? Harry looked over towards the kitchen window, where in April last year he and Rakel had gathered leaves and branches when they were clearing the garden. That was just after Finne had been released from prison, with a half-spoken threat to pay Harry's family a visit. If Finne had stood on that trailer one night, he could have seen right in between the bars over the kitchen window, where he would have seen the breadboard on the wall, and could have read the writing on it if his eyesight was good enough. Finne had found out that the house was a fortress. And had hatched his plan.

Harry doubted Krohn was behind the decision to use the false confession to get rid of the rape charges. Krohn was more aware than anyone that anything he won in the short term by a maneuver of that sort was small change in comparison to the damage to the credibility that—even for a defense lawyer with a license to be manipulative—was his real stock-in-trade.

"You're aware that those categories of yours don't exactly narrow it down much?" Kaja said. She had turned and was looking down at the city. "At some point in our lives we all fit into one or other of those descriptions."

"Mm. But actually going through with a premeditated, cold-blooded murder?"

"Why are you asking, if you already know the answer?"

"Maybe I just want to hear someone else say it."

Kaja shrugged. "Killing is just a question of context. There's no problem taking a life if you see yourself as the city's respected butcher, the fatherland's heroic soldier or the long arm of the law. Or, potentially, the righteous avenger of justice."

"Thanks."

"Don't mention it, that came from your own lecture at Police College. So who killed Rakel? Someone with personality traits from one of those categories killing without any context, or a normal person killing for a reason they've come up with themselves?"

"Well, I think that even a crazy person needs some sort of context. Even in outbursts of rage there's a moment when we manage to convince ourselves that we're acting in a justifiable way. Madness is a lonely dialogue where we give ourselves the answers we want. And we've all had that conversation."

"Have we?"

"I know I have," Harry said, looking down the drive where the dark, heavy fir trees stood on watch on either side. "But to answer your question: I think the process of narrowing down potential suspects starts here. That's why I wanted you to see the scene. It's been cleaned up. But murder is messy, emotional. It's as if we're facing a murderer who is both trained and untrained at the same time. Or perhaps trained, but emotionally unbalanced, typical for a murder motivated by sexual frustration or personal hatred."

"And because there are no signs of sexual assault, you've concluded that we're dealing with hatred?"

"Yes. That's why Svein Finne looked like the perfect suspect. A man accustomed to using violence who wants to avenge the death of his son."

"In which case surely he should have killed *you*?"

"I reasoned that Svein Finne knows that living after losing the person you love is worse than dying. But it looks like I was wrong."

"The fact that you got the wrong person doesn't necessarily mean that you got the wrong motive."

"Mm. You mean it's hard to find anyone who hated Rakel, but easy to find people who hate me?"

"Just a thought," Kaja said.

"Good. That could be a starting point."

"Perhaps the investigative team have got something that we don't know about."

Harry shook his head. "I went through their files last night, and all they've got are separate details. No definite line of inquiry or actual evidence."

"I didn't think you had access to the investigation?"

"I know the access code of someone who has. Because he was pissed off that IT had given him his bust measurement: BH100. I guessed the password."

"His date of birth?"

"Almost. HW1953."

"Which is?"

"The year Hank Williams was found dead in a car on New Year's Day."

"So, nothing but random thoughts, then. Shall we go and think them somewhere warmer than this?"

"Yes," Harry said, about to take a last drag on the cigarette.

"Hold on," Kaja said, holding out her hand. "Can I . . . ?"

Harry looked at her before passing her the cigarette. It wasn't true that he was able to see. He was more blind than any of them, blinded by tears, but now it was as if he had managed to blink them away for a moment and, for the first time since they'd met again, actually *saw* Kaja Solness. It was the cigarette. And the memories flooded back, suddenly and unexpectedly. The young police officer who had travelled to Hong Kong to fetch Harry home so he could hunt a serial killer the Oslo Police hadn't managed to catch. She had found him on a mattress in Chungking Mansions, in a kind of limbo between intoxication and indifference. And it wasn't exactly clear who had needed rescuing most: the Oslo Police or Harry. But here she was again. Kaja Solness, who denied her own beauty by showing her sharp, irregular teeth as often as she could, thereby spoiling her otherwise perfect face. He remembered the morning hours they had spent in a large, empty house, the cigarettes they had shared. Rakel used to want the first drag of a cigarette, Kaja always wanted the last.

He had abandoned them both and fled to Hong Kong again. But he had come back for one of them. Rakel.

Harry saw Kaja's raspberry lips close around the yellow-brown filter and tense ever so slightly as she inhaled. Then she dropped the butt onto the damp brown earth between the puddle and the gravel, trod on it and set off towards the car. Harry was about to follow her, but stopped.

His eyes had been caught by the squashed cigarette butt.

He thought about pattern recognition. They say that the human brain's ability to recognise patterns is what distinguishes us from animals, that our automatic, never-ending search for patterns repeating is what allowed our intelligence to develop and made civilisation possible. And he recognised the pattern in the shoeprint. From the pictures in the file titled "Crime-scene photographs" in the investigative team's material. A short comment attached to the photograph said they hadn't found a match in Interpol's database of shoe-sole patterns.

Harry cleared his throat.

"Kaja?"

He saw her thin back stiffen as she made her way to the car. God knows why, perhaps she detected something in his voice that he himself hadn't heard. She turned towards him. Her lips were drawn back, and he could see those sharp teeth.

26

"All infantry soldiers have dark hair," the stocky, fit-looking man sitting in the low armchair at the end of the coffee table said. Erland Madsen's chair was positioned at a ninety-degree angle to Roar Bohr's, instead of directly opposite him. That was so Madsen's patients could decide for themselves if they wanted to look at him or not. Not having to see the person you were talking to had the same effect as talking in a confessional: it gave the patient a feeling of talking to themselves. When you don't see a listener's reactions in the form of body language and facial expressions, the threshold for what you tell them is lowered. He had toyed with the idea of getting hold of a couch, even if that would have a been a cliché, something of a showpiece.

Madsen glanced down at his notepad. At least they had been allowed to keep those. "Can you elaborate?"

"Elaborate on dark hair?" Roar Bohr smiled. And when the smile reached those slate-grey eyes, it was as if the tears in them—the silent, dry tears that just lay there—emphasised the smile, the way the sun shines extra strongly when it's at the edge of a cloud. "They have dark hair, and they're good at putting a bullet in your skull from a couple of hundred metres. But the way to recognise them when you approach a checkpoint is that they have dark hair and are friendly. Terrified and friendly. That's their job. Not to shoot the enemy as they've been trained, but the last thing they ever thought they'd have to do when they applied to join the corps and went through hell to be accepted into Special Forces. Smiling and being friendly to civilians passing through a checkpoint that has been blown to pieces by suicide bombers twice in the previous year. It's called winning hearts and minds."

"Did it ever win any?"

"No," Bohr said.

As a specialist in post-traumatic stress disorder, Madsen had become a sort of Doctor Afghanistan, the psychologist whom people who were struggling after their experiences in war-torn areas heard about and sought out. But even if Madsen had learned a lot about the life and feelings they talked about, he also knew from experience that it was better to be a blank page. To let the patients talk as long as they liked about concrete, simple things. Nothing could be taken for granted, he needed to get them to realise that they had to paint the *whole* picture for him. His patients weren't always aware of where their pressure points were; occasionally they lay in things the patients themselves regarded as trivial and unimportant, in things they may otherwise have skipped over, in things their unconscious was working through in secret, out of sight. But right now, it was a sort of limbering up.

"So no hearts?" Madsen said.

"No one in Afghanistan really understood why ISAF were there. Not even everyone in ISAF. But no one believes that ISAF were there solely to bring democracy and happiness to a country that has no concept of democracy, nor any interest in the values it represents. The Afghans say what they think we want to hear as long as we help them with drinking water, supplies and mine clearance. But apart from that, we can go to hell. And I'm not just talking about people sympathetic to the Taliban."

"So why did you go?"

"If you want to get on in the Army, you need to have been part of ISAF."

"And you wanted to get on?"

"There's no other way. If you stop, you die. The Army has a slow, painful and humiliating death in store for anyone who thinks they can stop striving to get ahead."

"Tell me about Kabul."

"Kabul." Bohr shifted position in his chair. "Strays."

"Strays?"

"They're everywhere. Stray dogs."

"You mean literally, not . . ."

Bohr shook his head with a smile. No sunlight in his eyes this time. "The Afghans have far too many masters. The dogs live off rubbish. There's a lot of rubbish. The city smells of exhaust fumes. And burning. They burn everything to keep warm. Rubbish, oil, wood. It snows in Kabul. It always seemed to make the city look greyer. There are a few decent buildings, of course. The Presidential Palace. The Serene Hotel is five-star, apparently. The Babur Gardens are nice. But what you see most of when you drive around the city are simple, shabby buildings, one or two storeys, and shops where they sell all manner of things. Or Russian architecture at its most depressing." Bohr shook his head. "I've seen pictures of Kabul before the Soviet invasion. And what they say is true, Kabul really was beautiful once."

"But not when you were living there?"

"We didn't really live in Kabul, but in tents just outside. Very nice tents, almost like houses. But our offices were in ordinary buildings. We didn't have air con in the tents, just fans. They weren't often on, anyway, because it gets cold at night. But the days could get so hot that it was impossible to move outside. Not as bad as fifty humid degrees in Basra in Iraq, but all the same, Kabul in summer could be hell."

"But you still went back . . ." Madsen looked down at his notes. "Three times? On twelve-month tours?"

"One twelve, two six."

"You and your family were obviously aware of the risks of going into a war zone. With regard to both mental health and close relationships."

"I was told about that, yes. That the only things you get from Afghanistan are shredded nerves, divorce, and a promotion to colonel just before you retire if you manage to avoid alcoholism."

"But . . ."

"My course was staked out. I had been invested in. Officer training at the Military Academy. There are no limits to what people are willing to do if you give them a feeling that they've been chosen. Getting sent to the moon in a tin can in the sixties was pretty much a suicide mission, and everyone knew it. NASA asked only the best pilots to volunteer for their astronaut programme, the ones who had brilliant prospects in an age when pilots—civilian as well as military—had the same sort of status as film stars and footballers. They didn't ask the fearless, thrill-seeking younger pilots, but the more experienced, steady ones. The ones who knew what risk was, and had no desire to seek it out. Married pilots, who had maybe just had a child or two. In short: the ones with everything to lose. How many of them do you think turned down their country's offer to commit suicide in public?"

"Was that why you went?"

Bohr shrugged. "It was probably a mixture of personal ambition and idealism. But I don't really remember the proportions anymore."

"What do you remember most about coming home again?"

Bohr gave a wry smile. "That my wife always had to retrain me. Remind me that I didn't have to say 'understood' when she asked me to buy milk. That I should dress properly. When you haven't worn anything but a field uniform for years because of the heat, a suit feels . . . constricting. And that in social situations you're expected to shake hands with women, even if they're wearing hijabs."

"Shall we talk about killing?"

Bohr tugged at his tie and looked at the time. He took a slow, deep breath. "Shall we?"

"We've still got time."

Bohr closed his eyes for a moment. Opened them again. "Killing is complicated. And extremely simple. When we select soldiers for an elite unit like Special Forces, they don't just have to fulfil a set of physical and mental criteria. They also have to be able to kill. So we're looking for people who are capable of maintaining enough distance to kill. You've probably seen films and television programmes about recruitment to specialist units, like the Rangers, where it's mostly about stress management, solving tasks without food or sleep, behaving like a soldier under emotional and physical stress. When I was a rank-and-file soldier, there wasn't much focus on killing, on the individual's ability to take a life and deal with that. We know more about that now. We know that people who are going to kill have to know themselves. They mustn't be surprised by their own feelings. It isn't true that it's unnatural to kill a member of the same species, it's actually perfectly natural. It happens in nature all the time. Most people obviously feel a certain reluctance, which is also logical from an evolutionary perspective. But that reluctance can be overcome when the circumstances demand it. In fact, being able to kill is actually a sign of good health, because it demonstrates a capacity for self-control. If there's one thing my soldiers in Special Forces had in common, it was the fact that they were extremely relaxed about killing. But I'd happily slap anyone who accused a single one of them of being a psychopath."

"Just slap them?" Madsen asked with a wry smile.

Bohr didn't answer.

"I'd like you to talk a little more directly about your own problem," Madsen said. "Your own killing. I see from my notes that you called yourself a freak last time. But you didn't want to go into that in any more depth."

Bohr nodded.

"I can see that you're concerned, and I can only repeat what I've said before about being under an oath of complete confidentiality."

Bohr rubbed his forehead with the palm of his hand. "I know, but I'm starting to run short of time if I'm going to make it to a meeting at work."

Madsen nodded. Apart from purely professional curiosity, the business of working out where the problem was, it was rare that he ever felt curious about his patients' stories per se. But this was different, and he hoped his face wasn't showing the disappointment he felt. "Well, let's call it a day, then. And if you'd rather not talk about it at all . . ."

"I *want* to talk about it, I . . ." Bohr stopped. Buttoned his jacket. "I *need* to talk about it to someone. If I don't . . ."

Madsen waited, but he didn't go on.

"See you on Monday, same time?" Madsen asked.

Yes, he was definitely going to get hold of a couch. Maybe even a confessional.

"I hope you like your coffee strong," Harry called towards the living room as he poured water from the kettle into their cups.

"How many records have you actually got?" Kaja called back.

"About fifteen hundred." The heat scorched Harry's knuckles as he stuck his fingers through the handles of the cups. With three quick, long strides he was in the living room. Kaja was kneeling on the sofa looking through the records. "About?"

Harry pulled one corner of his mouth up into a sort of smile. "One thousand, five hundred and thirty-six."

"And like most neurotic guys, obviously you've got them arranged alphabetically by artist, but I see that at least you haven't got each artists' albums arranged by release date."

"No," Harry said, putting the cups down beside the computer on the table and blowing on his fingers. "Just in order of when I bought them. The most recent acquisition by that artist on the far left."

Kaja laughed. "You're all mad."

"Probably. Bjørn says I'm the only mad one, because *everyone* else arranges theirs by release date." He sat down on the sofa and she slid down beside him and took a sip of the coffee.

"Mmm."

"Freeze-dried coffee from a freshly opened jar," Harry said.

"I'd forgotten how good it is." She laughed.

"What? Hasn't anyone else served you coffee like this since I last did?"

"Clearly you're the only one who knows how to treat a woman, Harry."

"And don't you forget it," Harry said, then pointed at the screen. "Here's the picture of the shoeprint in the snow outside Rakel's house. Do you see it's the same?"

"Yes," Kaja said, holding up her own boot. "But the print in the picture is from a bigger size, isn't it?"

"Probably size 43 or 44," Harry said.

"Mine are 38. I bought them in a second-hand market in Kabul. They were the smallest they had."

"And they're Soviet military boots from the occupation?"

"Yes."

"That must mean they're over thirty years old."

"Impressive, isn't it? We had one Norwegian lieutenant colonel in Kabul who used to say that if these bootmakers had been in charge of the Soviet Union, it would never have collapsed."

"Do you mean Lieutenant Colonel Bohr?"

"Yes."

"Does that mean he had a pair of these boots as well?"

"I don't remember, but they were popular. And cheap. Why do you ask?"

"Roar Bohr's number appeared so frequently in Rakel's phone log that they checked his alibi for the night of the murder."

"And?"

"His wife says he was at home all evening and all night. What strikes me about those phone calls from Bohr is that he seems to have called her about three times for each call she made to him. That may not count as stalking, but wouldn't a subordinate return their boss's calls more often?"

"I don't know. You're suggesting that Bohr's interest in Rakel could have been more than professional?"

"What do you think?"

Kaja rubbed her chin. Harry didn't know why, but it struck him as a masculine gesture, possibly something to do with stubble.

"Bohr's a conscientious boss," Kaja said. "Which means that he can sometimes come across as a bit too engaged and impatient. I can well imagine him calling three times before you get around to returning the first call."

"At one o'clock in the morning?"

Kaja grimaced. "Do you want me to argue, or . . ."

"Ideally."

"Rakel was assistant director of the NHRI, if I've understood correctly?"

"Technical director. But yes."

"And what did she do?"

"Reports for UN treaty organisations. Lectures. Advice to politicians."

"So, in the NHRI you have to fit in with other people's working hours and deadlines. UN Headquarters is six hours behind us. So it isn't that remarkable for your boss to call you a bit late every now and then."

"Where does . . . What's Bohr's address?"

"Somewhere in Smestad. I think it's the house he grew up in."

"Mm."

"What are you thinking?"

"Random thoughts."

"Come on."

Harry rubbed the back of his neck. "Seeing as I'm suspended, I can't call anyone to interview, request a search warrant or operate in any way that might attract attention from Kripos or Crime Squad. But we *can* do a bit of digging in the blind spot where they can't see us."

"Such as?"

"Here's the hypothesis. Bohr killed Rakel. Then he went straight home, and got rid of the murder weapon on the way. In which case he probably drove the same way we did to get back here from Holmenkollen. If you wanted to get rid of a knife between Holmenkollveien and Smestad, where would you choose?"

"Holmendammen is literally a stone's throw from the road."

"Good," Harry said. "But the files say they've already looked there, and the average depth is only three metres, so they would have found it."

"So where else?"

He closed his eyes, leaned his head back against the wall of albums behind him and reconstructed the road he had driven so many times. Holmenkollen to Smestad. It couldn't be more than three or four kilometres. But still offered endless opportunities to get rid of a small object. It was mostly gardens. A thicket just before Stasjonsveien was a possibility. He heard the metallic whine of a tram in the distance, and a plaintive shriek from one right outside. Caught a sudden glimpse of it. Green, this time. With a stench of death.

"Rubbish," he said. "The container."

"The container?"

"At the petrol station just below Stasjonsveien."

Kaja laughed. "That's one of a thousand possibilities, and you sound *so* certain."

"Sure. It's the first thing that came to mind when I thought what I'd have done."

"Are you OK?"

"What do you mean?"

"You look very pale."

"Not enough iron," Harry said, getting to his feet.

"The company that hires out the container comes and collects it when it's full," the bespectacled, dark-skinned woman said.

"And when was the last time that happened?" Harry said, looking at the big grey container standing next to the petrol station building. The woman—who had introduced herself as the manager—had explained that the skip was for the petrol station's use, and was mostly used to get rid of packaging, and that she couldn't recall seeing anyone dumping their own rubbish in it. The container had an open metal mouth at one end, and the woman had pressed a red button to demonstrate how the jaws compacted the rubbish and pressed it into the bowels of the container. Kaja was standing a few metres away making a note of the name and phone number of the container company, which was printed on the grey steel.

"The last time they replaced it was probably a month or so ago," the manager said.

"Have the police opened it up and looked inside?" Harry asked.

"I thought you were the police?"

"The right hand doesn't always know what the left hand is doing in such a large investigation. Could you open the container for us so we can take a look at what's inside?"

"I don't know. I'd have to call my boss."

"I thought you were the boss," Harry said.

"I said I was the manager of this petrol station, that doesn't mean—"

"We understand." Kaja smiled. "If you could call him or her, we'd be very grateful."

The woman left them and disappeared inside the red and yellow building. Harry and Kaja stood there looking down at the artificial grass pitch where a couple of boys were practising the latest Neymar tricks they'd no doubt seen on YouTube.

After a while, Kaja looked at her watch. "Shall we go in and ask how it's going?"

"No," Harry said.

"Why not?"

"The knife isn't in the container."

"But you said . . ."

"I was wrong."

"And what makes you so sure about that?"

"Look," Harry said, pointing. "Security cameras. That's why no one dumps anything in here. And a murderer who's had the presence of mind to remove a well-camouflaged wildlife camera from the crime scene isn't going to drive straight into a petrol station with cameras to get rid of the murder weapon."

Harry started to walk towards the football pitch.

"Where are you going?" Kaja called after him.

Harry didn't answer. Largely because he didn't have an answer. Not until he reached the back of the petrol station and saw a building with the logo of the Ready sports club above the entrance. There were six green plastic bins beside the building. Outside the reach of the cameras. Harry opened the lid of the largest one and was hit by the rancid smell of rotting food.

He tilted the bin onto the two wheels at the back and moved it out into the open. There he tipped it over, spilling its contents.

"What a terrible smell," Kaja said as she caught up with him.

"That's good."

"Good?"

"It means it hasn't been emptied in a while," Harry said, crouching down and starting to hunt through the waste. "Can you start with one of the others?"

"There was nothing about poking through rubbish in the job description."

"Given the terrible salary you're on, you should probably have realised that rubbish was going to crop up at some point."

"You're not paying me a salary at all," Kaja said as she tipped over the smallest bin.

"That's what I meant. And yours doesn't smell as bad as mine."

"No one can say you don't know how to motivate your staff." Kaja crouched down, and Harry noted that she started with the top left, the way they were taught to search at Police College.

A man had come out onto the steps and was standing under the Ready sign. In jeans with the Ready logo on. "What the hell do you think you're doing?"

Harry stood up, walked over to the man and showed him his police ID. "Do you know if anyone might have seen anyone here on the evening of the tenth of March?"

The man stared at the ID, then back at Harry with his mouth half open. "You're Harry Hole."

"That's right."

"The super-detective himself?"

"Don't believe everything—"

"And you're looking through our rubbish."

"Sorry if you're disappointed."

"Harry . . ." Kaja called.

Harry turned round. She was holding something between her thumb and forefinger. It looked like a tiny piece of black plastic. "What is it?" he asked, screwing his eyes up as he felt his heart start to beat faster.

"I'm not sure, but I think it's one of those . . ."

Memory cards, Harry thought. The sort you use in wildlife cameras.

The sun was shining into the kitchen on Lyder Sagens gate, to where Kaja was standing, removing her memory card from the slot of what looked to Harry like a cheap camera, but which Kaja had said was a Canon G9, bought in 2009 for a small fortune, and which had actually stood the test of time. She inserted the memory card from the rubbish bin into the empty slot, connected the camera to her MacBook with a cable and clicked on the Pictures folder. A series of thumbnails appeared. Some of them showed Rakel's house in various stages of daylight. Some were taken in darkness, and all Harry could see was the light from the kitchen window.

"There you go," Kaja said, and went over to the hissing espresso machine that was working on cup number two, but Harry realised that was mostly to leave him alone.

The thumbnails were marked with dates.

The second to last was marked *10 March*, the last *11 March*. The night of the murder.

He took a deep breath. What did he want to see? What was he worried about seeing? And what was he hoping to see?

His brain felt like a wasps' nest under attack, so it was just as well to get it done.

He clicked the Play symbol on the thumbnail for 10 March.

Four smaller thumbnails appeared, with the times marked.

The camera had been activated four times before midnight on the night of the murder.

Harry clicked on the first recording, which was labelled *20:02:10*.

Darkness. Light behind the curtain in the kitchen window. But someone, or something, was moving in the darkness and had triggered the recording. Damn, he should have followed the advice of the guy in the shop and bought a more expensive camera with Zero Blur technology. Or was it No Glow? Either way, something that meant you could see what was in front of the camera even in the middle of the night. Suddenly, there was light on the steps as the front door opened, and in the doorway stood a shape that could only be Rakel. She stood there for a couple of seconds before she let a different shape in, then the door closed behind them.

Harry was breathing hard through his nose.

Several long seconds passed, then the image froze.

The next recording started at 20:29:25. Harry clicked on it. The front door was open, but the lights in the living room and kitchen were switched off, or dimmed, so he could hardly see the shape that came out, closed the door behind it and went down the steps before disappearing into the darkness. But this was half past eight in the evening, an hour and a half before the window suggested by Forensics. The next clips were the important ones.

Harry could feel his palms sweating as he clicked on the third thumbnail, labelled *23:21:09*.

A car swept across the drive. The headlights lit up the wall of the house before it came to a stop right in front of the steps and the lights went out. Harry stared at the screen, trying in vain to make his eyes bore into the darkness.

The seconds ticked past on the clock, but nothing happened. Was the driver sitting inside the dark car waiting for someone? No, because the recording hadn't stopped, so the camera's sensor was still detecting movement. Then, at last, Harry saw something. Faint light fell across the steps as the front door opened and what looked like a hunched figure went inside. The door closed, and the image went dark again. And froze a few seconds later.

He clicked on the last recording before midnight. 23:38:21.

Darkness.

Nothing.

What had the camera's PIR sensor detected? Something that was moving and had a pulse, at least; a different temperature to everything else.

After thirty seconds the recording stopped.

It could have been someone moving across the drive in front of the house. But also a bird, a cat, a dog. Harry rubbed his face hard. What the hell was the point of a wildlife camera with sensors that were far more sensitive than the lens? He vaguely remembered the sales assistant in the shop saying something along those lines when he was trying to persuade Harry to spend a bit more money on the camera. But that was back when Harry was first starting to have trouble financing his drinking and still keeping a roof over his head.

"Have we got anything?" Kaja asked, putting one of the cups down in front of him.

"Something, but not enough." Harry clicked the thumbnail for 11 March. One recording. 02:23:12.

"Cross your fingers," he said, and pressed Play.

The front door opened, and a shape could just be made out in the weak grey light from the hall. It stood there for a few seconds, looked like it was swaying. Then the door closed and everything was completely dark again.

"He's leaving," Harry said.

Light.

The car's headlights came on; the rear lights glowed red as well. The reversing light came on. Then they all went out again and everything was dark.

"He's switched the engine off again," Kaja said. "What's happening?"

"I don't know." Harry leaned closer to the screen. "There's someone approaching, can you see?"

"No."

The picture jolted, and the outline of the house became crooked. Another jolt, and it was even more crooked. Then the recording stopped.

"What was that?"

"He pulled the camera down," Harry said.

"Surely we should have seen him if he walked from the car to the camera?"

"He approached it from the side," Harry said. "You could just see him approach, from off to the left."

"Why walk around? If he was going to get rid of the recordings, I mean?"

"He was avoiding the area with most snow. Less work to get rid of his footprints afterwards."

Kaja nodded slowly. "He must have reconnoitred carefully in advance if he knew about the camera."

"Yes. And he carried out the murder with almost military precision."

"*Almost?*"

"He got in the car first, and came close to forgetting the camera."

"He hadn't planned it?"

"Yes," Harry said, lifting the cup to his lips. "Everything was planned, down to the last detail. Such as the fact that the light inside the car didn't come on when he got in and out of the car. He'd switched it off beforehand in case any of the neighbours heard the car and looked over to see who it was."

"But they'd still have seen his car."

"I doubt it was his car. If it had been, he'd have parked farther away. It looked almost as if he *wanted* to have the car at the scene."

"So that any eventual witnesses could mislead the police?"

"Mm." Harry swallowed the coffee and pulled a face.

"Sorry I haven't got any freeze-dried," Kaja said. "So what's the conclusion? Was it perfectly executed or not?"

"I don't know." Harry leaned back to pull his cigarettes from his trouser pocket. "Almost forgetting about the camera doesn't fit with the rest of it. And it looked like he was swaying in the doorway, did you see? Almost as if the person coming out isn't the same person who went in. And what was he doing in there for two and a half hours?"

"What do you think?"

"I think he was high. Drugs or drink. Does Roar Bohr take any pills?"

Kaja shook her head and fixed her gaze on the wall behind Harry.

"Is that a no?" he asked.

"It's an I-don't-know."

"But you're not ruling it out?"

"Ruling out the possibility that a Special Forces officer who's been on three tours to Afghanistan is on pills? Absolutely not."

"Mm. Can you remove the memory card? I'll take it to Bjørn, maybe Forensics can get something out of the images."

"Sure." Kaja took hold of the camera. "What are your thoughts about the knife? Why doesn't he get rid of it in the same place as the memory card?"

Harry inspected the remains of his coffee. "The crime scene indicates that he had some idea of how the police work. So he probably also knows the way we search the area around the scene for a possible murder weapon, and that the chances that we'd find a knife in a rubbish bin less than a kilometre from the scene is relatively large."

"But the memory card . . ."

". . . was OK to get rid of. He wasn't counting on us even looking for that. Who would know that Rakel had a camouflaged wildlife camera in her garden?"

"So where's the knife?"

"I don't know. But I'd guess it's in the perpetrator's home."

"Why?" Kaja asked as she looked at the camera screen. "If it gets found there, he's as good as convicted."

"Because he doesn't think he's a suspect. A knife doesn't rot, it doesn't melt, it needs to be hidden somewhere it will *never* be found. And the first place we can think of good hiding places is where we live. Having it nearby also gives us a sense of being in control of our own fate."

"But if he used a knife he took from the scene and wiped his prints off it, the only way it could be traced back to him is if it's found in his home. Home is the last place I'd have chosen."

Harry nodded. "You're right. Like I said, I don't know, I'm just guessing. It's just . . ." He tried to find the right word.

"Gut feeling?"

"Yes. No." He pressed his fingers to his temples. "I don't know. Do you remember the warnings we were given when we were young before we took LSD, that we could have flashbacks and start tripping again without any warning later in life?"

Kaja looked up from the camera. "I never took or was offered LSD."

"Smart girl. I was a rather less clever boy. Some people say those flashbacks can be triggered. Stress. Heavy drinking. Trauma. And that sometimes those flashbacks are actually a new trip, that the remnants of old drugs get activated because LSD is synthetic and doesn't get broken down in the same way as cocaine, for instance."

"So now you're wondering if you're having an LSD trip?"

Harry shrugged his shoulders. "LSD is consciousness-raising. It makes the brain work in top gear, interpret information on such a detailed level that it gives you a feeling of cosmic insight. That's the only way I can describe why I felt we had to check those green rubbish bins. I mean, you don't just find such a tiny piece of plastic in the first rather odd place you look in, one kilometre from the crime scene *by chance*, do you?"

"Maybe not," Kaja said, still staring at the camera screen.

"OK. Well, the same cosmic insight is telling me that Roar Bohr isn't the man we're looking for, Kaja."

"And what if I tell you that my cosmic insight is saying you're wrong?"

Harry shrugged. "I'm the one who took LSD, not you."

"But I'm the one who's looked at the recordings from before the tenth of March, not you."

Kaja turned the camera around and held the screen up in front of Harry.

"This is a week before the murder," she said. "The person obviously approaches from behind the camera, so when the recording starts we only see his back. He stops right in front of the camera, but unfortunately he doesn't turn around and show his face. Nor when he leaves two hours later."

Harry saw a large moon hanging directly above the roof of the house. And silhouetted against the moon Harry saw all the details of the barrel of a rifle and parts of the butt sticking up over the shoulder of someone standing between the camera and the house.

"Unless I'm mistaken," Kaja said, and Harry already knew that she wasn't mistaken, "that's a Colt Canada C8. Not exactly your standard rifle, to put it mildly."

"Bohr?"

"It's the sort of rifle Special Forces used in Afghanistan, anyway."

"Are you aware of the situation you've put me in?" Dagny Jensen asked. She had kept her coat on and was sitting bolt upright on the chair in front of Katrine Bratt's desk as she hugged her handbag in her arms. "Svein Finne has walked free of all charges, he doesn't even have to hide. And now he knows that I reported him for rape."

Outside the door, Katrine saw the muscular frame of Kari Beal. She was one of three officers who were working shifts to protect Dagny Jensen.

"Dagny—" Katrine began.

"Jensen," the woman interrupted. "*Miss* Jensen." Then she covered her face with her hands and started to cry. "He's free forever, and you can't protect me for that long. But *he* . . . he'll watch me like . . . like a farmer watching a pregnant cow!"

Her crying turned to hiccoughing sobs, and Katrine wondered what she ought to do. Should she go around her desk and try to comfort the woman, or leave her be? Do nothing. See if it blew over. If it went away.

Katrine cleared her throat. "We're looking at the possibility of charging Finne for the rapes anyway. To get him behind bars."

"You'll never manage that, he's got that lawyer. And he's smarter than all of you, anyone can see that!"

"He may be smarter, but he's on the wrong side."

"And you're on the right side? Harry Hole's side?"

Katrine didn't answer.

"You persuaded me not to press charges," Dagny said.

Katrine opened her desk drawer and handed Dagny a tissue. "Obviously it's up to you if you want to change your mind, Miss Jensen. If you want to file a formal complaint against Hole for claiming to be a police officer on active duty and for the way he put you in danger, I'm sure he would be dismissed and charged to your full satisfaction."

Katrine saw from Dagny Jensen's expression that that had come out rather sharper than she intended.

"You don't know, Bratt." Dagny wiped the makeup running from her eyes. "You don't know what it's like, bearing a child that you don't want . . ."

"We can help arrange an appointment to see a doctor who—"

"Let me finish!"

Katrine closed her mouth.

"Sorry," Dagny whispered. "I'm just so exhausted. I was going to say that you don't know how it feels . . ." She took a deep, trembling breath. ". . . to still want the baby anyway."

In the silence that followed, Katrine could hear footsteps hurrying up and down the corridor outside her office. But they had been moving faster yesterday. Tired feet.

"Don't I?" Katrine said.

"What?"

"Nothing. Of course I can't know how you feel. Look, I want to get Finne as much as you. And we will. The fact that he tricked us with that deal won't stop us. That's a promise."

"The last time I got a promise like that from a police officer, it came from Harry Hole."

"This is a promise from *me*. From this office. This building. This city."

Dagny Jensen put the tissue down on the desk and stood up. "Thanks."

When she had gone, it struck Katrine that she had never heard a single syllable express so much and yet so little. So much resignation. So little hope.

Harry stared at the memory card he had put down on the bar counter in front of him.

"What can you see?" Øystein Eikeland asked. He was playing Kendrick Lamar's *To Pimp a Butterfly*. According to Øystein, that was where the bar was at its lowest for old men who wanted to overcome their prejudices against hip-hop.

"Night recordings," Harry said.

"Now you sound like St. Thomas when he puts a cassette to his ear and says he can hear it. You've seen the documentary?"

"No. Good?"

"Good music. And a few interesting clips and interviews. Way too long, though. Looks like they had too much footage and couldn't manage to focus."

"Same here," Harry said, turning the memory card over.

"Direction is everything."

Harry nodded slowly.

"I've got a dishwasher to empty," Øystein said, and disappeared into the back room.

Harry closed his eyes. The music. The references. The memories. Prince. Marvin Gaye. Chick Corea. Vinyl records, the scratch of a needle, Rakel lying on the sofa at Holmenkollveien, sleepy, smiling as he whispers: "Listen now, this bit . . ."

Perhaps she had been lying on the sofa when he arrived.

Who was he?

Maybe it wasn't a he; not even that much was possible to determine from the recordings.

But the first person, who had arrived on foot at eight o'clock and left again half an hour later, that had been a man, Harry was fairly certain of that. And he hadn't been expected. She had opened the door and stood there for two or three seconds instead of letting him in at once. Perhaps he had asked if he could come in, and she had let him in without hesitation. So she had known him well. How well? So well that he had let himself out just under half an hour later. Perhaps that visit had nothing to do with the murder, but Harry couldn't help the questions from popping up: What can a man and a woman do in just under half an hour? Why had the lights in the kitchen and living room been dimmed when he left? Bloody hell, he didn't have time to let his thoughts wander off in that direction now. So he hurried on instead.

The car that had arrived three hours later.

It had parked right in front of the steps. Why? A shorter walk to the house, less chance of being seen. Yes, that fitted with the fact that the automatic light inside the car was switched off.

But there was slightly too much of a gap between the car arriving and the front door of the house opening.

Perhaps the driver had been looking for something inside the car.

Gloves. A cloth to wipe fingerprints off with. Perhaps he checked that the safety was on on the pistol he was going to threaten her with. Because obviously he wasn't going to kill her with that; ballistics analysis can identify the pistol, which identifies the owner. He would use a knife he found at the scene. The perfect knife, the one the murderer already knew he would find in the knife block on the kitchen counter.

Or had he improvised in there, had the knife at the scene been a matter of chance?

The thought had struck Harry because it seemed careless to spend so long in the car in front of the steps. Rakel could have woken up and become alarmed, the neighbours could have chanced to look out of their windows. And when the man finally opened the front door and enough light filtered out for them to see the silhouette of an oddly hunched figure disappear inside, what was that? Someone who was intoxicated? That might fit with the clumsy parking, and the fact that he had taken so long getting to the door, but not the light inside the car and the clean crime scene.

A mixture of planning, intoxication and chance?

The person in question had been in there for almost three hours, from just before midnight until around half past two in the morning. Given the Forensic Department's estimate of the time of death, he had been in there for a long time after committing the murder, and had taken plenty of time to clean up.

Could it be the same person who was there earlier that evening, and he had come back later in his car?

No.

The images had been too poor to see anything clearly, but there was something about the shape—the person who had been hunched over when he went in had looked broader. But, on the other hand, that could be thanks to a change of clothes, or even a shadow.

The person who had come out at 02:23 had stood for a couple of seconds in the doorway, and had looked as if he were swaying. Injured? Intoxicated? Momentary dizziness?

He had got in the car, the lights had come on, then gone off again. He had walked around behind the wildlife camera. End of recording.

Harry rubbed the memory card, hoping that a genie might appear.

He was thinking about this wrong. All wrong! Damn, damn.

And he needed a break. He needed a . . . coffee. Strong, Turkish coffee. Harry reached behind the bar for the *cezve*, the Turkish coffeepot Mehmet had left, and realised that Øystein had changed the music. Still hip-hop, but the jazz and intricate bassline were gone.

"What's this, Øystein?"

"Kanye West, 'So Appalled,'" Øystein called from the back room.

"And just when you almost had me. Please, turn it off."

"This is good stuff, Harry! Give it time. We mustn't let our ears get stale."

"Why not? There are thousands of albums from the last millennium I haven't heard, and that's enough to last the rest of my life." Harry swallowed. What a relief it was to take a break from the heavy stuff, with these feather-light, meaningless exchanges with someone you knew inside out, like table tennis with a three-gram ball.

"You need to make more of an effort." Øystein came back into the bar with a broad, toothless grin. He had lost his last front tooth in a bar in Prague, it had just fallen out. And even if he had discovered the gap in the airport toilet, called the bar and had the brownish-yellow tooth returned to him by post, there was nothing that could be done. Not that Øystein seemed particularly bothered.

"These are the classics hip-hop fans will be listening to when they're old, Harry. This isn't just form, it's *content*."

Harry held the memory card up to the light. He nodded slowly. "You're right, Øystein."

"Tell me something I don't know."

"I'm thinking wrong because I'm focusing on form, on how the murder was carried out. I'm ignoring what I always used to go on about to my students. *Why*. The motive. The content."

The door opened behind them.

"Oh, shit," Øystein said in a low voice.

Harry glanced up at the mirror in front of him. A man was approaching. Short, with a light step, shaking his head, with a grin under his black, greasy fringe. It was the sort of grin you see on golfers or footballers when they've just shot the ball high into the stands, a grin that's probably supposed to suggest that it was such a fuck-up that all they can do is smile.

"Hole." A high, disconcertingly friendly voice.

"Ringdal." Not high. Not disconcertingly friendly.

Harry saw Øystein shiver, as if the temperature in the bar had just plunged below zero.

"So, what are you doing in my bar, Hole?" There was a jangle of keys and coins in Ringdal's pockets as he took off his blue Catalina jacket and hung it on the hook behind the door to the back room.

"Well," Harry said. "Would 'seeing how the inheritance is being managed' be a satisfactory answer?"

"The only satisfactory answer is 'getting out of here.'"

Harry put the memory card in his pocket and pushed himself off the bar stool. "You don't look as badly hurt as I'd hoped, Ringdal."

Ringdal was rolling up his shirtsleeves. "Hurt?"

"To deserve a lifetime ban I should have broken your nose at the very least. But perhaps you haven't got any bones in your nose?"

Ringdal laughed as if he genuinely thought Harry was funny. "You landed your first punch because I wasn't expecting it, Hole. A bit of a nosebleed, but not enough to break anything, I'm afraid. And after that you hit nothing but air. And that wall over there." Ringdal filled a glass with water from the tap behind the bar. Perhaps it was a paradox that a teetotaller was running a bar. Perhaps not. "But all credit to you for trying, Hole. Maybe you should try to be a bit less drunk next time you attempt to take on a Norwegian judo champion."

"And there we have it," Harry said.

"What?"

"Have you ever heard of anyone involved in judo who has good taste in music?"

Ringdal sighed, Øystein raised his eyebrows and Harry realised that the ball had ended up in the stand.

"Getting out of here," Harry said, and stood up.

"Hole."

Harry stopped and turned around.

"I'm sorry about Rakel." Ringdal raised his glass of water in his left hand as if in a toast. "She was a wonderful person. A shame she didn't have time to carry on."

"Carry on?"

"Oh, didn't she tell you? I asked her to stay on as chair after you were gone. Well, let's draw a line under all that, Harry. You're welcome here, and I promise to listen to Øystein here when it comes to the choice of music. I can see that takings have dropped a bit, although of course that could be due to something other than a slightly less . . ."—he searched for the right words—"strict music policy."

Harry nodded and opened the door.

He stopped in the doorway and looked around.

Grünerløkka. The scraping sound of a skateboard, ridden by a guy closer to forty than thirty, wearing Converse and flannels. Harry guessed design studio, clothing boutique or one of the hipster burger joints that Helga, Oleg's girlfriend, had said "sold the same shit, same wrapping as everywhere else, but they put truffles on the fries so they can charge three times the price and still be on-trend."

Oslo. A young man with an impressive, unkempt beard—like an Old Testament prophet—hanging like a bib over his tie and impeccable suit, his Burberry coat open. Finance? Irony? Or just confusion?

Norway. A couple in Lycra suits, jogging with skis and sticks in their hands, ski wax worth a thousand kroner, energy drinks and protein bars in their bumbags, on their way to the last patches of snow in the highest shadows of Nordmarka.

Harry pulled out his phone and called Bjørn's number.

"Harry?"

"I've found the memory card from the wildlife camera."

Silence.

"Bjørn?"

"I just needed to get away from everyone. That's crazy! What can you see?"

"Not much, sadly. I was wondering if you could help me get it analysed. It's dark, but you've got methods of getting more out of the images than I can manage. There are a few silhouettes and reference points, the height of the door frame, that sort of thing. A 3-D specialist might be able to come up with a decent description." Harry rubbed his chin. He was itching somewhere, he just didn't know where.

"I can try," Bjørn said. "I can use an external expert. Because I'm assuming you'd like this done discreetly?"

"If I'm to have any chance of following this line of inquiry undisturbed, yes."

"Have you made copies of the recordings?"

"No, it's all on the memory card."

"OK. Leave it in an envelope at Schrøder's and I'll call in and pick it up later today."

"Thanks, Bjørn." Harry ended the call. Tapped in R for Rakel. The other entries in his contacts were O for Oleg, Ø for Øystein, K for Katrine, B for Bjørn, S for Sis and A for Ståle Aune. That was all. That was enough for Harry, even if Rakel had told Ståle that Harry was open to meeting new people. But only if those letters weren't already taken.

He keyed in Rakel's work number without her extension.

"Roar Bohr?" he said when the receptionist answered.

"It looks like Bohr isn't here today."

"Where is he, and when will he be back?"

"It doesn't say anything about that here. But I've got a mobile number."

Harry made a note of the number and tapped it into the app for directory inquiries. It came up with an address between Smestad and Huseby, and a landline number. He looked at his watch. Half past one. He called the number.

"Yes?" a woman's voice said after the third ring.

"Sorry, wrong number." Harry hung up and started to walk towards the tram stop at the top of Birkelunden. He rubbed his upper arm. That wasn't where the itch was either. It wasn't until he was on the metro heading towards Smestad that he realised that the itch was probably in his head. And that it had almost certainly been triggered by Ringdal's possibly well-meant, possibly calculated gesture. And that he would actually have preferred to have gone on being barred, rather than be the recipient of irritating, broad-minded benevolence. And that he might possibly have underestimated judo.

The woman who opened the door of the yellow house exuded the sort of sharp vitality that was typical of women between thirty and fifty in the upper social segment here on the west side of the city. It was difficult to know if it was an ideal they were trying to live up to, or their true energy level, but Harry had a suspicion that there was something status-related about the effortless, loud way they marshalled their two children, gun dog and husband, preferably in a public place.

"Pia Bohr?"

"How can I help you?" No confirmation, and gently dismissive politeness, but said with a confident smile. She was short, wasn't wearing makeup, and her wrinkles suggested she was closer to fifty than forty. But she was as slim as a teenager. A lot of time at the gym and plenty of outdoor living, Harry guessed.

"Police." He held up his ID.

"Of course, you're Harry Hole," she said without looking at it. "I've seen your face in the paper. You were Rakel Fauke's husband. My condolences."

"Thank you."

"I presume you're here to talk to Roar? He isn't here."

"When . . ."

"This evening, possibly. Give me your number and I'll ask him to contact you."

"Mm. Perhaps I could talk to you, Mrs. Bohr?"

"To me? What for?"

"It won't take long. There are just a couple of things I need to know." Harry's eyes roamed across the shoe rack behind her. "Can I come in?"

Harry noticed the hesitation. And found what he was looking for on the bottom shelf of the rack. A pair of black, Soviet military boots.

"Now isn't a good time, I'm in the middle of . . . something."

"I can wait."

Pia Bohr smiled quickly. Not obviously beautiful, but cute, Harry decided. Possibly what Øystein would call a Toyota: not the boys' first choice when they were teenagers, but the one that stayed in the best shape as the years passed.

She looked at her watch. "I need to go and get something from the chemist. We can talk while we walk, OK?"

She grabbed a coat from a hook, came out onto the steps and closed the door behind her. Harry had noted that the lock was the same sort as Rakel's, no self-locking mechanism, but Pia Bohr didn't bother to look for a key. Safe neighbourhood. No strange men who'd just walk into your house.

They walked past the garage, through the gate and down the road, where the first Tesla cars were humming home from their short days at work.

Harry put a cigarette between his lips without lighting it. "Are you going to pick up sleeping pills?"

"Sorry?"

Harry shrugged his shoulders. "Insomnia. You told our detective that your husband was at home all night of the tenth and eleventh of March. To know that for certain, you can't have slept much."

"I . . . Yes, it's sleeping pills."

"Mm. I needed sleeping pills after Rakel and I split up. Insomnia eats away at your soul. What have they put you on?"

"Er . . . Imovane and Somadril." Pia was walking faster.

Harry lengthened his stride as he clicked the lighter beneath the cigarette but failed to get it to light. "Same as me. I've been on them for two months. You?"

"Something like that."

Harry put the lighter back in his pocket. "Why are you lying, Pia?"

"I'm sorry?"

"Imovane and Somadril are heavy stuff. If you take them for two months, you're hooked. And if you're hooked, you take them *every* night. Because they work. So well that if you did take them that night, you were in a coma and would have no idea what your husband was doing. But you don't strike me as the sort of person who's hooked on sedatives. You're a little too energetic, a little too quick-witted."

Pia Bohr slowed down.

"But of course you could easily prove me wrong," Harry said. "By showing me the prescription."

Pia stopped walking. She put her hand in the back pocket of her tight jeans. Pulled out and unfolded a piece of blue paper.

"See?" she said with a light vibrato in her voice, holding it up and pointing. "So-ma-dril."

"I see," Harry said, taking the paper from her before she had time to react. "And when I look more closely, I see that it's been prescribed for Bohr. Roar Bohr. He evidently hasn't told you how strong the medication he needs is."

Harry handed the prescription back to her.

"Perhaps there are other things he hasn't told you, Pia?"

"I . . ."

"Was he at home that night?"

She swallowed. The colour in her cheeks was gone, her energetic vitality punctured. Harry adjusted his estimate of her age by five years.

"No," she whispered. "He wasn't."

They skipped the chemist and walked down to Smestaddammen, then sat down on one of the benches on the slope on the eastern side, looking out at the little island that had room for a single willow tree.

"Spring," Pia said. "Anything but spring. In the summer it's so green here. Everything grows like mad. Loads of insects. Fish, frogs. It's so full of life. And when the trees get their leaves and the wind plays through the willow, they dance and rustle loud enough to drown out the motorway." She smiled sadly. "And autumn in Oslo . . ."

"Finest autumn in the world," Harry said, lighting his cigarette.

"Even winter's better than spring," Pia said. "At least it used to be, when you could count on it being properly cold, with solid ice. We used to bring the children here to go skating. They loved it."

"How many . . . ?"

"Two. One girl and one boy. Twenty-eight and twenty-five. June's a marine biologist in Bergen, and Gustav's studying in the U.S."

"You started early."

She smiled wryly. "Roar was twenty-three and I was twenty-one when we had June. Couples who get moved around the country on Army postings often become parents early. So the wives have something to do, I suppose. As an officer's wife you have two options. To let yourself be tamed and accept life as a breeding cow. Stand in your stall, give birth to calves, give milk, chew the cud."

"And the second option?"

"Not to become an officer's wife."

"But you chose option number one?"

"Looks like it."

"Mm. Why did you lie about that night?"

"To spare us from questions. From becoming the focus. You can imagine how it would have damaged Roar's reputation if he'd been called in for questioning in a murder investigation, surely? He doesn't need that, if I can put it like that."

"Why doesn't he need that?"

She shrugged. "No one needs that, do they? Especially not in our neighbourhood."

"So where was he?"

"I don't know. Out."

"Out?"

"He can't sleep."

"Somadril."

"It was worse when he got home from Iraq; they gave him Rohypnol for his insomnia that time. He got hooked in two weeks and it gave him blackouts. So now he refuses to take anything. He puts his field uniform on, says he has to go out on reconnaissance. Keep watch. Keep an eye out. He says he just walks from place to place, like a night patrol, staying out of sight. I suppose it's typical of people with post-traumatic stress disorder that they're frightened the whole time. He usually comes home and gets a couple of hours' sleep before he goes to work."

"And he manages to keep this hidden at work?"

"We see what we want to see. And Roar has always been good at making whatever impression he wants to make. He's the sort of man people trust."

"You too?"

She sighed. "My husband isn't a bad person. But sometimes even good people fall to pieces."

"Does he take a gun with him when he's out on night patrol?"

"I don't know. He goes out after I've gone to bed."

"Do you know where he was on the night of the murder?"

"I asked him after you'd asked me. He said he slept in June's old room."

"But you didn't believe him?"

"Why do you say that?"

"Because then you would have told the police that he'd slept in another room. You lied because you were worried we had something else. Something that meant he needed a stronger alibi than the truth."

"You're not seriously suggesting that you suspect Roar, Hole?"

Harry looked at a pair of swans that were paddling towards them. He glimpsed a flash of light from the hillside beyond the motorway. A window opening, perhaps.

"Post-traumatic," Harry said. "What's the trauma?"

She sighed. "I don't know. A combination of things. Rough stuff from his childhood. And Iraq. Afghanistan. But when he came home from his last tour and told me he'd left the Army, obviously I realised that something had happened. He'd changed. Was more shut off. After a lot of nagging, I finally got it out of him that he'd killed someone in Afghanistan. Of course that's what they were there for, but this one had got to him, and he didn't want to talk about it. But he was able to function, at least."

"And he isn't now?"

She looked at Harry with the eyes of someone who'd been shipwrecked. And he realised why she had opened up to him, a stranger, so easily. *Not in our neighbourhood.* She had wanted this, had been longing desperately for it, she just hadn't had anyone to talk to about it until now.

"After Rakel Fauke . . . after your wife's death, he went completely to pieces. He . . . he's not functioning, no."

That flash of light again. And it struck him that it must be coming from roughly the same part of the hillside where the Bohrs' house was. Harry stiffened. He had seen something from the corner of his eye, something between them on the white backrest of the bench, something trembling that had moved and disappeared, like a quick, red, silent insect. There were no insects here in March.

Harry leaned forward instantly, dug his heels in the slope, pushed off and threw himself against the back of the bench. Pia Bohr screamed as the bench tipped over and they fell backwards. Harry wrapped his arms round her as they slid off the backrest, pressing her down into the shallow ditch behind the bench. Then he began to snake his way across the mud, pulling Pia behind him. He stopped and peered up towards the hillside. He saw that the willow tree was between them and where he had seen the flash of light. Farther away on the path, a man in a hooded sweater walking a Rottweiler had stopped, and looked like he was considering getting involved.

"Police!" Harry cried. "Get back! There's a sniper!"

Harry saw an elderly lady turn and hurry away, but the man with the Rottweiler didn't move.

Pia tried to pull free, but Harry lay with the whole of his body weight on top of the slight woman so that they were lying face to face.

"Looks like your husband's at home after all," he said, pulling out his phone. "That's why I couldn't come in. That's why you didn't lock the door when we left." He called a number.

"No!" Pia cried.

"Emergency Control," a voice said on the phone.

"Inspector Harry Hole here. Reporting an armed man—"

The phone was snatched from his hand. "He's just using the rifle sight as a telescope." Pia Bohr put the phone to her ear. "Sorry, wrong number." She ended the call and gave the phone back to Harry. "Isn't that what you said when you called me?"

Harry didn't move.

"You're quite heavy, Hole. Could you . . ."

"How do I know I'm not going to get a bullet in my forehead when I stand up?"

"Because you've had a red dot on your forehead since we sat down on the bench."

Harry looked at her. Then he put his hands down on the cold mud and pushed himself up. Got to his feet. Squinted towards the hillside. He turned to help Pia, but she was already up. Her jeans and jacket were black and dripping with mud. Harry pulled a bent cigarette from his packet of Camels. "Is your husband going to disappear now?"

"I imagine so," she sighed. "You need to understand that he's in a bad way mentally, and very jittery right now."

"Where does he go?"

"I don't know."

"You know you can be prosecuted for obstructing the police, Mrs. Bohr?"

"Are you talking about me or my husband?" she asked, brushing her thighs. "Or yourself?"

"Sorry?"

"You'd hardly be allowed to investigate the murder of your own wife, Hole. You're here as a private detective. Or should we say *pirate* detective?"

Harry tore off the bent tip of the cigarette and lit what was left. He looked down at his own filthy clothes. His coat was torn where one of the buttons had been pulled off. "Will you tell me if your husband comes back?"

Pia nodded towards the water. "Watch out for that one, it doesn't like men."

Harry turned and saw that one of the swans had set off towards them.

When he turned back, Pia Bohr was already heading up the slope.

"A *pirate* detective?"

"Yep," Harry said, holding the door to Bjølsenhallen open for Kaja.

The hall lay nestled among the more ordinary buildings around it. Kaja had said that Kjelsås Table Tennis Club was based above the large supermarket on the ground floor.

"Still not keen on the whole lift concept?" Kaja asked as she struggled to keep up with Harry on the stairs.

"It's not the concept, it's the size," Harry said. "How did you find out about this military police officer?"

"There weren't that many Norwegians in Kabul, and I've talked to most of the people I know there now. Glenne is the only person who sounds like he might have something to tell us."

The girl in reception told them where to go. The sound of shoes on hard floors and the clatter of ping-pong balls reached them before they turned the corner and found themselves in a large, open room where a few people, most of them men, were dancing and crouching and swinging at either end of green table-tennis tables.

Kaja set off towards one of them.

Two men were hitting a ball diagonally across the net at each other, the same trajectory every time, forehand with topspin. They were barely moving, just repeating the same movement, striking the ball with their arms bent and a flick of the wrist, accompanied by a hard step with one foot. The ball was moving so fast that it looked like a white line between the men, who seemed locked into this duel, like a computer game that had got stuck.

Then one of them hit the ball too far and it bounced away across the floor between the tables.

"Damn," the player said. He was a fit-looking man in his forties or fifties, with a black headband over cropped, silver-grey hair.

"You're not reading the spin," the other man said as he went to fetch the ball.

"Jørn," Kaja said.

"Kaja!" The man with the headband grinned. "Here's a sweaty soldier for you." They hugged each other.

Kaja introduced him to Harry.

"Thanks for agreeing to see us," Harry said.

"No one turns down a meeting with this young lady," Jørn Glenne said with his smile still in his eyes, squeezing Harry's hand just hard enough for it to be taken as a challenge. "But if I'd known she was going to be bringing backup . . ."

Kaja and Glenne laughed.

"Let's grab a coffee," Glenne said, putting his paddle on the table.

"What about your partner?" Kaja asked.

"My trainer, bought and paid for," he said, showing them the way. "Connolly and I are going to be meeting up in Juba this autumn. I need to get in practice."

"An American colleague," Kaja explained to Harry. "They had a never-ending table-tennis tournament while we were in Kabul."

"Fancy coming along?" Glenne asked. "I'm sure your lot could find a job for you there."

"South Sudan?" Kaja asked. "What's it like there now?"

"Same as before. Civil war, famine, Dinkas, Nuers, cannibalism, gang rape and more weapons than the whole of Afghanistan put together."

"Let me think about it," Kaja said, and Harry could see from the expression on her face that she wasn't joking.

They got coffee in the canteen-like cafeteria and sat down at a table next to a grimy window looking out onto Bjølsen Valsemølle and the Akerselva. Jørn Glenne started speaking before Harry and Kaja had a chance to ask any questions.

"I agreed to talk to you because I fell out with Roar Bohr in Kabul. A woman was raped and murdered; she was Bohr's personal interpreter. A Hazara woman. The Hazaras are mostly poor, simple peasants with no education. But this young woman, Hela—"

"Hala," Kaja corrected. "It means the circle around the full moon."

". . . had taught herself English and French pretty much unaided. And she was in the process of learning Norwegian as well. Brilliant at languages. She was found right outside the house where she lived with other women who worked for the coalition and various aid agencies. Of course, you lived there too, Kaja."

Kaja nodded.

"We suspected it was the Taliban or someone from her home district. Honour is obviously a huge thing for Sunni Muslims, and even more so for the Hazaras. The fact that she was working for us infidels, socialised with men and dressed like a Westerner may have been enough for someone to want to make an example of her."

"I've heard about honour killings," Harry said. "But honour rape?"

Glenne shrugged his shoulders. "One could have led to the other. But who knows? Bohr stopped us investigating it."

"Really?"

"Her body was found a stone's throw from the house where we're responsible for security. It was basically an area that was under our control. Despite that, Bohr handed the investigation to the local Afghan police. When I objected, he pointed out that the military police, which in this case meant me and one other guy, were under his command and charged with the security of Norwegian troops in the country, and that was all. Even if he knew perfectly well that the Afghan police lacked the resources and forensic tools that we take for granted. Fingerprinting was a new-fangled concept, and DNA-testing the stuff of dreams."

"Bohr had to consider the political implications," Kaja said.

"There was already a lot of ill will about Western forces taking too much control, and Hala was Afghan."

"She was a *Hazara*," Glenne snorted. "Bohr knew the case wouldn't be given the same priority it would have got if she'd been a Pashtun. OK, there was a post-mortem, and they found traces of fluni-something-or-other. The stuff men put in women's drinks if they want to rape—"

"Flunitrazepam," Kaja said. "Also known as Rohypnol."

"Right. And do you think any Afghan would spend money drugging a woman before he raped her?"

"Mm."

"No, damn it, it was a foreigner!" Glenne hit the table with his hand. "And was the case ever solved? Of course not."

"Do you think . . ." Harry took a sip of coffee. Tried to find an alternative, more indirect way to phrase the question, but changed his mind when he looked up and met Jørn Glenne's gaze. ". . . that Roar Bohr could have been behind the murder, and made sure that the people with the least chance of catching him were given responsibility for the investigation? Is that why you wanted to talk to us?"

Glenne blinked and opened his mouth. But nothing came out.

"Listen, Jørn," Kaja said. "We know Bohr told his wife he killed someone in Afghanistan. And I've talked to Jan . . ."

"Jan?"

"The camp instructor for Special Forces. Tall, blond . . ."

"Oh, him. He was crazy about you too!"

"Anyway," Kaja said, lowering her eyes, and Harry suspected she was acting embarrassed to give the laughing Glenne what he wanted. "Jan says they have no record of any confirmed or claimed kill for Roar. As the officer in command, obviously he wasn't on the front line much, but the fact is that he has no kills from earlier in his career when he was actually on the front line."

"I know," Glenne said. "Officially, Special Forces weren't in Basra, but Bohr was there for training with an American unit. According to rumour he saw a lot of action, but still remained a virgin. And the closest he got to the action in Afghanistan was that time Sergeant Waage was taken by the Taliban."

"Yes, that," Kaja said.

"What was that?" Harry asked.

Glenne shrugged. "Bohr and Waage were on a long drive and stopped in the desert so the sergeant could have a shit. The sergeant went behind some rocks, and when he didn't come back after twenty minutes and didn't answer when he was called, Bohr said in his report that he got out of the car to look for him. But I'm pretty sure he didn't budge."

"Why do you think that?"

"Because there's not that fucking much that can happen in a desert. Because one or two Taliban farmers with basic rifles and a knife were sitting behind the rocks waiting for Bohr to come looking. And Bohr obviously knew that. And he was safe in the bulletproof car with open ground between him and the rocks. He knew there wouldn't be any witnesses to prove he was lying. So he locked all the doors and called the camp. They told him it was a five-hour drive from there. Two days later an Afghan unit found a trail of blood on the pavement, several kilometres long, a few hours farther north. Sometimes the Taliban torture prisoners by dragging them behind a cart. And outside a village even farther north, a head was found on a stake stuck in the ground by the side of the road. His face had been scraped off on the pavement, but DNA analysis in Paris confirmed that it was Sergeant Waage, of course."

"Mm." Harry toyed with his coffee cup. "Do you think that about Bohr because you'd have done the same thing if it had been you, Glenne?"

The military police officer shrugged his shoulders. "I'm not under any illusions. We're human, we all take the path of least resistance. But it wasn't me."

"So?"

"So I judge other people just as hard as I would have judged myself. And maybe Bohr did that as well. It's tough for a commanding officer to lose any of his troops. Bohr was never the same after that, anyway."

"So you think he raped and murdered his interpreter, but what broke him was the fact that the Taliban took his sergeant?"

Glenne shrugged again. "Like I said, I wasn't allowed to investigate, so all I've got are theories."

"And what's your best one?"

"That the business of the rape was just a cover-up to make it look like sexually motivated murder. To get the police to look among the usual suspects and perverts. Which is a fairly thin file in Kabul."

"A cover-up for what?"

"For Bohr's real project. To kill someone."

"*Someone?*"

"Bohr had a problem with killing, as you already know by now. And when you're in Special Forces, that's a *big* problem."

"Really? I didn't think they were *that* bloodthirsty."

"They're not, but . . . how can I explain it?" Glenne shook his head. "The old school in Special Forces, the ones who came through paratrooper training, were picked because of their long-term intelligence-gathering behind enemy lines, where patience and stamina are the most important qualities. They were the Army's long-distance runners, OK? That's where Bohr fitted in. Now, the focus is on antiterrorism in urban settings. And you know what? The new Special Forces look like ice hockey players, if you see what I mean? And in this new environment, a rumour had gone around saying Bohr was . . ." Glenne pulled a face, as if he didn't like the taste of the word on his tongue.

"A coward?" Harry asked.

"Impotent. Imagine the shame. You're in command, but you're still a virgin. And not a virgin because you've never had the opportunity, because there are still soldiers in Special Forces who have never found themselves in a situation where it's been necessary to kill. But because you couldn't get it up when it mattered. See what I mean?"

Harry nodded.

"As an old hand, Bohr knew that the first kill is the hardest," Glenne went on. "After that first blood it gets easier. Much easier. So he chose an easy first victim. A woman who wouldn't put up a fight, who trusted him and wouldn't suspect anything. One of the hated Hazaras, a Shia in a Sunni Muslim country, someone plenty of people might have a motive to kill. And then maybe he got a taste for it. Killing is a very special feeling. Better than sex."

"Is it?"

"So they say. Ask people in Special Forces. And tell them to answer honestly."

Harry and Glenne looked at each other for a few moments before Glenne looked at Kaja. "All of this is just things I've thought to myself. But if Bohr has admitted to his wife that he killed Hela—"

"Hala."

". . . then you can count on my help." Glenne drank the last of his coffee. "Connolly never rests. I need to get back to training."

. . .

"Well?" Kaja asked when she and Harry were standing outside in the street. "What do you think about Glenne?"

"I think he hits too long because he doesn't read the spin."

"Funny."

"Metaphorically. He's drawing overblown conclusions from the trajectory of the ball, but without analysing what his opponent has just done with the paddle."

"Is the lingo supposed to tell me you know all about table tennis?"

Harry shrugged. "Øystein's basement from when we were ten. Him, me and Tresko. And King Crimson. To be honest, by the time we were sixteen we knew more about screwballs and prog rock than girls. We . . ." Harry stopped abruptly and grimaced.

"What?" Kaja asked.

"I'm babbling, I . . ." He closed his eyes. "I'm babbling so I don't wake up."

"Wake up?"

Harry took a deep breath. "I'm asleep. As long as I'm asleep, as long as I can manage to stay in the dream, I can carry on looking for him. But every so often it starts to slip away from me. I need to concentrate on sleeping, because if I wake up . . ."

"What?"

"Then I'll know that it's true. And then I'll die."

Harry listened. The clatter of studded tires on pavement. The sound of a small waterfall in the Akerselva.

"Sounds like what my psychologist called lucid dreaming," he heard Kaja say. "A dream where you can control everything. And that's why we do all we can not to let it go."

Harry shook his head. "I can't control anything. I just want to find the man who killed Rakel. Then I'll wake up. And die."

"Why not try to sleep properly?" Her voice was soft. "I think it would do you good to get some rest, Harry."

Harry opened his eyes again. Kaja had raised her hand, probably to put it on his shoulder, but instead she brushed a strand of hair from her face when she saw the look in his eyes.

He cleared his throat. "You said you'd found something in the property register?"

Kaja blinked a couple of times.

"Yes," she said. "A cabin listed under Roar Bohr's name. In Eggedal. An hour and forty-five minutes away, according to Google Maps."

"Good. I'll see if Bjørn can drive."

"Sure you don't want to talk to Katrine and put an alert out for him?"

"What for? The fact that his wife didn't see with her own eyes that he was asleep in their daughter's old room that night?"

"If she wouldn't think what we've got is enough, why do you?"

Harry buttoned his coat and got his mobile out. "Because I've got a gut feeling that's caught more murderers than any other gut in this country."

He felt Kaja looking at him in astonishment as he called Bjørn.

"I can drive," Bjørn said after a short pause for thought.

"Thanks."

"One other thing. That memory card of yours . . ."

"Yes?"

"I forwarded the envelope in your name to Freund, our external 3-D expert. I haven't spoken to him, but I've sent you an email with his contact details, so you can talk to him yourself."

"I get it. You'd rather not have your name mixed up in this."

"This is the only job I know how to do, Harry."

"Like I said, I get it."

"If I get fired now, with a kid and everything . . ."

"Stop it, Bjørn, you're not the one who should be apologising. I should, for dragging you into this mess."

A pause. In spite of what he'd just said, Harry could almost feel Bjørn's guilty conscience down the phone.

"I'll pick you up," Bjørn said.

Detective Inspector Felah was sitting with the fan on his back, but his shirt was still sticking to his skin. He hated the heat, hated Kabul, hated his bombproof office. But most of all he hated the lies he had to listen to, day in, day out. Like the ones from the pathetic, illiterate, opium-addicted Hazara sitting in front of him now.

"You've been brought to see me because you claimed under questioning that you can give us the name of a murderer," Felah said. "A foreigner."

"Only if you protect me," the man said.

Felah looked at the man cowering in front of him. The battered cap the Hazara was rubbing between his hands wasn't a *pakol*, but it had at least covered his filthy hair. The dribbling, ignorant Shia bandit evidently thought that escaping the death penalty and getting a long prison sentence instead would be a mercy. A slow, painful death, that was what that was, and he himself would have chosen a quick death by hanging without hesitation.

Felah wiped his forehead with his handkerchief. "That depends on what you've got to say to me. Spit it out."

"He killed . . ." the Hazara said in a shaky voice. "He didn't think anyone saw him, but I did. With my own eyes, I swear, as Allah is my witness."

"A foreign soldier, you said."

"Yes, sir. But this wasn't in battle, this was murder. Murder, plain and simple."

"I see. And who was this military foreigner?"

"The leader of the Norwegians. I know that because I recognised him. He'd been in our village, talking about how they're here to help us, that we'd get democracy and jobs . . . all the usual."

Felah felt a moment of longed-for excitement. "You mean Major Jonassen?"

"No, that wasn't his name. Lieutenant Colonel Bo."

"Do you mean Bohr?"

"Yes—yes I do, sir."

"And you saw him murder an Afghan man?"

"No, not that."

"What, then?"

Felah listened as he felt his excitement and interest fade away. Firstly, Lieutenant Colonel Bohr had gone home, and the chances of getting him extradited were as good as nonexistent. Secondly, a commander who was out of the game was no longer a particularly valuable chess piece in Kabul's political game, a game that Felah actually hated more than everything else put together. Thirdly, the victim wasn't someone who qualified for the amount of resources it would require to investigate this opium addict's claims. And then there was the fourth thing. It was a lie. Of course it was a lie. Everyone was out to save their own skin. And the more detail the man in front of him gave about the murder—and Felah was confident it matched what little they already knew—the more certain Felah was that the man was describing a murder he himself had committed. A crazy idea, and Felah wasn't about to use the few resources he had at his disposal to investigate the hypothesis. Opium addiction or murder—either way, you still couldn't hang a man more than once.

27

"Can it really not go any faster?" Harry asked, staring out into the darkness beyond the slush and the hard-working windshield wipers.

"Yes, but I'd rather not go off the road with so much irreplaceable brain capacity in the car." As usual, Bjørn had his seat so far back that he was more lying than sitting. "Especially in a car with old-fashioned seat belts and no airbags."

A truck coming around a bend in the opposite direction on Highway 287 passed them so close that Bjørn's 1970 Volvo Amazon shook.

"Even I've got airbags," Harry said, looking past Bjørn at the low crash barriers and still-frozen river that had been running alongside the road for the past ten kilometres. The Haglebu River, according to the GPS on the phone in his lap. When he looked the other way he saw the steep, snow-covered side of the valley and dark fir forest. Ahead of them: the paved road that swallowed up the light of the headlamps and wound, narrow and predictable, towards mountains, more forest and wilderness. He had read that there were supposed to be brown bears in the area.

And as the sides of the valley towered above them, the voice on the radio—which in between tracks announced that they were listening to *nationwide* P10 Country—lost all credibility when it was intermittently replaced by static or disappeared altogether.

Harry turned the radio off.

Bjørn turned it back on again. Adjusted the dial. Crackling and a sense of post-apocalyptic empty space.

"DAB killed the radio star," Harry said.

"Not at all," Bjørn said. "They've got a local station here." A razor-sharp steel guitar suddenly cut through the static. "There!" He grinned. "Radio Hallingdal. Best country channel in Norway."

"You still can't drive without country music, then?"

"Come on, driving and country music are like gin and tonic," Bjørn said. "And they have radio bingo every Saturday. Just listen!"

The steel guitar faded away and, sure enough, a voice announced that it was time to have your bingo cards ready, especially in Flå, where, for the first time ever, all five winners two Saturdays before had lived. Then the steel guitar was back at full volume again.

"Can we turn it down?" Harry said, looking at the glowing screen of his phone.

"You can handle a bit of country, Harry. I gave you that Ramones album because it's country in disguise. You really need to listen to 'I Wanted Everything' and 'Don't Come Close.'"

"Kaja's calling."

Bjørn turned the radio off and Harry put the phone to his ear. "Hi, Kaja."

"Hi! Where are you?"

"Eggedal."

"Where in Eggedal?"

Harry looked outside. "Somewhere near the bottom."

"You don't know?"

"No."

"OK. I haven't found out anything specific on Roar Bohr. He hasn't got a criminal record, and none of the people I've spoken to have said anything to suggest that he's a potential murderer. Quite the reverse, in fact, they all describe him as a very considerate man. Almost overprotective when it comes to his own children and troops. I spoke to an employee at the NHRI who said the same."

"Hang on. How did you get them to talk?"

"I told them I'm working on a flattering profile piece about Roar Bohr's time in Afghanistan for the Red Cross magazine."

"So you're lying to them?"

"Not really. I might be working on that article. Maybe I just haven't asked the Red Cross if they're interested yet."

"Sneaky. Go on."

"When I asked the member of staff at the NHRI how Bohr had taken Rakel Fauke's murder, she said he had seemed upset and exhausted, that he'd taken a lot of time off in the past few days and had reported sick today. I asked what sort of relationship Bohr and Rakel had, and she said Bohr had kept an extra eye on Rakel."

"An extra eye? Did she mean that he looked out for her?"

"I don't know, but that's how she put it."

"You said you didn't have anything *specific* on Bohr. Does that mean you've something non-specific?"

"Yes. Like I said, Bohr hasn't got a criminal record, but I did find one old case when I searched for his name in the archive. It turns out that a Margaret Bohr went to the police in 1988 because her seventeen-year-old daughter, Bianca, had been raped. The mother claimed her daughter was showing behaviour typical of a rape victim, and had cuts on her stomach and hands. The police interviewed Bianca, but she denied she'd been raped and said she had inflicted those cuts herself. According to the report there were suspicions of incest, and Bianca's father and her older brother, Roar Bohr, who was then in his twenties, were among the suspects mentioned. Later on, both the father and Bianca were briefly admitted to hospital for psychiatric treatment. But it was never discovered what—if anything—had happened. When I searched for Bianca Bohr, a report from Sigdal Police Station popped up from five years later. Bianca Bohr had been found dead on the rocks at the bottom of the twenty-metre-high falls at Norafossen. The Bohr family's cabin is four kilometres farther up the river."

"Sigdal. Is that the same cabin we're on our way to?"

"I assume so. The post-mortem showed that Bianca died from drowning. The police concluded that she could have fallen into the river by accident, but that it was more likely that she had taken her own life."

"Why?"

"A witness had seen Bianca running barefoot through the snow along the path between the cabin and the river, wearing only a blue dress. It's several hundred metres from the cabin to the river. And she was naked when she was found. Her psychiatrist also confirmed that she had previously shown suicidal tendencies. I managed to find his phone number, and left a message on his answer machine."

"OK."

"Still in Eggedal?"

"Presumably."

Bjørn turned the radio back on, and a voice monotonously reading out numbers, repeating them digit by digit, merged with the sound of the studded tires on the pavement. The forest and darkness seemed to be getting denser, the sides of the valley steeper.

Bohr rested the rifle on the thickest, lowest branch and looked through the telescopic sight. Saw the red dot dance across the wooden wall before it found the window. It was dark in there, but the man was on his way. The man who needed to be stopped before he ruined everything was going to come, Bohr just knew it. It was simply a matter of time. And time was the only thing Roar Bohr had left.

"It's right up this hill," Harry said, looking at the phone screen, where a red teardrop-shaped symbol marked the coordinates Kaja had given him. They were parked by the side of the road and Bjørn had switched the engine and lights off. Harry leaned forward and peered out through the windshield, where light rain had started to fall. There were no lights anywhere on the black hillside. "Looks pretty sparsely populated."

"We'd better take some beads for the natives," Bjørn said, taking a flashlight and his service pistol from the glove compartment.

"I was thinking I'd go up there alone," Harry said.

"And leave me here on my own when I'm scared of the dark?"

"You remember what I said about laser sights?" Harry put his index finger to his forehead. "I'm still marked after Smestaddammen. This is my project, and you're on paternity leave."

"You've seen those discussions in films where the woman nags the hero to let her join in something dangerous?"

"Yes . . ."

"I usually fast-forward those bits, because I know who's going to win. Shall we go?"

28

"Sure it's this cabin?" Bjørn asked.

"According to the GPS, yes," said Harry, who was holding his coat over his phone. Partly to shield it from the rain that had replaced the snow showers, and partly to stop the glow from giving away their position if Bohr was looking out for them. Because *if* he was in the cabin, the darkness inside suggested that that was precisely what he was doing. Harry screwed his eyes up. They had found a trail that ran partially across bare ground, and the brown marks where there was snow indicated that it had been used recently. It hadn't taken more than fifteen minutes to find. The snow on the ground reflected the light, but it was still too dark for them to be able to make out what colour the cabin was. Harry was putting his money on red. The rain had camouflaged the sound as they approached, but now it was also muffling any noises from inside the cabin.

"I'll go in, you wait here," Harry said.

"I need a bit more instruction, I've been in Forensics too long."

"Shoot if you see someone who isn't me shooting," Harry said, then got out from under the low, dripping branches and strode towards the cabin.

There were regulations for how to enter a house if you thought you might encounter armed resistance. Harry knew some of them. Roar Bohr probably knew them all. So there was no point overthinking it. Harry walked up to the door and tried the handle. Locked. He moved to the side of the door and banged on it twice.

"Police!"

He leaned against the wall and listened. All he could hear was the persistent rain. And a twig snapping somewhere. He stared out into the darkness, but it was like a solid black wall. He counted to five, then hit the pane of glass beside the door with the butt of his pistol. The glass shattered. He reached inside and loosened the window catch. The frame had swollen, and he had to grab it hard and pull. He climbed inside. Inhaled the spice-like smell of fresh birch wood and ash. He turned on his flashlight, holding it away from his body in case anyone felt like using it as a target. He swept the beam around the room until it found a light switch by the door. Harry clicked it and the ceiling lamp came on, and he hurried to stand with his back against the wall between the windows. He looked around the room, from left to right, like he would at a crime scene. He was in the living room, from which two doors led to bedrooms containing bunk beds. No bathroom. A kitchen worktop with a sink and a radio at one end of the room. An open fireplace. Typical Norwegian cabin furniture—pine—a painted wooden chest, and a submachine gun and automatic rifle leaning against the wall. A table with a crocheted tablecloth and candlesticks, a sports magazine, two glinting hunting knives and a game of Yahtzee. Printed sheets of A4 were pinned to the walls all around the room. Harry stopped breathing when he saw Rakel beside the fireplace. The picture showed her standing behind a barred window. The kitchen window at Holmenkollveien. It must have been taken from right in front of the wildlife camera.

Harry forced himself to carry on looking round.

Above the dining table were photographs of more women, some with newspaper cuttings beneath them. And when Harry turned to look at the wall behind him he saw more pictures. Of men. Around a dozen, pinned in three columns, numbered according to some sort of ranking system. He recognised three of them at once. Number 1 was Anton Blix, who had been convicted of several rapes and a double murder ten years ago. Number 2 was Svein Finne. And further down, at number 6, Valentin Gjertsen. Now Harry thought he recognised some of the others as well. Well-known violent criminals, at least one of them dead and a couple more still in prison, as far as he was aware. He peered over at the newspaper cuttings on the other side of the room, and managed to make out one bold headline: *Raped in Park*. The print of the others was too small.

If he stepped closer, he would make himself a target from outside. But, of course, he could switch the lamp off and just use his flashlight. Harry's eyes turned towards the switch, but found Rakel again.

He couldn't see her face, but there was something about the way she was standing inside the window. Like a deer that had raised its head, pricked up its ears. That scented danger. Perhaps that was why she looked so alone. While she's waiting for me, Harry thought. The way I waited for her. Two of us, waiting.

Harry realised he'd stepped out into the room, into the light, visible to anyone and everyone. What the hell was he doing? He closed his eyes.

And waited.

Roar Bohr had the crosshairs on the back of the person in the illuminated room. He had switched off the laser sight that had given him away when Pia and Hole were sitting on the bench beside Smestaddammen. The raindrops rustled in the trees above him, dripping from the brim of his cap. He waited.

Nothing happened.

Harry opened his eyes. Started breathing again.

And read the newspaper clippings.

Some of them had turned yellow, some were just a couple of years old. Reports of rapes. No names, just ages, locations, an outline of what happened. Oslo, Østlandet. One in Stavanger. God knows how Bohr had got hold of the photographs, but Harry had no doubt that they were the rape victims. So what about the pictures of the men? A sort of top-ten list of the worst—or possibly best—rapists in Norway? Something for Roar Bohr to aspire to, to measure himself against?

Harry unlocked the front door and opened it. "Bjørn! The coast's clear!"

He looked at the picture that was pinned up beside the door. Sharp sunlight in squinting green eyes, a hand brushing aside a strand of honey-brown hair, a white vest with the Red Cross on it, desert landscape, Kaja smiling with those pointed teeth.

Harry looked down. Saw the same military boots he had seen in Bohr's hallway.

The rocks in the desert. The Taliban waiting for number two to get out of the bulletproof car.

"No, Bjørn! No!"

"Kaja Solness," the almost exaggeratedly deep voice from the black stone slab beside the stove.

"Officer in the Oslo Police," Kaja said loudly as she scanned the shelves of the fridge in vain for something to eat.

"And how can I help you, Officer Solness?"

"We're looking for a serial attacker." She poured herself a glass of apple juice in the hope of getting her blood sugar up a bit. She checked the time. A relaxed local restaurant had opened on Vibes gate since she was last home. "Obviously I'm aware that as a psychiatrist you're under an oath of confidentiality when it comes to patients who are still alive, but this concerns a deceased patient . . ."

"Same rules."

". . . whom we suspect may have been raped by someone we want to prevent from raping others."

There was silence at the other end.

"Let me know when you've finished thinking, London." She didn't know why the man's surname, one of the biggest cities in the world, seemed to suggest loneliness. She switched off the speaker function on her phone, and took it and the glass of juice back into the living room.

"Go ahead and ask, and we'll see," he said.

"Thanks. Do you remember a patient called Bianca Bohr?"

"Yes." He said this in a tone that told Kaja that he also remembered what had happened to her.

"When you were seeing her as a patient, did you think she had been raped?"

"I don't know."

"OK. Did she show any behaviour that might indicate—"

"The behaviour of psychiatric patients can indicate a lot of things. I wouldn't rule out rape. Or assault. Or other traumas. But that's just speculation."

"Her father was also admitted for mental health problems. Did she ever talk about him?"

"During conversations between psychiatrists and patients we almost always talk about their relationship to their parents, but I can't recall anything that struck me in particular."

"OK." Kaja tapped a key on her computer and the screen came back to life. The frozen image showed the silhouette of a person leaving Rakel's house. "What about her older brother, Roar?"

Another long pause. Kaja took a sip from the glass and looked out at the garden.

"You're talking about a serial attacker who's still on the loose?"

"Yes," Kaja said.

"During the period that Bianca was an inpatient with us, one of the nurses noted that she had repeatedly screamed a name in her sleep. The name you just mentioned."

"Do you think that Bianca could have been raped, not by her father, but by her older brother?"

"Like I said, Solness, I can't rule out—"

"But the thought has occurred to you, hasn't it?"

Kaja listened to the sound of his breathing in an attempt to interpret it, but all she heard was the rain outside.

"Bianca did tell me something, but I have to stress that she was psychotic, and when suffering from psychosis patients say all sorts of things."

"What did she say?"

"That her brother had performed an abortion on her at the family's cabin."

Kaja shuddered.

"Naturally, that needn't necessarily have happened," London said. "But I remember a drawing she had pinned up above the bed in her room. It was a large eagle swooping down over a little boy. And out of the bird's beak came the letters R-O-A-R."

"As in the English verb?"

"That was how I chose to interpret it at the time, yes."

"But in hindsight?"

Kaja heard him sigh loudly, out there in telephone-land. "It's quite typical that when a patient takes their own life, you imagine that you misinterpreted everything, that everything you did and thought was wrong. When Bianca died, we thought she was actually getting better. So I looked through my old notes to see what I had misunderstood, where I'd gone wrong. And I discovered that on two occasions—which I had dismissed as psychotic babbling—she told me that they had killed her big brother."

"Who are 'they'?"

"She herself, and her older brother."

"What does that mean? That Roar took part in killing himself?"

Roar Bohr lowered the butt of the rifle, but left the barrel resting on the branch.

The person he'd had in his sights had moved away from the illuminated window.

He took in the sounds of the darkness around him.

Rain. The sound of tires on wet pavement not far away. He guessed a Volvo. They liked Volvos here on Lyder Sagens gate. And Volkswagens. Estates. The expensive models. In Smestad it was more Audis and BMWs. The gardens here weren't as obsessively neat as in his neighbourhood, but the more relaxed look didn't necessarily take any less work and planning. Kaja's wilderness of a garden was the exception; anarchy ruled here. In her defence, she hadn't lived at home much in the past few years. And he wasn't complaining. The overgrown shrubs and trees gave him better camouflage than in Kabul. Once he'd had to hide behind a burned-out car on top of a garage roof, where he had been far too exposed, but it was the only place where he had a complete view of the hostel where the girls lived. He had spent enough hours there watching Kaja Solness through the sights of his rifle to know that she wouldn't let a garden get overgrown unless she had more important things to do. And she did. People do so many peculiar things when they think they're not being seen, and Roar Bohr knew things about Kaja Solness that other people had no idea about. With his Swarovski rifle sight he could easily read the text on the screen of the computer on her desk when Kaja wasn't sitting in the way. And now she had just tapped a key to make the screen light up. There was an image on the screen. Taken at night, it showed a house with one window lit up.

It took Bohr a few moments to realise that he was looking at Rakel's house.

He adjusted the sight and brought the screen into focus. He saw that it wasn't a still picture but a recording. It must have been filmed from where he used to stand. What the hell? Then the door of Rakel's house opened and a figure was silhouetted in the opening. Bohr held his breath so that the rifle was completely still and he could read the date and time at the bottom of the clip.

It was from the night of the murder.

Roar Bohr let the air out of his lungs and leaned his rifle against the trunk of the tree.

Was the image good enough for the person to be identified?

He ran his left hand over his hip. Over the *karambit* knife.

Think. Think, then act.

His fingertip slid over the cold, serrated edge of the steel. Up and down. Up and down.

. . .

"Watch out," Harry said by way of warning.

"What now?" Bjørn asked. Harry didn't know if Bjørn was referring to his exclamation up at the cabin, which had turned out to be groundless.

"Freezing rain."

"I can see," Bjørn said, and braked gently before turning onto the bridge in front of them.

It had stopped raining, but a film of ice was glinting on the road ahead of them. The road straightened out again after they crossed the river, and Bjørn accelerated. A sign. *Oslo 85 kilometres.* There weren't many vehicles on the road, and if they got a bit of dry road under their tires they could be back in the city in just over an hour.

"Are you *quite* sure you don't want to issue an alert?" Bjørn asked.

"Mm." Harry closed his eyes. Roar Bohr had been at the cabin recently, the newspaper in the wood basket was six days old. But he wasn't there now. No tracks in the snow outside the door. No food. Mould on the dregs of coffee in the cup on the table. The boots by the door were dry, he must have several pairs. "I called that 3-D expert, Freund. His first name's Sigurd, by the way."

Bjørn chuckled. "Katrine suggested we should name the kid after the singer in Suede. Brett. Brett Bratt. What did Freund have to say?"

"That he was going to look at the memory card, and that I could expect a response at the weekend. I explained what was on it, and he said there wasn't much he could do about the lack of light. But by measuring the height of the doorway and the tread of the steps at Holmenkollveien he reckoned he could give me the height of the person down to the nearest centimetre. If I say that we need to bring Bohr in as a result of what we found after breaking into his cabin without a search warrant, you'd get into trouble as well, Bjørn. It makes more sense to use the fact that the height of the guy in the doorway matches Bohr's, because there's no way you can be linked to those images. I'll call Kripos, explain that I've got pictures proving that Bohr was at the crime scene, and suggest that they search his cabin. They'll find a broken window, but anyone could have done that."

Harry saw flashing blue lights at the end of the straight stretch of road in front of them. They passed a warning triangle. Bjørn slowed down.

An articulated truck was parked by the verge on their side of the road. On the other side lay the wreckage of a car next to the crash barrier in front of the river. What had once been a car reminded Harry of a crushed tin can.

A policeman waved them past.

"Hang on," Harry said, winding his window down. "That car's got Oslo plates."

Bjørn stopped the Amazon next to a policeman with a face like a bulldog, a neck and arms that looked too short sticking out from his over-pumped upper body.

"What's happened?" Harry asked, holding up his ID.

The policeman looked at it and nodded. "The truck driver's being questioned, so we should know soon enough. It's icy, so it *could* just be an accident."

"It's a bit straight for that, isn't it?"

"Yes," the police officer said, composing his face into a professional sombre expression. "At worst, we have one a month. We call this stretch of road the green mile. You know, that last walk people sentenced to death in America take on their way to the chair."

"Mm. We're looking for a guy who lives in Oslo, so it would be interesting to know who was driving the car."

The policeman took a deep breath. "To be honest, when a car weighing one thousand three hundred kilos drives at eighty or ninety kilometres an hour into the front of an almost-fifty-ton truck, seat belts and airbags aren't a lot of use. I couldn't tell you if my own brother had been driving that car. Or my sister, come to that. But the car's registered to a Stein Hansen, so for the time being we're working on the assumption that it's him."

"Thanks," Harry said, and closed the window.

They drove on in silence.

"You seem relieved," Bjørn said after a while.

"Do I?" Harry said in surprise.

"You think it would be too easy if Bohr had got away like that, don't you?"

"Dying in a car crash?"

"I mean, leaving you in this world to suffer alone every day. That wouldn't be fair, would it? You want him to suffer the same way."

Harry looked out of the window. Moonlight was shining through a gap in the clouds, colouring the ice on the river silver.

Bjørn turned the radio on.

The Highwaymen.

Harry listened for a while, then he got his phone out and called Kaja.

No answer.

Weird.

He tried again.

He waited until her voicemail kicked in. Her voice. The memory of Rakel's. The bleep. Harry cleared his throat. "It's me. Call me."

She probably had her headphones on, listening to loud music again.

The wipers cleared the windshield. Over and over again. A fresh start, a blank page every three seconds. The never-ending absolution of sin.

Two-tone yodelling and banjo music played on the radio.

29

Two and a half years earlier

Roar Bohr wiped the sweat from his forehead and looked up at the sky above the desert.

The sun had melted, that was why he couldn't see it. It had dissolved, spreading out like a layer of golden copper across the hazy blue. And beneath it: a monk vulture, its three-metre wingspan etching a black cross on the yellow copper.

Bohr looked around again. There were only the two of them out here. The two of them, and open, empty, stony desert, sloping hillsides and rocky outcrops. Obviously it was a breach of operational safety manuals to drive out into the field without more protection, just two men in one vehicle. But in his report he would say he judged it to be a gesture to Hala's home village, an appeal to Afghan hearts, that Hala's boss had driven her body home in person, with no more protection than she herself had had.

One more month, then he'd be going home, home from his third and final tour in Afghanistan. He was longing to go home, he always longed to go home, but he wasn't happy. Because he knew that when he got home, after just two or three weeks he would start longing to be back here again.

But there weren't going to be any more tours, he had applied and been accepted to fill the post of head of the NHRI in Oslo, a newly established national institute for human rights. The NHRI was subject to Parliament, but operated as an independent body. They would be investigating human rights issues, providing information and advice to the national assembly, though beyond that their remit was rather vague. But that just meant that he and the eighteen other members of staff could influence what their purpose should be. In many ways it was a sort of continuation of what he had been doing in Afghanistan, just without guns. So he was going to take the job. He wasn't going to end up being a general, in any case. That was the sort of thing they let you know in a very respectful, discreet manner. That you weren't one of the chosen few. But that wasn't why he had to get away from Afghanistan.

In his mind's eye he could see Hala lying on the ground. She was usually dressed in Western clothes and a modest hijab, but that night she had been wearing a blue *shalwar kameez* tunic that was pulled up around her waist. Bohr remembered her bare hips and stomach, the skin with that glow that would slowly fade. The way the life in those beautiful, beautiful eyes had faded. Even when she was dead, Hala had looked like Bianca. He had noticed when she introduced herself as his interpreter, that Bianca was looking out through those eyes, that she had come back from the dead, from the river, to be with him again. But obviously Hala couldn't know that, it wasn't the sort of thing he could ever have explained to her. And now she was gone too.

But he had found someone else who resembled Bianca. The head of security at the Red Cross. Kaja Solness. Maybe that was where Bianca lived now, inside her? Or in someone else. He'd have to keep his eyes open.

"Don't do it," the man begged as he knelt on the ground behind the Land Rover, parked by the side of the road. His light-coloured camouflage uniform had three stripes on the chest to indicate that he was a sergeant, and on his left arm was the insignia of the Special Forces Division: a winged dagger. His hands were clasped. But perhaps that was only because his wrists were bound together with the narrow white cable ties they used on prisoners of war. A five-metre-long chain ran from the cable ties to a hook on the back of the Land Rover.

"Let me go, Bohr. I've got money. An inheritance. I can keep quiet if you can. No one needs to know what's happened, ever."

"And what has happened?" Bohr asked, without taking the barrel of his Colt Canada C8 from the sergeant's forehead.

The officer swallowed. "An Afghan woman. A Hazara. Everyone knows you and she were close, but as long as no one makes a fuss it will soon be forgotten."

"You shouldn't have told anyone what you saw, Waage. That's why I have to kill you. You wouldn't forget. I wouldn't forget."

"Two million. Two million kroner, Bohr. No, two and a half. In cash, when we get to Norway."

Roar Bohr started to walk towards the Land Rover.

"No! No!" his soldier screamed. "You're not a murderer, Bohr!"

Bohr got in, started the engine and began to drive. He didn't notice any resistance when the chain jerked the sergeant to his feet and he started to run after the vehicle.

Bohr slowed down. He speeded up again whenever the chain started to slacken. He watched the sergeant as he ran along in a sort of stumbling jog with his hands held out as if in prayer.

Forty degrees. Even at walking pace the sergeant would soon dehydrate. He wouldn't be able to stay on his feet, he'd collapse. A farmer with a horse and cart was driving towards them on the road. As he passed them the sergeant cried out to him, begging for help, but the farmer merely bowed his turbaned head and looked down at the reins. Foreigners. Taliban. Their war wasn't his—his war was against drought, against starvation, against the never-ending demands and torments of daily life.

Bohr leaned forward and looked at the sky.

The monk vulture was following them.

No one's prayers were granted. No one's.

"Sure you don't want me to wait?" Bjørn asked.

"Get home, they'll be waiting," Harry said, peering out of the car window at Kaja's house. The lights in the living room were on.

Harry got out and lit the cigarette he hadn't been allowed to smoke in the car.

"New rules with kids," Bjørn had explained. "Katrine doesn't want any trace of smoke anywhere."

"Mm. They sort of seize power the moment they become mothers, don't they?"

Bjørn had shrugged. "I don't know about seizing it. Katrine pretty much had it already."

Harry took four deep drags. Then he pinched the cigarette out and put it back in the packet. The gate creaked when he opened it. Water dripped from the iron, it had been raining here too.

He walked up to the door and rang the bell. Waited.

After ten seconds of silence he tried the handle. Unlocked, like last time. With a feeling of déjà vu he went inside, past the open door to the kitchen. He saw a phone charging on the kitchen worktop. That explained why she hadn't answered his calls. Maybe. He opened the door to the living room.

Empty.

He was about to call Kaja's name when his brain registered a sound behind him, the creak of a floorboard. In the space of a nano-second, his brain had reasoned out that it was obviously Kaja coming downstairs or out of the toilet, so it didn't sound the alarm.

Not until an arm was squeezing his throat and a cloth was pressed against his mouth and nose. As his brain registered the danger it sent an automatic command to take a deep breath before the cloth completely blocked the supply of air. And by the time his slower cognitive process told him that was precisely the point of the cloth, it was too late.

30

Harry looked around. He was in a ballroom. An orchestra was playing, a slow waltz. He caught sight of her. She was sitting at a white-clothed table under one of the crystal chandeliers. The two men in dinner jackets standing on either side of her were trying to get her attention. But her eyes were focused on him, on Harry. They were telling him to hurry up. She was wearing the black dress, the one of several black dresses that she called *the* black dress. And when Harry looked down at himself he saw that he was wearing the black suit, his only one, the one he wore for christenings, weddings and funerals. He put one foot in front of the other and made his way through the tables, but it went slowly, as if the room were filled with water. There must be a lot of swell on the surface, because he pulled forward, then back, and the S-shaped chandeliers were swinging in time to the waltz. Just as he got there, just as he was about to say something and let go of the table, his feet lifted from the floor and he began to rise up. She stretched out her hand towards his, but he was already out of reach, and even if she stood up from her chair and stretched towards him, she remained where she was as he rose higher and higher. And then he discovered that the water was starting to turn red, so red that she receded from view, red and warm, and the pressure in his head began to rise. He didn't realise at first that he couldn't breathe, of course he couldn't, and he began to flail about, he had to get to the surface.

"Good evening, Harry."

Harry opened his eyes. The light cut like a knife and he closed them again.

"Trichloromethane. Better known as chloroform. A bit old-school, of course, but effective. We used it in E14 whenever someone needed kidnapping."

Harry opened his eyes a crack. A lamp was shining directly into his face.

"You probably have a lot of questions." The voice was coming from the darkness behind the lamp. "Like 'What happened?' and 'Where am I?' and 'Who is he?'"

They had only exchanged a few words at the funeral, but Harry still recognised the voice and the hint of rolled "r"s. "But let me answer the question you're wondering about most, Harry: 'What does he want with me?'"

"Bohr," Harry said hoarsely. "Where's Kaja?"

"Don't worry about that, Harry."

Harry could tell from the acoustics that he was seated in a large room. Probably wooden walls. Not a basement, then. But it was cold and raw, as if it wasn't in use. The smell was neutral, like in a meeting hall or open-plan office. That could make sense. His arms were taped to the armrests of the chair and his feet to the wheeled base of an office chair. No smell of paint or building work, but he saw the light reflect off transparent plastic that had been laid on the parquet floor beneath and in front of the chair.

"Have you killed Kaja as well, Bohr?"

"As well?"

"Like Rakel. And the other girls you've got pictures of in your cabin."

Harry heard the other man's footsteps behind the lamp.

"I have a confession to make, Harry. I have killed. I didn't think I could do it, but it turned out I was wrong." The steps stopped. "And they say that once you've started . . ."

Harry leaned his head back and looked up at the ceiling. One of the panels had been removed, and a load of severed cables were sticking out. IT stuff, presumably.

"I heard a rumour that one of my guys in Special Forces, Waage, knew something about the murder of my interpreter, Hala. And when I checked and found out what he knew, I realised I was going to have to kill him."

Harry coughed. "He was on your trail. So you killed him. And now you're planning to kill me. I have no interest in being your confessor, Bohr, so just get on with the execution."

"You misunderstand me, Harry."

"When everyone misunderstands you, Bohr, it's time to ask yourself if you're mad. Get on with it, you poor bastard, I'm done."

"You're in a hell of a hurry."

"Maybe it's better there than here. Might be more pleasant company too."

"You misunderstand me, Harry. Let me explain."

"No!" Harry tugged at the chair, but the tape held him down.

"Listen. Please. I didn't kill Rakel."

"I *know* you killed Rakel, Bohr. I don't want to hear about it, and I don't want to hear any pathetic excuses—"

Harry stopped when Roar Bohr's face suddenly came into view, lit up from below, like in a horror film. It took Harry a moment to realise that the light was coming from a phone on the table between them, and that it had just started to ring.

Bohr looked at it. "Your phone, Harry. It's Kaja Solness."

Bohr touched the screen, picked the phone up and held it to Harry's ear.

"Harry?" It was Kaja's voice.

Harry cleared his throat. "Where . . . where are you?"

"I just got in. I saw you'd called, but I needed to eat so I went to the new restaurant around the corner and left my phone charging at home. Tell me, have you been here?"

"Here?"

"My computer has been moved from the desk to the living-room table. Tell me it was you, or I'll start to worry."

Harry stared into the lamplight.

"Harry? Where are you? You sound so—"

"It was me," Harry said. "Nothing to worry about. Listen, I'm in the middle of something right now. I'll call you later, OK?"

"OK," she said, sounding doubtful.

Bohr tapped to end the call and put the phone on the table. "Why didn't you sound the alarm?"

"If there was any point in doing that, you wouldn't have let me speak to her."

"I think it's because you believe me, Harry."

"You've got me taped to a chair. What I think is completely irrelevant."

Bohr stepped into the light again. He was holding a large, broad-bladed knife. Harry tried to swallow but his mouth was too dry. Bohr moved the knife closer to Harry. To the underside of the right armrest of the chair. Cut. Did the same with the left armrest. Harry lifted his arms and took the knife.

"I taped you to the chair so you wouldn't attack me before you'd heard everything," Bohr said as Harry cut through the tape around his ankles. "Rakel told me about the problems you and she had had in relation to a couple of your murder investigations. From people who were on the loose. So I kept an eye on you both."

"Us?"

"Mostly her. I kept watch. Like I kept watch on Kaja in Kabul after Hala was raped and murdered. And now in Oslo."

"You know that's called paranoia?"

"Yes."

"Mm." Harry straightened up and rubbed his lower arms. He kept hold of the knife. "Tell me."

"Where do you want me to start?"

"Start with the sergeant."

"Understood. No one in Special Forces is an idiot, exactly. The entrance criteria are too strict for that. But Sergeant Waage was one of those soldiers with more testosterone than brains, if I can put it like that. In the days following Hala's death, when everyone was talking about her, I heard that someone had said Hala must like Norway because she had a Norwegian word tattooed on her body. I looked into the matter and found out that it was Sergeant Waage who had said this after a few drinks in the bar. But Hala was always covered up, and that tattoo was right above her heart. There was no way she would have got mixed up with Waage. And I know Hala kept the tattoo secret. Even if the use of henna is widespread, many Muslims regard permanent tattoos as a 'sin of the skin.'"

"Mm. But the tattoo wasn't a secret from you?"

"No. I was the only person apart from the tattooist who knew about it. Before she got the tattoo, Hala asked me about the correct spelling, and any possible double meanings she might not have been aware of."

"What was the word?"

Bohr smiled sadly. "'Friend.' She had such a fascination with languages, she wanted to know if the different spellings of the word meant different things, had different connotations."

"Waage could have heard about the tattoo from the people who found her or conducted the post-mortem."

"That's the point," Bohr said. "Two of the knife wounds . . ." He stopped, took a deep, shuddering breath. "Two of the *sixteen* knife wounds had pierced the tattoo, making the word illegible unless you already knew what it said."

"Unless you were the person who raped her and saw the tattoo before you began to stab her."

"Yes."

"I understand, but that doesn't exactly count as proof, Bohr."

"No. Under the immunity regulations covering international forces, Waage would have been sent back to Norway, where any half-decent lawyer would have got him off the hook."

"So you appointed yourself judge and jury?"

Roar Bohr nodded. "Hala was my interpreter. My responsibility. The same with Sergeant Waage. My responsibility. I contacted Hala's parents and told them that I would personally be taking her earthly remains to their village. It was a five-hour drive from Kabul. Mostly empty desert. I ordered Waage to drive. After a couple of hours' driving I told him to stop, held a pistol to his head and got a confession. Then I tied him to the Land Rover and drove. So-called D and Q."

"D and Q?"

"Drawing and quartering. The penalty for high treason in England between 1283 and 1870. The condemned man was hanged until he was almost dead, then they cut his stomach open, pulled out his innards and burned them while he watched. Before they cut his head off. But before all that he was dragged to the gallows behind a horse, the *drawing*. And if it was a long way from the prison to the gallows, he might be fortunate enough to die at that point. Because when he could no longer walk or run after the horse, he got dragged along on his chest. The flesh got scraped off, layer by layer. It was a slow and extremely painful death."

Harry thought about the long trail of blood they had found on the ground.

"Hala's family were extremely grateful to have her body back home," Bohr said. "And for the corpse of her murderer. Or what was left of it. It was a beautiful burial ceremony."

"And the sergeant's body?"

"I don't know what they did with it. Quartering is probably an English thing. But decapitation is evidently pretty international, because his head was found on a pole outside the village."

"And you reported that the sergeant went missing on the way back?"

"Yes."

"Mm. Why do you watch over these women?"

Silence. Bohr had sat down on the edge of the table, and Harry tried to read the expression on his face.

"I had a sister." His voice was toneless. "Bianca. My younger sister. She was raped when she was seventeen. I should have been looking after her that evening, but I wanted to go and see *Die Hard* at the cinema. It was rated 18. It wasn't until several years later that she told me she was raped that evening. While I was watching Bruce Willis."

"Why didn't she tell you straightaway?"

Bohr took a deep breath. "The rapist threatened to kill me, her older brother, if she said anything. She didn't know how the rapist could have known she had an older brother."

"What did the rapist look like?"

"She never got a good look at him, she said it was too dark. Unless her mind had blocked it. I saw that happen in Sudan. Soldiers who experienced such terrible things that they simply forgot about them. They could wake up the next day and, perfectly sincerely, deny having been there and seen anything. For some people suppression works absolutely fine. For others it pops up later, in the form of flashbacks. Nightmares. I think everything came back to Bianca. And she couldn't handle it. The terror of it broke her."

"And you think it was your fault?"

"Of course it was my fault."

"You know you're damaged, don't you, Bohr?"

"Of course. Aren't you?"

"What were you doing in Kaja's house?"

"I saw that she had a video on her computer, a man leaving Rakel's house on the night of the murder. So when she went out, I went in to take a closer look at it."

"What did you find out?"

"Nothing. Poor-quality images. Then I heard the door. I left the living room and went into the kitchen."

"So you could approach me from behind in the hallway. And you just happened to have some chloroform on you?"

"I always have chloroform on me."

"Because?"

"Anyone who tried to break into any of my ladies' houses ends up in the chair where you're sitting."

"And?"

"And pays the price."

"Why are you telling me all this, Bohr?"

Bohr clasped his hands. "I have to admit that I thought you'd killed Rakel at first, Harry."

"Oh?"

"The spurned husband. It's the classic, isn't it? The first thing you think. And I thought I could tell from the look in your eyes at the funeral. A mixture of innocence and remorse. The look that belongs to someone who's killed for no other motive than their own hatred and lust, and who regrets it. Who regrets it so much that he's managed to suppress it. Because that's the only way he can survive, the truth is too unbearable. I saw that look in Sergeant Waage. It was as if he'd managed to forget what he'd done to Hala, and only remembered it again when I confronted him with it. But then, when I found out that you had an alibi, I realised that the guilt I'd seen in your eyes was the same I felt. Guilt because you hadn't been able to prevent it happening. And the reason why I'm telling you this . . ."—Bohr got up from the table and disappeared into the darkness as he went on—"is because I know you want the same thing as me. You want to see them punished. They took someone we loved away from us. Prison isn't enough. An easy death isn't enough."

The fluorescent lights flickered a few times, then the room was bathed in light.

Sure enough, it was an office. Or had been. The six or seven desks, the pale patches where computers had stood, the wastepaper bins, random office equipment, a printer—everything suggested that the office had been abandoned in some haste. There was a picture of the king hanging on the white wooden wall. Military people, Harry thought automatically.

"Shall we go?" Bohr asked.

Harry stood up. He felt dizzy and walked rather unsteadily towards the wooden door where Bohr was waiting, holding Harry's phone, pistol and lighter out towards him.

"Where were you?" Harry asked as he put the phone and lighter away and weighed the pistol in his hand. "The night Rakel was killed? Because you weren't at home . . ."

"It was a weekend, I was at the cabin," Bohr said. "In Eggedal. Alone, I'm afraid."

"What were you doing there?"

"Yes, what was I doing? Polishing weapons. Keeping the stove alight. Thinking. Listening to the radio."

"Mm. Radio Hallingdal?"

"Yes, actually, it's the only station you can get there."

"They had radio bingo that night."

"They did. Do you spend a lot of time in Hallingdal?"

"No. Do you remember anything special?"

Bohr raised an eyebrow. "About the bingo?"

"Yes."

Bohr shook his head.

"Nothing?" Harry said, feeling the weight of the pistol. He concluded that the bullets hadn't been removed from the magazine.

"No. Is this an interview?"

"Think."

Bohr frowned. "Maybe something about all the winners being from the same place? Ål. Or Flå."

"Bingo," Harry said quietly, and put the pistol in his coat pocket. "You're hereby removed from my list of suspects."

Roar Bohr looked at Harry. "I could have killed you in there without anyone finding out. But *radio bingo* is what got me off your list?"

Harry shrugged. "I need a cigarette."

They walked down some worn, creaking wooden steps and out into the night as a clock started to chime.

"Bloody hell," Harry said, breathing in the cold air. In the square in front of them people were hurrying towards bars and restaurants, and above the rooftops he could see the City Hall. "We're in the middle of the city."

Harry had heard the City Hall bells play both Kraftwerk and Dolly Parton, and once Oleg had been delighted to recognise a tune from the game Minecraft. But this time they were playing one of the regular tunes, "Watchman's Song" by Edvard Grieg. Which meant it was midnight.

Harry turned around. The building they had come out of was a barrack-like wooden building just inside the gates of Akershus Fortress.

"Not exactly MI6 or Langley," Bohr said. "But this did actually used to be the headquarters of E14."

"E14?" Harry dug out his packet of cigarettes from his trouser pocket.

"A short-lived Norwegian espionage organisation."

"I vaguely remember it."

"Started in 1995, spent a few years doing James Bond–style action stuff, then there were power struggles and political rows about its methods, until it was shut down in 2006. The building's been empty since then."

"But you've got the keys?"

"I was here for its last few years. No one ever asked for them back."

"Mm. A former spy. That explains the chloroform."

Bohr smiled wryly. "Oh, we did more interesting things than that."

"I don't doubt it." Harry nodded towards the clock on the City Hall tower.

"Sorry I ruined your evening," Bohr said. "Can I bum a cigarette off you before we call it a night?"

"I was a young officer when I was recruited," Bohr said, blowing smoke up towards the sky. He and Harry had found a bench on the ramparts behind the cannons pointing out across the Oslo Fjord. "It wasn't just people from the military in E14. There were diplomats, waiters, carpenters, police officers, mathematicians. Beautiful women who could be used as bait."

"Sounds like a spy film," Harry said, sucking on his own cigarette.

"It *was* a spy film."

"What was the mandate?"

"Gathering information from places Norway could imagine having a military presence. The Balkans, the Middle East, Sudan, Afghanistan. We were given a lot of freedom; we were supposed to operate independently of the American intelligence network and NATO. For a while it actually looked like we might manage it. A strong sense of camaraderie, a lot of loyalty. And maybe a bit too much freedom. In closed environments like that you end up developing your own standards for what is acceptable. We paid women to have sex with our contacts. We equipped ourselves with unregistered High Standard HD 22 pistols."

Harry nodded. That was the pistol he had seen in Bohr's cabin, the pistol CIA agents preferred because it had a lightweight and efficient silencer. The pistol the Soviets found on Francis Gary Powers, the pilot of the U2 spy plane that was shot down over Soviet territory in 1960.

"With no serial numbers, they couldn't be traced back to us if we ever had to use them for liquidation."

"And you did all that?"

"Not the bit about paying for sex or liquidating anyone. The worst thing I did . . ." Bohr rubbed his chin thoughtfully. "Or the one that *felt* worst . . . was the first time I deliberately got someone to trust me, then betrayed them. Part of the admission test was to get from Oslo to Trondheim as quickly as possible with only ten kroner in your pocket. The point was to show you had the social skills and imagination that an active situation might require. I offered the money to a kind-looking woman at the Central Station in return for borrowing her phone to call my mortally ill younger sister in the district hospital in Trondheim, to tell her that my luggage had just been stolen, along with my wallet, train ticket and phone. I called one of the other agents and managed to cry on the phone. When I hung up the woman was crying as well, and I was just about to ask to borrow money for the train fare when she offered to drive me in her car, which was in the car park next to the station. We drove as fast as we could. The hours passed, and we talked about everything, our deepest secrets, the way you only do with strangers. My secrets were lies I had learned, good training for someone hoping to be a spy. We stopped at Dovre after four hours. Watched the sun go down over the plateau. Kissed. Smiled through the tears and said we loved each other. Two hours later, just before midnight, she dropped me off in front of the main entrance to the hospital. I told her to find somewhere to park while I found out where my sister was. I said I'd wait in reception. I walked straight through the reception area, out through the other side, and ran as fast as I could to the statue of Olav Tryggvason where the head of recruitment for E14 was waiting with a stopwatch. I was the first person to get there, and was celebrated as a hero that night."

"No bitter aftertaste?"

"Not at the time. That came later. Same thing with Special Forces. You're under the sort of pressure normal people never experience. And after a while you start to think that the rules for normal people don't apply to you. In E14 it started with a bit of gentle manipulation. Exploitation. A few little breaches of the law. And ended with moral questions about life and death."

"So you're saying that those rules do actually apply to people with jobs like that?"

"On paper . . ." Bohr tapped his thigh with his finger. "Of course. But up here . . ." He tapped his forehead. "Up here you know you're going to have to break a few rules in order to protect them. Because it's your watch, the whole time. And it's a lonely watch—us watchers only have each other. No one else is ever going to thank us, because most people never know that they've been watched over."

"The rule of law—"

"Has its limitations. If the rule of law had its way, a Norwegian soldier who raped and murdered an Afghan woman would have been sent home to serve a short sentence in a prison that would have seemed like a five-star hotel to a Hazara. I gave him what he deserved, Harry. What Hala and her family deserved. An Afghan punishment for a crime committed in Afghanistan."

"And now you're hunting the man who killed Rakel. But if you follow the same principle, a crime committed in Norway should be punished according to Norwegian law, and we don't have the death penalty."

"Norway might not, but *I* have the death penalty, Harry. And so do you."

"Do I?"

"I don't doubt that you, along with the majority of people in this country, have a genuine belief in humane punishment and fresh starts. But you're also human, Harry. Someone who's lost someone you loved. Someone I loved."

Harry sucked hard on his cigarette.

"No," Bohr said. "Not like that. Rakel was my younger sister. Just like Hala. They were Bianca. And I've lost them all."

"What is it you want, Bohr?"

"I want to help you, Harry. When you find him, I want to help you."

"Help me how?"

Bohr held up his cigarette. "Killing someone is like smoking. You cough, you don't want to, you don't think you'll ever be able to do it. And deep down I never believed the guys in Special Forces who said that killing an enemy is the ultimate kick. If Rakel's murderer is killed after he's been arrested, you need to be beyond all suspicion."

"I pass the death sentence, and you're offering to be the executioner?"

"Oh, we've already passed judgement, Harry. Hatred is burning us to our foundations. We're aware of it, but we're already alight, and it's too late to stop it." Bohr tossed the cigarette butt on the ground. "Shall I drive you home?"

"I'll walk," Harry said. "I need to air out the chloroform. Just two questions. When your wife and I were sitting by Smestaddammen, you aimed at us with a laser sight. Why, and how did you know that's where we would go?"

Bohr smiled. "I didn't know. I often sit in the basement keeping watch. I make sure the mink don't take any more cygnets from the two swans who live there. Then the pair of you showed up."

"Mm."

"The second question?"

"How did you get me out of the car and up all those stairs this evening?"

"The way we carry anyone who's fallen. Like a rucksack. That's the easiest way."

Harry nodded. "I suppose it is."

Bohr stood up. "You know how to get hold of me, Harry."

Harry walked past City Hall, crossed Stortingsgata and stopped in front of the National Theatre. He noted that he had walked past three open, lively bars without much difficulty. He got his phone out. A message from Oleg.

Anything new? Head above water?

Harry decided to call after he'd spoken to Kaja. She answered on the first ring.

"Harry?" He could hear the concern in her voice.

"I've been speaking to Bohr," he said.

"I *knew* something was going on!"

"He's innocent."

"Really?" He heard the sound of a duvet scraping the phone as she rolled over. "What does that mean?"

"That means we're back at square one. I can give you a full report first thing tomorrow, OK?"

"Harry?"

"Yes."

"I was worried."

"I noticed."

"And now I feel a bit lonely."

A pause.

"Harry?"

"Mm."

"You don't have to."

"I know."

He ended the call. Tapped O for Oleg. Just as he was about to press the Call button he hesitated. He clicked the message symbol instead and typed: *Call you tomorrow.*

31

Harry was lying on his back on top of the duvet, almost fully dressed. His Dr. Martens boots were standing on the floor beside the bed, his coat draped over the chair. Kaja was lying under the duvet, but right beside him with her head on his arm.

"You feel exactly the same," she said, running her hand over his sweater. "All these years, and nothing's changed. It's not fair."

"I've started to smell of BO," he said.

She stuck her face into his armpit and sniffed. "Rubbish, you smell good, you smell of Harry."

"That's the left one. It's the right one that's changed. Maybe it's age."

Kaja laughed quietly. "You know research has shown that it's a myth that old people smell worse? According to a Japanese study, the aroma component 2-nonenal is only found in people over forty, but in blind tests the sweat of older people was found to smell better than people in their thirties."

"Bloody hell," Harry said. "You've just theorised away the fact that I smell like shit on the other side."

Kaja laughed. The soft laugh he had been longing for. *Her* laughter.

"So tell me," she said. "You and Bohr."

Harry was granted a cigarette and started at the beginning. He told her about Roar Bohr's cabin, and how Bohr had overpowered him in the room below them. About coming to in the empty premises that used to belong to E14, and his conversation with Bohr. He repeated it more or less in detail, minus the last part. The offer to carry out the execution.

Oddly, Kaja didn't seem particularly shocked that Bohr had executed one of his own soldiers. Or that he had kept watch over her both in Kabul and here in Oslo.

"I thought you might freak out a bit when I told you you'd been under observation without knowing it."

She shook her head and borrowed his cigarette. "I never saw him, but sometimes I just had a feeling. You see, when Bohr found out I'd lost my older brother the same way he lost his younger sister, he started to treat me a bit like a surrogate younger sister. It was only little things, like the fact that I got a bit more backup than the others when I went out on jobs beyond the secure zones. I pretended never to notice. And being watched is something you get used to."

"Do you?"

"Oh, yes." She put the cigarette back between his lips. "When I was working in Basra, there were mostly British people in the coalition forces around the hotel where the Red Cross team were living. And the British are different, you know. The Americans work broadly, they sweep streets and talk about 'snake procedure' when they're out to get someone; they go straight forward and literally smash through walls that are in their way. They claim it's quicker as well as more terrifying, which shouldn't be undervalued. Whereas the British . . ."—she traced her fingers across his chest—"they sneak along by the walls, they're invisible. There was a curfew after eight o'clock, but sometimes we used to go out onto the hotel roof outside the bar. We never saw them, but occasionally I would see a couple of red dots on the person I was standing next to. And he saw the same on me. Like a discreet message from the Brits that they were there. And that we should go back inside. It made me feel safer."

"Mm." Harry took a drag on his cigarette. "Who was he?"

"Who?"

"The guy you saw the dots on."

Kaja smiled. But her eyes looked sad. "Anton. He was with the ICRC. Most people don't realise it, but there are two Red Crosses. There's the IFRC, who are regular health workers under the command of the UN. And then there's the ICRC, which mostly consists of Swiss nationals and has its headquarters outside the UN building in Geneva. They're the Red Cross equivalent of the Marines and Special Forces. You don't often hear about them, but they're the first in and the last out. They do everything the UN can't do because of safety considerations. It's the ICRC who go around at night counting bodies, that sort of thing. ICRC staff keep a low profile, but you can recognise them by the fact their shirts are more expensive and they exude a feeling that they're a bit superior to the rest of us."

"Because they are?"

Kaja took a deep breath. "Yes. But they're just as liable to die of shrapnel from a mine."

"Mm. Did you love him?"

"Are you jealous?"

"No."

"*I* was jealous."

"Of Rakel?"

"I hated her."

"She hadn't done anything wrong."

"That was probably why." Kaja laughed. "You left me because of her, that's all the reason a woman needs to hate someone, Harry."

"I didn't *leave* you, Kaja. You and I were two people with broken hearts who were able to comfort each other for a while. And when I left Oslo, I was running away from both of you."

"But you said you loved her. And when you came back to Oslo the second time, it was because of her, not me."

"It was because of Oleg, he was in trouble. But yes, I always loved Rakel."

"Even when she didn't want you?"

"*Especially* when she didn't want me. That seems to be how we're made, doesn't it?"

Kaja's four fingers began to retreat.

"Love's complicated," she said, curling up closer and laying her head on his chest.

"Love's the root of everything," Harry said. "Good and bad. Good and evil."

She looked up at him. "What are you thinking about?"

"Was I thinking about something?"

"Yes."

Harry shook his head. "Just a story about roots."

"Come on. Your turn to talk."

"OK. Have you heard about Old Tjikko?"

"What's that?"

"It's a pine tree. One time Rakel, Oleg and I drove to Fulufjället in Sweden because Oleg had learned in school that's where Old Tjikko, the oldest tree in the world, was growing—it was almost ten thousand years old. In the car Rakel explained that the tree was born back when human beings first invented agriculture and Britain was still part of the continent. When we reached the mountain, we discovered to our disappointment that Old Tjikko was a scruffy, windblown, rather small spruce tree. We were told by a ranger that the tree itself is only a few hundred years old, and that it was one of several trees, and that the root system that these trees had grown from was the part that was ten thousand years old. Oleg was sad, he'd been looking forward to telling the rest of the class that he'd seen the world's oldest tree. And of course we couldn't even see the roots of the scrappy little tree. So I told him that he'd be able to tell his teacher that roots aren't a proper tree, and that the world's oldest known tree is in the White Mountains in California and is five thousand years old. That cheered Oleg up, and he ran the whole way down because he couldn't wait to get home and lord it over his classmates. When we went to bed that night, Rakel curled up next to me and told me she loved me, and that our love was like that root system. The trees might rot, get struck by lightning, we might argue, I might get drunk. But no one, not us or anyone else, could touch the part that was underground. That would always be there, and a new tree would always emerge and grow."

They lay in silence in the darkness.

"I can barely hear your heartbeat," Kaja said.

"Her half," Harry said. "It's supposed to stop once the other half is gone."

Kaja suddenly lay on top of him.

"I want to smell your right armpit," she said.

He let her. She lay there with her cheek close to his, and he felt the warmth of her body through her washed-out pyjamas and his own clothes.

"Maybe you need to take your jeans off for me to be able to smell it," she whispered with her lips close to his ear.

"Kaja . . ."

"Don't, Harry. You need it. I need it. Like you said. Comfort." She moved just enough to make room for her hand.

Harry grabbed it. "It's too soon, Kaja."

"Think about her while you do it. I mean it. Just do it. Think about Rakel."

Harry swallowed.

He let go of her hand. Closed his eyes.

It was like slipping into a warm bath with his suit on and his phone in his pocket: completely wrong, and completely wonderful.

She kissed him. He opened his eyes again, looked directly into hers. For a moment it was as if they were watching each other, like two animals that had run into each other in the forest and had to figure out if the other was friend or foe. Then he returned her kiss. She undressed him, then herself, and sat on top of him. Gripped his cock. She didn't move her hand, just held him hard. Possibly fascinated to feel the blood throb in his erection, the way he could feel it. Then—without any further ado—she guided him inside her.

They found each other's rhythm, remembered it. Slow, heavy. Harry saw her rocking above him in the thin red glow from the clock radio. He ran his hand over what he thought was a necklace shaped like a symbol or sign, but which turned out to be a tattoo, a sort of S with two dots under it, and something that made him think of Fred Flintstone in his car. Kaja's moaning grew louder, she wanted to speed up, but Harry didn't let her, he held her down. She let out an angry cry, but let him lead the dance. He closed his eyes and looked for Rakel. He found Alexandra. He found Katrine. But he couldn't find Rakel. Not until Kaja stiffened, her moaning stopped, he opened his eyes and saw the red light running down her face and upper body. Her eyes were fixed on the wall, her mouth was open as if in a mute scream, and her sharp, wet teeth were glinting.

And his half a heartbeat.

32

"Sleep well?" Kaja asked, handing Harry one of the two steaming cups of coffee and creeping back into bed beside him. Light from the pale sun was filtering through the curtains that were swaying gently in front of the open window. The morning air still had a chill to it, and Kaja shivered happily as she stuck a pair of ice-cold feet between his legs.

Harry pondered. Yes, damn it, he *had* slept well. No nightmares that he could remember. No withdrawal symptoms he couldn't suppress. No sudden visions or signs of a panic attack.

"Looks that way," Harry said, sitting up in bed and taking a sip. "You?"

"Like a log. The idea of you being here works well for me. But it did last time too, of course."

Harry stared into space and nodded. "What do you say, shall we give it another go? Start again on a new page." He turned around and saw from the look of astonishment on her face that she had misunderstood. "OK, we haven't got any suspects lined up," he said quickly. "So where do we start?"

Her face tightened, in an unspoken "you couldn't even leave Rakel alone for five minutes after we woke up together?"

He saw Kaja compose herself, then clear her throat. "Well, Rakel had told Bohr about the threats that had been made against her because of your work. But we also know that in nine out of ten murders committed in the home, the murderer is someone known to the victim. So it was someone she knew. Or someone who knows you."

"The first list is a long one. The second one very short."

"Which men did she know, apart from Bohr and other people from work?"

"She knew my colleagues. And . . . no."

"What?"

"She helped out when I owned the Jealousy Bar. Ringdal, the guy who took it over, wanted her to carry on. She said no, but that's hardly a motive for murder."

"Is it worth considering that it could be a woman?"

"Fifteen percent probability."

"Statistically, yes, but think about it. Jealousy?"

Harry shook his head.

They heard a phone vibrate in the room. Kaja leaned over her side of the bed, fished the mobile from Harry's pocket, looked at the screen and pressed Answer.

"He's a bit busy right now, in bed with Kaja, so please keep it short."

She handed the phone to a resigned-looking Harry. He looked at the screen.

"Yes?"

"Not that it's any of my business, but who's Kaja?" Alexandra's voice sounded ice-cold.

"Sometimes I find myself wondering the same thing," Harry said, watching Kaja as she slipped out of bed, took off her pyjamas and went into the bathroom. "What is it?"

"*What is it?*" Alexandra mimicked. "I thought I might let you know about the last DNA report we sent the investigating team."

"Oh?"

"But now I'm not so sure."

"Because I'm in Kaja's bed?"

"You *admit* it!" Alexandra exclaimed.

"'Admit' is the wrong word, but yes. I'm sorry if you think that sucks, but I'm just a booty call to you, so you'll get over it pretty quickly."

"No more booty calls from me, pretty boy."

"OK, I'll have to try to live with that."

"You could at least try to sound a bit sad."

"Listen, Alexandra, I haven't been anything but sad for several months, and I don't feel up to playing this sort of game right now. Are you going to tell me about the report or not?"

A pause. Harry heard the sound of the shower in the bathroom.

Alexandra sighed. "We've analysed anything that might be

thought to contain DNA from the scene, and obviously there are loads of matches with the police officers we've got in the database. You, Oleg, the investigating officers."

"Did they really manage to contaminate the crime scene?"

"Not too much, but this was a very thorough search for evidence, Harry. From the whole house, including the basement. We brought in so much that the team at the scene gave us a list of what to prioritise. That's why this has only just cropped up. The unwashed glasses and cutlery in the dishwasher were some way down the list."

"What's cropped up?"

"DNA from an unknown individual in dried saliva on the edge of the glass."

"Male?"

"Yes. And they said there were fingerprints on the glass as well."

"Fingerprints? Then they'll have pictures." Harry swung his legs out of bed. "Alexandra, you're a good friend, thanks!"

"Friend," she snorted. "Who wants to be *friends*?"

"Will you call me when you've got anything else?"

"I'll call when I've got a well-hung man in my bed, that's what I'm going to do." She ended the call.

Harry got dressed, took his cup of coffee, coat and boots down to the living room, opened Kaja's laptop and logged into the investigation section of the Oslo Police District website. He found images of the glass in the final report, among the pictures of the contents of the dishwasher. Two plates and four glasses. That meant that the glass had probably been used not long before the murder. Rakel never let things sit in the dishwasher for more than a couple of days, and if it was still less than half full she would sometimes take things out again and wash them by hand.

The glass containing the fingerprints was one of the ones Rakel had bought from a small glassworks in Nittedal, run by a Syrian family who had come to Norway as refugees. Rakel had liked the blue-tinted glasses and wanted to help the family, so she had suggested the Jealousy Bar should buy a load, saying they'd give the bar a distinctive quality. But before Harry had time to make a decision he had been thrown out of both the house in Holmenkollen and ownership of the bar. Rakel had kept the glasses in a cupboard in the living-room section of the large, open space. Not the first place a killer would look for a glass if he wanted a drink after the murder. The report also said that Rakel's own fingerprints had been found on the glass. So she had given this person something to drink, had handed him the glass.

Water, probably, because according to the report there were no traces of anything else. And Rakel hadn't drunk anything herself; there was only one of the blue-tinted glasses in the dishwasher.

Harry rubbed his face.

So she had known whoever had arrived well enough to let him in, but not so well as to use one of the IKEA glasses from the kitchen cupboard above the tap when he asked for a glass of water. She had made more of an effort. A lover? A new date, if so, because the cupboard containing those glasses was a bit of a detour. And he hadn't been there before. When Harry had checked the rest of the recordings from the wildlife camera, Rakel was the only person seen coming and going, she hadn't had any visitors at all. It must be him. Harry thought about the person Rakel had seemed surprised to see but had still let in a few seconds later. The report said that no matching fingerprints had been found in the database. So, not an active police officer—at least, not one who had worked at the scene—and not a known felon. Someone who hadn't been in the house much, seeing as this was the only print he had left.

Whoever had lifted the fingerprint from the glass had used the old method: coloured powder spread evenly over the surface with a brush or magnet. Harry could see prints from five fingers. In the middle of the glass, four prints in a pattern that indicated that the four fingers, with the little finger at the bottom, had been pointing to the left. At the bottom of the glass was the print from the thumb. Rakel's, from when she handed him the glass with her right hand. Harry looked further down the report and found confirmation of what he already knew: the prints were from Rakel's right hand and the unknown man's left hand. Harry's brain sounded the alarm when it detected the same creaking on the floor as the previous evening.

"Made you jump!" Kaja laughed as she padded barefoot into the living room wearing a worn blue dressing gown that was far too big for her. Her father's. Or her older brother's. "I've only got enough breakfast for one, but we can go out and—"

"Don't worry," Harry said, closing the laptop. "I need to get home and change clothes." He stood up and kissed her forehead. "Nice tattoo, by the way."

"Do you think? I seem to remember that you don't like tattoos?"

"Really?"

She smiled. "You said that human beings are by definition idiots, and therefore shouldn't inscribe anything in either stone or skin, and should only use water-soluble paint. That we needed to be able to erase the past and forget who we used to be."

"Christ. Did I say that?"

"A blank page, you said. The freedom to become someone new, something better. That tattoos define you, force you to stick to old values and opinions. You used the example of having a tattoo of Jesus on your chest, which would then be an incentive to cling to old superstitions, because the tattoo would look ridiculous on an atheist."

"Not bad. I'm impressed you remember that."

"You're a thoughtful man with many peculiar ideas, Harry."

"I used to be better, maybe I should have had them tattooed." Harry rubbed the back of his neck. The alarm didn't want to stop, like an old-style car alarm that kept blaring outside the bedroom window, waiting for someone to come and turn it off. Had something other than a creaking floorboard set it off?

Kaja followed him into the hallway as he put his boots on.

"You know what?" she said when he was about to open the door. "You look like you've decided to survive."

"What?"

"When I saw you at the church, you looked like you were waiting for the first decent excuse to die."

Katrine looked at the screen of her phone to see who was calling. She hesitated, looked at the heap of reports on her desk and sighed.

"Good morning, Mona. So you're working on a Sunday?"

"ISB," Mona Daa said.

"Sorry?"

"*In the same boat.* Text speak."

"Yes, I'm at work. Without trucks, Norway stops."

"Sorry?"

"Old saying. Without women . . . Never mind, how can I help *VG*?"

"An update on the Rakel case."

"That's what we have press conferences for."

"And it's getting to be quite a while since you last had one of those. And Anders seems—"

"The fact that you're living with a forensics officer doesn't mean you can jump the queue, Mona."

"No, it puts me at the *back* of the queue. Because you're all so terrified it'll look like I'm getting special treatment. What I was about to say is that Anders obviously isn't saying anything, but he seems moody. Which I interpret as meaning that you're treading water."

"Investigations are never treading water," Katrine said, massaging her forehead with her free hand. Dear God, she was tired. "We and Kripos are working systematically and tirelessly. Every line of inquiry that doesn't take us closer to our goal takes us closer to our goal."

"Great, but I think I've had that quote from you before, Bratt. Have you got anything a bit more sexy?"

"Sexy?" Katrine felt something come loose, something that had been threatening to come out for a long time. "OK, here's sexy. Rakel Fauke was a wonderful person. And that's more than I can say about you and your colleagues. If you can't keep the day of rest sacred, then at least try to keep her memory and whatever remnants of integrity you've got left sacred, you fucking bitch. There, is that sexy enough for you?"

In the seconds that followed, Katrine was as speechless at what she had just said as Mona Daa.

"Do you want me to quote you on that?" Mona asked.

Katrine leaned back in her chair and cursed silently. "I don't know, what do you think?"

"Bearing in mind future cooperation," Mona said, "I think this conversation never happened."

"Thanks."

They hung up, and Katrine leaned her head on the cool desktop. It was too much. The responsibility. The headlines. The impatience of the people on the top floor. The baby. Bjørn. The uncertainty. The certainty. Certainty about so much, about knowing she was at work because she didn't want to be at home, with *them*. And it was too little. She could read as many reports as she liked, her own and those from Winter and Kripos, but it didn't help. Because Mona Daa was right: they were treading water.

Harry stopped abruptly in the middle of Stensparken. He had taken a slight detour to give himself time to think, but had forgotten it was Sunday. Angry barking competed with the excited cries of children, which in turn competed with the shouted commands of the owners of the dogs and children. Yet all this hadn't managed to drown out the alarm that wouldn't stop ringing. Until he suddenly remembered. Because he *did* remember. Remembered where he had seen a left hand holding a glass of water.

"What do you think about the fact that you can get sent to prison for ordering a sex doll in the shape of a child?" Øystein Eikeland asked as he leafed through the newspaper on the counter in the Jealousy Bar. "I mean, it's disgusting, but thoughts ought to be free, surely?"

"There have to be boundaries for disgusting things," Ringdal said, then licked a finger and went on counting the notes from the till. "We had a good night last night, Eikeland."

"It says here that experts disagree about whether messing about with child sex dolls increases the likelihood of assaults on children."

"But we're not getting enough babes. Maybe we should advertise cheaper drinks for ladies under thirty-five."

"If that's the case, why don't parents get sent to prison for buying toy guns for their kids and teaching them to carry out school massacres?"

Ringdal put a glass under the tap. "Are you a pedophile, Eikeland?"

Øystein Eikeland stared out into space. "I've considered it, naturally. Just out of curiosity, you know? But no, no tingling anywhere. What about you?"

Ringdal filled the glass. "I can assure you that I'm an extremely normal man, Eikeland."

"What does that mean?"

"What does what mean?"

"*Extremely* normal. It sounds kind of creepy."

"Extremely normal means I like babes above legal age. Just like our male clientele." Ringdal raised his glass. "And that's why I've employed a new bartender."

Øystein's mouth fell open.

"She'll be in addition to the two of us," Ringdal said. "So we can have a bit more time off. Rotate the team, so to speak. Mourinho-style." He drank.

"Firstly, it was Sir Alex who introduced the rotation system. Secondly, José *Moronho* is a pompous jerk who may have won a few titles with the most expensive players in the world, but like most people he's been deceived by the comments of so-called experts into believing that his own unique gifts were the cause. Even if all research shows that it's a myth that the coach has anything to do with a football team's results. The team with the highest-paid players wins, it's as easy as that. So if you want the Jealousy to come top of the bar league in Grünerløkka, all you have to do is increase my wages, Ringdal. Simple as that."

"You're entertaining, I'll give you that, Eikeland. That must be why the customers seem to like you. But I don't think it would do any harm to mix things up a bit."

Øystein flashed his brown stumps of teeth in a grin. "Mix bad teeth with big tits? She's got big tits, hasn't she?"

"Well . . ."

"You're an idiot, Ringdal."

"Careful now, Eikeland. Your position here isn't *that* secure."

"You need to decide what sort of bar this is going to be. A place with integrity and self-respect, or Hooters?"

"If that's the choice, I'd—"

"Don't answer until you've added this to your tactical considerations, Moronho. According to statistics from the porn website Pornhub, the customers of the future—aged between eighteen and twenty-four—are almost 20 percent less likely to search for tits than any other group. While those who are closest to dying, the ones between fifty-five and sixty-four, are most likely to search for your big-titted ladies. Tits are on the way out, Ringdal."

"What about bad teeth?" Harry asked.

They turned towards the new arrival.

"Perhaps you could get me something to drink, Ringdal?"

Ringdal shook his head. "It's not time yet."

"I don't want anything strong, just—"

"No beer or wine served before twelve on Sundays, Hole. We'd like to keep our license."

". . . a glass of water," Harry said, finishing his sentence.

"Oh," Ringdal said, putting a clean glass under the tap and turning it on.

"You said you asked Rakel if she wanted to carry on working for the Jealousy," Harry said. "But you're not in her email folder or in the list of calls made to her phone in the past few months."

"No?" Ringdal said, handing the glass to Harry.

"So I was just wondering where, when and how you were in contact with her?"

"*You* were wondering? Or the police?"

"Does that make any difference to your answer?"

Ringdal stuck his bottom lip out and tilted his head. "No. Because I can't actually remember."

"You can't remember if you met her in person or if you sent an email?"

"No, actually."

"Or if it was recent or a long time ago?"

"I'm sure you can appreciate that sometimes there are gaps in our memories."

"You don't drink," Harry said, raising the glass of water to his lips.

"And I have busy days when I meet a lot of people and there's a lot going on, Harry. Speaking of which . . ."

"You're short of time *now*?" Harry looked around the empty bar.

"Before it happens, Harry, that's when you should be busy. Preparation is everything. That stops you having to improvise. A good plan has nothing but advantages. Have you?"

"Have I what? Got a plan?"

"Think about it, Harry. It pays off. Now, if you'll excuse us . . ."

When they saw the front door close behind Harry, Øystein looked around automatically—and in vain—for Harry's empty glass.

"He must be desperate," Ringdal said, nodding towards the newspaper in front of Øystein. "They're saying the police haven't got anything new. And everyone knows what they do then."

"What do they do then?" Øystein asked as he stopped looking.

"They go back to their old lines of inquiry. The ones they've already dismissed."

It took a while for Øystein to realise what Ringdal meant. Harry wasn't desperate because the police didn't have anything. Harry was desperate because the police would be looking more closely at their previous lines of inquiry. Such as Harry's alibi.

The Criminal Forensics Unit laboratory out in Bryn was almost deserted. But two men were bent over a computer screen in the fingerprint lab.

"It's a match," Bjørn Holm concluded, and straightened up. "The same prints as the blue-tinted glass in Rakel's house."

"Ringdal was there," Harry said, studying the marks on the glass from the Jealousy.

"Looks that way."

"Apart from the people coming and going on the night of the murder, no one apart from Rakel had entered or left the house in several weeks. No one."

"Right. So this Ringdal guy could have been the first one. The one who arrived earlier that evening and then left again."

Harry nodded. "Of course. He could have paid her an unannounced visit, and drank a glass of water while he asked Rakel if she wanted to carry on working for the Jealousy. She said no, and he left. That would all fit with the recordings. What doesn't fit is Ringdal saying he can't remember. Of course you remember if you visited a woman somewhere you find out two days later in the paper was the scene of a murder just hours after you were there."

"Maybe he's lying because he doesn't want to become a suspect. If he was alone with Rakel on the night of the murder, he'd obviously have a lot to explain. And even if he knows he's innocent, he may be aware that he can't prove it, and stands to risk both being held in custody and being the subject of unwelcome media attention. You'll have to confront him with the evidence and see if that jogs his memory."

"Mm. Unless perhaps we should hold our cards closer to our chest until we've got more."

"Not *we*, Harry. This is your thing. Like Ringdal, I'm aiming for a strategy of not getting involved."

"Sounds like you think he's innocent."

"I'll leave the thinking to you. But I'm on paternity leave, and I'd like to have a job to come back to afterwards."

Harry nodded. "You're right, it's very selfish of me to expect that people who don't owe me anything should risk everything to help me."

A subdued whimper came from the pram. Bjørn looked at the time, pulled his sweater up and pulled out a baby's bottle. He had told Harry about the trick of squeezing the bottle between two rolls of fat under a tight sweater as a way of keeping it at around body temperature.

"Ah, I've just realised which musician Ringdal reminds me of," Harry said as he watched the little boy with his three comically large fair curls suck and chew on the teat. "Paul Simon."

"Paul *Frederic* Simon?" Bjørn exclaimed. "You just realised?"

"It's your son's fault. He looks like Art Garfunkel."

Harry was expecting Bjørn to look up and say something about that being an insult, but he just sat there with his head bowed, concentrating on the feed. Perhaps he was contemplating where Art Garfunkel was on his barometer of musical taste.

"Thanks again, Bjørn," Harry said, doing his coat up. "I'd better get going."

"That thing you said about me not owing you anything," Bjørn said, without looking up. "That isn't true."

"I don't know what it could be."

"If it hadn't been for you, I'd never have met Katrine."

"Of course you would."

"You were the one who guided her into my arms. She could see what happened in the relationships you were in, so you represented everything she *didn't* want in a man. And I was as far from you as she could get. So in a way, you were my matchmaker, Harry." Bjørn looked up with a broad smile and moist eyes.

"Oh, shit," Harry said. "Is this that famous paternal sensitivity talking?"

"Probably," Bjørn laughed, and wiped his eyes with the back of his hand. "So what are you going to do now? About Ringdal, I mean."

"You said you didn't want to get involved."

"Right. I don't want to know."

"So I'd better get out before there are two people crying here." Harry looked at his watch. "The two of you, obviously."

On his way to the car, Harry called Kaja.

"Peter Ringdal. See what you can find out."

At seven o'clock that evening it was already dark, and the invisible, silent twilight rain draped itself like a cold spider's web on Harry's face as he walked up the gravel path to Kaja's house.

"We've got a lead," he said into his phone. "I'm not entirely sure it deserves to be called that, though."

"Who is 'we'?" Oleg asked.

"Haven't I said?"

Oleg didn't answer.

"Kaja Solness," Harry said. "A former colleague."

"Are you two—"

"No. Nothing like that. Nothing . . ."

"Nothing I need to know?" Oleg filled in.

"No, I don't think so."

"OK."

A pause.

"Do you think you're going to find him?"

"I don't know, Oleg."

"But you know what I need to hear."

"Mm. We're probably going to find him."

"OK." Oleg sighed deeply. "Speak soon."

Harry found Kaja on the sofa in the living room, where she was sitting with her laptop on her knees and her phone on the coffee table. She had found out the following: Peter Ringdal was forty-six years old, had been divorced twice, had no children, his relationship status was unclear, but he lived alone in a house in Kjelsås. His career had been mixed. He had studied economics at the Norwegian Business School, and had once launched a new transportation concept.

"I found two interviews with him, both in *Finansavisen*," Kaja said. "In the first, from 2004, he was looking for investors for what he claimed was going to revolutionise the way we think about individual transport. The headline was *Killer of the Private Car*." She tapped her laptop. "Here it is. A quote from Ringdal: 'Today we convey one or two people in vehicles weighing a ton on roads that demand huge amounts of space and a lot of maintenance to handle the traffic they have to carry. The amount of energy required to get these machines rolling with their wide tires on rough pavement is laughable when you consider the alternatives available to us. In addition there's also the resources that go into making these outsized driving machines. But that isn't the biggest cost to humanity of today's private transport. It's *time*. The loss of time when a potential contributor to society has to spend four hours each day focusing solely on steering his own private machine through the Los Angeles traffic. That isn't just a pointless use of a quarter of a person's waking life, it also means a loss in GDP that in this city alone would be enough to finance another trip to the moon—every year!' "

"Mm." Harry ran his forefinger over the worn varnish on the armrest of the wingback chair he had sat down on. "What's the alternative?"

"According to Ringdal, masts with small carriages hanging off them, containing one or two people, not unlike cable cars. The carriages are parked at platforms on every street corner, like bicycles. You get inside, tap in your personal code and where you want to go. Your debit card is charged a small amount per kilometre, and a computerised system sends the carriages off, gradually accelerating to up to two hundred kilometres an hour, even in the centre of Los Angeles. While you carry on working, reading, watching television, barely noticing the corners. Or *the* corner, because on most journeys there would only be one. No traffic lights, no concertina effect, the carriages are like electrons drifting through a computer system without ever colliding. And beneath the carriages, all the roads are freed up for the use of pedestrians, cyclists, skateboarders."

"What about heavy transport?"

"Anything that's too heavy for the masts is carried in trucks that would have to drive at a snail's pace in cities, in allocated time slots at night or early in the morning."

"Sounds expensive, having to build both masts and roads."

"According to Ringdal, the new masts and rails would cost between 5 and 10 percent of what a new road costs. The same with maintenance. In fact a transition to masts and rails would be paid for within ten years simply from the reduction in road maintenance. In addition to that, there would be the human and financial saving of fewer accidents. The target is no accidents at all, not a single one."

"Mm. Sounds sensible in the city, but out in the sticks . . ."

"The cost of building masts to your cabin would be a fifth of an ordinary gritted road."

Harry gave her a wry smile. "Sounds as if you like the idea."

Kaja laughed. "If I'd had the money in 2004, I'd have invested in it."

"And?"

"And would have lost it. The second interview with Ringdal is from 2009, and has the headline *Black belt bankrupt*. The investors lost everything and are furious with Ringdal. He for his part claims that he's the victim, and that people with no vision for the future have ruined things for him by cutting off the money. Did you know he used to be Norwegian judo champion?"

"Mm."

"He says something funny, actually . . ." Kaja scrolled down and read out loud with laughter in her voice: " 'The so-called financial elite are a gang of parasites who think it takes intelligence to get rich in a country with fifty successive years of growth. Whereas in fact the only thing you need is an inferiority complex, a willingness to risk other people's money, and being born after 1960. Our so-called financial elite are a gaggle of blind hens in a corn silo, and Norway is the paradise of mediocrity.' "

"Strong words."

"It doesn't stop there, he's got a conspiracy theory as well."

Harry watched steam rise from the cup on the table in front of her. That meant fresh coffee in the kitchen. "Let's hear it."

" 'This development is inescapable, and who has most to lose from it?' "

"Are you asking me?"

"I'm reading from the interview!"

"You'd better use your funny voice, then."

Kaja shot him a warning glance.

"Car manufacturers?" Harry sighed. "Road builders? Oil companies?"

Kaja cleared her throat and looked back at the screen: " 'Just like the big arms manufacturers, the car companies are extremely powerful players, and they live or die with private motoring. So they're fighting desperately against development by pretending to be trailblazers. But when they try to convince people that driverless cars are the solution, of course it isn't because they want better transport solutions, but because they want to slow things down as long as possible and carry on producing one-ton monsters even if they know that this is of no benefit to the world, and actually uses up its limited resources. And they're trying to smother any other initiatives with everything they've got. They've been out to get me from day one. They haven't managed to put me off, but they've obviously managed to frighten my investors.' " She looked up.

"And after that?" Harry asked.

"Not much. A short piece in 2016, also in *Finansavisen*, about the Norwegian Musk-wannabe Peter Ringdal, who is currently running a small tobacconist's in Hellerud, but who once ruled a castle in the air that didn't last long despite the fact that experts at the Institute of Transport Economics praised it as the most sensible proposal for the future of personal transportation, especially in cities."

"Criminal record?"

"One report for beating up a guy when he was working as a bouncer while he was a student, and one for careless driving, also when he was a student. He wasn't convicted in either instance. But I've found something else. An abandoned missing person case."

"Oh?"

"His second ex-wife, Andrea Klitchkova, was reported missing last year. Because the case was dropped, the files have been deleted, but I found a copy of an email from the Norwegian friend who reported Andrea missing. She wrote that Andrea had told her that before she left Ringdal, he had threatened her several times with a knife when she criticised him about the bankruptcy. I found the friend's number and had a chat with her. She says the police spoke to Ringdal, but then she got an email from Russia, from Andrea, in which she apologised for not telling her she was going leave so suddenly. Because Andrea was a Russian citizen, the matter was passed on to the Russian police."

"And?"

"Presumably Andrea was found, because there's nothing more about the case in the police's files."

Harry stood up and walked towards the kitchen. "How come you've got access to police files?" Harry asked. "Did IT forget to cancel your access?"

"No, but I've still got my access chip, and you told me your friend's user ID and password."

"Did I?"

"BH100 and HW1953. Have you forgotten?"

It's gone, Harry thought as he got a cup out of the kitchen cupboard and poured himself some coffee from the cafetière. Ståle Aune had warned him about Wernicke–Korsakoff syndrome, which was when alcoholics slowly but surely drank away their ability to remember things. Well, at least he could remember the names Wernicke and Korsakoff. And he hardly ever forgot things he'd done when he was sober. And there were rarely such long, totally blank gaps as there were for the night of the murder. Passwords.

He looked at the pictures hanging on the wall between the cupboards and worktop.

A faded photograph of a boy and a girl in the back seat of a car. Kaja's sharp teeth were smiling for the photographer, the boy had his arm round her, he must be her older brother, Even. Another picture showed Kaja with a dark-haired woman who was a head shorter than her. Kaja was wearing a T-shirt and khaki trousers, the other woman in Western dress with a hijab over her head, with a desert landscape behind them. The shadow of a camera tripod was etched on the ground in front of them, but no photographer. Taken using a timer. It was just a photograph, but something about the way they were standing, so close together, put Harry in mind of the same sense he got from the picture taken in the car. An intimacy.

Harry moved on to a photograph of a tall fair man in a linen jacket, sitting at a restaurant table with a whisky glass in front of him and a cigarette dangling from one hand. A playful, self-assured look in his eyes, not focused on the camera but slightly above it. Harry thought about the Swiss guy, the one in the hardcore version of the Red Cross.

The fourth picture was of him, Rakel and Oleg. The same one Harry had in his own flat. He didn't know how Kaja had got hold of it. This version wasn't as sharp as his, the dark bits were darker and there was a reflection on one side, as if it was a photograph of a photograph. Obviously she could have taken the picture during the short time they had been together, if that could actually be called being "together." They were two people who had huddled up next to each other for a bit of warmth during the winter night, seeking shelter from the storm. And when the storm had eased, he had got up and gone off to warmer climes.

Why did anyone stick photographs from their life on the kitchen wall? Because they didn't want to forget, or because drink or the passage of time had drained colour and definition from the memories? Photographs were a better record, more accurate. Was that why he—apart from this single one—didn't have any pictures? Because he preferred to forget?

Harry took a sip from the cup.

No, photographs weren't more accurate. The pictures you chose to hang on the wall were fragments torn from life the way you wished it had been. Photographs revealed more about the person who had hung them up than the images in them. And if you read them right, they could tell you more than any interview. The newspaper cuttings on the wall of Bohr's cabin. The guns. The picture of the boy with the Rickenbacker guitar on the wall of the girl's bedroom on Borggata. The trainers. The father's single wardrobe.

He needed to get into Peter Ringdal's home. Read his walls. Read about the man who was furious with his investors for not holding out for longer. The man who had threatened his wife with a knife because she criticised him.

"Category three," he called as he studied Rakel, Oleg and himself. They had been happy. That was true, wasn't it?

"Category three?" Kaja called back.

"Categories of killer."

"Which one was number three again?"

Harry carried his cup of coffee to the doorway and leaned against the frame. "The resentful. The ones who can't handle criticism and direct their rage at people they bear grudges against."

She was sitting there with her legs tucked beneath her, her cup in one hand as she brushed the hair from her face with the other. And it struck him once again how beautiful she was.

"What are you thinking about?" she asked.

Rakel, he thought.

"A break-in," he said.

Øystein Eikeland lived a simple life. He got up. Or not. If he got up, he walked from his flat in Tøyen down to Ali Stian's kiosk. If it was shut, that meant it was Sunday, and he would automatically check the first thing that stuck in his long-term memory: Vålerenga football club's fixture list, because he had arranged to have every Sunday when they played a home match off work from the Jealousy. If Vålerenga weren't playing in their new stadium at Valle-Hovin that day, he went home and lay down again for another half hour before the Jealousy opened. But if it was a weekday, he would get a cup of coffee from Ali Stian, who had a Pakistani father, a Norwegian mother, and—as his name suggested—one foot firmly planted in each culture. One year, Norwegian National Day, 17 May, had fallen on a Friday, and he was seen kneeling on his prayer mat in the local mosque dressed in full national costume.

After leafing through Ali Stian's newspapers and discussing the most important stories with him, then sticking the papers back in the stand, Øystein would walk to a café where he would meet Eli—an older, overweight woman who was only too pleased to buy him breakfast in return for him talking with her. Or *at* her, because she didn't have much to say, she just smiled and nodded no matter what he was running on about. And Øystein didn't feel remotely guilty. She valued his company, and that value was equivalent to a roll and a glass of milk.

After that, Øystein would walk from Tøyen to the Jealousy Bar in Grünerløkka, and that was his exercise for the day. Even if it took no more than twenty minutes, sometimes he decided it merited a glass of beer. Not a large glass, but he was happy to make do. And that was fine, because that hadn't always been the case. But having a secure job did him good. Even if he didn't like Ringdal, his new boss, he liked the job and wanted to keep it. The way he wanted to keep his life simple. As a result, he was deeply unhappy with the phone conversation he was having with Harry.

"No, Harry," he said. He was standing in the back room of the Jealousy with his phone pressed to one ear and a finger stuck in the other to block out Peter Gabriel, who was singing "The Carpet

Crawlers" out in the bar, where Ringdal and the new girl were serving the early evening rush. "I'm *not* going to steal Ringdal's keys."

"Not steal," Harry said. "*Borrow.*"

"OK, borrow. That's what you said when we were seventeen and stole that car in Oppsal."

"*You* were the one who said that, Øystein. And it was Tresko's father's car. And that was all fine, if you remember?"

"Fine? We got away with it, but Tresko was grounded for two months."

"Like I said, fine."

"Idiot."

"He keeps them in his jacket pocket, you hear them rattle when he hangs it up."

Øystein stared at the old Catalina jacket hanging on the hook right in front of him. In the eighties those short, overpriced cotton jackets had been the uniform of young Social Democrats in Oslo. In other parts of the world they had been adopted by graffiti artists. But Øystein mostly found himself thinking of Paul Newman. How some people could make even the blandest item of clothing look so cool that you simply had to have one. Even if you already had an idea of the disappointment that would come when you looked at yourself in the mirror. "What do you want his keys for?"

"I just want to take a look in his house," Harry said.

"Do you think he killed Rakel?"

"Don't think about that."

"No, because that's really easy to do," Øystein groaned. "OK, if I was stupid enough to say yes, what's in it for me?"

"The satisfaction of knowing that you've done your best and only friend a favour."

"And unemployment benefit when the Jealousy's owner ends up in prison."

"OK, good. Say you're taking the rubbish out, then meet me in the backyard at nine o'clock. That's in . . . six minutes."

"You know this is a really bad idea, don't you, Harry?"

"Let me think about it. OK, I've thought about it. And you're right. A really bad idea."

Øystein hung up and told Ringdal he was taking a cigarette break, went out through the back door, stopped between the parked cars and rubbish bins, lit a cigarette and pondered the same two eternal mysteries: how could it be that the more expensive players Vålerenga bought, the greater their chances of fighting to avoid relegation rather than competing for medals seemed to be? And how come the more hair-raising things Harry asked Øystein to do, the greater the chances were of him saying yes? Øystein rattled the key ring he had taken from the Catalina jacket and tucked in his pocket as he thought about Harry's concluding argument: *A really bad idea. But it's the only one I've got.*

33

It took Harry barely ten minutes to drive from Grünerløkka, across Storo, to Kjelsås. He parked the Escort on one of the side streets off Grefsenveien, on a street named after a planet, and walked around to one named after another one. The drizzle had turned into a steady downpour and the dark streets were deserted. A dog started barking on a balcony as Harry approached the house where Peter Ringdal lived. Kaja had found his address in the population register. Harry pulled up the collar of his coat, turned in through the gate and walked up the paved drive to the blue-painted house that consisted of one traditional rectangular section and another part shaped like an igloo. Harry wasn't sure if the neighbourhood had taken a collective decision to have space as their theme, but in the garden there was a sculpture that looked like a satellite. Harry assumed it was supposed to look as if it was floating around the blue, dome-shaped part of the house: the earth. Home. The impression was only strengthened by the half-moon-shaped window in the front door. There was no sticker warning that the house was alarmed. Harry rang the bell. If anyone answered, he would say he'd got lost and ask the way to the street where his car was parked. No answer. He put the key in the lock and turned it. He opened the door and stepped into the dark hallway.

The first thing that struck him was the smell. That there was no one there. Every home Harry had been in had a smell: clothes, sweat, paint, food, soap or something else. But walking in from the torrent of smells outside felt like it did when you *left* most houses: the smells stopped.

There was no Yale lock, so you had to turn the knob from the inside to lock the door. He turned on the light on his mobile phone, then swept it across the walls of the hallway that ran like an axis through the centre of the house. The walls were lined with artistic photographs and paintings, bought with what looked to Harry like a keen eye for taste. It was the same with food: Harry couldn't cook, he couldn't even put together a sensible three-course meal when he was sitting in a restaurant with an extensive menu. But he had the sense to recognise a good order when he watched Rakel smile and tell the waiter quietly what she wanted, and would copy her without embarrassment.

There was a chest of drawers just inside the door. Harry opened the top drawer. Gloves and scarves. He tried the next one down. Keys. Batteries. A flashlight. A judo magazine. A box of bullets. Harry picked it up: 9mm. Ringdal had a pistol somewhere. He put the box back and was about to close the drawer when he noticed something. There was no longer a total absence of smell; an almost imperceptible smell was rising from the drawer.

A smell of sun-warmed forest.

He moved the judo magazine.

There was a red silk scarf under it. He stood frozen to the spot for a moment. Then he picked it up and held it to his face, inhaling its smell. There was no doubt. It was hers, it was Rakel's.

Harry stood there for a few seconds before he pulled himself together. He thought for a moment, then put the scarf back under the magazine, closed the drawer and carried on along the hallway.

Instead of going into what he assumed was the living room, he went upstairs. Another passageway. He opened a door. Bathroom. Seeing as there were no windows that could be seen from outside, he turned the light on. Then it struck him that if Ringdal had had one of those new electricity monitors fitted, and if what the work-man from Hafslund had said was right, they would be able to tell if someone had been inside the house by checking the meter and seeing that the electricity usage had gone up a tiny bit just before half past nine in the evening. Harry checked the shelf under the mirror and the bathroom cabinet. Just the usual toiletries a man would need. No interesting pills and potions.

Same thing with the bedroom. A clean, neatly made bed. No skeletons in the closets. The light on his mobile evidently used a lot of power, he could see that the charge in the battery had already sunk alarmingly quickly. He sped up. A study. Barely used, it looked almost abandoned.

He went down to the living room. The kitchen. The house was silent, it wasn't telling him anything.

He found a door leading to the cellar. His phone died as he was about to go down the narrow staircase. He hadn't seen any basement windows from the outside of the house facing the road. He switched the light on and went down.

There was nothing that spoke to him there either. A freezer, two pairs of skis, tins of paint, some white and blue rope, worn hiking boots, a board of tools beneath an oblong basement window, the same sort Rakel's house had, facing the back of the building. Four separate, fenced-off compartments. The house had probably been semi-detached once upon a time, with the igloo and the more conventional part of the house as separate homes. So why were there padlocks on the compartment doors if there was only one person living there? Harry looked through the wire mesh towards the top of one of them. Empty. The same with two of the others. But the last one had chipboard over the opening.

That was where it was.

The first three compartments were locked and visibly empty, to fool an intruder into thinking that the fourth was as well.

Harry thought. He wasn't hesitating, he was just taking a bit of time to think through the consequences, weighing up the advantages of finding something against the disadvantages of the break-in being discovered, meaning that whatever he found couldn't be used as evidence. There had been a crowbar hanging on the board. He reached a conclusion, went back to the tools, grabbed a screwdriver and returned to the door. It took him three minutes to remove the screws from the door hinges. He lifted the door aside. The light inside must have been connected to the switch at the top of the stairs, because the compartment was lit up. An office. Harry's eyes scanned the desk and computer, the shelves of files and books. He stopped at the picture that was fixed to the bare grey wall above the desk with a piece of red tape. Black and white. Maybe it had been taken using a flash, which was why the contrast between the white glare of the skin and the darkness of the blood and shadows was so noticeable, like an ink drawing. But the drawing showed her oval face, her dark hair, her lifeless eyes, her mutilated, dead body. Harry closed his eyes. And there, on the red skin on the inside of his eyelids, there it was again. Burned on. Rakel's face, the blood on the floor. It felt like a knife being driven into his chest, with such force that it made him stagger back.

"What did you say?" Øystein Eikeland called over David Bowie, staring at his boss.

"I said the two of you can manage!" Ringdal cried, putting his hand on the back of the door of the back room and pulling on his jacket.

"B-but . . ." Øystein stammered. "She's only just started!"

"And she's proved to us that she's worked behind a bar before," Ringdal said, nodding at the girl who was pouring two glasses of beer at the same time as she chatted to a customer.

"Where are you going?" Øystein asked.

"Home," Ringdal said. "Why?"

"So early?" Øystein muttered desperately.

Ringdal laughed. "That's kind of the point of employing someone else, Eikeland." He zipped his jacket up and took his car keys out of his trouser pocket. "See you tomorrow."

"Hold on!"

Ringdal raised an eyebrow. "Yes?"

Øystein just stood there, scratching the back of his hand hard, trying to think fast, which wasn't one of his strong points. "I . . . I was wondering if I could leave early this evening instead. Just this once."

"What for?"

"Because . . . the clan are practising some new songs tonight."

"Vålerenga's supporters club?"

"Er, yes."

"They can manage without you."

"Manage? We could get *relegated*!"

"Two matches into the season? I doubt that. Ask me again in October." Ringdal smiled as he walked through the back room towards the door. Then he was gone.

Øystein pulled out his phone, leaned back against the inside of the bar and called Harry.

A woman's voice answered after two rings.

"The person you have called has turned their phone off . . ."

"No!" Øystein exclaimed, ending the call and trying again. Three rings this time. But the same woman's voice and the same message. Øystein tried for a third time, and thought he could detect a note of irritation in the woman's voice this time.

He tapped out a text message.

"Øyvind!" A woman's voice. Definitely irritated. The new bargirl was mixing a cocktail as she nodded towards the queue of impatient, thirsty drinkers behind him.

"Øystein," he said quietly, before turning and glaring at a young woman who ordered a beer with a resigned, patronising sigh. Øystein's hand was shaking so much that he spilled the drink, so he wiped the glass and put it down on the bar as he looked at the time. Kjelsås? All hell would break loose in ten minutes. Harry locked up and him with no job. Fuck Harry, the crazy idiot! The young woman had evidently tried to communicate with him, because now she was leaning forward and shouting into his ear: "I said a small glass, you jerk, not half a litre!"

"Suffragette City" was blaring from the speakers.

Harry was standing in front of the photograph. Taking in the details. The woman was lying in the boot of a car. Now that he was standing closer, he could see two things. That it wasn't Rakel, but a younger woman with the same colouring and facial features as Rakel. And that what had initially made him think it was a drawing and not a photograph was that there were several things wrong with the body. It had indentations and protrusions where it shouldn't, as if the artist didn't quite know his anatomy. This body wasn't just dead, it had been shattered, with rage and force, as if it had been thrown off a mountain. There was nothing about the picture to indicate where it had been taken, or who had taken it. Harry turned the picture over without removing the tape. Glossy photographic paper. Nothing on the back.

He sat down at the desk, which was strewn with drawings of small, two-person carriages hanging from rails running between masts. In one someone was using a laptop, in another someone was sleeping on a chair that had been folded back, and in a third an elderly couple were kissing. There were ramps for people to get on every hundred metres or so along the street, with empty carriages waiting beside them. Another drawing showed a bird's-eye view of a cross, the rails forming a four-pointed star. One large sheet of paper showed a map of Oslo with a grid that Harry assumed was the network of rails.

He opened the desk drawers. Pulled out futuristic sketches of aerodynamically shaped carriages hanging from cables or rails, bright colours, extravagant lines, smiling people, an optimistic view of the future that made Harry think of adverts from the sixties. Some of them had captions in English and Japanese under them. The pictures evidently weren't Ringdal's own idea, just related proposals. But no more pictures of bodies, just the one stuck to the wall right in front of him. What did it mean, what were the walls telling him this time?

He tapped the keyboard in front of him and the screen lit up. No password. He clicked the email icon. Tapped Rakel's address into the search box, but got no results. Not surprising, seeing as all the folders turned out to be empty. Either they weren't used, or he emptied them as he went along, which might explain why he wasn't worried about protecting access to his computer. The police's IT experts might be able to reconstruct Ringdal's email correspondence, but Harry was aware that had become harder rather than easier in the past few years.

He looked through the list of documents, opened a couple of them. Notes about transport. An application for increased opening hours for the Jealousy Bar. Six-monthly accounts that showed the bar had made a healthy profit. Nothing of interest.

Nothing on the shelves of files—about transport theory, research into urban development, traffic accidents, game theory—either. But one worn hardback book. Friedrich Nietzsche's *Also Sprach Zarathustra*. When he was younger, Harry had leafed through this mythologised book out of curiosity without finding anything about Übermensch or the purported Nazi ideology, just a story about an old man in the mountains who—except for the bit about God being dead—said completely incomprehensible things.

He looked at the time. He had been there half an hour. With no charge in his phone he couldn't take a picture of the dead girl so he could find out who she was. But there was no reason to believe that the photograph and Rakel's scarf would be gone when they came back with a search warrant.

Harry stood up and left the office, screwed the door hinges back in place, hung the screwdriver on the board, jogged up the stairs, switched off the light and went out into the hallway. He heard the neighbour's dog barking outside. On his way to the front door, he opened the door to the only room he hadn't been in. A combination of toilet and utility room. He was about to close it again when he caught sight of a white sweater lying on the tiled floor in the heap of dirty underwear and T-shirts in front of the washing machine. The sweater had a blue cross on the chest. And flecks of what looked like blood. To be more precise: sprays of blood. Harry closed his eyes. The cross had triggered something in his memory. He saw himself walk into the Jealousy Bar, Ringdal behind the counter. That was the sweater Ringdal had been wearing that night, the night Rakel died.

Harry had punched Ringdal. They had both bled. But *that* much?

If the sweater got washed before the house was searched, they would never know.

Harry hesitated for a moment. The dog had stopped barking. Then he bent down, carefully rolled the sweater up and squeezed it into his coat pocket. He stepped back out into the passageway.

And stopped abruptly.

The sound of footsteps on gravel.

Harry moved back, into the darkness farther along the passageway.

Through the half-moon glass he saw a shape step into the light out on the steps.

Shit.

The glass was too low for him to see the other man's face, but he saw a hand searching in the pockets of a blue Catalina jacket, followed by subdued swearing. The door handle was pushed down. Harry tried to remember: had he turned the lock?

The man outside tugged at the door. Cursed more loudly now.

Harry silently let the air out of his lungs. He had locked it. And, once again, it was as if something had been triggered. Rakel's lock. He had checked it, as if to make sure it was locked.

Something lit up outside. A mobile. A pale face was pressed against the half-moon in the door, nose and cheek pressed flat against the glass, lit up by the phone being held to his ear. Ringdal was almost unrecognisable, his face like a bank robber's under a nylon stocking, demonic, but his eye was staring into the darkness of the hallway.

Harry stood motionless, holding his breath. They were five metres apart, at most. Could Ringdal really not see him? As if in response, Ringdal's voice echoed through the half-moon window with an odd, muffled resonance, low and calm.

"There you are."

Shit, shit.

"I can't find the keys to the house," Ringdal said. The heat of his mouth settled as grey condensation on the glass.

"Eikeland," Øystein had said rather stiffly when, after a moment of panic, he had gone into the back room to take Ringdal's call.

"There you are," Ringdal had said. Then: "I can't find the keys to the house."

Øystein closed the door so he could hear better.

"Oh?" Øystein did his best to sound calm. Where the hell was Harry, and why the hell had he turned his phone off?

"Can you see if they're lying on the floor under the hook where I hang my jacket?"

"OK, hang on a moment," Øystein said, and took the phone from his mouth. He was breathing hard, as if he'd been holding his breath, which he might well have been. Think, think!

"Eikeland? Are you there, Eikeland?" Ringdal's voice sounded thin and less threatening when Øystein was holding the phone farther away from him. Reluctantly he moved it closer to his ear again.

"Yes. No, I can't see any keys. Where are you?"

"I'm standing outside my house."

Harry's inside, Øystein thought. If he's heard Ringdal approach, he needs time to get away, a window at the back, a back door.

"Maybe the keys are out in the bar," Øystein said. "Or in the toilet. Give me a couple of minutes and I'll go and check."

"I never put my keys down anywhere, Eikeland." This was said with such certainty that Øystein realised there was no point trying to sow any doubt. "I'll just have to break the glass."

"But . . ."

"I can get the window mended tomorrow, it's no big deal."

Harry was looking right into Ringdal's eyes behind the glass, and it was a complete mystery to him that the other man couldn't see him. He thought about retreating towards the door to the cellar and crawling out through one of the basement windows. But he knew that the slightest movement would give him away. Ringdal's face moved away from the window. Harry saw Ringdal put his hand inside his jacket, under a dark pullover. He pulled out something black. A pistol with what Bjørn called a "stuck-up nose," an extremely short barrel, possibly a Sig Sauer P320. Easy to fire, easy to use, quick trigger, effective at short range.

Harry gulped.

He imagined he could hear Ringdal's defense lawyer. *The accused thought a burglar was coming towards him through the darkness in the hallway, so he fired in self-defense.* The defense lawyer asking Katrine Bratt in the witness stand: "On whose orders was Hole inside the house?"

He saw the pistol being raised, then the hand swing back.

. . .

"I can see them!" Øystein shouted into his phone.

Silence at the other end.

"That was in the nick of time," Ringdal's voice finally said. "Where—"

"On the floor. Below the hook, where you said. They're behind the broom."

"Broom? There's no broom . . ."

"I put it in there, I kept kicking it behind the bar," Øystein said, leaning through the doorway to look at the bar, where a throng of unserved, thirsty customers was waiting. He grabbed the brush and put it behind the door, beneath the hook.

"OK, hang on to them, I'm on my way."

The line went dead.

Øystein called Harry's number. Still the same woman's voice reciting her mantra about the phone being switched off. Øystein wiped the sweat from his brow. Relegation. The season had hardly begun, but it was already decided, it was the law of gravity, which could at best be counterbalanced rather than avoided.

"Øyvind! Where are you, Øyvind?"

"Øy-STEIN!" Øystein bellowed towards the crowd on the other side of the doorway. "I'm definitely an Øy, but I'd much prefer to be a -stein, OK?"

Harry watched the shape move away from the window. He heard quick footsteps down the steps. The dog started barking again.

Keep them there, I'm on my way.

Øystein must have persuaded Ringdal that he had his keys.

He heard a car start, then disappear.

His own car was parked on a different planet. There was no way he could get to the Jealousy Bar ahead of Ringdal. And his phone was dead, so he couldn't contact Øystein. Harry tried to think. It was as if his brain had lost its steering, and kept thinking about the photograph of the dead girl. And something Bjørn had said about developing pictures from crime scenes back when they still had a darkroom in Forensics. That new staff always tended to use too much contrast, meaning that there was less detail in both black and white. The contrast in the photograph in the basement wasn't exaggerated because of the flash, but because it had been developed by an amateur. Harry was suddenly sure. Ringdal had taken the picture himself. Of a girl he had killed himself.

34

Øystein saw the door swing open from the corner of his eye. It was him, Ringdal. He walked in, but was so short that he immediately vanished in the crowd of customers. But Øystein could see them moving, could tell he was on his way over, like the jungle moving above the Tyrannosaurus rex in *Jurassic Park*. Øystein went on pouring beer. He saw the brown liquid fill the glass, then the head form on top of it. The tap spluttered. An air bubble, or was it time to change the barrel again already? He didn't know. He didn't know if this was the end, or just a bump in the road. All he could do was wait and see. Wait and see if everything was going to go to hell. No question about that "if," really. Everything always went to hell, it was all just a question of time. At least if your best friend was called Harry Hole.

"It's the barrel," he said to the girl. "I'll go and change it, tell Ringdal I'll be back in a moment."

Øystein went into the back room, locked himself inside the staff toilet, which also functioned as a storage space for everything from glasses and napkins to coffee and filters. He took out his phone and made one last attempt to call Harry. With the same deflating result.

"Eikeland?"

Ringdal had come into the back room. "Eikeland!"

"In here," Øystein mumbled.

"I thought you were changing the barrel?"

"It wasn't empty after all. I'm on the bog."

"I'll wait."

"On the bog, as in having a shit." Øystein underlined the claim by straining his stomach muscles and pressing the air from his lungs in a long, loud groan. "Help out in the bar and I'll be out soon."

"Push the keys under the door. Come on, Eikeland, I want to get home!"

"I've got a magnificent cable halfway out, boss, we could be talking a world record here, so I'm reluctant to pinch it off halfway."

"Keep your toilet humour for people who appreciate it, Eikeland. Now."

"OK, OK, just give me a minute."

Silence.

Øystein wondered how long he could delay things. Delaying was everything. Wasn't that what life came down to in the end, anyway?

After counting slowly to twenty and still not managing to come up with a better excuse than the ten hopeless ones he had already thought of, he flushed the toilet, unlocked the door and went out into the bar.

Ringdal was handing a customer a glass of wine, took his bank card and turned towards Øystein, who had put his hands in his pockets and adopted an expression that he hoped conveyed surprise and dismay. That wasn't far from what he was actually feeling.

"I had them right here!" Øystein called over the music and buzz of conversation. "I must have lost them somewhere."

"What's going on, Eikeland?" More abstract than interested.

"Going on?"

Ringdal's eyes narrowed. "Go-ing on," he said. Slowly, almost in a whisper, yet it still cut through the noise like a knife.

Øystein swallowed hard. And decided to give up. He had never understood people who let themselves be tortured and *then* told the truth. He couldn't help thinking that was just lose-lose.

"OK, boss. It's—"

"Øystein!"

It wasn't the girl this time, finally getting his name right. The cry came from over by the door, and this person didn't pass below the canopy of customers, but stood a head taller than them, as if he were swimming through them. "Øystein, my Øystein!" Harry repeated, with a wild grin. And seeing as Øystein had never seen Harry with that sort of grin before, it was quite a disconcerting sight. "Happy birthday, old friend!"

The other customers turned towards Harry, and a few glanced at Øystein. Harry reached the bar and threw his arms round Øystein, pressing him to him with one hand between his shoulder blades and the other at the base of his spine. In fact it slid even lower down, and came dangerously close to his buttocks.

Harry let him go and straightened up. Someone began to sing. And someone—it must have been the girl—turned the music off. Then more of them joined in.

"Happy birthday to you . . ."

No, Øystein thought, not that, I'd prefer the rack and having my fingernails pulled out.

But it was too late, even Ringdal joined in, somewhat reluctantly, presumably keen to show everyone what a great guy he was. Øystein bared his brown teeth in a stiff smile as embarrassment burned his cheeks and ears, but that just made them laugh and sing even louder.

The song ended with everyone raising their glasses to Øystein, and with Harry giving him a hard slap on the backside. And only when he noticed something sharp pressing into his buttock did he realise what the opening hug had been about.

The music came back on, and Ringdal turned to Øystein and offered him his hand. "Happy birthday, Eikeland. Why didn't you say it was your birthday when you asked to have the evening off?"

"Well, I didn't want . . ." Øystein shrugged. "I suppose I just like to keep things to myself."

"Really?" Ringdal said, looking genuinely surprised.

"Oh, by the way," Øystein said. "I remembered where I put your keys." With what he hoped didn't look like too exaggerated a gesture, he put his hand in the back pocket of his trousers.

"Here."

He held up the key ring. Ringdal stared at it for a moment, then glanced at Harry. Then he snatched it from Øystein.

"Have a good night, boys."

Ringdal strode towards the door.

"Fucking hell, Harry," Øystein hissed as he watched him leave. "*Fucking* hell!"

"Sorry," Harry said. "A quick question. After Bjørn got me out of here on the night of the murder, what did Ringdal do?"

"Do?" Øystein thought. He stuck one finger in his ear as if the answer might be in there. "That's right, he went straight home. He said his nose wouldn't stop bleeding."

Øystein felt something wet against his cheek. He turned towards the girl, who was standing there, her lips still in a pout. "Happy birthday. I'd never have guessed you were an Aries, Øyvind."

"You know what they say." Harry smiled, putting one hand on Øystein's shoulder. "Up like a lion, down like a ram."

"What did he mean by that?" the girl asked as she watched Harry march off towards the door in Ringdal's wake.

"You tell me. He's a man of mystery," Øystein mumbled, hoping Ringdal wouldn't pay any attention to his date of birth on his next wage slip. "Let's put some Stones on and get this place going, OK?"

His phone woke up after a few minutes' charging in the car. Harry brought up a name, pressed Call and got an answer as he braked at a red light on Sannergata.

"No, Harry, I don't want to have sex with you!"

The acoustics suggested Alexandra was in her office at the Forensic Medical Institute.

"Great," Harry said. "But I've got a bloodstained sweater that—"

"No!"

Harry took a deep breath. "If Rakel's DNA is in the blood, that puts the owner of the sweater at the scene on the night Rakel died. Please, Alexandra."

There was silence at the other end of the line. A noisy drunk stopped on the crossing in front of the car, swayed, stared at Harry with a dark, foggy look in his eyes, hit the hood with his fist, then wandered off into the darkness.

"You know what?" she said. "I hate bed-hoppers like you."

"OK, but you *love* solving murders."

Another pause.

"Sometimes I wonder if you even like me at all, Harry."

"Of course I do. I may be a desperate man, but not when it comes to who I go to bed with."

"Someone you go to bed with? Is that all I am?"

"No, don't be daft. We're professional colleagues who catch criminals who would otherwise plunge our society into chaos and anarchy."

"Ha ha," she groaned drily.

"Obviously I'm willing to lie to you to get you to do this," Harry said. "But I like you, OK?"

"Do you want to have sex with me?"

"Well. No. Yes, but no. If you get what I mean."

It sounded like there was a radio playing quietly in her office. She was on her own.

She let out a deep sigh. "If I do this, Harry, you need to be clear that it isn't for your sake. But I still can't do a full DNA analysis for a while—there's a long queue, and Kripos and Bratt's team are breathing down my neck the whole time."

"I know. But a partial profile that excludes matches against certain other profiles takes less time, doesn't it?"

Harry heard Alexandra hesitate. "And who do you want to have excluded?"

"The owner of the sweater's DNA. Mine. And Rakel's."

"*Yours?*"

"The owner of the sweater and I had a little boxing match. He had a nosebleed, my knuckles were bleeding, so it isn't impossible that that's where the blood on the sweater comes from."

"OK. You and Rakel are in the DNA database, so you're fine. But if I need to exclude a match with the sweater's owner, I'll need something I can get his DNA profile from."

"I've thought about that. I've got a pair of bloodstained jeans in my laundry basket, and there's too much blood for it all to have come from my knuckles, so some of that must be from his nose. Sounds like you're still at work?"

"I am."

"I'll be there in twenty minutes."

Alexandra was waiting when Harry pulled up outside the entrance to the Rikshospital, freezing with her arms wrapped round her. She was wearing high-heeled shoes, tight trousers and a lot of make-up. Alone at work, but looking like she was going to a party. He'd never seen her any other way. Alexandra Sturdza said life was too short not to make yourself look as good as you could all the time.

Harry wound the window down. She bent over.

"Evening, mister." She smiled. "Five hundred for a hand job, seven for—"

Harry shook his head and handed her two plastic bags: one containing Ringdal's sweater, the other with his own jeans. "You know no one in Norway works at this time of the night?"

"Oh, is that why I'm alone here? You Norwegians truly have a lot to teach the rest of the world."

"Working less?"

"Lowering the bar. Why go to the moon when you've got a cabin in the mountains?"

"Mm. I really appreciate this, Alexandra."

"In that case, you ought to choose something from the price list," she said without smiling. "Is it that Kaja who's lured you away? I'll kill her."

"Her?" Harry leaned over and looked at her more closely. "I thought it was people like me you hated?"

"I hate you, but she's the one I want to kill. If you get that?"

Harry nodded slowly. Killing. He was about to ask if that was a Romanian saying, something that sounded worse when it was translated into Norwegian, but decided against it.

Alexandra took a step back from the car and looked at him as the window slid silently closed.

Harry looked in the mirror as he drove off. She was still standing there, arms by her sides, under the light of the street lamp, getting smaller and smaller.

He called Kaja as he was passing under Ring 3 and told her about the sweater. And the scarf in the drawer. About Ringdal showing up, and his pistol. He asked her to check if he had a gun license, as soon as she could.

"One more thing—" Harry said.

"Does this mean you're not on your way here?" she interrupted.

"What?"

"You're five minutes away from me and you say 'one more thing' like we're not going to be seeing each other soon."

"I need to think," Harry said. "And I think best on my own."

"Of course. I didn't mean to nag."

"You're not nagging."

"No, I . . ." She sighed. "What's the last thing?"

"Ringdal has a photograph of the shattered body of a woman on the wall above his computer. You know, so he can see her the whole time. Like a certificate or something."

"Bloody hell. What does that mean?"

"I don't know. But do you think you could find a photograph of his ex-wife, the Russian one who disappeared?"

"Shouldn't be too hard. If there's nothing on Google, I'll call her friend again. I'll text it to you."

"Thanks." Harry drove slowly down Sognsveien, between the brick houses in the quiet, English-style garden district. He saw a pair of headlights coming towards him. "Kaja?"

"Yes?"

It was a bus. Pale, ghostly faces looked out at him from inside the illuminated vehicle as it passed. And among them Rakel's face. They were coming more frequently now, the flashes of memory, like loose stones before a landslide.

"Nothing," Harry said. "Goodnight."

Harry was sitting on the sofa listening to the Ramones.

Not because the Ramones meant anything special to him, but because the album had been sitting on the record player ever since Bjørn had given it to him. And he realised he'd been steering clear of music since the funeral, that he hadn't turned the radio on once, not here at home or in the Escort, and seemed to have preferred silence. Silence to think. Silence while he tried to hear what it was saying, the voice out there, on the other side of the darkness, behind a half-moon-shaped window, behind the windows of the ghostly bus, saying something he could almost hear. Almost. But now it needed to be drowned out instead. Because now it was talking too loudly, and he couldn't bear to hear it.

He turned the volume up, closed his eyes and leaned his head back against the shelves of records behind the sofa. The Ramones. *Road to Ruin.* Joey's punchy lyrics. Even so, it still sounded more pop than punk. That was what tended to happen. Success, the good life, age, they all made even the angriest of people more conciliatory. The way they had with Harry, making him milder, kinder. Almost sociable. Happily tamed by a woman he loved in a marriage that worked. Not perfect. Well, fuck it, as perfect as anyone could bear. Until one day, like a bolt from the blue, she picked at a sore point. Confronted him with her suspicions. And he had confessed. No, not confessed. He always told Rakel what she wanted to know, it was just up to her to ask. And she had always known better than to ask about more than she needed to know. So she must have thought she needed to know. One night with Katrine. Katrine had taken care of him on a night when he was so drunk that he couldn't look after himself. Had they had sex? Harry didn't remember, he had been rat-arsed, probably so drunk that even if he had tried he wouldn't have managed it. But he told Rakel the truth, that it couldn't be ruled out entirely. And then she had said that it didn't make any difference, that he had betrayed her anyway, that she didn't want to see him again, and told Harry to pack his things.

Just the thought of it now hurt so much that it left Harry gasping for breath.

He had taken a bag of clothes, his bathroom stuff and his records, leaving the CDs behind. Harry hadn't drunk a drop of alcohol since the night Katrine picked him up, but the day Rakel threw him out he went straight to the liquor store. And was stopped by one of the staff when he started to unscrew one of the bottles before he was out of the shop.

Alexandra would be working on the sweater by now.

Harry put the pieces together in his head.

If it was Rakel's blood, then the case was sorted. On the night of the murder, Peter Ringdal left the Jealousy Bar around 22:30 and paid Rakel an unannounced visit, possibly under the pretext of trying to persuade her to remain as chairperson. She let him in, gave him a glass of water. She turned down his offer. Unless perhaps she said yes. Perhaps that was why he stayed longer, because they had things to discuss. And perhaps the conversation had slipped on to more personal subjects. Ringdal probably told Rakel about Harry's outrageous behaviour in the bar earlier, and Rakel would have told him about Harry's problems and—this was the first time Harry had considered this—that Harry had set up a wildlife camera that he didn't think Rakel knew anything about. Rakel might even have told Ringdal where the camera was mounted. They had shared their troubles, and possibly their joys, and at some point Ringdal evidently thought the time was right to make a more physical move. But this time he was definitely rejected. And in the rage that followed this humiliation, Ringdal grabbed the knife from the block on the kitchen counter and stabbed her. Stabbed her several times, either in ongoing rage or because he realised it was too late, the damage was done, and he had to finish the job, kill her and get rid of the evidence. He managed to keep a clear head. Do what had to be done. And when he left the scene, he took a trophy with him, a certificate, like when he took a photograph of the other woman he had killed. The red scarf that was hanging next to Rakel's coat under the hat rack. Then, when he was sitting in his car, he remembered just in time about the camera Rakel had mentioned, got out and removed it. He got rid of the memory card at the petrol station. Tossed the sweater with Rakel's blood on it on the floor with his dirty washing. Maybe he hadn't even seen the blood, because presumably then he would have washed it at once. *That* was what had happened.

Maybe. Maybe not.

Twenty-five years' experience as a murder detective had taught Harry that the chain of events was almost always more complicated and incomprehensible than it seemed at first.

But that the motive was almost always as simple and obvious as it seemed at first glance.

Peter Ringdal had been in love with Rakel. Hadn't Harry seen the desire in his eyes the first time he came to view the Jealousy? Maybe he had been viewing Rakel as well. Love and murder. The classic combination. When Rakel rejected Ringdal in her home, maybe she told him she was going to take Harry back. And we're all stuck in our ways. Bed-hoppers, thieves, drunks, murderers. We repeat our sins and hope for forgiveness, from God, other people, ourselves. So Peter Ringdal had killed Rakel Fauke the way he killed his ex-wife, Andrea Klitchkova.

Harry had originally been thinking along different lines. That it was the same person who had been there earlier that evening, that the murder had happened then, and then the perpetrator—who knew Rakel would be alone—had come back later to clean up. From the images on the wildlife camera they had seen Rakel in the doorway when she opened the door, but not the second time. Could that be because she was already dead. Maybe the murderer had taken her keys, let himself in, cleaned up and then left the keys behind when he left the house? Or had the murderer sent someone else to clean up after him? Harry had a vague notion that the silhouettes of the two visitors couldn't belong to the same person. Either way, Harry had rejected that theory because the Forensic Medical Institute's written report had been so certain about the time of the murder, that because of the temperature of the body and the room, the murder must have taken place *after* the first visit. In other words, while the second visitor was there.

Harry heard the needle of the record player bump gently against the label, as if to point out discreetly that the record needed to be turned over. His brain was suggesting more loud, numbing hard rock, but he resisted, the way he routinely resisted the same bastard brain's suggestion to have a drink, just a sip, a few drops. Time to go to bed. And if he managed to get some sleep, that would be a bonus. He lifted the record from the deck without touching the grooves, without leaving any fingerprints. Ringdal had forgotten to clean the glass in the dishwasher. Odd, really. Harry slid the album into the inner sleeve, then the cover. He ran his finger over the spines of his records. Alphabetical by artist's name, then chronologically by date of acquisition. He inserted his hand between the eponymous albums *The Rainmakers* and *Ramones* to make space for the new acquisition. He caught sight of something tucked between the albums. He pushed them aside a bit harder to see better. Shut his eyes. His heart began to beat faster, as if it had understood something his brain hadn't yet taken in.

His phone rang.

Harry answered.

"It's Alexandra. I've done a first sweep and I can already see differences in the DNA profiles that mean the blood on this Ringdal guy's sweater can't possibly be Rakel's."

"Mm."

"And it doesn't match yours either. And the blood on your jeans isn't yours either."

Silence.

"Harry?"

"Yes."

"Is something wrong?"

"I don't know. I suppose it must be blood from his nose on his sweater and my jeans, then. We've still got fingerprints tying him to the scene. And Rakel's scarf in the drawer in his home, it smells of her, it's bound to have her DNA on it. Hair, sweat, skin."

"OK. But there's a difference between the DNA profiles of the blood on the sweater and on your trousers as well."

"Are you saying that the blood on the sweater *doesn't* belong to Rakel, me or Ringdal?"

"It's a possibility."

Harry realised she was giving him time to figure out the other possibilities for himself. *The* other possibility. It was a matter of logic.

"The blood on my trousers isn't Ringdal's. And you began by saying it wasn't mine. So whose is it, then?"

"I don't know," Alexandra said. "But . . ."

"But?" Harry stared in between the records. He knew what she was going to say. There were no longer any loose stones warning of a landslide. That had already happened. The whole mountainside had given way.

"So far, the blood on your trousers doesn't show any deviation from Rakel's DNA," Alexandra said. "Obviously there's a lot of work left before we get to the 99.999 percent probability that we count as a complete match, but we're already up to 82 percent."

Eighty percent. Four out of five.

"Of course," Harry said. "I was wearing the trousers when I was at the scene after Rakel was found. I knelt down beside her body. There was a pool of blood there."

"That explains that, if it really *is* Rakel's blood on your trousers. Do you want me to carry on with the analysis that could rule out the possibility that the blood on the sweater is Rakel's?"

"No, there's no need," Harry said. "Thanks, Alexandra. I owe you one."

"OK. You're sure everything's OK? You sound so—"

"Yes," Harry interrupted. "Thanks, and goodnight." He ended the call.

There *had* been a pool of blood. He *had* knelt down. But that wasn't what had triggered the scream inside Harry's head, the landslide that was already starting to bury him. Because he hadn't been wearing those trousers when he was in Rakel's house with the crime-scene investigators, he had left them in the laundry basket the morning after the night she was murdered. That much he *did* remember. Until now, his memory had been as blank as a crystal ball when it came to that night, from the time he walked into the Jealousy Bar at seven in the evening until the time the woman collecting for charity rang on the door and woke him the next day. But images were starting to appear, connect, become a sequence. A film with him in the lead role. And what was screaming inside his head, in a trembling, broken voice, was his own voice, the soundtrack from Rakel's living room. He had been there on the night of the murder.

And squeezed between The Rainmakers and the Ramones lay the knife Rakel had loved. A Tojiro knife with an oak handle and a white guard of water-buffalo horn. The blade was smeared with something that could only be blood.

35

Ståle Aune was dreaming. At least, he assumed it was a dream. The siren that had been cutting through the air had stopped abruptly, and now he could hear the distant rumble of bombers as he ran through the empty street to the air-raid shelter. He was late, everyone else had got inside long before, and now he could see that a man in uniform was closing the metal door at the end of the street. He could hear himself panting for breath, he should have tried to lose some weight. But on the other hand, it was only a dream, everyone knew Norway wasn't at war. But perhaps we've been attacked suddenly? Ståle reached the door and discovered that the opening was much smaller than he had thought. "Come on!" the man in uniform yelled. Ståle tried to get in, but it was impossible, all he could do was get his shoulder and one foot inside. "Get in or get lost, I have to close the door!" Ståle kept pushing. And now he was stuck, he couldn't get in or out. The air-raid siren started to blare again. Damn. But he could comfort himself with the fact that all the evidence suggested that this was a dream, nothing more.

"Ståle . . ."

He opened his eyes and felt his wife Ingrid's hand shaking his shoulder. There you go, the professor was right again.

The bedroom was dark, and he was lying on his side with the alarm clock on the bedside table right in front of him. The luminous numbers said it was 3:13.

"Someone's at the door, Ståle."

And there it was again. The siren.

Ståle heaved his overweight body out of bed and into his silk dressing gown, and pushed his feet into the matching slippers.

He was downstairs and on his way to the front door when the thought struck him that whoever was outside might be less than welcome. A paranoid schizophrenic patient with voices in his head telling him to kill his psychologist, for instance. But on the other hand, perhaps the air-raid shelter had been a dream within a dream, perhaps this was the real dream. So he opened the door.

And once again the professor was proved right. The person outside was less than welcome. It was Harry Hole. More precisely: the Harry Hole you don't want to see. The one with eyes that were more bloodshot than usual, with the hunted, desperate expression that could only mean trouble.

"Hypnosis," Harry said. He was out of breath, and his face was wet with sweat.

"Good morning to you too, Harry. Would you like to come in? Assuming the door isn't too small, of course."

"Too small?"

"I dreamed I couldn't get through the door to an air-raid shelter," Ståle said, then followed his stomach through the hallway and into the kitchen. When his daughter Aurora was little, she used to say it always looked like Daddy was walking uphill.

"And the Freudian interpretation of that is?" Harry asked.

"That I need to lose weight." Aune opened the fridge. "Truffle salami and cave-aged Gruyère?"

"Hypnosis," Harry said.

"Yes, so you said."

"The husband in Tøyen, the one we thought had killed his wife. You said he had suppressed his memories of what happened. But that you could bring them back with hypnosis."

"If the subject was susceptible to hypnosis, yes."

"Shall we find out if I am?"

"You?" Ståle turned towards Harry.

"I've started to remember things from the night Rakel died."

"Things?" Ståle closed the fridge door.

"Images. Random pictures."

"Fragments of memory."

"If I can get them to link up, or dig out more of them, I think I might know something. Know something I don't know, if you see what I mean."

"Put them together into a sequence? I can try, obviously, but there are no guarantees. To be honest, I fail more often than I succeed. It's hypnosis as a method rather than me that's at fault, of course."

"Of course."

"When you say you think you know *something*, what sort of knowledge are we talking about?"

"I don't know."

"But it's clearly urgent."

"Yes."

"OK. Do you remember anything definite from these fragments of memory?"

"The crystal chandelier in Rakel's living room," Harry said. "I'm lying right under it, looking up, and can see the pieces of glass form the letter S."

"Good. That gives us a location and a situation, so we can try associative memory retrieval. Just let me get my pocket watch first."

"You mean the sort you can swing in front of me?"

Ståle Aune raised an eyebrow. "Any objections?"

"No, not at all, it just seems . . . a bit old-school."

"If you'd rather be hypnotised in a more modern way, I can recommend a number of respected but obviously less qualified psychologists who—"

"Get the watch," Harry said.

"Fix your eyes on the face of the watch," Ståle said. He had sat Harry on the tall-backed armchair in the living room, and was himself sitting on a footstool alongside. The old watch was swinging on its chain, back and forth, twenty centimetres in front of the detective's pale, anguished face. Ståle couldn't remember ever having seen his friend in such a state before. And he felt guilty about not going to see Harry since the funeral. Harry wasn't the sort of person who found it easy to ask other people for help, and when he did it meant that things were pretty bad.

"You're safe and relaxed," Ståle chanted slowly. "Safe and relaxed."

Had Harry ever been that? Yes, he had. When he was with Rakel, Harry had become someone who seemed to be at peace with both himself and his surroundings. He had—however much of a cliché it might sound—found the right woman for him. And on the occasions when Harry had invited Ståle to give guest lectures at Police College, Ståle got the distinct impression that Harry was genuinely happy with his job and his students.

So what had happened? Had Rakel thrown Harry out, had she left him just because he had fallen off the wagon? When you choose to marry a man who has been an alcoholic for so long, who has fallen apart so many times, you know that the chances of him doing so again are pretty high. Rakel Fauke had been an intelligent and realistic woman, would she really wreck a driveable car just because there was a dent in it, because it had gone into the ditch? The thought had obviously occurred to him that Rakel might have met someone else, and that she had used Harry's alcohol abuse as an excuse to leave him. Maybe the plan was to wait until the dust had settled, until Harry had come to terms with the break-up, before showing herself in public with her new man.

"You're sinking deeper and deeper into a trance each time I count down from ten."

Ingrid had had lunch with Rakel after they broke up, but Rakel hadn't mentioned another man. On the contrary, when she got home Ingrid had said Rakel seemed sad and lonely. They weren't close enough friends for Ingrid to feel comfortable asking Rakel, but she said that if there had been another man, she thought Rakel had already dumped him and was trying to find a way back to Harry. Nothing Rakel had said gave any basis for that sort of speculation, but the professor of psychology was under no illusions that when it came to reading other people, Ingrid was far superior to him.

"Seven, six, five, four . . ."

Harry's eyelids were half closed now, and his irises looked like pale blue half-moons. People's susceptibility to hypnosis varied. Only 10 percent were what were regarded as extremely unreceptive, and some didn't react at all to this sort of intervention. In Ståle's experience, you could pretty much assume that people with imagination, who were open to new experiences, and who often worked in the creative industries, were the easiest to hypnotise. Anyone who had anything to do with engineering was harder. This made it tempting to believe that murder detective Harry Hole, who wasn't exactly a tea-drinking daydreamer, would be a tough nut to crack. But without Ståle ever having performed any of the more popular personality tests on Harry, he had a suspicion that he would score unusually highly on one point: imagination.

Harry's breathing was even, like someone asleep.

Ståle Aune counted down one more time.

There was no doubt, Harry was in a trance.

"You're lying on a floor," Ståle said slowly and calmly. "You're on the floor of the living room in Rakel's and your house. And above you, you see a crystal chandelier where the crystals form the letter S. What else can you see?"

Harry's lips moved. His eyelids fluttered. The first two fingers on his right hand flexed in an involuntary twitch. His lips moved again, but no sound came out, not yet. He started to move his head back and forth at the same time as he pushed himself harder against the back of the chair, with a look of pain on his face. Then, like someone having a fit, two strong jolts ran through his long body, and Harry sat there with his eyes wide open, staring in front of him.

"Harry?"

"I'm here." Harry's voice was hoarse, thick. "It didn't work."

"How do you feel?"

"Tired." Harry stood up. Swayed. He blinked hard and stared into space. "I need to go home."

"Maybe you should sit down for a while," Ståle said. "If you don't finish the session properly, it can leave you feeling dizzy and disorientated."

"Thanks, Ståle, but I have to go. Goodnight."

"In the worst cases it can lead to anxiety, depression and other unpleasantness. Let's just take a little while to make sure you're back on your feet, Harry."

But Harry was already on his way to the door. Ståle got to his feet, but by the time he reached the hall the front door was already closing.

Harry managed to get to his car and bend over behind it before he threw up. Then again. Only when his half-digested breakfast, the only thing he had eaten that day, was completely out of his stomach did he stand up, wipe his mouth with the back of his hand, blink away the tears and unlock the car. He got in and stared through the windshield.

He took out his phone. Called the number Bjørn had given him.

After a few seconds, a groggy male voice muttered his surname, like a tic, a habit from the stone age of telephony.

"Sorry to wake you, Freund. This is Inspector Harry Hole again. Something's cropped up that's made things urgent, so I was wondering if you can let me have your preliminary findings from the wildlife camera?"

The sound of a long yawn. "I'm not finished."

"That's why I said preliminary, Freund. Anything at all would be a help."

Harry heard the expert at 3-D analysis of 2-D images talk in a whisper to someone else before he came back.

"It's tricky to determine the height and width of the man entering the house because he's crouching," Freund said. "But it could—and I emphasise *could*—look like the person who comes back out again—assuming that this person is standing upright in the doorway and isn't wearing heels or anything like that—is between one metre ninety and one ninety-five. And it looks like the car, based on the design and distance between the brake and rear lights, could be a Ford Escort."

Harry took a deep breath. "Thanks, Freund, that's pretty much all I needed to know. Take as long as you need with the rest, there's no longer any rush. In fact, you can leave it at that. Send me the memory card and your invoice at the return address that was on the envelope."

"Addressed to you personally?"

"It's more practical that way. We'll be in touch if we need a more detailed description."

"Whatever you want, Hole."

Harry ended the call.

The 3-D expert's conclusion merely confirmed what Harry already knew. He had already seen everything when he was sitting in Ståle Aune's armchair. He remembered everything now.

36

The white Escort was parked in Berg, where the clouds were chasing across the sky as if they were fleeing something, but the night wasn't yet showing any signs of retreat.

Harry Hole rested his forehead against the inside of the damp, ice-cold windshield. He felt like turning the radio on, Stone Hard FM, hard rock, turning the volume as loud as it would go and blasting his head empty for a few seconds. But he couldn't, he needed to think.

It was almost incomprehensible. Not the fact that he had suddenly remembered. But the fact that he had managed *not* to remember, to shut it out. It was as if Ståle's command about the living room and the S-shape, the sound of Rakel's name, had forced his eyes open. And in that instant it was there, all of it.

It was night, and he had woken up. He was staring directly up at the crystal chandelier. He realised he was back, back in the living room on Holmenkollveien. But he didn't know how he had ended up there. The lighting was subdued, the way he and Rakel liked it when they were alone. He could feel that his hand was lying in something wet, sticky. He lifted it. Blood? Then he had rolled over. Rolled over and looked right into her face. She hadn't looked like she was sleeping. Or like she was staring blankly at him. Or like she had lost consciousness. She looked like she was dead.

He was lying in a pool of blood.

Harry had done what you're always supposed to do—he pinched himself in the arm. He dug his fingernails into his skin as hard as he could, hoping that the pain would make the vision go away, that he would wake up, yawn with relief and thank the God he didn't believe in that it had only been a nightmare.

He hadn't tried to revive her, he had seen too many dead bodies and knew it was too late. It looked like she'd been stabbed with a knife, her cardigan was soaked with blood, darker around the stab wounds in her stomach. But it was the blow to the back of her neck that had killed her. An efficient and deadly wound, inflicted by someone who knew that was what it would be. Someone like him.

Had he killed Rakel?

He had looked around the room in search of evidence to the contrary.

There was no one else there. Just him and her. And the blood. Could that be right?

He had got to his feet and stumbled over to the front door.

It was locked. If anyone had been there and left, they must have used a key to lock it from the outside. He had wiped his bloody hand on his trousers, opened the drawer in the chest. Both sets of keys were there. Hers and his. The ones he had given back to her one afternoon at Schrøder's, when he had pestered her to take him back, even though he had promised himself that he wasn't going to do that.

The only other keys were a little way south of the North Pole, in Lakselv with Oleg.

He had looked around. There was too much to take in, too much to grasp, too much for him to be able to find any sort of explanation. Had he killed the woman he loved? Destroyed what he valued more than anything? When he expressed it the first way, when he whispered Rakel's name, it seemed impossible. But when he said it the other way, about destroying everything he had, it didn't seem impossible at all. And all he knew, all he had learned from experience, had taught him that facts beat gut feeling. Gut feeling was just a collection of ideas that could be trumped by a single, crushing fact. And the fact here was this: he was a spurned husband who was in a room with his murdered spouse, a room that had been locked from the inside.

He knew what he was doing. That, by going into detective mode, he was trying to protect himself against the unbearable pain he couldn't yet feel but knew was on its way, like an unstoppable train. That he was trying to reduce the fact that Rakel was lying there dead on the floor to a murder case, something he could handle, the way he had—before he had started to drink alone—made his way to the nearest bar the moment he felt that the pain of living needed to be combated with his talent for drinking, with performing in an arena where he had once imagined himself its master. And why not? Why not assume that the part of the brain governed by instinct is making the only logical, necessary choice when you see your life, your only reason for living, lying broken in front of you? When it chooses to take flight. Alcohol. Detective mode.

Because there was still someone who could be—who needed to be—saved.

Harry already knew he wasn't afraid of any personal punishment. On the contrary, any punishment, especially death, would feel like liberation, like finding a window on the hundredth floor of a burning skyscraper when you're surrounded by flames. And no matter how irrational, crazy or simply unfortunate he had been at the moment of the deed, he knew he deserved this punishment.

But Oleg didn't deserve it.

Oleg didn't deserve to lose his father, his real, non-biological father, at the same time as he had lost his mother. To lose the beautiful story of his life, the story of growing up with two people who loved each other so much, the story that in and of itself was proof that love did exist, *could* exist. Oleg, who was now standing on the threshold of settling down with someone, perhaps of having a family of his own. He may have had to watch Rakel and Harry split up a few times, but he had also been the closest witness to the fact that two people loved each other, two people who always wanted what was best for the other. And that they had therefore always found their way back to each other. Taking that idea—no, that *truth*, damn it!—away from Oleg would destroy him. Because it wasn't *true* that he had murdered Rakel. There was no doubt that she was lying there on the floor, and that he had caused her death, but all the associations, the conclusions that followed automatically when it was discovered that a spurned husband had murdered his wife, were lies. That wasn't why.

The chain of events was always more complicated than you assumed at first, but the motives were simple and clear. And he hadn't had any motive, any desire to kill Rakel, never! That was why Oleg needed to be protected from this lie.

Harry had cleaned up after him as well as he could without looking at Rakel's body, telling himself it would only shake his resolve, and that he had seen what he needed to see: that she wasn't here, that all that was left was an uninhabited body. Harry couldn't give a detailed account of what this cleaning had entailed, he had been feeling dizzy and was now trying in vain to remember the critical moment, to push through the total darkness that shrouded the hours from when he reached a certain level of intoxication in the Jealousy Bar until he woke up here. How much does anyone really know about themselves? Had he gone to see her, had she, as she stood there in the kitchen with this raving, drunk man, realised that she couldn't actually do what she had intimated to Oleg that she might do: take Harry back? Had she said as much to Harry? Was that what had tipped him over the edge? The rejection, the sudden awareness that he would never, ever get her back, had that managed to turn love into uncontrollable hatred?

He didn't know, he didn't remember.

All he could remember was that after he woke up, as he was cleaning up, an idea had started to take shape. He knew he would be the police's first prime suspect, that much was obvious. So to mislead them, to save Oleg from the lie about the classic murder, to save his young, unsullied faith in love, save him from the realisation that he'd had a murderer as his role model, he needed someone else. A lightning rod. An alternative suspect, someone who could and should be hung on the cross. Not a Jesus, but a sinner worse than him.

Harry stared out through the windshield, where the condensation from his breath made the lights of the city below him look like they were dissolving.

Was that what he had been thinking? Or had his brain, like the manipulative illusionist it was, merely invented this business about Oleg, clutching at any excuse instead of admitting the real, simpler motive: to escape. To evade punishment. To hide somewhere and suppress the whole thing because it was a memory, a certainty that it was impossible to live with, and survival was, when it came down to it, the only real function of the body and brain.

That, at any rate, was what he had done. Suppressed it. Suppressed the fact that he had left the house, making sure to leave the door unlocked so it couldn't be concluded that the killer must have a key to the house. He had got in his car, then remembered that the wildlife camera could give him away if the police found it. He tore it down. Removed the memory card and ditched it in one of the bins outside the Ready sports club. Later, a fragment had swirled up from the suppressed sludge when, in a moment of deep concentration, he reconstructed the killer's probable line of retreat and where he might have got rid of the memory card. How could he have imagined it was a coincidence that he had guided Kaja and himself back there, when there were a million other possibilities? Even Kaja had been astonished at his confidence.

But then Harry's suppressed memories had turned against him, threatened to bring him down. Without a moment's hesitation he had handed the memory card to Bjørn, and as a result Harry's meticulous investigation, the intention of which had been to find another deserving culprit—a violent rapist like Finne, a killer like Bohr, an enemy like Ringdal—had begun to close in on himself.

Harry's thoughts were interrupted when his phone rang.

It was Alexandra.

On his way to see Ståle he had stopped off to see Alexandra and given her a cotton bud with blood on it. He hadn't told her it was blood from the presumed murder weapon, the knife he had found among his records. While he was driving he had realised why he had left the knife between The Rainmakers and the Ramones. Simple. Rakel.

"Did you find anything?" Harry asked.

"It's the same blood group as Rakel's," she said. "A."

The most common, Harry thought. Forty-eight percent of the Norwegian population belong to blood group A. A match was like tossing a coin, it didn't mean anything. All the same, right now it did mean something. Because he had decided in advance—like Finne and his dice—to let this toss of a coin decide.

"There's no need to do a full DNA analysis," Harry said. "Thanks. Have a good day."

There was just one loose thread, one other possibility, one thing that could save Harry: breaking an apparently solid alibi.

It was ten o'clock in the morning when Peter Ringdal woke up in his bed.

It wasn't his alarm clock that had woken him, that was set for eleven. It wasn't the neighbour's dog, the neighbour's car setting off to work, kids on their way to school or the garbage truck—his sleeping brain had learned to ignore all those noises. It was something else. It had been a loud noise, like a cry, and it sounded like it had come from the floor below him.

Ringdal got up, pulled on a pair of trousers and a shirt and grabbed the pistol that he kept on the bedside table every night. He felt a cold draft around his bare feet as he crept down the stairs, and when he reached the hall he discovered the cause. There was broken glass on the floor. Someone had smashed the half-moon-shaped window in the front door. The door to the basement was standing half open, but the light was off. They had arrived. It was time.

The scream, or whatever it had been, had sounded like it had come from the living room. He crept in, holding the pistol out in front of him.

He realised at once that the sound hadn't been made by someone screaming, but that the noise that had woken him had been made by a chair leg scraping against the parquet floor. One of the heavy armchairs had been moved, turned around so its back was facing him, with a view of the picture window and the garden containing the satellite sculpture. A hat was sticking up above the back of the chair. Peter assumed that the man in the chair hadn't heard him coming, but obviously it was possible he had positioned the chair like that so he could see anyone entering the room reflected in the window without them seeing him. Peter Ringdal took aim at the back of the chair. Two bullets to the base of the spine, two higher up. The neighbours would hear the shots. It would be difficult to get rid of the body without being discovered. And even more difficult to explain why he had done it. He could tell the police it was self-defence, that he had seen the broken glass, that his life had been threatened.

He squeezed the trigger more tightly.

Why was it so difficult? He couldn't even see the face of the person in the chair. For all he knew there might be no one there, just a hat.

"It's only a hat," a hoarse voice whispered in his ear. "But what you can feel against the back of your head is a very real pistol. So drop yours and stand very still, or I'll shoot you with a very real bullet right through the brain I'm suggesting you now use for your own good."

Without turning round, Ringdal dropped the pistol, which hit the floor with a thud.

"What do you want, Hole?"

"I want to know why your fingerprints are on a glass in Rakel's dishwasher. Why you've got her scarf in the drawer in your hallway. And who this woman is."

Ringdal stared at the black-and-white photograph the man behind him held up in front of his face. The photograph from his office in the basement. The photograph of the woman he, Peter Ringdal, had killed. And then stuffed into a cold car boot and photographed as she lay there.

37

Peter Ringdal was staring bitterly through the front windshield of the car, into the snowdrift. He couldn't see much, but put his foot down anyway. There wasn't much traffic up here on the mountain on a Saturday night, not in this weather, anyway.

He had set off from Trondheim two hours earlier, and realised from the weather reports on the radio that he must have been one of the last vehicles allowed onto the E6 across Dovrefjell before it was closed to traffic because of the bad weather. He'd had a hotel room in Trondheim, but couldn't bear the thought of the banquet. Why not? Because he was a bad loser and had just lost the final of the featherweight class at the Norwegian Judo Championship. If only he had lost against someone better than him instead of sabotaging himself in such an unnecessary way. There had been only seconds to go in the match, and he was leading by two *yuko* to one *koka*, and all he had to do was see it through. And he had been in control, he really had! But then he had started thinking about his victory interview, and something funny he could say, and had lost concentration for a fraction of a second, and suddenly he was flying through the air. He managed to avoid landing on his back, but his opponent was awarded a *waza-ari*, and therefore emerged victorious when the match was over a few seconds later.

Peter hit the steering wheel hard.

In his locker room afterwards he opened the bottle of champagne he had bought for himself. Someone had made a comment, and he had replied that the point of holding the senior finals on a Saturday afternoon for once instead of on Sunday morning was surely that they could have a bit of a party, so what the hell? He had managed to drink more than half the bottle before his coach came in, snatched the bottle away from him and said he was sick of seeing Peter drunk after every meeting, whether he won or lost. And then Peter had said he was sick of having a coach who couldn't even help him beat people who were obviously worse than him. His coach had started with the philosophical bullshit about *judo* meaning "soft power," that Peter needed to learn to give way, let his opponent find himself, show humility, not believe he was best, because after all it was only two years since he had been a junior, and that pride came before a fall. And Peter had replied that judo was all about fake humility. About tricking your opponent by pretending to be weak and submissive, luring him into a trap and then striking without mercy, like a beautiful, wide-open carnivorous plant, a lying whore. It was a stupid, fake sport. And Peter Ringdal had stormed out of the locker room, yelling that he'd had enough. How many times had he done that?

Peter steered the car around a bend as the headlights swept across banks of snow that were still one and a half metres high, even though it was the end of March, so close to the edge of the road that it felt like driving through a tunnel that was far too narrow.

He emerged onto a straight section and accelerated, more out of anger than haste. Because he had been planning to make a move on Tina at the banquet. He knew she had her eye on him as well. But the fair-haired girl had won gold in the lightweight class, and a female Norwegian champion doesn't fuck a loser, especially not one who's half a head shorter than her, and who she might now think she could floor on the judo mat. That's how evolution works.

As if by magic it stopped snowing, and the road—which stretched off between the banks of snow like a long, black pencil line on a white page—lay bathed in moonlight. Was this the eye of the storm? No, for fuck's sake, this wasn't some tropical storm, it was just a Norwegian one, and they didn't have eyes, just teeth.

Peter looked at the speedometer. He felt tiredness settling over him, the result of the long drive to Trondheim yesterday after his lectures at business school, the matches today, the champagne. Hell, he'd thought out some fucking funny remarks for his victory interview, he was going to say—

And there she was. Tina. Right in front of him in the light of the headlamps, with her long fair hair, a flashing red star above her head, waving her arms as if to welcome him. She wanted him after all! Peter smiled. Smiled because he realised he was only imagining this, and his brain told his foot to press the brake pedal. It wasn't Tina, he thought, it couldn't be her, Tina was at the banquet dancing with one of the winners, probably welterweight, and his foot pressed the pedal, because it wasn't his imagination that there was a girl standing in the middle of the road, in the middle of Dovrefjell, in the middle of the night, with a red star above her head, a real-life girl with fair hair.

And then the car hit the girl.

There were two quick thuds, one of them from the roof, and she was gone.

Peter took his foot off the brake, pulled the seat belt away from his chest and drove on slowly. He didn't look in the mirror. Didn't want to look in the mirror. Because maybe he had imagined it after all? The windshield had a large white rose on it where it had hit Tina. Tina or another girl.

He reached a bend where he wouldn't be able to see if there was anyone lying on the road behind him. He kept his eyes fixed ahead of him, then slammed the brakes on. A car that had evidently lost its grip or got caught by a gust of wind was standing with its front pressed into the bank of snow, sideways, blocking the road.

Peter sat there until he got his breath back before putting the car into reverse. He accelerated, heard the engine complain, but he wasn't about to turn back, he was going to Oslo. He stopped when he saw something in the road, something glinting in the glare of the rear lights. He got out. It was the red star. Or rather, it was a warning triangle. The girl was lying on the windswept pavement just beyond it. An unmoving, shapeless bundle, like a sack of wood someone had stuck a fair-haired head on. Parts of her trousers and jacket had been torn off. He sank to his knees. The whistling of the wind rose and fell in an ominous melody over the moonlit banks of snow.

She was dead. Shattered. In pieces.

Peter Ringdal felt sober now. More sober than he had ever felt in his twenty-two-year life. Which was already over. He had been driving at 140 before he started to brake, sixty above the speed limit, and for all he knew they could probably work out what speed the car had been going from the extent of her injuries. Or the length of the trail of blood, the distance between where her body had first hit the ground and where it had ended up. His brain automatically began to identify the variables in that sort of calculation, as if he could somehow escape the more pressing realities that way. Because his speed wasn't the worst of it. Or the fact that he hadn't reacted quickly enough. He could blame the weather, he could say visibility had been poor. But what he couldn't deny, and what was a measurable fact, was the amount of alcohol in his blood. The fact that he had been driving drunk. That he had made a choice, and that choice had killed someone. No, *he* had killed someone. Peter Ringdal repeated it to himself, he didn't know why: *I* have killed someone. And his blood would be tested for alcohol; it always was in car accidents when someone got hurt.

His brain began its calculations again, couldn't help it.

And when it had finished, he stood up and looked out across the desolate, windswept landscape. He was struck by how alien it looked, so different from when he had been driving in the opposite direction the day before. Now it might as well be a desert in a foreign country, apparently empty of people but where enemies might be hiding in every depression in the terrain.

He reversed his car alongside the girl, took his white judo outfit from his bag, spread it out across the back seat. Then he tried to lift her. He may have been a former Norwegian judo champion, but she still slid out of his grasp. In the end he carried her like a rucksack and bundled her onto the back seat. He turned the heater up full and drove up to her car. A Mazda. The keys were in the ignition. He got out a tow rope, pulled the Mazda out of the snow and parked it beside the bank of snow on the straight section where other vehicles would be able to see it in time to brake. Then he got back into his own car, turned around and drove back towards Trondheim. After two kilometres he reached a turning that probably led to one of the cabins you could see out on the plateau in better weather. He parked the car ten metres along the track, unwilling to drive any farther in case he got stuck. He took off his jacket and sweater because the hot air from the heater was making him sweat. He looked at the time. Three hours had passed since he had drunk almost a full bottle of champagne with a 12 percent alcohol content. He did the quick calculation he'd had plenty of opportunities to practise in the past few years. Alcohol measured in grams divided by his own weight, times 0.7. Minus 0.15 times the number of hours. He concluded it would be another three hours before he was safe.

It started to snow again. A heavy shower that hung like a wall on all sides of the car.

Another hour passed. Out on the main road a car passed at a snail's pace. It was hard to guess where it might have come from, seeing as the radio had said the E6 was closed.

Peter looked up the emergency number, the one he was going to call when the time was right, once the alcohol had been burned up.

He glanced in the mirror. Weren't dead bodies supposed to leak? But there was no smell. Maybe she'd been to the toilet just before she set off to drive across Dovrefjell. Lucky for her, lucky for him. He yawned. Fell asleep.

When he woke up the weather was still the same, the darkness was still the same.

He looked at the time. He had been asleep for an hour and a half. He called the number.

"My name is Peter Ringdal, I want to report a car accident on Dovrefjell."

They said they'd be there as soon as possible.

Peter waited a bit longer. Even if they were coming from the Dombås side, it would take them at least an hour.

Then he moved the body into the boot and drove out onto the main road. He parked and waited. An hour passed. He opened his bag and took out his Nikon camera, the one he'd won at a tournament in Japan, got out of the car into the storm and opened the boot. There was plenty of space for the little body in there. He took a few pictures every time the wind eased and there was a slight pause in the snow. He made sure he took a picture of her watch, which, miraculously enough, was undamaged. Then he closed the boot again.

Why had he taken pictures?

To prove she had been lying in the boot for a long time rather than inside the car? Or was there some other reason, a thought he hadn't yet managed to decipher, a sense of something he hadn't yet realised?

When he caught sight of the flashing light, like a lighthouse on top of the snowplough, he switched the heater off altogether. And hoped that his calculations were correct, when it came to both her and him.

A police car and ambulance were following the snowplow. The paramedics concluded at once that the girl in the boot was dead.

"Feel her," Peter said, putting his hand on the girl's forehead. "She's still warm."

He noticed the policewoman looking at him.

After the paramedics had taken a blood sample from him inside the ambulance, he was asked to get in the back of the police car.

He explained how the girl had come rushing out of the snowdrift and ran into his car.

"More like you ran into her," the policewoman said, looking down at the pad she was making notes in.

Peter explained about the warning triangle, about the car that was stuck across the road on the bend, how he had moved it to prevent anyone else driving into it.

The older policeman nodded approvingly. "It's good that you had the sense to think about others in a situation like this, lad."

Peter felt something in his throat. He tried to clear it before realising that it was a sob. So he swallowed it instead.

"The E6 was closed six hours ago," the policewoman said. "If you called us as soon as you hit the girl, you took a hell of a long time to get from the barrier to here."

"I had to stop several times because of the visibility," Peter said.

"Yes, this is a real spring storm," the policeman rumbled.

Peter looked out of the window. The wind had eased, and the snow was settling on the road now. They wouldn't find any sign of where the girl had hit the road. Nor any other tire tracks crossing the trail of blood on the pavement that might prompt them to look for any vehicles that had crossed Dovrefjell at the time in question. They wouldn't get a witness statement from someone saying that yes, he had seen a car parked along the straight section, and yes, it was the same make as the girl's, but no, that had been several hours before Peter Ringdal claimed he hit the girl.

"You got away with it," Harry said.

He had sat Peter Ringdal on the sofa and was himself sitting astride the high-backed armchair. Harry's right hand was resting on his lap, still holding the pistol.

Ringdal nodded. "There were traces of alcohol in my blood, but not enough. The girl's parents filed charges against me, but I was acquitted."

Harry nodded. He remembered what Kaja had said about Ringdal's criminal record, and the charge of reckless driving when he was a student.

"That was lucky," Harry said drily.

Ringdal shook his head. "I thought so too, but I was wrong."

"Oh?"

"I didn't sleep for three years. And by that I mean that I didn't sleep a single hour, a single minute. That hour and a half I slept up on the plateau, that was the last time I slept. And nothing helped, pills just made me crazy and unhinged, alcohol made me depressed and angry. I thought it was because I was frightened I was going to get caught, that the person who drove across Dovrefjell was going to come forward. And I didn't get anywhere until I realised that wasn't the problem. I'd started to have suicidal thoughts and was seeing a psychologist. I told her a different, made-up story but with the same content, with me causing another person's death. And she told me that the problem was that I hadn't made amends. You have to make amends. So I made amends. I stopped taking pills, stopped drinking. Started to sleep. Got better."

"How did you make amends?"

"Same way as you, Harry. By trying to save enough innocent lives to make up for the ones you're responsible for losing."

Harry looked at the short, dark-haired man on the sofa.

"I devoted my life to a project," Ringdal said, looking out at the satellite sculpture, which the rays of sunlight had now reached, casting sharp shadows into the living room. "A future where lives aren't ruined by pointless, unnecessary traffic accidents. And by that I don't just mean the girl's life, but my own."

"Self-driving cars."

"Carriages," Ringdal corrected. "And they're not self-driving, they're controlled centrally, like the electronic impulses in a computer. They can't crash, they maximise speed and choice of route from the position of the other carriages right from the start. Everything follows the logic of the matrix and physics, and eliminates human drivers' fatal fallibility."

"And the photograph of the dead girl?"

". . . I've had that in front of me right from the start so I never forget why I'm doing this. Why I've let myself be ridiculed in the media, yelled at by investors, why I've gone bankrupt and had trouble from car manufacturers. And why I still sit up at night working, when I'm not working in a bar that I hope will make enough profit to finance the project and employ engineers and architects and get the whole thing back on the agenda."

"What sort of trouble?"

Ringdal shrugged. "Letters with a certain subtext. People showing up at the door a few times. Nothing you could ever use against them, but enough to make me get hold of *that*." He nodded towards the pistol that was still lying on the floor.

"Mm. This is a lot to take in, Ringdal. Why should I believe you?"

"Because it's true."

"When did that become a reason?"

Ringdal let out a short laugh. "You might not believe this either, but when you were standing behind me with your arm out and the pistol against my head, you were standing in the perfect position for a *seoi nage*. If I'd wanted to, you would have been lying on the floor before you realised what was happening, disarmed and with all the air knocked out of you."

"So why didn't you do it?"

Ringdal shrugged again. "You showed me the photograph."

"And?"

"It was time."

"Time for what?"

"To talk. To tell the truth. The whole truth."

"OK. So would you like to go on?"

"What?"

"You've already confessed to one murder. How about confessing to the other one?"

"What do you mean?"

"Rakel's."

Ringdal jerked his head back in a movement that made him look like an ostrich. "You think I killed Rakel?"

"Tell me quickly and without giving yourself time to think, why your fingerprints were found on a blue glass in Rakel's dishwasher, a dishwasher where nothing dirty is allowed to sit for more than a day, and why you haven't told the police you were there. And why you've got this in a drawer in your hall?" Harry pulled Rakel's red scarf out of his jacket pocket and held it up.

"That's easy," Ringdal said. "They both have the same explanation."

"Which is?"

"That she was here the morning of the day before she was killed."

"Here? What for?"

"Because I'd invited her. I wanted to persuade her to carry on chairing the committee at the Jealousy. You remember?"

"I remember you mentioning it, yes. But I also know she'd never have been interested, she only helped out with the bar because of me."

"Yes, that's what she said when she came."

"So why did she come at all?"

"Because she had her own agenda. She wanted to persuade me to buy these glasses, which I understand are made by a Syrian family who have a small glass workshop just outside Oslo. Rakel had brought one glass with her in an attempt to convince me that they were the perfect drinking glasses. I thought it was a bit too heavy."

Harry could see Peter Ringdal holding the glass, weighing it in his hand. Giving it back to Rakel. Who took it home again and put it in the dishwasher. Unused, but not quite clean.

"And the scarf?" he asked, already guessing the answer.

"She left it on the coat rack when she left."

"Why did you put it in the drawer?"

"The scarf smelled of Rakel's perfume, and my lady friend has a strong sense of smell and is extremely prone to jealousy. She was coming by that evening, and we both have a better time when she doesn't suspect me of playing the field."

Harry drummed the fingers of his left hand on the armrest. "Can you prove that Rakel was here?"

"Well." Ringdal scratched his temple. "If you haven't already wiped everything off, her fingerprints should still be on the armrests of the chair you're sitting in, I suppose. Or on the kitchen table. No, hang on! The coffee cup she used. It's in the dishwasher, I never run it before it's full."

"Good," Harry said.

"I also went to see that glassworks in Nittedal. Nice glasses. They offered to make them a bit lighter. With the Jealousy's logo on them. I ordered two hundred."

"Last question," Harry said, even though he knew the answer to this as well. "Why didn't you tell the police that Rakel was here a day and a half before she was murdered?"

"I weighed up the consequences of becoming involved in a murder inquiry against the benefit the police might get from the information. Because the police suspected me once before, when my ex-wife suddenly took off back to Russia without telling anyone and was reported missing here in Oslo. She showed up, but it wasn't a pleasant experience being in the police spotlight, I can assure you. So I concluded that if what Rakel was doing a day and a half before the murder was important to the police, they'd track her phone's movements, see that she'd been in this neighbourhood and put two and two together. In short, I reasoned it was up to the police, not me. So I chose the selfish option. But I realise I should have told them."

Harry nodded. In the silence that settled he heard a clock ticking somewhere inside the house, and wondered how he hadn't noticed it last time he was there. It sounded like a countdown. And it struck

him that that could well be what it was, a clock inside his head counting down his last hours, minutes, seconds.

It felt like he needed all his strength to get to his feet. He took out
his wallet. Opened it and looked inside. He pulled out the only note,
five-hundred kroner, and put it on the table.

"What's that for?"

"The broken glass in your door," Harry said.

"Thanks."

Harry turned to leave. He stopped and turned back, and looked
thoughtfully down at the picture of Sigrid Undset on the note. "Mm.
Have you got any change?"

Ringdal laughed. "It's going to cost at least five hundred to—"

"You're right," Harry said, and picked the money up again. "I'll
have to owe you. Good luck with the Jealousy Bar. Goodbye."

The sound of the whining dog faded away, but the ticking sound
grew louder as Harry walked down the road.

38

Harry was sitting in the car, listening.

He had realised that the ticking was his own heart beating. Rakel's half.

Racing away.

And it had been doing that ever since the moment he saw the bloody knife on his shelf.

That was ten hours ago now, and his brain had spent those hours frantically searching for an answer, for a way out, for alternatives to the only explanation he could think of, skittering hither and thither like a rat below deck on a sinking ship, finding nothing but closed doors and dead ends as the water rose higher and higher towards the ceiling. And that half of his heart was beating faster and faster, as if it knew what was coming. Knew it was going to have to speed up if it was going to have time to use up the two billion heartbeats the average human life was made up of. Because he had woken up now. Had woken up, and was going to die.

That morning—after the hypnosis, but before he went to see Ringdal—Harry had rung the doorbell of the flat immediately below his, on the first floor. Gule—who worked nights on the trams—had come to the door in just his boxers, but if he thought it was early he didn't mention it. Gule hadn't been living in the building back when Harry had his own flat on the third floor, so Harry didn't really know him. Perched on his nose was a pair of round, steel-rimmed glasses that must somehow have survived the seventies, eighties and nineties and had therefore achieved retro status. A bit of wispy hair that wasn't entirely sure what it was doing meant that he could just about avoid being described as bald. He spoke in a jerky, toneless way, like the voice of a satnav. Gule confirmed what he had told the police, which was in the report. He had got home from work at quarter to eleven in the evening, when he had met Bjørn Holm who was on his way down the stairs, having put Harry to bed. When Gule went to bed at three o'clock in the morning, he still hadn't heard a sound from Harry's flat.

"What were you doing that night?" Harry had asked.

"I was watching *Broadchurch*," Gule said. When Harry showed no reaction, he added: "It's a British television series. Crime."

"Mm. Do you watch a lot of television at night?"

"Yes, I suppose so. My daily routine is a bit different to most people's. I work late and it always takes me a while to wind down after I finish."

"It takes a while to wind down after driving trams?"

"Yes. But three o'clock is bedtime. Then up at eleven. You don't want to fall outside normal society altogether."

"If the soundproofing here is as bad as you say, and you watch television at night, how come I live right above you, and sometimes go up and down the stairs late at night, and have never heard anything from your flat?"

"That's because I'm considerate and wear headphones." A couple of seconds passed before Gule asked: "Is there anything wrong with that?"

"Tell me," Harry said. "How can you be so sure you would have heard me going out if you were wearing headphones?"

"It was *Broadchurch*," Gule said. Then, when he remembered his neighbour hadn't seen it: "It's not exactly loud, if I can put it like that."

Harry persuaded Gule to put on his headphones and start watching *Broadchurch*, which he said he could find on the NRK website, then see if he could hear anything from Harry's flat or the stairwell. When Harry rang the doorbell again, Gule answered and asked him if they were going to start the test soon.

"Something's come up, we'll have to do this some other time," Harry had said. He decided not to tell Gule that he'd just walked from his bed, downstairs to the front door, then back again.

Harry didn't know much about panic attacks. But what he had heard fitted pretty well with what he was feeling right now. His heart, the sweating, the feeling of not being able to sit still, thoughts that wouldn't settle and kept swirling around his head to the beat of his racing heart, as he careered towards the wall. The daily wish to carry

on living, not forever, but another day, and therefore forever, like
a hamster constantly running faster so the wheel doesn't overtake
it, and dying of a heart attack long before it realises that that's all it
is, a wheel, a meaningless race against time where time has already
reached the finish line and is waiting for you, waiting for you, counting down, tick-tock, tick-tock.

Harry hit his head on the steering wheel.

He had woken up from his slumber, and now it was true.

He was guilty.

In the blackness of that night, on that windswept hillside in a storm
of alcohol and God knows what else—because of course it was still a
total, utter blank—it had happened. He had got home and was put to
bed. He had got up as soon as Bjørn had left. He had driven to Rakel's,
arriving there at 23:21, according to the wildlife camera, which all fitted. Still so drunk that he was hunched over as he walked up to the
house and straight in through the unlocked door. He had gone down
on his knees and begged, and Rakel told him she had thought about
it, but had made her mind up: she didn't want him back. Or had he,
in the full madness of drink, already decided before he went in that
he was going to kill her, and himself, because he didn't want to live
without her? Then stuck the knife into her before she had time to tell
him what he didn't know at the time, that she had spoken to Oleg and
had made up her mind to give Harry another chance? The thought of
that was unbearable. He hit his head against the wheel again and felt
the skin on his forehead tear.

Killing himself. Had he been thinking about that even then?

Even if the hours before he woke up on the floor of Rakel's house
were still blank, he had realised—and then suppressed the fact—that
he was guilty. And had immediately started looking for a scapegoat.
Not for his own sake, but for Oleg's. But now, when it had proved
impossible to find a scapegoat, or at least one who deserved to be the
victim of a miscarriage of justice, Harry had played out his role. He
could leave the stage. Leave everything.

Kill himself. It wasn't the first time he'd thought about it.

He had stood over bodies where as a murder detective he had to
decide if this was someone who had taken their own life, or if someone else had done it. He was rarely in any doubt. Even where brutal
means of death had been chosen, and the scenes were chaotic and
bloody, most suicides had something simple and lonely about them: a

decision, an act, no interaction, few complicated forensic issues. And the scenes tended to be still. Not that the scenes of suicides didn't speak to him, because they did, but it wasn't a cacophony of voices and conflict. Just an internal monologue that he—on a particularly good or a particularly bad day—could hear. And that always made him think about suicide as a possibility. A way of exiting the stage. An escape route for the rat on a sinking ship.

During the course of some of those investigations, Ståle Aune had guided Harry through the most common motives for suicide. From the infantile—revenge on the world, now-you'll-be-sorry—through self-loathing, shame, pain, guilt, loss, all the way to the "small" motive—people who saw suicide as a comfort, a consolation. Who weren't seeking an escape route, but just liked knowing it was there, the way a lot of people live in big cities because they offer everything from opera to strip clubs that they never think of making use of. Something to fend off the claustrophobia of being alive, of living. But then, in an unbalanced moment, prompted by drink, pills, romantic or financial problems, they take a decision, as heedless of the consequences as having another drink or punching a bartender, because the consolation thought has become the only thought.

Yes, Harry had considered it. But it had never—until now—been the only thought. He might be suffering from angst, but he was sober. And the thought had more to it than merely a conclusive end to pain. There was consideration of others, those who would go on living. He had thought it through. A murder investigation was supposed to serve several purposes. To bring certainty and peace to those left behind and society in general was only one of them. Others—such as removing a dangerous person from the streets, maintaining order by showing potential criminals that criminals got punished, or by fulfilling society's tacit need for vengeance—fell by the wayside if the perpetrator was dead. In other words: society expended fewer resources on an investigation that they suspected would at best give them a dead perpetrator, than on one where they risked the perpetrator remaining at large. So if Harry were to disappear now, there was a good chance that the investigation would focus on everything except the dead man Gule had already given an alibi for at the time of the murder. The only thing that could come out—and that pointed vaguely in Harry's direction—was a 3-D expert who claimed that the perpetrator *could* be taller than one metre ninety, and that the car *could* be a Ford Escort. But for all Harry knew, that information may get no further than Bjørn Holm, whose loyalty to Harry was

unshakeable and who over the years had crossed the line of professional ethics on more than one occasion. If Harry died now, there
would be no trial; Oleg would be the focus of a lot of publicity, but
he wouldn't be stigmatised for the rest of his life, nor would Harry's
younger sister Sis, or Kaja, or Katrine, Bjørn, Ståle, Øystein or anyone else whose name was marked by a single letter in his phone. It
was for them he had composed the three-sentence letter it had taken
him an hour to write. Not because he thought the words in themselves would mean much either way, but because his suicide could
obviously rouse suspicions that he was guilty, and because he wanted
to give the others—the police—the answer they needed to put the
case to bed.

*I'm sorry for the pain this will cause you, but I can't bear the loss
of Rakel and life without her. Thanks for everything. I've enjoyed
knowing you. Harry.*

He had read the letter three times. Then he had taken out his
cigarettes and lighter, lit a cigarette, then the letter, and flushed it
down the toilet. There was a better solution. Dying in an accident.
So he had got in his car and driven to Peter Ringdal's, to tug at the
last thread, extinguish his last hope.

And now it had been extinguished. In some ways it was a relief.

Harry had another think. Thought things through to see if he
had remembered everything. Last night he had sat in his car, like
he was now, and had seen the city below him, its lights shining
in the darkness, bright enough to join the dots. But now he could
see the whole picture, the city laid out beneath a high, blue sky,
bathed in the sharp spring light of the new day.

His heart was no longer beating as fast. Unless that was just the
way it felt, that the countdown slowed down as it approached zero.

Harry put his foot on the clutch, turned the key in the ignition
and put the car in gear.

39

Highway 287.

Harry was driving north.

The glare from the snow-covered hillsides was so bright that he had taken his sunglasses out from the glove compartment. His heart had begun to beat more normally after he left Oslo, on roads where there was less and less traffic the farther he got from the city. The sense of calm was presumably because the decision was made, that he in some ways was already dead, that one relatively simple act was all that remained. Or it could be because of the Jim Beam. He had made one stop on his way out of the city, the liquor store on Thereses gate where he had given them the note with Sigrid Undset on it in return for a half-bottle and some change. Then another stop at the Shell garage in Marienlyst where he used up the change to put some petrol in his almost empty tank. Not that he needed that much petrol. But he wasn't going to need the change either. Now the bottle was lying three-quarters empty on the passenger seat, next to his pistol and phone. He had tried calling Kaja again but there was still no answer. He couldn't help thinking that was probably just as well.

He'd had to drink almost half the bourbon before he noticed any effect, but now he felt just detached enough from what was going to happen, but not so much that he risked killing anyone who shouldn't be killed.

The green mile.

The police officer at the site of the accident two days earlier hadn't told them exactly where on Highway 287 the crash had taken place, but that didn't really matter. Any of the long straight sections would do the job.

There was a truck in front of him.

After the next bend Harry accelerated, pulled out, slipped past, saw that it was an articulated truck. He pulled in ahead of it. Glanced in the mirror. A tall cab.

Harry sped up a bit more, staying above 120 even though the speed limit was 80. A couple of kilometres farther on he reached another long straight. Towards the end of it was a lay-by on the left-hand side. He indicated, crossed the road and drove into the empty lay-by, past a toilet and some bins, then turned the car around so it was facing south again. He pulled over to the side of the road and let the engine idle in neutral as he looked back down the road. He saw the air shimmering above the pavement, as if it were crossing a desert rather than a Norwegian valley in March with an ice-covered river beyond the crash barriers on the right-hand side. Maybe the alcohol was playing tricks on him. Harry looked at the bottle of Jim Beam. The sunshine made its golden contents shimmer.

Something was telling him that it was cowardly to take his own life.

Possibly, but it still demanded courage.

And if you didn't have that courage, it could be bought in a bottle for 209.90 kroner.

Harry unscrewed the lid, drank the rest of the bourbon and replaced the lid.

There. Detached enough. Courage.

But, more important: the post-mortem would show that the notorious drunk had such a high percentage of alcohol in his blood when he crashed that it couldn't be ruled out that he had simply lost control of the car. And there would be no suicide note or anything else to suggest that Harry Hole had planned to kill himself. No suicide, no suspicions, no shadow of the wife-killer falling on anyone who didn't deserve it.

He could see it way off to the south now. The articulated truck. A kilometre away.

Harry checked in the left wing mirror. They had the road to themselves. He put the engine into first gear and released the clutch, then pulled out onto the road. He looked at the speedometer. Not too fast, because that would encourage suspicions of suicide. And it wasn't necessary anyway, as the police officer had said at the scene of the accident: when a car drives into the front of a truck at eighty or ninety, seat belts and airbags didn't count for much. The steering wheel would end up behind the back seat.

The speedometer hit ninety.

One hundred metres in four seconds, a kilometre in forty. If the truck was going at the same speed, they'd meet in less than twenty seconds.

Five hundred metres. Ten . . . nine . . .

Harry wasn't thinking about anything, apart from his intention: to hit the truck in the middle of its radiator. He was grateful he lived in an age where it was still possible to steer your car straight into your own and other people's deaths, but this funeral was going to be his alone. He would damage the truck and leave its driver scarred for life, prone to recurrent nightmares, but as the years passed hopefully that would happen less and less frequently. Because ghosts really did fade.

Four hundred metres. He steered the Escort onto the other side of the road. Tried to make it look like he was swerving, so the truck driver could tell the police it looked like the driver of the car had simply lost control of his car or fallen asleep at the wheel. Harry heard the howl of the truck's horn rise in volume and tone. The Doppler effect. It cut into his ear like a knife of disharmony, the sound of approaching death. And to drown out its shriek, to stop himself dying to that music, Harry reached out his right hand and turned the radio on, full blast. Two hundred metres. The speakers were crackling.

Farther along we'll know more about it . . .

Harry had heard the slow version of the gospel song before. The violins . . .

Farther along we'll understand why.

The front of the truck was growing larger. Three . . . two . . .

Cheer up, my brother, live in the sunshine.

So completely right. So completely . . . wrong. Harry wrenched the wheel hard to the right.

The Ford Escort veered back onto its own side of the road, only just missing the left-hand corner of the front of the truck. Harry was heading straight towards the crash barriers and braked, turning the wheel sharply to the left. He felt the tires lose their grip, the back of the car slide right, and felt the centrifugal force push him into his seat as the car spun round, aware that this couldn't possibly end well. He had time to see the truck disappear ahead of him, it was already a long way away, before the back of the car hit the crash barrier and he became weightless. Blue sky, light. For a moment he thought he was dead, that it was like they said: that you left your body and rose up towards paradise. But the paradise he was heading towards was spinning, as were the forest-covered hillside, the road and the river, while the sun was going up and down like a time-lapse film about the seasons, to the accompaniment of a voice that, in the sudden, strange silence, sang "*We'll understand it all . . .*" before it was interrupted by another crash.

Harry was pushed back into his seat, looked at the sky above him, which had stopped spinning, but now it seemed to be dissolving, taking on a greenish hue before a pale, transparent curtain was pulled across it. It was getting darker, they were sinking, down, underground. It's hardly that surprising, he found himself thinking, that I'm heading to hell instead. Then he heard a muffled thud, like the door of an air-raid shelter closing. The car straightened out, then slowly turned around, and he realised what had happened. The car had landed in the river, rear end first, had gone through the ice, and now he was underneath it. It was like landing on an alien planet with a strange, green landscape lit up by rays of sunlight filtered through ice and water, where everything that wasn't rock or the rotting remains of trees swayed dreamily as if dancing to the music.

The current had caught hold of the car, and it floated slowly down the river like a hovercraft as it rose gently to the surface. There was a scraping sound as the roof hit the ice. Water was pouring in from the bottom of the car doors, so cold that it numbed Harry's feet. He undid the seat belt and tried to shove the door open. But the water pressure just one metre below the surface made it impossible. He'd have to get out through the window. The radio and the headlights were still working, so the water hadn't yet short-circuited the electrics. He pressed the button to open the window, but nothing happened. A short circuit, or the water pressure. The water had risen to his knees. The roof of the car was no longer scraping against the ice, the car had stopped rising, he was floating between the bottom and the surface of the river. He would have to kick the front windshield out. He leaned back in his seat, but there wasn't enough room, his legs were too long, and he could feel the alcohol making his movements sluggish, his thoughts slow, his coordination clumsy. His hand fumbled under the seat and found the lever to push it backwards. Above it another lever, and he lowered the back of the seat until he was almost lying down. A fragment of memory. From when he had last adjusted the seat. At least now he could pull his legs out from beneath him. The water had almost reached his chest now, the cold clutching at his lungs and heart like a claw. Just as he was about to kick both feet against the windshield, the car hit something and he lost his balance, fell towards the passenger seat and his kick struck the steering wheel instead. Fuck, fuck! Harry saw the rock he had collided with glide past as the car spun around in a slow waltz before it carried on, backwards, hit another rock and turned the right way around again. The song fell silent in the middle of another *"We'll understand it all. . . ."* Harry took a deep breath up by the roof, then ducked under to get in position to kick again. This time he hit the windshield, but he was surrounded by water now and he felt his feet hit the glass as gently and devoid of force as an astronaut's boots on the moon.

He crawled up onto the seat, had to press his head against the roof to get to the air. He inhaled deeply a couple of times. The car stopped. Harry ducked under again and saw through the windshield that the Escort had caught on the branches of a rotten tree. A blue dress with white dots was waving at him. Panic seized him. Harry beat his hand against the side window, tried to shove it open. In vain. Suddenly two of the branches snapped off and the car slid sideways and came loose. The light from the headlamps, which, bizarrely, were still working, swept across the bottom of the river, towards the shore, where he saw a flicker of something that could have been a beer bottle, something made of glass, anyway, before the car drifted on, faster now. He needed more air. But the car was now so full of water that Harry had to close his mouth and press his nose against the car roof, and breathe in through his nostrils. The headlights went out. Something drifted into his field of vision, rocking on the surface of the water. The Jim Beam bottle, empty, with its lid on. As if it wanted to remind him of a trick that had saved him once before, a long time ago. But that wouldn't make any difference now; the air in the bottle would only give him a few more seconds of painful hope after resignation had granted him a little peace.

Harry closed his eyes. And—just like the cliché—his life passed before his eyes.

The time when he got lost as a boy, and ran around the forest in terror just a couple of stones' throws from his grandfather's farm in Romsdalen. His first girlfriend, in her parents' bed with the house to themselves, the balcony door open, the curtain swaying, letting in the sun as she whispered that he had to look after her. And him whispering "yes," then reading her suicide note six months later. The murder case in Sydney, the sun off to the north, meaning that he got lost there as well. The one-armed girl who plunged into the pool in Bangkok, her body cutting through the water like a knife, the peculiar beauty of asymmetry and destruction. A long hike in Nordmarka, just Oleg, Rakel and him. Autumn sun falling on Rakel's face, smiling at the camera as they waited for the timer, Rakel noticing him looking at her, turning towards him, her smile growing even wider, reaching her eyes, until the light evens out and she's the one shining like the sun, and they can't take their eyes off each other and have to take the picture again.

Evens out.

Harry opened his eyes again.

The water hadn't risen any higher.

The pressure had finally evened out. The basic, complex laws of physics were permitting this strip of air to remain beneath the roof and the surface of the water, for the time being.

And there was—literally—light at the end of the tunnel.

Through the rear window, back where they had come from, what he saw had been coloured an increasingly dark green, but in front of him it was getting lighter. That had to mean that the river up ahead was no longer covered in ice, or was at least shallower, possibly both. And if the pressure had evened out, he should be able to open the car door. Harry was about to duck under and try when he realised he was still under the ice. That it would be a ridiculous way to drown, seeing as here in the car he had enough air to last until they reached what was hopefully a shallow section of the river, free from ice. And it wasn't far away now, they seemed to be drifting faster, and the light was getting brighter.

You don't drown if you're going to be hanged.

He didn't know why the old saying had popped into his head.

Or why he was thinking about the blue dress.

Or Roar Bohr.

A noise was getting closer.

Roar Bohr. Blue dress. Younger sister. Norafossen. Twenty metres. Smashed on the rocks.

And when he emerged into the light, the water became a white wall of bubbles ahead of him, and the noise rose to a rumbling roar. Harry felt beneath him, grabbed hold of the back of the seat, took a deep breath, pulled himself under the water as the front of the car tipped forward. He stared through the water, through the windshield, straight down into something black, where cascades of white water splintered into white nothingness.

Part 3

40

Dagny Jensen looked out at the schoolyard, at the rectangle of sunlight that had started over by the caretaker's house that morning, but that now—towards the end of the school day—had moved to right below the staffroom. A wagtail was hopping across the road. The large oak tree was in bud. What was it that had suddenly made her notice buds everywhere? She looked across the classroom, where the students were hunched over their English coursework and the only sound breaking the silence was the rhythmic scratch of pencils and pens. It was actually their homework, but Dagny's stomach had been hurting so badly that she hadn't felt up to doing what she had been looking forward to, a study of Charlotte Brontë's *Jane Eyre*. About Charlotte, who had worked as a teacher and had preferred an independent life to entering into a socially acceptable marriage with a man whose intellect she didn't respect, an almost unheard-of idea in Victorian England. About the orphaned Jane Eyre, who falls in love with the master of the house where she works as a governess, the apparently brusque and misanthropic Mr. Rochester. About how they declared their love for each other but that she—when they were about to get married—discovered that he was still bound to his wife. Jane leaves and meets another man who falls in love with her, but to Jane he is no more than a mediocre surrogate for Mr. Rochester. And the tragic, happy ending where Mrs. Rochester is killed so that Jane and Mr. Rochester can finally be together again. The famous exchange where Mr. Rochester, defaced by the fire that destroyed the house, asks: "Am I hideous, Jane?" And she replies: "Very, sir; you always were, you know."

And right at the end, the tear-jerking chapter in which Jane gives birth to their child.

Dagny felt sweat break out on her forehead when another jolt of pain cut through her stomach. The pains had been coming and going over the past couple of days, and the indigestion pills she had been taking hadn't helped. She had made an appointment to see her doctor, but that wasn't until next week, and the thought of having to spend a week in this much pain was anything but appealing.

"I'm just popping out for a couple of minutes," she said, and stood up.

A few faces looked up and nodded, then concentrated on their schoolwork again. They were good, industrious students. A couple of them were genuinely talented. And sometimes Dagny couldn't help herself dreaming about one day, after she had retired from teaching, when one of them—one of them would be enough—called to thank her. Thank her for showing them a world that was about more than vocabulary, grammar and the most basic nutrients of the linguistic world. Someone who had found and been inspired by something during her English lessons. Something that put them on the track to creating something themselves.

When Dagny came out into the corridor outside the classroom a policeman got up from his chair and followed her. His name was Ralf, and he had taken over guard duty from Kari Beal.

"Toilet," Dagny said.

Katrine Bratt had assured Dagny that she would have a bodyguard with her for as long as they thought Svein Finne was a threat to her. Katrine and Dagny hadn't spoken about the reality: that it wasn't a question of how long Finne was free, or alive, but how long Bratt's budget or Dagny's patience could last.

The school corridors had a peculiar silence when lessons were taking place, as if they were resting between the bursts of frantic activity that occurred whenever there was a break. Like the periodical cicadas that swarm around Lake Michigan precisely every seventeen years. She had been invited to the next swarm by an uncle over there who said you just had to experience it, both the intense music of billions of insects, and the taste. The cicadas were apparently related to prawns and other shellfish, and he had told her during a meal of prawns on his visit to Norway that they could be eaten the same way: hold the hard shell tightly, remove the feet and head, and pull out the soft, protein-rich parts. It didn't sound particularly appetising, though, and she never took invitations from Americans seriously, especially when they were—if she had calculated correctly—for 2024.

"I'll wait here," the policeman said, stopping outside the girls' bathroom.

She walked in. Empty. She went into the last of the eight cubicles.

She pulled down her trousers and underwear, sat down on the toilet, leaned forward, then pushed the door to lock it. She discovered that it wouldn't close properly. She looked up.

There was a hand sticking between the door and the frame, four large fingers, one of them with a ring in the shape of a snake. And in the palm of the hand she could see one edge of a hole that went right through.

Dagny just managed to take a deep breath before the door was thrown open and Finne's hand shot forward, grabbing her by the throat. He held the snake-like knife up in front of her face, and his voice whispered right next to her ear:

"So, Dagny? Morning sickness? Stomach ache? Weak bladder? Tender breasts?"

Dagny closed her eyes.

"We can soon find out," Finne said, then slipped down onto his knees in front of her and, putting the knife into a sheath inside his jacket without taking his hand from her throat, pulled something that looked like a pen from his pocket and stuck it between her thighs. Dagny waited for it to touch her, penetrate her, but it didn't happen.

"Be a good girl and pee for Daddy, will you?"

Dagny swallowed.

"What's wrong? That is what you came in here for, isn't it?"

Dagny wanted to do as he said, but it was as if all her bodily functions had frozen, she didn't even know if she'd be able to scream if he loosened his grip.

"If you don't pee before I count to three, I'll stick the knife in you, then into the idiot standing out in the corridor." His whispered voice made every word, every syllable, sound like an obscenity. She tried. She really did try.

"One," Finne whispered. "Two. Three . . . There, that's right! Clever girl . . ."

She heard the trickle hit the porcelain, then the water.

Finne pulled the hand holding the pen towards him and put it on the floor. He wiped his hand on the toilet roll hanging from the wall.

"In two minutes we'll know if we're pregnant," he said. "Isn't that wonderful, darling? Pens like this, they didn't exist, we couldn't even dream of things like this the last time I was free. And just imagine all the wonderful things the future is going to bring. Is it any wonder that we want to bring a child into this world?"

Dagny closed her eyes. Two minutes. Then what?

She heard voices outside. A short conversation before the door opened, running steps, a girl whose teacher had allowed her to go to the toilet went into the cubicle closest to the corridor, finished, washed her hands and ran out again.

Finne let out a deep sigh as he stared at the pen. "I'm looking for a plus on here, Dagny, but I'm afraid it shows a minus. Which means . . ."

He stood up in front of her, started to undo his trousers with his free hand. Dagny jerked her head back and pulled free of his other hand.

"I've got my period," she said.

Finne looked down at her. His face was in shadow. And casting a shadow. His whole being cast a shadow, like a bird of prey circling in front of the sun. He pulled the knife from its sheath again. She heard the door creak, then the policeman's voice:

"Everything OK, Dagny?"

Finne pointed at her with the knife as if it were a magic wand that forced her to do whatever he wanted.

"Just coming," she said, without taking her eyes off Finne's.

She stood up, pulled up her pants and trousers, standing so close to him that she breathed in the smell of sweat and something else, something rank and nauseating. Sickness. Pain.

"I'll be back," he said, holding the door open for her.

Dagny didn't run, but walked quickly past the other cubicles, past the washbasins, out into the corridor. She let the door close behind her. "He's in there."

"What?"

"Svein Finne. He's got a knife."

The policeman stared at her for a moment before he unfastened the holster on his hip and drew his pistol. He inserted an earpiece with his free hand, then pulled off the radio that was attached to his chest.

"Zero-one," he said. "I need backup."

"He's escaping," Dagny said. "You have to get him."

The policeman looked at her. Opened his mouth as if to explain that his prime objective was to protect her, not take offensive action.

"Otherwise he'll come back," Dagny said.

Maybe it was something about her voice, or the expression on her face, but he closed his mouth. He took a step towards the door, put his head next to it and listened for a few seconds, with both hands round the pistol, which was pointing at the floor. Then he shoved the door open. "Police! Hands above your head!" He disappeared into the bathroom.

Dagny waited.

She heard the cubicle doors being thrown open.

All eight of them.

The policeman came back out.

Dagny took a trembling breath. "The bird has flown?"

"God knows how," the policeman said, reaching for his radio again. "He must have climbed up the bare wall and out through the window right up by the ceiling."

"Flown," Dagny repeated quietly while the policeman called 01, central command, again.

"What?"

"Not climbed. *Flown*."

41

"Twenty metres, you said?" asked Kripos detective Sung-min Larsen.

He gazed up towards the top of Norafossen, where the torrent of water was gushing out. He wiped his face, which was wet from the spray the westerly wind carried all the way to the bank of the river. The roar of the falls drowned out the traffic on the main road that ran along the top of the slope they had scrambled down to reach the river.

"Twenty metres," the police officer confirmed. He had a bulldog face, and had introduced himself as Jan from Sigdal Sheriff's Office. "It only takes a couple of seconds, but by the time you hit the ground you're already going at seventy kilometres an hour. You don't stand a chance." He pointed one of his short, slightly protruding arms at the compressed wreckage of a white Ford Escort that was perched on top of a large, black rock that the water had worn smooth as it struck it and sprayed out in all directions. Like an art installation, Sung-min Larsen thought. An imitation of Lord, Marquez and Michels's ten half-buried Cadillacs in the desert at Amarillo in Texas, where he had driven with his father when he was fourteen. His father was a pilot, and had wanted to show his son the wonderful country where he had learned to fly the Starfighter, a plane that his father claimed was more of a danger to its pilot than the enemy, a joke that his father had repeated many times on that trip, between coughing fits. Lung cancer.

"There's no question at all," Jan from Sigdal said, pushing his police cap farther back on his head. "The driver shot out through the windshield, hit the rocks and died instantly. The body's been carried downstream in the river. The water's so high right now that it probably won't have stopped until it reached Solevatn. And that's still frozen, so we won't see any sign of him for a while."

"What did the truck driver say?" Sung-min Larsen asked.

"He said the Escort veered across into his lane, the driver must have been looking for something in the glove compartment, something like that, then suddenly realised what was about to happen and lurched back onto the right side of the road in the nick of time. The driver said it all happened so fast that he didn't really have time to see what happened, but when he looked in the mirror the car was gone. But, seeing as the road was straight, he should have been able to see it. So he stopped and called us. There's rubber on the road, white paint on the crash barrier and a hole in the ice where the Escort went through."

"What do you think?" Larsen asked. There was another gust of wind and he automatically put his hand over his tie, even if it was held in place with a tie clip with the Pan-Am logo on it. "Dangerous driving or attempted suicide?"

"Attempted? He's dead, I tell you."

"Do you think he intended to drive into the truck and lost his nerve at the last moment?"

The policeman stamped the mixture of mud and snow from his knee-length boots. Looked down at Sung-min Larsen's smartly polished Loake shoes. Shook his head. "They don't usually."

"*They?*"

"People who come here to the green mile. They've made their minds up. They're . . ." He took a deep breath. "Motivated."

Larsen heard a branch snap behind them and turned round to see the head of the Crime Squad Unit, Katrine Bratt, making her way down the slope in stages, bracing herself against the trees. When she reached them she wiped her hands on her black jeans. Sung-min studied her face as she held her freshly dried hand out to the local police officer and introduced herself.

Pale. Newly applied make-up. Did that mean she'd been crying on the way from Oslo and had put more on before she got out of the car? Obviously, she knew Harry Hole well.

"Have you found the body?" she asked, and nodded when Jan from Sigdal shook his head. Sung-min guessed her next question would be if there was any chance Hole might be alive.

"So we don't actually *know* that he's dead?"

Jan let out a deep sigh and adopted his tragic expression again. "When a car falls twenty metres, it reaches a speed of seventy kilometres an—"

"They're sure he's dead," Sung-min said.

"And presumably you're here because you think there's a connection to the murder of Rakel Fauke," Bratt said without looking at Sung-min, focusing instead on the grotesque sculpture of the wrecked car.

Aren't you? Sung-min was about to ask, but realised that it probably wasn't that strange for a head of department to visit the location where one of her colleagues had died. Maybe. Almost two hours' driving, fresh make-up. Maybe it was more than just a professional relationship?

"Shall we go back up to my car?" he asked. "I've got some coffee."

Katrine nodded, and Sung-min cast a quick glance at Jan as if to let him know that no, he wasn't invited as well.

Sung-min and Katrine got in the front seats of his BMW Gran Coupé. Even if he got a decent petrol allowance, he was still taking a loss by driving his own car instead of one of Kripos's, but as his father used to say: life's too short not to drive a good car.

"Hello," Bratt said, reaching her hand back between the seats to pat the dog lying on the back seat with its head on its front paws, looking up at them sadly.

"Kasparov's a retired police dog," Sung-min said as he poured coffee from a flask into two paper cups. "But he outlived his owner so I've taken him in."

"You like dogs?"

"Not especially, but he didn't have anyone else." Sung-min handed her one of the cups. "To get to the point. I was at the point of arresting Harry Hole."

Katrine Bratt spilled some of the coffee as she was about to take her first sip. And Sung-min knew it wasn't because the coffee was too hot.

"Arrest him?" she said, accepting the handkerchief he offered her. "Based on what?"

"We got a phone call. From a guy called Freund. Sigurd Freund, in fact. A specialist in 3-D analysis of film and photographs. We've used him before, as have you. He wanted to check the formalities regarding a job he'd done for Detective Inspector Harry Hole."

"Why did he call you? Hole works for us."

"Maybe that's why. Freund said Hole had asked him to send the invoice to his private address, which is obviously highly irregular. Freund just wanted to make sure it was all above board. He had also found out rather late that Harry Hole is between one metre ninety and one ninety-five tall, the same as the man in the footage in question. Then Freund checked with Police Headquarters to see if Hole drives a Ford Escort, the same as in the recording. He sent us the files. They were taken using a so-called wildlife camera outside Rakel Fauke's house. The time matches the presumed time of the murder. The camera has been removed, presumably by the only person who knew it was there."

"The only person?"

"When people install cameras like that in built-up areas, they're usually used to spy on people. Their partner, for instance. So we sent Hole's photograph to the people who sell wildlife cameras in Oslo, and Harry Hole was recognised by an elderly man who used to own Simensen Hunting and Fishing."

"Why would Har . . . Hole request analysis of the footage if he knew it would incriminate himself?"

"Why would he request analysis without anyone in the police knowing about it?"

"Hole is suspended. If he was going to investigate the murder of his wife, it would have to be in secret."

"In which case the brilliant Harry Hole has just achieved his greatest triumph by uncovering the brilliant Harry Hole."

Katrine Bratt didn't answer. She hid her mouth behind the paper cup, turning it in her hand as she stared out through the windshield at the dwindling daylight.

"I actually think it was the other way around," Sung-min said. "He wanted to check with an expert if it was technically possible to see that it was him being filmed on his way in and out of Rakel Fauke's home right in the middle of the presumed time of the murder. If Sigurd Freund hadn't been able to tell that it was Hole, Hole could have safely handed the footage over to us, because it proves that someone was in Rakel Fauke's house at the time when Hole apparently had an alibi. His alibi would have been strengthened because the images confirm the medical officer's conclusion that Rakel Fauke was murdered sometime between ten o'clock and two o'clock, more precisely after 23:21, which is when the person caught on film arrives."

"But he does have an alibi!"

Sung-min was about to state the obvious, that the alibi was reliant on a single witness, and that experience shows that witness statements couldn't always be relied upon. Not because witnesses are unreliable by nature, but because our memories play tricks and our senses are less reliable than we think. But he had heard the despair in her voice, seen the naked pain in her eyes.

"One of our detectives has gone to see Gule, Hole's neighbour," he said. "They're reconstructing the circumstances in which he gave Hole his alibi."

"Bjørn says Harry was dead drunk when he left him in his flat, that Harry couldn't possibly have . . ."

"Appeared to be dead drunk," Sung-min said. "I'm assuming an alcoholic is more than capable of acting intoxicated. But it's possible he overplayed it."

"Oh?"

"According to Peter Ringdal, the owner of—"

"I know who he is."

"Ringdal says he's seen Hole drunk before, but never in such a state that he had to be dragged out. Hole can handle his drink better than most, and Ringdal says he hadn't drunk that much more than he had seen him drink before. It may be that Hole wanted to look more incapacitated than he was."

"I haven't heard any of this before."

"Because it was assumed that Hole had an alibi, no one looked into it particularly thoroughly. But I paid a visit to Peter Ringdal this morning, after I'd spoken to Freund. It turns out that he'd just had a visit from Harry Hole, and from what Ringdal says, I get the impression Hole realised that the net was starting to close in around him, and was searching desperately for a scapegoat. But once he realised that Ringdal was no use, he'd run out of options, and . . ." Sung-min gestured towards the road in front of them, leaving Bratt to finish the sentence for herself if she wanted to.

Katrine Bratt raised her chin, the way men of a certain age do to pull the skin of their necks from shirt collars that are too tight, but here it made Sung-min think of an athlete trying to motivate herself mentally, shake off a lost point before launching into battle for the next. "What other lines of inquiry are Kripos looking into?"

Sung-min looked at her. Had he expressed himself imprecisely? Didn't she realise that this wasn't a line of inquiry, but a well-lit four-lane highway where even Ole Winter couldn't get lost, where they—apart from the fact that they weren't in possession of the culprit's earthly remains—had already reached their goal?

"There aren't any other lines of inquiry now," he said.

Katrine Bratt nodded and nodded as she alternated between closing her eyes and staring ahead of her, as if this simple fact was something that took a lot of brain power to process.

"But if Harry Hole is dead," she said, "there isn't really any rush to go public with the fact that he's Kripos's prime suspect."

Sung-min began to nod too. Not because he was promising anything, but because he realised why she was asking.

"The local police have issued a press statement saying something along the lines of 'man missing after a car ended up in the river next to Highway 287,'" Sung-min said, pretending he didn't know it was an exact quote, because experience had taught him that it made people nervous and less communicative if you let them see too much of your good memory, your ability to read people, your deductive brain. "I can't see any pressing reason for Kripos to issue any more information to the public, but of course that's a decision for my bosses."

"Winter, you mean?"

Sung-min looked at Bratt, wondering why she had felt it necessary to mention his boss by name. Her face revealed no ulterior motive, and there was no reason to suspect she knew how uncomfortable it made Sung-min every time he was reminded of the fact that Ole Winter was still his superior. Sung-min had never told a soul that he considered Ole Winter a mediocre detective and a distinctly weak leader. Not weak in the sense that he was too soft, quite the reverse, he was old-fashioned, authoritarian and stubborn. Winter lacked the confidence to admit when he was wrong, and to accept that he ought to delegate more of the management to younger colleagues with younger ideas. And, truth be told, sharper detectives. But Sung-min had kept all of this to himself because he assumed he was alone in these opinions within Kripos.

"I'll talk to Winter," Katrine Bratt said. "And Sigdal Sheriff's Office. They won't want to go public with the name of the missing man until his family have been informed, and if I undertake to inform them, that puts me in control of when the local police can identify Harry Hole."

"Good thinking," Sung-min said. "But sooner or later his name's going to get out, and neither you nor I can stop the public and media speculating when they find out that the dead man—"

"Missing man."

". . . is the husband of the woman who was murdered recently."

He saw a shiver run through Bratt. Was she going to start crying again? No. But when she was alone in her own car, almost certainly.

"Thanks for the coffee," she said, feeling for the door handle. "Let's keep in touch."

At Solevatn, Katrine Bratt pulled off the road into an empty lay-by. She parked and looked out across the large, ice-covered lake as she concentrated on her breathing. When she had got her pulse down she took out her phone and saw that she had received a text from Kari Beal, Dagny Jensen's bodyguard, but that could wait. She called Oleg. Told him about the car, the river, the accident.

There was silence at the other end. A long silence. And when Oleg spoke again, his voice sounded surprisingly calm, as if it wasn't as much of a shock to him as Katrine had anticipated.

"It wasn't an accident," Oleg said. "He's committed suicide."

Katrine was about to reply that she didn't know, then realised that it wasn't a question.

"It might take a while to find him," she said. "There's still ice on the lake."

"I'll come down," Oleg said. "I've got a diving certificate. I used to be afraid of water, but . . ."

Another silence, and for a moment she thought the line had been broken. Then she heard a deep, shaky breath, and when he went on, it was in a voice that was fighting back tears.

". . . he taught me how to swim."

She waited. And when he spoke again, his voice was steady. "I'll contact Sigdal Sheriff's Office and ask if I can join the diving team. And I'll talk to Sis."

Katrine told him to get in touch if there was anything she could do, gave him her direct office number, then hung up. There. It was done. No reason to fight it anymore, she was alone in her own car.

She leaned her head back and burst into tears.

42

It was half past four. The last client. Erland Madsen had recently had a discussion with a psychiatrist about the conceptual boundary between a client and a patient. Was it dependent upon the professional's own title, whether they were a psychologist or a psychiatrist? Or did the distinction run between medicated patients and non-medicated clients? As a psychologist, it sometimes felt like a disadvantage not to be able to prescribe medication when he knew exactly what his client needed but still had to refer them to a psychiatrist who knew less about post-traumatic stress disorder than he did, for instance.

Madsen clasped his hands together. He usually did that when he and the client were done with the pleasantries and were about to start what they were there for. He did it without thinking, but when he became aware of the ritual, he had done a bit of research and found a religious historian who claimed it dated back to the time when a prisoner's hands were tied with rope, so that clasped hands came to be seen as a symbol of submission. In the Roman Empire, a defeated soldier could surrender and plead for mercy by showing his clasped hands. Christians' prayers for mercy from an omnipotent God were presumably another aspect of the same thing. So when Erland Madsen clasped his hands together, did that mean he was subordinating himself to his client? Hardly. It was more likely that the psychologist, on behalf of his client as well as himself, was subordinating himself to the questionable authority and shifting dogma of psychology, the way priests, the weathervanes of theology, asked their congregations to cast off the eternal truths of the past in favour of those of today.

But while priests clasped their hands together and said "Let us pray," Madsen's opening line was: "Let's start where we left off last time."

He waited until Roar Bohr nodded before he went on.

"Let's talk about when you killed someone. You said you were . . ."—Madsen checked his notes—"a freak. Why is that?"

Bohr cleared his throat, and Madsen noted that he too had clasped his hands together. Unconscious mirroring, that was fairly common. "I realised fairly early that I was a freak," Bohr said. "Because I wanted to kill someone so badly . . ."

Erland Madsen tried to keep his face neutral, and not show that he was keen to hear the rest, just that he was open, receptive, safe, non-judgemental. Not curious, not eager to hear anything sensational, not keen to hear an entertaining story. But Madsen couldn't help but admit that he had been looking forward to this appointment, this session, this conversation. But who was to say that there couldn't be a confluence between a key experience for the client and an entertaining story for the therapist? Yes, after thinking it through, Madsen had concluded that whatever was good for the client ought automatically to trigger curiosity in any serious psychologist who had his client's best interests at heart. The fact that Madsen was curious depended upon the fact that these questions were important for his client, because of course he was a conscientious psychologist. And now that he had figured out which order cause and effect came in, he not only knitted his fingers, but pressed his palms together.

"I wanted to kill someone so badly," Roar Bohr repeated. "But I couldn't. That's why I was a freak."

He stopped. Madsen had to count in his head to stop himself intervening too quickly. Four, five, six.

"You couldn't?"

"No. I thought I could, but I was wrong. In the Army there are psychologists whose job is to teach soldiers to kill. But specialist units like Special Forces don't use them. Experience indicates that the people who apply to units like that are already so supremely motivated to kill that it would be a waste of time and money to employ psychologists. And I felt motivated. Nothing I thought or felt when we trained to kill suggested I would ever encounter any resistance. Quite the opposite, in fact."

"When did you discover that you were unable to kill another person?"

Bohr took a deep breath. "In Basra, in Iraq, during a raid with an American specialist unit. We'd used the snake tactic, had blown our way into the building where the lookouts said the shots had come from. Inside was a young girl of fourteen or fifteen. She was wearing a blue dress, her face was grey from the dust of the blast, and she was holding a Kalashnikov that was as big as she was. It was aimed at me. I tried to shoot her, but froze. I ordered my finger to pull the trigger, but it wouldn't do it. It was as if the problem wasn't in my head, but in my muscles. The girl started firing, but luckily she was still blinded by the dust, and the bullets hit the wall behind me. I remember feeling fragments of brick hit my back. And still I just stood there. One of the Americans shot her. Her little body fell backwards onto a sofa covered with colourful blankets, and a small table with a couple of photographs on it, they looked like her grandparents."

He paused.

"What did that make you feel?"

"Nothing," Bohr said. "I felt nothing for the next few years. Apart from abject panic at the thought of finding myself in the same situation and messing up again. Like I said, there was nothing wrong with my motivation. There was just something inside my head that wouldn't work. Or was working *too* well. So I focused on leadership instead of active duty, I thought I was better suited to that. And I was."

"But you didn't *feel* anything?"

"No. Apart from those panic attacks. And seeing as they were the alternative to not feeling anything, it felt fine not to feel anything."

"'Comfortably Numb.'"

"What?"

"Sorry. Go on."

"When I was first made aware that I was showing signs of PTSD—insomnia, irritability, rapid heart rate, lots of little things—it didn't really bother me much. Everyone in Special Forces knew about PTSD, obviously, but even if the official version is that we take it very seriously, it wasn't something we ever spoke about much. No one said out loud that PTSD was for weaklings, but Special Forces troops are pretty self-aware, we know perfectly well that we have higher NPY levels and all that."

Madsen nodded. There was research that suggested the way soldiers were recruited to specialist units like Special Forces filtered out those with average or low levels of neuropeptide Y, or NPY, a neurotransmitter that lowers stress levels. Some Special Forces troops believed that this genetic disposition, together with their training and strong camaraderie, made them immune to PTSD.

"It was OK to admit you'd had a few nightmares," Bohr said. "That proved you weren't a complete psychopath. But apart from that I think we regarded PTSD a bit like our parents regarded smoking: as long as almost everyone had a go, it couldn't be *that* dangerous. But then it got worse . . ."

"Yes," Madsen said, leafing back through his notes. "We talked about that. But you also said that it got better at one point."

"Yes. It got better when I finally managed to kill someone."

Erland Madsen looked up. He took his glasses off, without it being a particularly dramatic gesture.

"Who did you kill?" Madsen could have bitten his tongue. What sort of question was that for a professional therapist? And did he really want to know the answer?

"A rapist. It doesn't really make much difference who he was, but he raped and killed a woman named Hala. She was my interpreter in Afghanistan."

A pause.

"Why do you say 'rapist'?"

"What?"

"You say he killed your interpreter. Isn't that worse than rape? Wouldn't it be more natural to say that you'd killed a murderer?"

Bohr looked at Madsen as if the psychologist had said something he'd never thought of himself. He moistened his lips as if he was about to say something. Then he did it again.

"I'm searching," he said. "I'm searching for the man who raped Bianca."

"Your younger sister?"

"He needs to make amends for what he did. We all need to make amends for what we've done."

"Do you need to make amends for what you've done?"

"I need to make amends for the fact that I didn't manage to protect her. The way she protected me."

"How did your sister protect you?"

"By holding on to her secret." Bohr took a deep, shaky breath. "Bianca was ill when she finally told me that she'd been raped when she was seventeen years old, but I knew it was true, it all fitted. She told me because she was convinced she was pregnant, even though it was several years later. She said she could feel it, it was growing very slowly, that it was like a swelling, a stone, and that it would kill her in order to get out. We were at the cabin, and I said I would help her to get rid of it, but she said that then he—the rapist—would come and kill her, like he'd promised. So I gave her a sleeping pill, and the next morning I told her it was an abortion pill, that she was no longer pregnant. She became hysterical. Later, when she was in hospital again and I went to visit her, the psychiatrist showed me a sheet of paper where she'd drawn an eagle calling my name, and told me she'd said something about an abortion and that she and I had killed *me*. I chose to keep our secret. I don't know if it made any difference. Either way, Bianca would rather die herself than let me, her big brother, die."

"And you were unable to prevent that. So you had to make amends?"

"Yes. And I could only do that by avenging her. By stopping men who rape. That was why I joined the Army, why I applied to Special Forces. I wanted to be prepared. And then Hala was raped as well . . ."

"And you killed the man who did the same thing to Hala that had been done to your sister?"

"Yes."

"And how did that make you feel?"

"Like I said. Better. Killing someone made me feel better. I'm no longer a freak."

Madsen looked down at the blank page in his notebook. He had stopped writing. He cleared his throat.

"So . . . have you made amends now?"

"No."

"No?"

"I haven't found the man who took Bianca. And there are others."

"Other rapists who have to be stopped, you mean?"

"Yes."

"And you'd like to stop them?"

"Yes."

"Kill them?"

"Looks like it. It makes me feel better."

Erland Madsen hesitated. Here was a situation that needed to be dealt with, from both a therapeutic and a judicial perspective.

"These killings, are they something you mostly just like to think about, or are they something you're actively planning to carry out?"

"I don't really know."

"Would you like someone to stop you?"

"No."

"What would you like, then?"

"I'd like you to tell me if you think it will help next time as well."

"Killing someone?"

"Yes."

Madsen looked at Roar Bohr. But all his experience told him that you could never find answers in faces, expressions, body language, too much of that is learned behaviour. It was in people's words that you found the answers. And now he had been asked a question that he couldn't answer. Not openly. Not honestly. Madsen looked at his watch.

"Time's up," he said. "Let's continue with this on Thursday."

"I'm going now," a woman's voice said from the doorway.

Erland Madsen looked up from the folder he had found in his clients' archive that was now lying on his desk. It was Torill, the receptionist shared by the six psychologists in the practice. She had her coat on, and was looking at Erland with an expression he knew meant there was something he needed to remember, but that she was too tactful to broach directly.

Erland Madsen looked at the time. Six o'clock. He remembered what it was. He was supposed to be putting the children to bed that evening; his wife was helping her mother clear out her loft.

But first he needed to figure this out.

Two clients. There were several points of contact. They had both worked in Kabul, partly overlapping there. Both had been referred to him because they had shown signs of PTSD. And now he had found it in the notes: they had both had a close relationship with some-one called Hala. Obviously it could be a common woman's name in Afghanistan, but the chance that there could be more than one Hala working as an interpreter for Norwegian forces in Kabul struck him as unlikely.

With Bohr it had been the usual thing when it came to his rela-tionships with women who were either his subordinates or younger than him: he felt responsible for them, in the same way he had for his younger sister, a responsibility that bordered on the obsessive, a form of paranoia.

The other client had had an even closer relationship to Hala. They had been lovers.

Erland Madsen had taken detailed notes, and read that they had both got the same tattoo. Not their names, because that would have been dangerous if it had been discovered by the Taliban or anyone else with a strict faith. Instead they'd had the word "friend" tattooed on their bodies, something that would bind them together for the rest of their lives.

But none of this was the most important point of connection.

Madsen ran his finger down the page and found what he was looking for, just as he thought he'd remembered it: both Bohr and the other client had said that they had felt *better* after killing someone. At the bottom of the page he had made a note for future reference: *NB! Dig deeper into this next time. What does "better after killing someone" mean?*

Erland Madsen looked at his watch. He would have to take the notes home and read the rest after the children were asleep. He closed the folder and put a red rubber band around it. The band ended up running across the name written on the folder.

Kaja Solness.

43

Three months earlier

Erland Madsen snuck a glance at his watch. The hour was almost over. That was a shame, because even if it was only their second therapy session, there was no doubt that the client, Kaja Solness, was an interesting case. She was responsible for security in the Red Cross, a post that shouldn't necessarily have exposed her to the traumas that triggered PTSD in soldiers. All the same, she had told him how she had experienced acts of war and the daily horrors that only soldiers on active duty usually experience, and that sooner or later end up damaging their psyche. It was interesting—but not unusual—that she didn't seem to recognise that she had not only ended up in these dangerous situations, but that she herself had more or less consciously sought them out. It was also interesting that she hadn't shown any symptoms of PTSD during her debriefing in Tallinn, but had taken the initiative to seek therapy herself. Most soldiers who came were referrals, they were more or less forced to have counselling. And most of them didn't want to talk, some of them came straight out and said they thought therapy was for sissies, and became irritable when they realised Madsen couldn't prescribe the sleeping pills they had come for. "I just want to sleep!" they said, unaware of how ill they actually were until the day they sat with their mouth over the end of the rifle and tears streaming down their cheeks. Those who refused to have therapy got their pills, of course, their antidepressants and sleeping tablets. But Madsen's experience told him that what he was engaged in, trauma-based cognitive therapy, helped. It wasn't the acute crisis therapy that had been so popular until research showed that it didn't work at all, but long-term treatment in which the client worked through the trauma and gradually learned to tackle and live with their physical responses. Because believing that there was a quick fix, that you could heal those wounds overnight, was naive and, at worst, dangerous.

But that seemed to be what Kaja Solness was after. She wanted to talk about it. Quickly, and a lot. So quickly, and so much, that he'd had to try to slow her down. But it felt like she didn't have time, she wanted answers straightaway.

"Anton was Swiss," Kaja Solness said. "A doctor, working for the ICRC, the Swiss branch of the Red Cross. I was deeply in love with him. And he loved me. I thought he did, anyway."

"Do you think you were wrong?" Madsen asked as he took notes.

"No. I don't know. He left me. Well, 'left' probably isn't the right word. When you work together in a war zone, it's difficult to physically leave someone—we live and work in close proximity. But he told me he'd met someone else." She let out a short laugh. "'Met' isn't the right word either. Sonia was a nurse in the Red Cross. We literally ate, slept and worked together. She was also Swiss. Anton prefers beautiful women, so it goes without saying that she was beautiful. Intelligent. Perfect manners. From a good family. Switzerland's still the sort of country where that kind of thing matters. But the worst thing was that she was nice. A genuinely likeable person who threw herself into her work with energy, courage and love. I used to hear her crying in her sleep on days when they'd had to deal with a lot of dead and serious injuries. And she was nice to me. She gave the impression that I was the one who was being nice to her. *Merci vilmal*, she used to say. I don't know if that's German, French or both, but she said it all the time. Thank you, thank you, thank you. As far as I know, she never knew that Anton and I had been together before she came into the picture. He was married, so we'd kept it quiet. And then it was Sonia's turn to keep their relationship secret. Ironically, I was the only person she confided in. She was frustrated, said he'd promised to leave his wife, but that he kept putting it off. I listened and comforted her and hated her more and more. Not because she was a bad person, but because she was a good person. Don't you think that's odd, Madsen?"

Erland Madsen started slightly at the mention of his name. "Do *you* think it's odd?" he asked.

"No," Kaja Solness said, after thinking for a few moments. "It was Sonia—not Anton's chronically ill, wealthy wife—who was standing between me and Anton. That makes sense, doesn't it?"

"It sounds logical. Go on."

"It was outside Basra. Have you ever been to Basra?"

"No."

"The hottest city on earth, you have to drink or die, as the journalists in the hotel bar at the Sultan Palace used to say. At night, huge, carnivorous honey badgers would come in from the desert and roam the streets, eating whatever they could find. People were terrified of them; farmers outside the city said the badgers had started eating their cows. You can get great dates in Basra, though."

"At least that's something."

"Well, we got called to a farm where some cows had trampled the badly maintained fence around a minefield. The farmer and his son had run after them to get them out. Afterwards we found out that they thought there were only anti-personnel mines there. They look like flowerpots with spikes sticking out of them, and are easy to see and avoid. But there were PROM-1s there as well, and they're much harder to spot. And PROM-1s are also called Bouncing Betties."

Madsen nodded. Most landmines hit their victims' legs and groins, but these bounced up when you triggered them and exploded at chest height.

"Almost all the animals had emerged unscathed, I don't know if that was by luck or instinct. The father had almost managed to get out of the minefield when he triggered a PROM-1 right next to the fence. It flew up and peppered him with shrapnel. But because these mines fly up, the shrapnel often hits people a long way away. The son had run thirty or forty metres into the minefield to rescue the last cow, but he still got hit by a piece of shrapnel. We'd managed to get the father out and were trying to save his life, but the boy was lying in the minefield screaming. Those screams were unbearable, but the sun was going down and we couldn't go into a field of PROM-1s without metal detectors; we had to wait for backup. Then one of the ICRC's vehicles turned up. Sonia jumped out. She heard the screams, ran over to me and asked what sort of mines they were. She put her hand on my arm the way she always did, and I saw she was wearing a ring that hadn't been there before. An engagement ring. And I knew he'd done it, that Anton had finally left his wife. We were standing a little way from the others, and I told her there were anti-personnel mines. And as I took a breath and was about to say there were PROM-1s as well, she was already on her way into the minefield. I called after her, obviously not loud enough, the boy's screams must have drowned me out."

Kaja picked up the cup of tea Erland had given her. She looked at him, and he saw her realise that he was waiting for the end of the story.

"Sonia died. The father too. But the boy survived."

Erland drew three vertical lines on his notepad. Struck through two of them.

"Did you feel guilty?" he asked.

"Obviously." Her face looked surprised. Was that a trace of irritation in her voice?

"Why is it obvious, Kaja?"

"Because I killed her. I killed someone who didn't have an ounce of malice in her."

"Don't you think you're being a bit hard on yourself now? Like you say, you tried to warn her."

"Don't you get paid enough to think you have to listen carefully, Madsen?"

Erland noted the aggression in her voice, but also that there was no trace of it in the mild expression on her face.

"What do you think I didn't hear, Kaja?"

"It doesn't take so long to breathe in and shout 'PROM-1' that someone has time to turn away from you, jump over a fence and stand on one of those fuckers. Your voice doesn't get drowned out by a boy lying half a football pitch away, Madsen."

Silence settled on the office for a few moments.

"Have you spoken to anyone else about this?"

"No. Like I said, Sonia and I kept to ourselves. I told the others I had warned her about both types of mine. They didn't think it odd, they knew how selfless Sonia was. During the memorial service in the camp, Anton told me he thought that Sonia's desire to be accepted, to be loved, had led to her demise. I've thought about that since then, how dangerous it can be for us, this longing to be loved. I'm the only person who knows what really happened. And now you." Kaja smiled. With small, pointed teeth. As if they were two teenagers sharing a secret, Erland thought.

"What consequences did Sonia's death have for you?"

"I got Anton back."

"You got Anton back. Was that all?"

"Yes."

"Why do you think you got back together with someone who had betrayed you like that?"

"I wanted him close so I could see him suffer. See him mourn his loss, devoured by it the way I had been. I held on to him for a while, then I told him I didn't love him anymore and left him."

"You'd got your revenge?"

"Yes. And it had also dawned on me why I had actually wanted him in the first place."

"And that was?"

"Because he was married and unavailable. And because he was tall and fair-haired. He reminded me of someone I used to love."

Erland noted that this was evidently also important, but it was something they would have to come back to at a later stage of the therapy.

"Let's get back to the trauma, Kaja. You said you felt guilty. Can I ask what might sound like the same question, even though it isn't: Do you regret it?"

Kaja put one finger under her chin, as if to show him she was thinking about it.

"Yes," she said. "But at the same time it gave me a strange sense of relief. I felt better."

"You felt better after Sonia died?"

"I felt better after I'd *killed* Sonia."

Erland Madsen made a note. *Felt better after killing.* "Can you describe what you mean by that?"

"Free. I felt free. Killing someone was like crossing some sort of border. You think there's a fence, some sort of wall, but when you cross it you realise that it's just a line someone's drawn on a map. Sonia and I, we had both crossed a boundary. She was dead, and I was free. But first and foremost, I felt better because the man who had betrayed me was suffering."

"You're talking about Anton?"

"Yes. He was suffering, so I didn't have to. Anton was my Jesus. My personal Jesus."

"In what way?"

"I crucified him so he could take on my suffering, the way we did with Jesus. Because Jesus didn't put himself on the cross, *we* hung him up there, that's the whole point. We achieved salvation and eternal life by killing Jesus. God couldn't do much, God didn't sacrifice his son. If it's true that God gave us free will, then we killed Jesus against God's will. And the day we realise that, that we defied God's will, that's the day we set ourselves free, Madsen. And then everything can happen."

Kaja Solness laughed, and Erland Madsen tried in vain to formulate a question. Instead he sat there looking at the peculiar glint in her eyes.

"My question is," she said, "if it was so liberating last time, should I try it again? Should I crucify the real Jesus? Or am I just mad?"

Erland Madsen moistened his lips. "Who's the real Jesus?"

"You didn't answer my question. Have you got an answer for me, Doctor?"

"That depends what you're really asking."

Kaja smiled and let out a deep sigh. "Quite true," she said, then looked at the watch on her slender wrist. "Looks like we're out of time."

After she had gone, Erland Madsen sat there looking at his notes. He wrote at the bottom of the page: *NB! Dig deeper into this next time. What does "better after killing someone" mean?*

Two days later Torill passed on a phone message she had received at the reception desk. A Kaja Solness had said they could cancel her next appointment, that she wouldn't be coming back, and that she'd found a solution to her problem.

44

Alexandra Sturdza was sitting at one of the window tables in the empty canteen at the Rikshospital. In front of her lay a cup of black coffee and another long day at work. She had worked until midnight the previous day, slept for five hours, and needed all the stimulants she could get.

The sun was on its way up. This city was like the sort of woman who could be dazzlingly beautiful in the right light, only to look so ordinary a moment later that she becomes utterly unremarkable, even ugly. But right now, at this early hour of the morning, before the average Norwegian got to work, Oslo was hers, like a secret lover she was sharing a stolen hour with. And it was a rendezvous with someone who was still unfamiliar and exciting.

The hills to the east lay in shadow, while those to the west were bathed in soft light. The buildings in the city centre down by the fjord were black silhouettes behind black silhouettes, like a cemetery at sunrise. Just a few glass buildings were lit up, like silver-coloured fish beneath the dark surface of the water. And the sea glinted between islands and skerries that would soon be green. How she longed for spring! They called March the first month of spring here, even if everyone knew it was still winter. Washed-out, cold, with isolated, sudden bursts of warm passion. April was at best a deceitful flirt. May was the first month you could rely on. May. Alexandra wanted a May. She knew that on the occasions when she had had a man like that, a warm, gentle man who gave her all she could ask for, even in suitable doses, she just became spoiled and demanding and ended up betraying him with June or, even worse, July, who was completely unreliable. How about a good, grown-up man like August next time, one with a bit of grey in his hair and a marriage and family behind him? Yes, she would have welcomed someone like that. So how come she had ended up falling in love with November? A gloomy, dark, rain-drenched man with prospects of getting even darker, who was either so quiet that you couldn't even hear any birds, or felt like he was going to tear the roof off your house with his crazy, rumbling autumn gales. Sure, he rewarded you with sunny days of unexpected warmth that you valued all the more as a result, revealing a strangely beautiful, ruined, ravaged landscape where a few buildings were still standing. Solid and unshakeable, like the bedrock itself, which you knew would still be standing on the last day of the month, and where Alexandra—in the absence of anything better—had sought refuge from time to time. But something better would surely have to come along soon. She stretched and tried to yawn the tiredness out of her body. It must be spring soon. May.

"Miss Sturdza?"

She spun round in surprise. It wasn't just the time of the encounter that was un-Norwegian, but the mode of address. And, sure enough, the man standing there wasn't quite Norwegian. Or rather, he didn't *look* Norwegian. Not only did he have Asiatic features, but his outfit—suit, crisp white shirt and a tie with a tie clip—definitely wasn't usual work attire for a Norwegian. Unless the Norwegian in question was one of those overconfident idiots with a job description ending in "agent" or "broker," which was usually one of the first things they told you if you met them in a bar, where they tried to look like they'd just come from the office because they had to work so hard. That, at least, was the signal they hoped to give off. And when they "revealed" their job after discreetly maneuvering the conversation to a place where it wasn't utterly ridiculous to mention it, they did so with feigned embarrassment, as if she had just uncovered some fucking crown prince in disguise.

"Sung-min Larsen," the man said. "I'm a detective at Kripos. Can I sit down?"

Well. Alexandra studied him. Tall. He went to the gym. Not too much, everything in proportion, he was aware of the cosmetic value, but enjoyed the exercise itself. Like her. Brown eyes, of course. A little over thirty? No ring. Kripos. Yes, she'd heard a couple of the girls mention his name, that odd combination of Asian and Norwegian. Strange that she'd never met him before. At that moment the sun reached the canteen window of the Rikshospital, lit up Sung-min Larsen's face and warmed one of Alexandra's cheeks with surprising intensity. *Miss Sturdza*. Perhaps spring was coming early this year? Without putting her cup down she pushed a chair out with her foot.

"Be my guest."

"Thanks."

As he leaned forward to sit down, he instinctively put his hand over his tie, even though he was wearing a tie clip. There was something familiar about the clip, something that reminded her of her childhood. She remembered what it was. The bird-like logo of the Romanian airline, TAROM.

"Are you a pilot, Larsen?"

"My father was," he said.

"My uncle was too," she said. "He flew IAR-93 fighters."

"Really? Produced in Romania."

"You know the plane?"

"No, I just remember that they were the only Communist planes that weren't made in the Soviet Union in the seventies."

"Communist planes?"

Larsen gave a wry smile. "The sort my father was supposed to shoot down if they came too close."

"The Cold War. So you dreamed of becoming a pilot yourself?"

He looked surprised. Something about him told her that didn't happen very often.

"It's fairly unusual to know about IAR-93s and wear a TAROM tie clip," she added.

"I applied to the Air Force," he admitted.

"But didn't get in?"

"I would have got in," he said with such natural confidence that she didn't doubt it. "But my back was too long. I couldn't fit in the cockpit of the fighters."

"You could have flown other things. Transport planes, helicopters."

"I suppose so," he said.

Your father, she thought. He flew fighters. You couldn't be happy being a lesser version of him, someone lower down on the uncomplicated pilots' hierarchy than your father. Sooner something else altogether. So he was an alpha male. Someone who might not have got to where he was going, but was on the way. Like her.

"I'm investigating a murder . . ." he said, and she realised from his quick glance that the introduction was intended as a warning. "I've got some questions about a Harry Hole."

It felt like the sun outside had gone behind a cloud, as if Alexandra's heart had stopped.

"From the call log on his phone I see that the two of you have called each other several times in the past few weeks, the past few days."

"Hole?" she said, as if she needed to dig the name out, and saw from the look on his face how fake it sounded. "Yes, we've talked on the phone. He's a detective."

"Maybe you've done more than talked?"

"More?" She tried to raise an eyebrow, but wasn't sure if she managed it, it felt like all the muscles in her face were out of control. "What makes you think that?"

"Two things," Larsen said. "That you instinctively pretended not to remember his name even though you've spoken to him six times and called his number twelve times in the past three weeks, two of them on the evening before Rakel Fauke was found murdered. And that during those same three weeks, his phone has been tracked to base stations that overlap with your home address."

He said this without aggression, suspicion or anything else that gave her any sense of manipulation or game-playing. Or rather, he said it as if the game was already over, like a croupier who had no stake in the game reading out the number before raking in the chips.

"We're . . . we *were* lovers," she said. And realised when she heard herself say it that that's exactly how it was. That they had been lovers, no more, no less. And that it was over.

But the second implication only dawned on her when Sung-min Larsen said: "Before we go on, I ought to advise you to consider if you'd like a lawyer present."

She must have looked aghast, because Larsen hurried to add: "You're not suspected of anything, this isn't an official interview, and I'm primarily trying to get information about Harry Hole, not you."

"So why would I need a lawyer?"

"For advice not to talk to me, seeing as your close relationship to Harry Hole could potentially connect you to a murder."

"You mean I might have murdered his wife?"

"No."

"Ah! You think I murdered her out of jealousy."

"Like I said, no."

"I told you we weren't seeing each other anymore."

"I don't think you've killed anyone. But I'm cautioning you because the answers you give could lead to you being suspected of having helped him to avoid being charged with the murder of his wife."

Alexandra realised that she had made the most classic of all drama-queen gestures, and had clutched the string of pearls that she was actually wearing.

"So," Sung-min Larsen said, lowering his voice when the first of the Norwegian early birds entered the canteen. "Shall we continue this conversation?"

He had informed her that she could have a lawyer present, even if it would make his job more complicated. He would have lowered his voice out of consideration to her even if they'd been alone in the room. Maybe he could be trusted. Alexandra looked into his warm brown eyes. She let her hand fall. Straightened her back, pushing—perhaps unconsciously—her breasts forward.

"I've got nothing to hide," she said.

Again, that half-smile of his. She realised she was already looking forward to seeing the rest of it.

Sung-min looked at the time. Four o'clock. He needed to take Kasparov to an appointment at the vet's, so this summons to Winter's office was doubly inconvenient.

But he was finished with the investigation. He didn't have absolutely everything, but he had all he needed.

Firstly, he had proved that Hole's alibi—provided by his neighbour, Gule—was worthless. The reconstruction had proved that he couldn't possibly have heard if Hole was in his flat, or if he had arrived or then left. Hole had evidently also thought about this, because Gule had said he had been there asking exactly the same questions.

Secondly, the 3-D expert, Freund, had completed his analysis. There wasn't much to be gleaned from the hunched figure who had stumbled into Rakel's house at almost half past eleven on the night of the murder. The figure looked twice as fat as Harry Hole, but Freund said that was probably because he was leaning forward and his coat was hanging down in front of him. His posture also made it impossible to determine his height. But when he came out again three hours later, at half past two in the morning, he was clearly more sober, was standing upright in the doorway, showing his true, slim self, and he was the same height as Harry Hole, around 1.92 metres.

He had got into a Ford Escort before remembering to remove his wildlife camera, then he drove away.

Thirdly, he had got hold of a final, decisive piece of evidence from Alexandra Sturdza.

There had been a look of quiet despair on that hard but lively face when he told her about the evidence they had against Harry Hole. And gradually a look of resignation. In the end he had seen her let go of the man she claimed to have already given up. Then he had gently prepared her for some even worse news. And told her that Hole was dead. That he had taken his own life. That—looking at the situation as a whole—perhaps it was for the best. At that point there had been tears in her dark eyes, and he had considered putting his hand on hers as it lay motionless and dead on the table. Just a gentle, comforting touch, then take his hand away again. But he hadn't. Perhaps she sensed his half-intention, because the next time she lifted her coffee cup, she did so with her left hand, leaving her right motionless, like an invitation.

Then she had told him—as far as he could judge—everything. And that reinforced Sung-min's suspicion that Hole had committed the murder when he was drunk and lost his temper, and that he had forgotten large parts of it and had spent the last days of his life investigating himself, hence the business with Gule.

A tear had trickled down one of Alexandra's cheeks, and Sung-min had passed her his handkerchief. He had seen her surprise, presumably because she wasn't used to Norwegian men carrying freshly ironed handkerchiefs.

They had left the canteen, which was starting to fill up, and went to the Forensic Medical Institute laboratory, where she showed him the bloodstained trousers Hole had given her. She told him that the analysis was almost finished, and that there was a more than 90 percent probability that the blood was Rakel Fauke's. She had repeated Harry's explanation as to how the blood had got there, that he had knelt down beside the body after Rakel had been found, and that his trousers had come into contact with the pool of blood.

"That's not correct," Sung-min had said. "He wasn't wearing those trousers when he was at the scene."

"How do you know that?"

"I was there. I spoke to him."

"And you *remember* what sort of trousers he was wearing?"

Sung-min suppressed a spontaneous "of course" and made do with a simple "yes."

So he had all he needed. Motive, opportunity, and forensic evidence that placed the suspect at the scene at the time of the crime. He had considered contacting someone else who, according to Harry Hole's call log, he had spoken to several times, a Kaja Solness, but decided it wasn't a priority seeing as their interaction hadn't started until after the murder. The important thing now was to find one of the pieces that were missing. Because even if he had everything he *needed*, he didn't have everything. He didn't have the murder weapon.

With so much concrete evidence, the police lawyer had had no hesitation in granting Larsen a warrant to search Harry Hole's flat, but they hadn't found the murder weapon or anything else of interest there. Except for that fact in itself: that they *hadn't* found anything of interest. Such a striking absence of incriminating evidence suggested one of two things. That the person living in the flat was a robot. Or that he knew his home would be searched and had removed anything potentially incriminating.

"Interesting," lead investigator Ole Winter said, leaning back behind his desk as he listened to Sung-min Larsen's minutely detailed report.

Not impressive, then, Sung-min thought. Not astonishing, not brilliant, not even so much as good police work.

Just interesting.

"So interesting that it surprises me that you haven't reported any of this to me before now, Larsen. And that I probably wouldn't have this information now either if I hadn't, as lead detective, asked for it. When were you planning to share this with the rest of us who have been working on this case?"

Sung-min ran one hand over his tie and moistened his lips.

He felt like saying that here he was, serving up Harry Hole, the biggest fish around, to Kripos, neatly wrapped up with a bow. That he had single-handedly outmaneuvered the legendary detective in his own field: murder. And that was all Winter had to say, that he could have reported a bit earlier?

There were three reasons why Sung-min decided not to say this.

The first was that there were only the two of them in Winter's office, so there was no third person whose common sense he could appeal to.

The second was that as a rule there's nothing to be gained by contradicting your boss, whether or not there's a third person present.

Thirdly, and most important, Winter was right.

Sung-min *had* delayed reporting on developments in the case.

Who wouldn't have done, when they'd got the fish on the hook, had reeled it back in close to the shore and all that remained was to get it in the net? When you knew that the murder of the decade, to be known in perpetuity as the Harry Hole case, would bear your name, and yours alone. It was the police lawyer who had mentioned it to Winter, when he congratulated him on having caught Harry Hole himself. Yes, Sung-min had to admit that he was selfish, and no, he hadn't stood in front of an open goal looking around for a Messi he could pass the ball and the goal to, because there was no Messi on this team. If there was, it was probably him. It certainly wasn't Winter, who was sitting there with veins throbbing in his temples and eyebrows like thunderclouds over his eyes.

Sung-min chose this response instead:

"It all happened so quickly, one thing kept leading to another, and I didn't want to risk any delay. There wasn't really any time to pause for breath."

"Until now?" Winter said, leaning back in his chair and looking as if he were using the ridge of his nose to take aim at Sung-min.

"The case is solved now," Sung-min said.

Winter let out a short, hard laugh, like a go-kart braking suddenly. "If it's OK with you, let's agree that it's the lead detective who decides when the case is solved. What do you say, Larsen?"

"Of course, Winter." Sung-min had intended to signal his submission, but realised that the older man had seen through him and decided to take offence at the fact the younger man had returned the sarcastic, drawn-out pronunciation of his surname.

"Seeing as you consider the case solved, *Laaar-sen*, I assume you have no objection to me taking it away from you while we tie up a few loose ends."

"As you wish."

Sung-min could have bitten his tongue when he saw how Winter took this arrogantly submissive, bourgeois "as you wish."

Winter smiled. "Right now we need good heads like yours on another murder. The Lysaker case." It was a mean, thin smile, as if his mouth wasn't flexible enough to manage anything more expressive.

The Lysaker murder, Sung-min thought. A drug-related killing. Clearly an internal conflict between junkies. Those involved would talk at the slightest mention of a reduced sentence out of fear of being denied access to drugs. It was the lowest form of murder case, the sort of thing you left to new recruits and those of limited abilities. Winter couldn't be serious, saying he was going to take him, the lead investigator, off the case now, right in front of the line, snatching all the honour and glory away, and for what? For playing his cards a bit too close to his chest for a little too long?

"I want a written report with all the details, Larsen. In the meantime, the others will carry on working on the lines of inquiry you've uncovered. Then I'll have to see when we go public with what we've found out."

Lines of inquiry you've uncovered? He had *solved* the case, for fuck's sake!

Give me a bollocking, Sung-min thought. A reprimand. Winter couldn't just decapitate one of his detectives like this. Until he realised that Winter not only could do it, but wanted to and was going to do it. Because it had just dawned on Sung-min what this was all about. Winter was also aware that Sung-min was the only Messi they had on the team. And that meant he was a threat to Winter as leader, now and in the future. Winter was the alpha male who had spotted that a rival was on the move. Sung-min's solo performance had shown he was ready to challenge Winter's authority. So Winter had decided it was best to dispatch the younger man now, before he grew any bigger and stronger.

45

Johan Krohn and his wife, Frida, had met while they were studying law at the University of Oslo. He would never know what it was
about him that she had fallen for. Maybe he had just presented his
own case so well that she eventually had to give in. There weren't
many other people back then who understood why pretty, sweet
Frida Andresen had picked a socially inept nerd who showed little
interest in anything much apart from law and chess. Johan Krohn,
who was more aware than anyone that he had managed to get a girlfriend who was at least one division above him in the attractiveness
league, courted her, watched over her, chased away potential rivals.
In short, he clung on to her with everything he had. Even so, everyone thought it was only a matter of time until she found herself someone more exciting. But Johan was a brilliant student, and a brilliant
lawyer. He became the youngest lawyer since John Christian Elden
to earn the right to practise in the Supreme Court, and was offered
work others his age could only dream about. His social confidence
rose in line with his status and income. Suddenly new doors were
open to him, and Krohn—after due consideration—walked through
most of them. One of them led to a life he had missed out on in his
youth, and could be summarised by the words "women," "wine" and
"song." More precisely: women who actually became more amenable
when you introduced yourself as a partner at a well-known law firm.
Wine in the form of exclusive whisky from windswept places like the
Hebrides and Shetland Islands, as well as cigars and—in ever greater
quantity—cigarettes. He never quite got the hang of song, but there
were exonerated criminals who claimed that his defense statements

were more beautiful than anything that had ever come out of Frank Sinatra's mouth.

Frida looked after the children, and managed the family's social circle, which wouldn't have been there if it weren't for her, and she worked part-time as a lawyer for two cultural foundations. If Johan Krohn had gone past her in the attractiveness league table, it didn't alter the balance in their relationship. Because that balance had always been so unequal, he so grateful for his luck, she so used to being courted, that it had become part of the DNA of their relationship, the only way they knew how to relate to each other. They showed each other respect and love, and outwardly were comfortable letting it look like it was Johan who was steering the ship. But at home neither of them was in any doubt about who decided what went where. Or where Johan Krohn should smoke his cigarettes now that he—and he was secretly rather proud of this—was addicted to nicotine.

So when darkness had fallen, the children were in bed and the television news had told him what was going on in Norway and the U.S.A., he would take his cigarettes, go upstairs and out onto the terrace, which looked out upon Mærradalen and Ullern.

He leaned against the railing. The view included Hegnar Media's office complex and part of Smestaddammen that lay just beyond. He was thinking about Alise. And how he was going to solve the matter. It had become too intense, had gone on too long, it couldn't continue, they were going to be found out. Well, they had actually been found out long ago, the wry smiles from the other partners in the firm when they were sitting in meetings and Alise came in with a file or an important phone message for him left no room for doubt. But *Frida* didn't know, and that was what he meant by being found out, as he had explained to Alise. She had taken it with almost irritating pragmatism and said he shouldn't worry.

"Your secret's safe with me," she had said.

And perhaps it was this very statement that worried him.

Your secret, not *ours* (she was single), and *with me*, as if it were a legal document stored in her bank vault. Where it was *safe*, but only as long as she kept the vault locked. Not that he suspected that her choice of words was meant as a threat, but it still struck home. That she was protecting him. The way she might expect him to offer a protective hand to her. There was stiff competition between young, recently qualified lawyers, and the rewards for those who rose to the top were considerable, with a correspondingly merciless demise for those who sank to the bottom. Getting help to float could have a decisive effect.

"A lot on your mind?"

Johan Krohn started and dropped his cigarette, which fell like a falling star through the darkness down towards the orchard below him. It's one thing to hear a voice behind you when you think you're alone and unobserved. It's something else entirely when that voice belongs to someone who doesn't belong there, and the only way that person could have got onto the terrace on the second floor was either by flying or teleportation. The fact that the person in question is a brutal criminal who has been convicted of more assaults than anyone else in Oslo in the past thirty years only makes the situation more unexpected.

Krohn turned and saw the man leaning against the wall in the darkness on the other side of the terrace door. In the choice between "What are you doing here?" and "How did you get here?", he found himself asking the former.

"Rolling a cigarette," Svein Finne said, raising his hands to his mouth, and a grey tongue slipped out between his thick lips to lick the cigarette paper.

"Wh . . . what do you want?"

"A light," Finne said, sticking the cigarette between his lips and looking expectantly at Krohn.

The lawyer hesitated before holding out his hand and clicking his lighter. He saw the flame tremble. Saw it get sucked into the cigarette, as the glowing strands of tobacco curled up.

"Nice house," Finne said. "Nice view too. I used to hang out in this neighbourhood a lot, many years ago."

For a moment Krohn imagined his client literally hanging out, floating in the air.

Finne pointed towards Mærradalen with his cigarette. "I occasionally slept in that bit of forest, along with the other homeless. And I remember one particular girl who used to walk through there, she lived on the Huseby side. Old enough for sex, obviously, but no older than fifteen, sixteen. One day I gave her a crash course in how to make love." Finne laughed gruffly. "She was so frightened I had to comfort her afterwards, poor thing. She cried and cried, saying her father, who was a bishop, and her big brother would come and get me. I told her I wasn't afraid of bishops or big brothers, and that she didn't have to be either, because now she had a man of her own. And possibly a child on the way. And then I let her go. I let them go, you see. Catch and release, isn't that what anglers call it?"

"I'm not an angler," Krohn found himself saying.

"I've never killed an innocent person in my entire life," Finne said. "You need to respect innocence in nature. Abortion . . ." Finne sucked so hard on his cigarette that Krohn heard the paper crackle. "Tell me, you know all about the law, is there anything that's a worse crime against the laws of nature? Killing your own innocent offspring. Can you think of anything more perverse?"

"Can we get to the point, Finne? My wife's waiting for me inside."

"Of course she's waiting for you. We're all waiting for something. Love. Intimacy. Human contact. I waited for Dagny Jensen yesterday. No love, I'm afraid. And now it's going to be difficult for me to get close to her again. We get lonely, don't we? And we all need something . . ." He looked at his cigarette. "Something warm."

"If you need my help, I suggest we talk about it at the office tomorrow." Krohn realised he hadn't struck the authoritative tone he was aiming at. "I . . . I'll find time to see you whenever you like."

"You'll find time?" Finne let out a short laugh. "After all I've done for you, that feather you've got in your hat now, that's all you've got to offer me? Your *time*?"

"What is it you want, Finne?"

His client took a step forward, and the light from the window fell across half his face. He ran his right hand over the red-painted railing. Krohn shuddered when he saw the red paint through the large hole in the back of Finne's hand.

"Your wife," Finne said. "I want her."

Krohn felt his throat tighten.

Finne flashed him a grotesque grin. "Relax, Krohn. Even if I have to admit that I've thought a lot about Frida in the past few days, I'm not going to touch her. Because I don't touch other men's women, I want my own. As long as she's yours, she's safe, Krohn. But obviously you could hardly hold on to a proud, financially independent woman like Frida if she got to hear about the pretty little assistant you had with you when I was questioned. Alise. That was her name, wasn't it?"

Johan Krohn stared. Alise? *He* knew about Alise?

Krohn cleared his throat. It sounded like windshield wipers on dry glass. "I have no idea what you're talking about."

Finne pointed one finger towards his eye. "Eagle eyes. I've seen you. Watching you fucking is like watching a couple of baboons. Fast, efficient, without any great emotion. It won't last, but you don't want to go without it, do you? We all need warmth."

Where? Krohn wondered. At the office? In the hotel room he sometimes booked for them? In Barcelona in October? It was impossible. When they made love it was always high up, where they knew they couldn't be seen from the other side of the street.

"What will last, on the other hand, unless someone tells Frida about Alise, is this." Finne jerked his thumb over his shoulder at the house. "Family. That's the most important thing, isn't it, Krohn?"

"I don't know what you're talking about or what you want," Krohn said. He had put both elbows on the railing behind him. It was supposed to convey relaxed ambivalence, but he knew he probably looked more like a boxer who was already on the ropes.

"I'll leave Frida alone if I can have Alise," Finne said, flicking his cigarette into the air. Its glowing tip curved through the darkness like Krohn's a short while ago before going out in the darkness. "The police are looking for me, I can't move as freely as I'd like. I need a little . . ."—he grinned again—"*assistance* in order to get some warmth. I want you to arrange for me to have the young lady to myself, somewhere safe."

Krohn blinked in disbelief. "You want me to try to persuade Alise to see you alone? So you can . . . assault her?"

"Forget 'try' and 'assault.' You *will* persuade her, Krohn. And I'm going to seduce her, not assault her. I've never assaulted anyone, that's all a big misunderstanding. The girls don't always understand what's best for them, or the task nature has set them, that's all. But they come to their senses soon enough. Just as Alise will too. She'll come to realise that if she threatens this family, for instance, she'll have me to answer to. Hey, don't look so glum, Krohn, you're getting two for the price of one here: my silence, as well as the girl's."

Krohn stared at Finne. The words were echoing through his head. *Your secret's safe with me.*

"Johan?"

Frida's voice came from inside the house, and he heard her steps on the stairs. Then a voice whispered close to his ear, accompanied by the smell of tobacco and something rancid, bestial. "There's a grave in Vår Frelsers Cemetery. Valentin Gjertsen. I'll expect to hear from you within two days."

Frida reached the top of the stairs and started to walk towards the terrace, but stopped in the light inside the door.

"Brr, it's cold," she said, folding her arms. "I heard voices."

"Psychiatrists say that's a bad sign." Johan Krohn smiled, and began to walk towards her, but wasn't quick enough. She had already stuck her head out of the door and was looking in both directions.

She looked up at him. "Were you talking to yourself?"

Krohn looked around the terrace. Empty. Gone.

"I was practising a defence statement," he said. He breathed out and walked back in through the terrace door, into the warmth, into their house, into his wife's arms. When he noticed her let go to look up at him, he kept hold of her so she couldn't read his face, see that something was wrong. Because Johan Krohn knew that the defense speech he was thinking about would never win the case, not this one. He knew Frida and her thoughts about infidelity too well, she'd condemn him to a lifetime of loneliness, with access to the children but not to her. The fact that Svein Finne also appeared to know Frida so well only made the matter even more unsettling.

Katrine heard the baby crying in the stairwell. It made her quicken her steps, even though she knew the child was in the best of hands. Bjørn's hands. Pale hands with soft skin and thick, stubby fingers that could do everything that needed doing. No more, no less. She shouldn't complain. So she tried not to. She had seen what happened to some women when they became mothers, they became despots who thought the sun and all the planets orbited around mother and child. Who suddenly treated their husbands with resigned derision when they didn't demonstrate lightning-fast reactions and ideally a telepathic understanding of the needs of mother and child. Or, to be more accurate, what the mother decided were the needs of the child.

No, Katrine definitely didn't want to be one of those. But was that somewhere inside her anyway? Hadn't she occasionally felt like slapping Bjørn, watching him curl up and submit, humiliate himself? She had no idea why. Nor how on earth it could ever happen, seeing as Bjørn was always one step ahead of her and had already sorted out anything she might be able to base any criticism on. And obviously there's nothing more frustrating than someone who's better than you, who constantly holds up a mirror that makes you hate yourself.

No, she didn't hate herself. That was an exaggeration. She just thought Bjørn was too good for her from time to time. Not "too good" as in *too attractive*, but *too nice*, as in *annoyingly nice*. That they could both have had a slightly better life if he had chosen someone more like himself, a stable, gentle, down-to-earth, kind, slightly plump farmer's daughter from Østre Toten.

The crying stopped as she was putting the key in the lock. She opened the door.

Bjørn was standing in the hallway with Gert on his arm. The boy looked at her with big, blue, tear-moistened eyes from under those laughably long blond curls that stood out like coiled springs around his head. Gert was named after Katrine's father, even if it had been Bjørn's suggestion. And now the child's face lit up in a smile that was so wonderful that it made Katrine's heart ache and brought a lump to her throat. She let her coat fall to the floor and walked towards them. Bjørn kissed her cheek before handing her the child. She pressed the little body to her and inhaled the smell of milk, vomit, warm skin and something sweet, irresistible, something that was her child alone. She closed her eyes and was home. Completely at home.

She was wrong. They couldn't have it any better than this. It was the three of them, now and forever, that was just how it was.

"You're crying," Bjørn said.

Katrine thought he was saying it to Gert until she realised he meant her, and that he was right.

"It's Harry," she said.

Bjørn looked at her with a frown as she gave him some time. The time an airbag takes to deploy and hopefully muffle some of the impact. Obviously it's pointless when things really have gone to hell, because then an airbag can't save anyone, it's just left hanging in shreds like a deflated balloon out of the front windshield of a Ford Escort that's standing on end and looks like it tried to dive through the rock, bury itself, wipe itself out.

"No," Bjørn said, in an equally vain protest against what her silence was telling him. "No," he repeated in a whisper.

Katrine waited a little longer, still holding Gert, who was tickling her neck with his tiny hands. Then she told Bjørn about the car. About the truck on Highway 287, about the hole in the ice, about the waterfall, about the car. As she spoke, he put one of those pale hands with those stubby fingers to his mouth, and his eyes filled with tears that hung on his thin, colourless eyelashes before falling, one by one, like icicles dripping in the spring sun.

She had never seen Bjørn Holm like this, never seen the big, solid man from Toten lose it so completely. He cried, sobbed, shaking with a force as if something inside him was fighting to get out.

Katrine took Gert into the living room. It was a reflex, to protect the child from his father's dark grief. He would inherit enough darkness as it was.

An hour later she had put Gert to bed, and now he was asleep in their bedroom.

Bjørn had gone to sit in the office that would eventually become Gert's bedroom. She could still hear him crying in there. She was standing at the door, wondering if she should go in, when her phone rang.

She went into the living room and answered it.

It was Ole Winter.

"I know you'd prefer to postpone the announcement that Harry Hole is the dead man," he said.

"Missing," she said.

"The divers have found a smashed mobile phone and a pistol in the river below the falls. My team have just confirmed that both belonged to Harry Hole. We're putting together the last pieces that mean we have a watertight case, and that means we can't wait, Bratt, I'm sorry. But seeing as this was a personal wish . . ."

"Not personal, Winter, I'm thinking about the force. We need to be as well prepared as possible when it comes to presenting this to the public."

"As things stand, it will be Kripos presenting the results of Kripos's work, not the Oslo Police. But I can see your dilemma—the press will obviously want to ask you, as Hole's employer, a number of detailed questions, and I can appreciate that you all need some time to discuss among yourselves how to answer those. In order to meet you halfway, Kripos won't be calling a press conference tomorrow morning, as originally planned, but will delay it until tomorrow evening, at 19:00."

"Thanks," Katrine said.

"Assuming you can manage to stop Sigdal Sheriff's Office from publishing the name of the deceased . . ."

Katrine took a deep breath and managed to stop herself saying anything.

". . . until after we at Kripos have made our own announcement."

You want breaking news with your name on it, Katrine thought. If Sigdal goes public with the name of the deceased, the public will put two and two together, feel that they've solved the case themselves, and that Kripos have been slow, so slow that Hole managed to make a quick exit from life. But if you get your way, Winter, you'll make it look like it was your team's incisive detective work that outsmarted master detective Harry Hole, got him on the run and finally drove him to take his own life.

But she said none of this either.

Just a quick "OK." And: "I'll inform the Chief of Police."

They ended the call.

Katrine crept into the bedroom. Leaned over the worn, blue crib Bjørn's parents had given them, the crib all the family's children and grandchildren had slept in when they were little.

Through the thin wall she could still hear Bjørn crying in the office. Quieter now, but still with the same despair. And as she looked down at Gert's sleeping face, she thought that Bjørn's grief was, in a peculiar way, making hers easier to bear. Now she had to be the strong one, the one who couldn't allow herself the luxury of reflection and sentimentality. Because life went on, and they had a child to take care of.

A child who suddenly opened his eyes.

Blinked, looked around, trying to find something to focus on.

She ran her hand over those strange blond curls.

"Who would have thought that a black-haired girl from the west and a red-headed lad from Toten would have a blond Viking," Bjørn's grandmother had said when they took Gert to see her in her nursing home in Skreia.

Then the boy found his mother's eyes, and Katrine smiled. Smiled, stroked his hair and sang quietly until the child's eyes closed again. Only then did she shiver. Because the look in those eyes had been like someone looking up at her from the other side of death.

46

Johan Krohn had shut himself away in the bathroom. He was tapping on his phone. He and Harry Hole had communicated enough
over the years that he must have his number tucked away somewhere.
There it was! In an old email about Silje Gravseng, the police student
who tried to get revenge on Hole by accusing him of rape. She had
turned to Krohn, wanted him to take the case, but he had seen the
charges and managed to stop her. So even if he and Hole had had
their disagreements since then, surely Hole owed him a favour when
it came down to it? He hoped so. There were other people he could
call, police officers who owed him more than Hole, but there were
two reasons to ask him specifically. Firstly, Hole was guaranteed to
devote all his energy to finding and arresting a man who had recently
tricked and humiliated him. And secondly, Harry Hole was the only
person in the police who had managed to catch Finne. Yes, Hole was
the only person who could help him. Then he would just have to see
how long he could keep Finne locked away for threatening behaviour
and blackmail. It would obviously be one man's word against another's, but he would cross that bridge when he came to it.

"*Leave a message if you must*," a gravelly voice said, followed by a
bleep.

Krohn was so bemused that he almost hung up. But there was
something about that turn of phrase. *If you must.* He had to, didn't
he? Yes, he had to, and he had to say enough to be sure that Hole
would call him back. He swallowed.

"This is Johan Krohn. I need to ask you to keep this message
between the two of us. Svein Finne is engaged in blackmail." He

swallowed again. "Of me. And my family. I . . . er, please, get back to me. Thanks."

He hung up. Had he said too much? And was he doing the right thing, was asking a police officer for help the right solution? Oh, it was impossible to be sure! Well, until Hole called back, he could still change his mind, tell Hole it was the result of a misunderstanding with his client.

Krohn went into the bedroom, slipped under the covers, picked up his copy of *TfR*, the Norwegian legal periodical, from the bedside table and started to read.

"You said something out on the terrace," Frida said beside him. "That you were practising a defense statement."

"Yes," Johan said, and saw that she had put her book down on the covers and was looking at him over her reading glasses.

"Who for?" she said. "I didn't think you were working on a case at the moment."

Krohn adjusted his pillow. "The defense of a decent man who's got himself into a bit of a mess." He let his eyes rest on his own article about double jeopardy. Obviously he knew the article backwards, but he had found that he was able to pretend he'd never read it, and could enjoy its complex but lucid legal reasoning over and over again. "It's only a potential case at the moment. He's being blackmailed by a bastard who wants to get hold of his mistress. If he doesn't give in, his whole family will be taken from him."

"Hmm," Frida murmured. "That sounds more like a work of fiction than an actual case."

"Let's say it is fiction," Krohn said. "What would you do if you were him, and you knew that a defense statement wasn't going to save him?"

"A mistress in exchange for an entire family? That's fairly straightforward, surely?"

"No. Because if the good guy lets the bastard rape his mistress, the bastard would have even more on him. And then the bastard would come back, demanding more and more."

"OK," Frida said with a slight smile. "Then I'd pay a hitman to get rid of the bastard."

"A bit of realism, maybe?"

"I thought you said it was fiction?"

"Yes, but . . ."

"The mistress," Frida said. "I'd let the bastard have the mistress."

"Thanks," Krohn said, staring down at the page, fully aware that even the most ingenious formulations about double jeopardy wouldn't be able to take his mind off Svein Finne tonight. Or Alise. And when he thought of her, on her knees, looking beseechingly up at Johan Krohn with eyes full of tears because he was so big but she was still trying to fit him in her mouth, he knew that option was out of the question. Wasn't it? What if Harry Hole couldn't help him? No, even then, he couldn't do that to Alise. Not only was it morally repugnant, but he loved her! Didn't he? And now Krohn felt more of a swelling in his heart than his groin. Because what did you do if you loved someone? You took the consequences. You paid the price. If you loved someone, it didn't matter what it cost. Those were the rules of love, and there was no room for reinterpretation. He could see it so clearly now. So clearly that he had to hurry up before doubt took hold of him again, he had to hurry to tell his wife everything. Absolutely everything about Alise. *Alea iacta est.* The die is cast. Krohn put the journal down and took a deep breath as he formulated the opening phrases in his head.

"I forgot to say that I caught Simon red-handed today," Frida said. "He was sitting in his room looking at . . . well, you wouldn't believe it."

"Simon?" Krohn said, seeing their firstborn in front of him. "A porn magazine?"

"Almost," Frida laughed. "*Norway's Laws.* Your copy."

"Oh dear," Krohn said, as lightheartedly as he could, and swallowed. He looked at his wife as Alise's image faded away, like in a film. Frida Andresen, now Frida Krohn. Her face was still as pure, as pretty as the first time he had seen it in the lecture hall. Her body was a bit plumper, but the extra kilos had really only given it a more feminine shape.

"I was thinking of making Thai tomorrow, the kids would like that. They're still going on about Ko Samui. Maybe we could go back there sometime? Sun, warm weather and . . ." She smiled and let the rest hang in the air.

"Yes," Johan Krohn said, and swallowed. "Maybe."

He picked up the journal again and began to read. About double jeopardy.

47

"It was David," the man said, in a thin, faltering junkie voice. "He hit Birger in the head with an iron bar."

"Because Birger has stolen his heroin," Sung-min said, and tried to stifle a yawn. "And the reason your fingerprints are on the bar is because you took it off Birger, but by then it was already too late."

"Exactly," the man said, looking at Sung-min as if he'd just solved a third-grade maths problem. "Can I go now?"

"You can go whenever you like, Kasko." Sung-min gestured with one hand.

The man, who was known as Kasko because he had once sold car insurance, stood up, his legs swaying as if the floor of the Stargate bar was the lurching deck of a ship, and maneuvered towards the door where there was a newspaper cutting announcing where the cheapest beer in Oslo could be found.

"What are you doing?" Marcussen, another Kripos detective, hissed in alarm. "We could have got the whole story, all the details! We had him, damn it! Next time he might change his story. They do that, these smackheads."

"All the more reason to let him go now," Sung-min said, switching off the tape recorder. "Right now we've got a simple explanation. If we get more details, he'll either have forgotten them, or changed them by the time he gets to the witness stand. And that's exactly what a defense lawyer needs to sow doubt on the rest of the explanation. Shall we go?"

"No reason to hang around here," Marcussen said, getting to his feet. Sung-min nodded and let his gaze roam over the clientele of drinkers who had been queuing up outside when he and Marcussen arrived at the bar with the earliest opening time in Oslo, seven o'clock.

"Actually, I think I'll stay," Sung-min said. "I haven't had breakfast yet."

"*You* want to eat *here?*"

Sung-min knew what his colleague meant. He and Stargate didn't really go together. They hadn't done, anyway. But who knew, maybe he'd have to lower his standards? Downgrade his expectations. This was as good a place to start as any.

Once Marcussen had gone, Sung-min picked up the newspaper that was lying on the next table.

Nothing on the front page about the Rakel Fauke case.

And nothing about the accident on Highway 287.

Which must mean that neither Ole Winter nor Katrine Bratt had gone public with the news that Harry Hole was involved.

In Ole Winter's case, that was presumably because he wanted time to add a sheen of teamwork to what had been Sung-min's deductions. Trivial double-checking that would only confirm what Sung-min had already ascertained, but that Winter could later claim was a team victory under his wise leadership.

Sung-min had read Machiavelli's *The Prince* when he realised he didn't understand political game-playing and power strategies. One of Machiavelli's pieces of advice to a ruler who wanted to stay in power was to ally himself to and give support to weaker players in the country, those who weren't in a position to threaten him and who would therefore be happy with the status quo. But any stronger potential opponents had to be weakened by all means available. What applied in Italian city states in the 1500s evidently also applied within Kripos.

When it came to Katrine Bratt's motive for wanting to delay the announcement, Sung-min was in more doubt. She'd had twenty-four hours, Hole's family must have been informed by now, and she'd had time to prepare the news that one of their own colleagues was suspected of murder. The fact that she may have personal feelings for Hole didn't explain the fact that she was prepared to expose herself and the Crime Squad Unit to criticism and accusations of special treatment for police officers by protecting him from publicity in this way. It was as if there had to be something else, some consideration that ran deeper than that of a lover. But what could that be?

Sung-min brushed it aside. Perhaps it was something else. A desperate hope for a miracle. That Harry Hole was still alive. Sung-min took a sip of his coffee and looked out at the Akerselva, where the morning sun was starting to shine on the tops of the grey buildings on the other side. If Harry Hole was sharing any of this, it was because he was sitting on a cloud with a halo round his head, listening to the angels singing and watching it all from above.

He looked down at the cloud below him.

Held up the fragment of mirror and looked at his face. He had a white band round his head. He could hear singing.

He looked down at the cloud again.

Ever since it had got light, that little clump of cloud had been lying down in the valley, obscuring the view of the frozen river, colouring the forest grey. But as the sun rose higher it started to burn off the cloud, improving the visibility. And hopefully the intense birdsong around him would calm down a bit.

He was freezing. That was OK. It made it easier to see.

He looked in the piece of mirror again.

The halo or bandage he had found in one of the drawers in the cabin had a red stain where the blood had seeped through. He was probably going to end up with another scar, in addition to the one running from the corner of his mouth to his ear.

He stood up from the chair that was leaning against the wall of the cabin and went inside.

Past the newspaper cuttings on the wall, one of them bearing the same face he had just seen in the mirror.

He went into the bedroom where he had spent the night. Pulled off the bloody sheets and duvet cover, just as he had pulled off the bloody duvet cover two weeks ago in his own flat. But this time it was his blood, and his alone.

He sat down on the sofa.

Looked at the High Standard pistol lying beside the Yahtzee game. Bohr had said E14 had got hold of them without them being registered. He turned the pistol over in his hand.

Was he likely to need it?

Maybe, maybe not.

Harry Hole looked at the time. Thirty-six hours had passed since he had stumbled out of the forest towards the cabin, to the broken window, and let himself in. He had got out of his wet clothes, cleaned himself off, found clean clothes, a sweater, long johns, a camouflage uniform, thick woollen socks. He'd put everything on and laid down under a blanket on the bunk bed, and stayed there until the worst of the shivering stopped. He had considered lighting the stove but decided against it; someone might see the smoke from the chimney and get it into their head to investigate. He had looked through the cupboards until he found a first-aid kit, and managed to staunch the bleeding from the wound on his forehead. He wrapped a bandage around his head, then used the remainder to cover his knee, which was already so swollen it looked like it had eaten an ostrich egg. He breathed in and out, and tried to figure out if the pain meant his ribs were broken, or if he was just badly bruised. Otherwise he was in one piece. Some would doubtless call it a miracle, but it was really just simple physics and a bit of luck.

Harry breathed in again, heard it whistle and felt a stab of pain in his side.

OK, more than a bit of luck.

He had tried to avoid thinking about what had happened. That was the new advice for police officers who had suffered serious trauma: not to talk about it, not to think about it until at least six hours had passed. Recent research showed—in marked contrast to previous assumptions—that "talking things through" directly after a traumatic experience didn't reduce the probability of developing PTSD, but the opposite.

Obviously it hadn't been possible to shut it out altogether. It kept playing in his head like a YouTube clip that's gone viral. The way the car had toppled over the edge of the waterfall, the way he had hunched up in his seat to see out of the windshield; the weightlessness when everything was falling at the same speed, which had made it oddly easy to grip the seat belt with his left hand and the buckle with his right, it just made his movements slower because they were happening underwater. The way he had seen the white foam bursting from the huge black rock that was rushing towards him as he pushed the seat belt into the lock. And then the pressure. And then the noise.

And then he was dangling in the seat belt with his head against the airbag on the steering wheel, and realised he could breathe, that the sound of the waterfall was no longer muffled, but sharp, hissing as it crashed and spat at him through the shattered back window. It took him a few seconds to realise that he wasn't just alive, but remarkably unharmed.

The car was standing on end, the front and the steering wheel pressed towards the seats, or the other way around, but not so badly that his legs were cut or trapped. All the windows were broken, so the water inside the car must have drained out within a second or two. But the resistance of the dashboard and front windshield had probably stopped the water draining away just long enough for it to act as an extra cushion for Harry's body, counteracting the crumpling of the chassis. Because water's strong. The reason deep-sea fish don't get squashed flat in the depths of the ocean under pressure that would crumple an armoured tank to the size of a tin can is because the fishes' bodies largely consist of something that can't be compromised, no matter how much pressure it's put under: water.

Harry closed his eyes and played the rest of the film.

The way he had hung from his seat, unable either to undo the buckle or slip out of the belt, because both the buckle and the spool mechanism were wrecked. He had looked around, and in the broken wing mirror it looked as if two waterfalls were crashing down on him. He managed to free one piece of the mirror. It was sharp, but his hands were shaking so much that it seemed to take him an eternity to cut through the seat belt. He fell against the steering wheel and what was left of the airbag, tucked the piece of mirror into his jacket pocket in case he needed it again later, then climbed carefully out through the windshield and hoped the car wasn't going to fall on top of him. Then he swam the short distance from the black rock to the right-hand side of the river, waded ashore, and that was when he realised that his chest and left knee hurt. The adrenaline had probably acted as a painkiller, and the Jim Beam still was, so he knew it was only going to get worse. And as he stood there, so cold that his head was throbbing, he felt something warm running across his cheek and down his neck, pulled out the fragment of mirror and saw that he had a large cut on one side of his forehead.

He looked up at the hillside. Pine trees and snow. He waded one hundred metres down the river before he found somewhere the slope seemed easy enough to climb, and started to make his way upward, but his knee gave way and he slid on a mixture of mud and snow back towards the river again. The pain in his chest was so bad that he felt like screaming, but the air had gone out of him and all that came out was an impotent wheeze, like a puncture. When he opened his eyes again, he didn't know how long he'd been out, ten seconds or several minutes. He couldn't move. And it dawned on him that he was so cold that his muscles wouldn't obey him. Harry howled up at the blue, innocent, merciless sky above him. Had he survived all that, only to freeze to death here on dry land?

Like hell he would.

He staggered to his feet, broke a branch off a dead tree that was half lying in the river, and used it as a crutch. After struggling ten metres up the wretched slope, he found a path through the patches of snow. Ignoring the throbbing pain in his knee, he walked north, against the current. Because of the waterfall and the chattering of his own teeth he hadn't heard any traffic, but when he got a bit higher he saw that the road was on the other side of the river. Highway 287.

He saw a car drive past.

He wasn't going to freeze to death.

He stood there, breathing as carefully as he could to avoid the pain in his chest.

He could get back down to the river, cross it, stop a car and get back to Oslo. Or, even better, he could call Sigdal Sheriff's Office and get them to pick him up. Maybe they were already on their way; if the truck driver had seen what happened on 287 he had probably called them. Harry felt for his phone. Then he remembered it had been lying on the passenger seat along with the Jim Beam and his pistol, and was now lying dead and drowned somewhere in the river.

And that was when it struck him.

That he too was dead and drowned.

That he had a choice.

He walked back along the path, and stopped where he had scrambled up the slope. He used his hands and feet to shovel snow back over his tracks. Then he began to limp north again. He knew that the road followed the river, and if the path did the same, it wasn't far to Roar Bohr's cabin. As long as his knee held out.

His knee hadn't held out. It took two and a half hours.

Harry looked down at the swelling bulging out from either side of the tight bandage.

It had had one night's rest, and could have a few more hours.

Then it would just have to bear his weight.

He pulled on the woolen hat he had found, then took out the fragment of the Escort's mirror again to see if it covered the bandage. He thought about Roar Bohr, who'd had to make his way from Oslo to Trondheim with just ten kroner. He had no money at all, but the distance was shorter.

Harry closed his eyes. And heard the voice in his head.

Farther along we'll know more about it,
Farther along we'll understand why;
Cheer up, my brother, live in the sunshine,
We'll understand it all by and by.

Harry had heard the song many times. It wasn't just about the idea that the truth would come out one day. It was about how the deceitful lived happy lives, while those they had deceived suffered.

48

The driver of the new Eggedal Express to Oslo looked at the tall man who had just climbed up the steps into her bus. The bus stop was situated on a deserted stretch of Highway 287, and the man was wearing camouflage trousers, so she assumed he was one of the hunters who came up from Oslo to shoot their wildlife. There were three things that didn't quite make sense, though. It wasn't hunting season. His clothes were at least two sizes too small, and he had a white bandage sticking out from below the edge of his black woolly hat. And he had no money for a ticket.

"I fell in the river, injured myself and lost both my phone and my wallet," he said. "I'm staying in a cabin, and I have to get into the city. Can you let me have an invoice?"

She looked at him, considering the situation. The bandage and the ill-fitting clothes seemed to fit his story. And the express bus to Oslo hadn't been an overnight success; people still seemed to prefer taking the local bus to Åmot and changing to the hourly express service there, so there were plenty of free seats. The question was, what was likely to cause more trouble: turning him away from the bus, or letting him come on board?

He may have noticed her hesitation, because he cleared his throat and added: "If I could borrow a phone, I can arrange for my wife to meet me at the bus station with money."

She looked at his right hand. He had a prosthetic middle finger made of some sort of greyish-blue metal. On the next finger he was wearing a wedding ring. But she had no inclination to let that hand touch her phone.

"Sit down," she said, then pressed a button and the door closed behind him with a drawn-out hiss.

Harry limped towards the back of the bus. He noticed that the other passengers, or at least those who had overheard his conversation with the driver, averted their gaze. He knew they were praying silently that this slightly disconcerting man who looked like he had come straight from the battlefield wasn't going to sit down next to them.

He found a free double seat.

He looked out at the forest and landscape gliding past. He looked at his watch, which had confirmed what the advertisements had claimed: it could survive most things, including a waterfall or two. Five minutes to five. He'd be in Oslo just after it got dark. Darkness suited him fine.

Something was sticking into him just beneath his sore rib. He put his hand inside his jacket and moved the barrel of the High Standard pistol he had taken with him from the cabin. He closed his eyes when they passed the lay-by where he had turned the car around before. He felt the bus and his heart rate speed up.

It had come to him in a moment of clarity. The song with the line *"We'll understand it all"* hadn't been a piece of a puzzle, but a door that had swung open in the darkness and shown him the light. Not the whole picture, not the context, but enough for him to know that the story didn't make sense, that something was missing. Or, to be more accurate, that something had been inserted into it. Enough for him to change his mind and wrench the steering wheel.

He had spent the past twenty-four hours piecing the whole thing together. And he was now reasonably sure that he knew what had happened. It had been relatively easy to imagine how the crime scene could have been manipulated and cleaned by someone with a degree of insight into detection methods. And how the murder weapon with Rakel's blood had been planted in his record collection, seeing as only two other people had been to his flat since the murder. He just had to prove either the manipulation of the scene or the planting of evidence.

It had been trickier to figure out the motive.

Harry had ransacked his memory for signs, for an explanation. And this morning, when he was lying half awake, half asleep in the bunk bed, when he finally found it—or it found him—he had at first dismissed it as nonsense. That couldn't be it. He chewed it over. Could it? Could it really be so straightforward that the motive had come out that night he had been lying in bed in Alexandra's flat?

Sung-min Larsen slipped unseen into a seat at the back of the conference centre in Kripos's new premises at Nils Hansens vei 25.

In front of him sat an unusually large gathering of journalists and photographers, even though the press conference had been called outside normal working hours. He guessed Ole Winter had made sure someone had leaked the name that had lured them here: Harry Hole. Now Winter was sitting with Landstad—Winter's latest favourite detective—behind the table on the podium, checking the second hand on his watch. Presumably they wanted to synchronise the start with the news on some television channel or other. Beside Winter and Landstad sat another detective from the team, and the head of the Criminal Forensics Unit, Berna Lien. And, slightly apart from the others, on the far right, sat Katrine Bratt. She looked out of place, and was staring down at some papers in front of her. Sung-min doubted there was anything relevant there, or that she was even reading it.

He saw Ole Winter take a deep breath, literally inflating himself. Winter had swapped his cheap old suit for a new one Sung-min thought he recognised from the Swedish label Tiger. He guessed it had been bought specially after he had conferred with the recently appointed female head of PR, who seemed to have a degree of fashion sense.

"So, welcome to this press conference," Winter said. "My name is Ole Winter, and as head of the preliminary investigation I'd like to give an account of our work on the murder of Rakel Fauke, in which we have had a number of breakthroughs, and—after a lot of intensive teamwork—are now confident that we have solved."

Winter should have left a dramatic pause at that point, Sung-min thought, for maximum effect, but the detective ploughed on, and who knows, perhaps that came across as more professional, more credible. You shouldn't make a spectacle of murder. Sung-min made a mental note, storing it for later use. Because one day he would be the person sitting up there. If he hadn't known it before, he knew it now. He was going to pull that tired, grizzled old monkey down from his perch.

"We hope and believe that this will reassure those directly involved, those around them, and the public in general," Winter said.

"Tragically, it appears that the person we have now found evidence to link to Rakel Fauke's murder has taken his own life. I shan't speculate about the motives for that, but obviously we can't help wondering if it's connected to the fact that he realised that Kripos were closing in on him."

Sung-min noted that Winter said "the person we have now found evidence to link to Rakel Fauke's murder" rather than "the suspect," "taken his own life" rather than "missing," and "closing in on" rather than "about to arrest." And that Winter was churning out speculations in the same sentence as saying he wasn't going to speculate. Sung-min also noted that a more cautious, professionally sober choice of words would have worked better.

"When I say 'appears to have taken his own life,'" Winter said, "that's because the person in question is still officially missing. Some of you will be aware that a car drove into the river beside Highway 287 yesterday morning. We can now make public the fact that the car belonged to the suspect, Harry Hole . . ."

Here Winter didn't need to leave a dramatic pause, because he was stopped by the loud groans, gasps and exclamations that rose from the crowd of reporters.

Harry was woken by flickering lights and discovered that they were driving through the Lysaker tunnel and would soon be arriving. When they emerged at the other end, Harry noted that, sure enough, it was now dark. The bus climbed to the top of the hill, then headed down towards Sjølyst. He looked down at the armada of small boats in Bestumkilen. OK, not so small. And even if you could afford to buy one of those boats, how much would they cost in administration fees, maintenance and running costs per hour at sea during the mayfly Norwegian boating season? Why not hire a boat on those few decent days instead, then tie up at the end of the day and walk away without any worries? The largely empty bus was quiet, but from the seat in front of him he could hear the insect buzz of music in earphones, and in the gap between the two seats he could see the glow of a screen. They evidently had Wi-Fi on board, because he saw it was showing the news on *VG*'s website.

He looked out at the boats again. Maybe it wasn't the number of hours you spent at sea that was the important thing, maybe it was the fact of ownership. The fact that at any hour of the day, you could think that there was a boat out there that was *yours*. A carefully maintained, expensive boat that you knew people passing by would point at and say your name, say that it was *yours*. Because of course we aren't what we do, but what we own. And when we've lost everything, we no longer exist. Harry knew where his thoughts were heading, and pulled himself free of them.

He looked at the screen between the seats in front of him. He saw that it must be angled in such a way that it reflected his face, because from where he was sitting it looked like his own ravaged face was filling *VG*'s website. He looked down at the headline under the reflection.

LIVE report from press conference: SUSPECTED KILLER HARRY HOLE MISSING.

Harry screwed his eyes shut, both to assure himself he was awake and that he wasn't seeing things. He read the headline again. Looked at the picture, which wasn't a reflection, but a photograph taken after the vampirist case.

Harry sat back in his seat and pulled the front of his hat down over his face.

Fuck, fuck.

That picture would be everywhere within the next couple of hours. He'd be recognised in the street, because in the city a limping man in camouflage clothes that were too small for him would be the very opposite of camouflaged. And if he was arrested now, the whole plan would be shot to hell. So the plan needed to change.

Harry tried to think. He couldn't move about openly, so he would have to get hold of a phone as soon as possible, so he could call the people he needed to talk to. In five or six minutes they would be pulling into the bus station. There was a pedestrian walkway to Central Station. Around the station, in the bustling crowds, among junkies and beggars and the more eccentric elements of the city, he wouldn't stand out so badly. And, more important, since Telenor had shut down all their public phones in 2016, they had—almost as a curiosity—installed a few old-fashioned coin-operated payphones, one of them at Central Station.

But even if he made it that far, he still had the same problem.

How to get from Oslo to Trondheim.

Without a single krone in his pocket.

"No comment," Katrine Bratt said. "I can't comment on that at present." And: "That's a question for Kripos."

Sung-min felt sorry for her as she sat there letting the report-ers pepper her with questions. She looked like she was at her own funeral. Was that a good choice of expression, though? What reasons did we really have to assume that death was a worse place? Harry Hole evidently hadn't thought it was.

Sung-min slipped out from the otherwise-empty row of seats. He had heard enough. Enough to see that Winter had got what he wanted. Enough to see that he might not be able to challenge the alpha male for the foreseeable future. Because this case would strengthen Win-ter's position still further, and now that Sung-min had fallen out of favour he would have to ask himself if it was time to seek a transfer to a different club. Katrine Bratt seemed to be the sort of coach he could imagine working for. Working with. He could step into the gap left by Harry Hole. If he was Messi, then Hole had been Maradona. A divinely blessed cheat. And no matter how brightly Messi shone, he would never be as great a legend as Maradona. Because Sung-min knew that even if he faced resistance at the moment, his own story was going to lack the fall from grace, the tragedy of Hole and Mara-dona. His story was going to be one of boring success.

Kasko was wearing his Oakley sunglasses.

He had pinched them from the windowsill of a coffee bar he had gone in to get one of the paper cups he used to beg for money for gear. The owner of the sunglasses had put them down to study a girl in the street outside the bar. The sun was glinting off the snow outside, so it seemed a bit odd to be taking the sunglasses *off*. But presumably he wanted the girl to see that he was looking at her. Well, served the idiot right for being full of the joys of spring.

"Idiot!" Kasko groaned loudly to anyone and everyone.

His thighs and buttocks felt numb beneath him. It took its toll, sitting on your arse all day on a hard, stone floor looking like you were suffering. Well, he *was* suffering. And it was high time he got his evening fix.

"Thanks!" he sang out when a coin fell into the paper cup. It was important to show you were in good spirits.

Kasko had put the sunglasses on because he thought they made him less recognisable. Not that he was frightened of the police, he had told them what he knew. But they hadn't found and caught David yet, and if David had found out that Kasko had blabbed to the Chi-nese detective, there was a good chance he was looking for Kasko now. Which was why it made sense to sit here in the crowd in front of the ticket desk at Central Station, where at least no one could threaten to kill you.

And perhaps the mixture of decent spring weather and fewer delays on the trains had put people in a better mood. They had certainly dropped more money than usual into the paper cup in front of him. Even a couple of kids in the emo gang that usually hung around the steps down to Platform 19 had given him a bit of change. The evening fix was as good as sorted; he wouldn't have to sell the sunglasses tonight.

Kasko noticed a figure in camouflage uniform. Not because he was limping, had a bandage under his hat and generally looked dishevelled, but because he was walking in a way that broke the pattern, he was walking across everyone else, like a predator fish in a shoal of plankton-eaters. To be more precise, he was heading straight for Kasko. Kasko didn't like that. The people who gave him money were on their way *past* him, not *towards* him. *Towards* him wasn't good.

The man stopped in front of him.

"Can I borrow a couple of coins from you?" His voice was as rough as Kasko's.

"Sorry, mate," Kasko said. "You'll have to get your own, I've only got enough for myself."

"I only need twenty, thirty kroner."

Kasko gave a short laugh. "I can see you need medicine but, like I said, so do I."

The man crouched down beside him. Pulled something from his inside pocket. It was a police ID. Shit, not again. The man in the picture looked vaguely like the man in front of him.

"I am hereby seizing your takings from illegal begging in a public place," he said, reaching for the cup.

"Like fuck you are!" Kasko yelled, snatching the cup. He clutched it to his chest.

A couple of passersby glanced at them.

"You're giving that to me," the man said. "Or I'll take you down to the station, have you arrested, then there'll be no fix for you until sometime later on tomorrow. How does a night like that sound?"

"You're bluffing, you fucking junkie bastard! At a vote in the City Council on 16 December 2016, both primary and subsidiary proposals to ban fundraising in public, including begging, were chucked out."

"Mm," the man said, pretending to think this over. He moved closer to Kasko, screening him from people walking past, and whispered: "You're right. It was a bluff. But this isn't."

Kasko stared. The man had put his hand inside his camouflage jacket, and was now holding a pistol aimed at Kasko. A big, noisy fucking pistol in the middle of evening rush hour at Central Station! The guy must be completely fucking deranged. The bandage around his head and a scary fucking scar from his mouth to his ear. Kasko knew all too well what drug cravings could do to otherwise perfectly normal people—he'd only recently seen what an iron bar could do, and here was this guy with a gun. He would have to sell the sunglasses after all.

"Here," he groaned, giving the guy the paper cup.

"Thanks." The man took it and looked inside.

"How much for the shades?"

"Huh?"

"The sunglasses." The man pulled out all the notes that were in the cup and offered them to him. "Is this enough?"

Then he snatched the shades from Kasko, put them on, stood up and limped across the flow of people, towards the old phone box outside the 7-Eleven.

First Harry called his own voicemail, tapped in the code and checked that Kaja Solness hadn't left a message to suggest she had tried to answer any of his calls. The only message was from a shaken Johan Krohn: "*I need to ask you to keep this message between the two of us. Svein Finne is engaged in blackmail. Of me. And my family. I . . . er, please, get back to me. Thanks.*"

He'll have to call someone else, I'm dead, Harry thought as he watched the coins drop into the phone.

He called directory inquiries. Got the numbers he asked for, making a note of them on the back of his hand.

The first number he called was Alexandra Sturdza's.

"Harry!"

"Don't hang up. I'm innocent. Are you at work?"

"Yes, but—"

"How much do they know?"

He heard her hesitate. Heard her make a decision. She gave him a brief summary of her conversation with Sung-min Larsen. She sounded close to tears by the time she finished.

"I know how it looks," Harry said. "But you have to believe me. Can you do that?"

Silence.

"Alexandra. If I believed I'd killed Rakel, would I have bothered to rise from the dead?"

Still silence. Then a sigh.

"Thanks," Harry said. "Do you remember that last evening I was at yours?"

"Yes," she sniffed. "Or no."

"We were lying on your bed. You asked me to use a condom because you were sure I didn't want another kid. There was a woman who rang."

"Oh yes. Kaja. Nasty name."

"Right," Harry said. "Now I need to ask you something I'm sure you don't want to answer."

"OK?"

Harry asked a yes/no question. He heard Alexandra pause. That was almost enough of an answer. Then she said yes. He had what he needed.

"Thanks. One more thing. Those trousers with blood on them. Can you run an analysis of it?"

"Rakel's blood?"

"No. I was bleeding from my knuckles, so there's my blood on the trousers as well, if you remember."

"Yes."

"Good. I want you to analyse my blood."

"Yours? What for?"

Harry explained what he was after.

"That's going to take a bit of time," Alexandra said. "Let's say an hour. Can I call you somewhere?"

Harry thought for a moment. "Send the results by text to Bjørn Holm."

He gave her Bjørn's number, then hung up.

Harry fed more money into the phone, noting that the coins were going faster than his words. He needed to be more efficient.

He knew Oleg's number.

"Yes?" His voice sounded distant. Either because he was a long way away, or because his thoughts were. Possibly both.

"Oleg, it's me."

"Dad?"

Harry had to swallow.

"Yes," Harry said.

"I'm dreaming," Oleg said. It didn't sound like a protest, just a sober statement of fact.

"You're not," Harry said. "Unless I'm dreaming too."

"Katrine Bratt said you'd driven into a river."

"I survived."

"You tried to kill yourself."

Harry could hear his stepson's astonishment start to give way to rising anger.

"Yes," Harry said. "Because I thought I had killed your mother. But at the last moment I realised that that's what I was supposed to think."

"What are you saying?"

"It's too much to explain now, I haven't got enough money. I need you to do something for me."

A pause.

"Oleg?"

"I'm here."

"The house is yours now, which means you can check the electricity consumption online. It shows the usage from hour to hour."

"So?"

Harry explained what he needed, and told him to text the results to Bjørn Holm.

When he was done, he took a deep breath and called Kaja Solness's number.

The phone rang six times. He was about to hang up, and almost jumped when he heard Kaja's voice.

"Kaja Solness."

Harry moistened his mouth. "It's Harry."

"Harry? I didn't recognise the number." She sounded stressed. Talking quickly.

"I tried calling you several times from my own phone," Harry said.

"Did you? I haven't checked. I . . . I have to go. The Red Cross. I've had to drop everything, that's how it is when you're on standby."

"Mm. Where are they sending you?"

"To . . . it's all happened so quickly that I don't even remember the name. Earthquake. A small island in the Pacific, a hell of a long journey. That's why I haven't called you back, I've basically been sitting in a transport plane."

"Mm. You sound like you're nearby."

"Phones are pretty good these days. Listen, I'm in the middle of something. What did you want?"

"I need somewhere to sleep."

"Your flat?"

"Too risky. I need somewhere to hide." Harry could see the amount of money left on the phone shrinking. "I can explain later, but I need to find somewhere else fast."

"Hang on!"

"What?"

A pause.

"Come to mine," Kaja said. "To my house, I mean. There's a key under the doormat."

"I can sleep at Bjørn's."

"No! I insist. I want you to go there. Really."

"OK. Thanks."

"Great. See you soon. I hope."

Harry stood there looking in front of him for a few moments after he hung up. He found himself looking at a television screen above the counter of a café that jutted out into the concourse. It showed a clip of him walking into Oslo Courthouse. From the vampirist case, again. Harry quickly turned back towards the phone. Called Bjørn's number, which he also knew by heart.

"Holm."

"Harry."

"No," Bjørn said. "He's dead. Who are you?"

"Don't you believe in ghosts?"

"I said, who are you?"

"I'm the person you gave *Road to Ruin* to."

Silence.

"I still like *Ramones* and *Rocket to Russia* better," Harry said. "But it was a bloody good thought."

Harry heard a noise. It took him a few moments to realise that it was crying. Not a child's crying. A grown man's.

"I'm at Central Station," Harry said, pretending he hadn't heard. "They're looking for me, I've got a wounded knee, not a single krone to my name, and I need free transport to Lyder Sagens gate."

Harry heard heavy breathing. A half-stifled "bloody hell" muttered to himself. Then Bjørn Holm said in a voice so thin and shaky it was as if Harry had never heard it before.

"I'm on my own with the lad. Katrine's at a press conference up at Kripos. But . . ."

Harry waited.

"I'll bring the baby, he needs to get used to cars," Bjørn said. "Shopping centre entrance in twenty?"

"A couple of people have been looking at me a bit too closely, so if you could manage fifteen?"

"I'll try. Stand by the tax—"

His voice was cut off by a long bleeping tone. Harry looked up. His last coin was gone. He put his hand inside his jacket and stroked his chest and rib.

Harry was standing in the shade outside the north-side entrance to Oslo Central Station when Bjørn's red Volvo Amazon slid past the armada of waiting taxis and stopped. A couple of the drivers who were standing talking glanced over suspiciously, as if they thought the vintage car was a black-market taxi or, even worse, Uber.

Harry limped over to the car and got in the passenger seat.

"Hello, ghost," Bjørn whispered from his usual half-lying position. "To Kaja Solness's?"

"Yes," Harry said, realising that the whispering was because of the baby carrier that was strapped to the back seat.

They pulled out onto the roundabout next to Spektrum, where Bjørn had persuaded Harry to go to a Hank Williams tribute concert last summer. Then Bjørn had called Harry on the morning of the concert to say he was at the maternity ward, and that things had started a bit earlier than expected. And that he suspected the little kid was eager to get out so he could go with his dad to hear his first Hank Williams songs.

"Does Miss Solness know you're on your way?" Bjørn asked.

"Yes. She says she's left a key under the doormat."

"No one leaves keys under the doormat, Harry."

"We'll see."

They passed beneath Bispelokket and the government buildings. Past the mural of *The Scream* and Blitz, past Stensberggata where Bjørn and Harry had driven on the way to Harry's flat early on the night of the murder. When Harry had been so out of it that he wouldn't have noticed a bomb going off. Now he was concentrating hard, hearing every change in the sound of the engine, every creak of the seats, and—when they stopped at a red light on Sporveisgata close to Fagerborg Church—the child's almost silent breathing in the back seat.

"You'll have to tell me, when you think the time is right," Bjørn Holm said quietly.

"I will," Harry said, and heard how odd his voice sounded.

They drove through Norabakken and turned into Lyder Sagens gate.

"Here," Harry said.

Bjørn stopped. Harry didn't move.

Bjørn waited a bit, then switched the engine off. They looked at the dark house behind the fence.

"What do you see?" Bjørn asked.

Harry shrugged his shoulders. "I see a woman one-metre-seventy-something tall, but everything else about her is bigger than me. Bigger house. More intelligent. Better morals."

"Are you talking about Kaja Solness, or the usual?"

"The usual?"

"Rakel."

Harry didn't answer. He looked up at the black windows behind the bare witches' fingers of the branches in the hedge. The house was saying nothing. But it didn't look like it was asleep. It looked like it was holding its breath.

Three short notes. Don Helms's steel guitar on "Your Cheatin' Heart." Bjørn pulled his phone from his jacket pocket. "Text message," he said, and went to put his phone back.

"Open it," Harry said. "It's for me."

Bjørn did as Harry said.

"I don't know what this is or who it's from, but it says benzodiazepine and flunitrazepam."

"Mm. Familiar substances in rape cases."

"Yes. Rohypnol."

"Can be injected into a sleeping man, and if the dose is strong enough he'd be out for at least four or five hours. He wouldn't even notice if he was being bundled about and carried all over the place."

"Or raped."

"Quite. But what makes flunitrazepam such an effective drug for rape is of course that it induces amnesia. Total blackout, the victim doesn't remember a thing about what happened."

"Which is presumably why it isn't manufactured anymore."

"But it's sold on the street. And someone who's worked in the police would know where to get hold of it."

The three notes rang out again.

"Christ, rush hour," Bjørn said.

"Open this one too."

There was a whimper from the back seat and Bjørn turned to look at the baby carrier. Then the breathing settled down again and Harry saw the tension leave Bjørn's body, and his colleague tapped at his phone.

"It says electricity usage went up by 17.5 kilowatts per hour between 20:00 and 24:00 hours. What does that mean?"

"It means that whoever killed Rakel did it at around 20:15."

"What?"

"Recently I spoke to a guy who pulled the same trick. He ran over and killed a girl when he was drunk, put her in the car and turned up the heat to keep her body temperature up. He wanted to trick the medical officer into thinking she died later than she did, at a time when he didn't have an illegal amount of alcohol in his blood."

"I don't follow you, Harry."

"The murderer is the first person we see in the recording, the one who arrives on foot. They get to Rakel's at 20:02, kill her with a knife from the block in the kitchen, turn up the thermostat that all the radiators on the ground floor are connected to, then leave without locking the door. Come to mine later, where I'm still so out of it I don't notice myself being dosed up with Rohypnol. The killer plants the murder weapon between the records on my shelves, finds the keys to the Ford Escort, drives me to the scene and carries me inside. That's why it takes so long on the video, and looks like a fat person, or someone with their coat hanging down as they go inside, hunched over. The killer is carrying me like a rucksack. 'The way we carry anyone who's fallen,' as Bohr said they did in Afghanistan and Iraq. And I was put down in the pool of blood beside Rakel and left to my own devices."

"Bloody hell." Bjørn scratched his red beard. "But we don't see anyone leaving the scene."

"Because the perpetrator knew I'd be convinced I'd killed Rakel when I woke up. Which meant I'd have to find both sets of keys inside the house, with the door locked from the inside. Which would lead me to conclude that no one but me could have committed the murder."

"A variation on the locked-room mystery?"

"Exactly."

"So . . . ?"

"After the murderer put me down beside Rakel, they locked the door from the inside and left the scene through one of the basement windows. That's the only one without bars. They don't know about the wildlife camera, but they're lucky. The camera is activated by movement, but nothing shows up because the murderer is moving through total darkness on the far side of the drive when they leave the scene. We assumed it must have been a cat or a bird and didn't really pay it much thought."

"You mean it was all just . . . to fuck with you?"

"Manipulated into thinking I'd killed the woman I loved."

"Christ, that's worse than the most brutal death sentence, that's just torture. Why . . . ?"

"Because that's exactly what it was. A punishment."

"Punishment? For what?"

"For my betrayal. I realised that when I was about to kill myself and turned the radio on. *'Farther along we'll know more about it. . . .'*"

"*'Farther along we'll understand why,'*" Bjørn said, nodding slowly.

"*'Cheer up, my brother,'*" Harry said. "*'Live in the sunshine. We'll understand it all by and by.'*"

"Beautiful," Bjørn said. "A lot of people think that's a Hank Williams song, but it was actually one of the few cover versions he ever recorded."

Harry took out the pistol. He saw Bjørn shuffle uncomfortably in his seat.

"It's unregistered," Harry said as he screwed the silencer onto the barrel. "It was acquired for E14, a disbanded intelligence unit. Can't be traced to anyone."

"Are you thinking of . . ."—Bjørn nodded nervously towards Kaja's house—"using that?"

"No," Harry said, handing the pistol to his colleague. "I'm going in without it."

"Why are you giving it to me?"

Harry looked at Bjørn for a long time.

"Because you killed Rakel."

49

"When you called Øystein at the Jealousy Bar early on the night of the murder and found out that I was there, you realised I was going to be there for a while," Harry said.

Bjørn was clutching the pistol as he stared at Harry.

"So you drove to Holmenkollen. Parked the Amazon a little way away so the neighbours or other witnesses wouldn't see and remember the unusual car. You walked to Rakel's house. Rang the bell. She opened the door, saw it was you, and obviously let you in. At the time you didn't know you were being recorded by a wildlife camera, of course. Back then, all you knew was that everything was in place. There were no witnesses, nothing unforeseen had happened, the block of knives was standing where it had been the last time you visited us, when I was still living there. And I was sitting in the Jealousy Bar drinking. You grabbed the knife from the block and killed her. Efficiently and without any pleasure, you're not a sadist. But brutally enough for me to know that she had suffered. When she was dead, you turned up the thermostat, took the knife, drove to the Jealousy, put Rohypnol in my drink while I was busy fighting with Ringdal. You bundled me into your car and drove home with me. Rohypnol works fast, I was well away by the time you parked next to the Escort in the car park behind my building. You found the keys to my flat in my pocket, pressed my hand round the knife so it had my fingerprints on it, then planted it in my flat between The Rainmakers and the Ramones, in the right place for Rakel. You searched until you found the car keys. On your way down the stairs you bumped into Gule, on his way home from work. That wasn't part of the plan, but you improvised well. Told him you'd put me to bed and were on your way home. Back in the car park you moved me from the Amazon to the Escort, then drove it up to Rakel's. You managed to get me out, but it took a bit of time. You carried me on your back up the steps, in through the unlocked door, and put me down in the pool of blood beside Rakel. You cleaned the scene of any evidence that you'd been there, then left the house through the basement window. Obviously the window catch couldn't be fastened from the outside. But you'd thought about that too. I'm guessing you walked home from there. Down Holmenkollveien. Sørkedalsveien to Majorstua, maybe. Avoiding anywhere with security cameras, taxis that would need paying by card, anything that could be traced. Then you just had to wait, keeping your TETRA terminal nearby, following developments. That was why you—even though you were on paternity leave—were one of the first on the scene when there was a report that a woman's body had been found at Rakel's address. And you took charge. You went around the house looking for possible escape routes, something the others hadn't thought to do seeing as the main entrance had been open when they found Rakel. You went down into the basement, put the catch back on the window, then went up into the attic for appearance's sake, then came back and said everything was locked up. Any objections so far?"

Bjørn Holm didn't answer. He was sitting slouched in his seat, his glassy eyes looking in Harry's direction, but apparently unable to focus.

"You thought you were home and dry. That you'd committed the perfect crime. No one could accuse you of not being ambitious. Obviously things got a bit tricky when you realised my brain had suppressed the fact that I'd woken up in Rakel's house. Suppressed the fact that I was convinced I must have killed her seeing as the door was locked from the inside. Suppressed the fact that I had removed any evidence that I had been there, taken down the wildlife camera and thrown the memory card away. I couldn't remember anything. But that wasn't going to save me. You'd hidden the murder weapon in my flat as insurance. Insurance that if I didn't recognise my own guilt and punish myself enough, if it looked like I was going to escape, you could discreetly arrange for the police to get a search warrant and find the knife. But when you realised I couldn't remember anything, you made sure I found the knife you'd planted. You wanted me to become my own torturer. So you gave me a new record and you knew exactly where in my record collection I'd put it, seeing as you know my system. The Ramones' *Road to Ruin* was precisely that. I daresay you didn't take any perverse pleasure from giving it to me at the funeral, but . . ." Harry shrugged. "That's what you did. And I found the knife. And I began to remember."

Bjørn's mouth opened and closed.

"But then a couple of real flies appeared in the ointment," Harry said. "I found the memory card containing the recordings from the wildlife camera. You realised there was a serious danger that you could be identified and uncovered. You asked if the contents had been copied before you told me to hand the card over to you. I thought you were asking because it would be easier to send the contents by Dropbox. But you just wanted to make sure that you were getting the only copy in existence, and could destroy or modify the recordings so that you couldn't be recognised. When, to your relief, you saw that the recordings didn't reveal much, you sent the card on to a 3-D expert, but without your name being involved. In hindsight it's easy to see that I should have asked myself why you didn't just ask me to send it straight to him in the first place."

Harry looked at the pistol. Bjørn wasn't holding it by the handle with his finger on the trigger, but by the trigger guard, like it was a piece of evidence that he didn't want to leave any fingerprints on.

"Have you . . ." Bjørn's voice sounded like a sleepwalker's, as if his mouth were full of cotton wool. "Have you got some sort of recording device?"

Harry shook his head.

"Not that it matters," Bjørn said with a resigned smile. "How . . . how did you figure it out?"

"The thing that always bound us together, Bjørn. Music."

"Music?"

"Just before I drove into the truck, I turned the radio on and heard Hank Williams and those violins. It should have been playing hard rock. Someone had changed the channel. Someone other than me had used the car. And when I was in the river I realised something else, that there was something about the seat. It wasn't until I got to Bohr's cabin that I had time to figure it out. It was the first time I got in the car after Rakel's death, when I was about to drive to the old bunkers in Nordstrand. I felt it then as well, that something wasn't right. I even bit my false finger, the way I do when I can't quite remember something. Now I know it was the back of the seat. When I got in the car, I had to adjust it, raise it. Sometimes I had to adjust it when Rakel and I were sharing the car, but why would I have to adjust the seat of a car that no one but me drives? And who do I know who has the seat pushed so far back that he's almost lying down?"

Bjørn didn't answer. There was that same, distant look in his eyes, as if he were listening to something going on inside his own head.

Bjørn Holm looked at Harry, saw his mouth move, registered the words, but they didn't sound the way they ought to. He felt almost like he was drunk, watching a film, was underwater. But this was happening, it was real, only there was a filter over it, as if it didn't really concern him. Not anymore.

He had known it ever since he heard dead Harry's voice on the phone. That he had been found out. And that it was a relief. Yes, it was. Because if it had been torture for Harry to think he had killed Rakel, it had been hell for Bjørn. Because he not only thought, but *knew* he had killed Rakel. And he remembered almost every detail of the murder, reliving it practically every moment, without pause, like a monotonous, throbbing bass drum against his temple. And with each beat came the same shock: no, it isn't a dream, I *did* it! I did what I dreamed about, what I planned, what I was convinced would somehow bring balance back to a world that's spun out of control. Killing what Harry Hole loved more than anything, the way Harry had killed—ruined—the only thing Bjørn cherished.

Of course Bjørn had been aware that Katrine was attracted to Harry; no one who had worked closely with the pair of them could have failed to notice. She hadn't denied it, but claimed she and Harry had never got it together, had never so much as kissed each other. And Bjørn had believed her. Because he was naive? Maybe. But primarily because he wanted to believe her. Besides, that was all a long time ago, and now she was with Bjørn. Or so he had thought.

When was the first time he had suspected anything?

Was it when he had suggested to Katrine that Harry should be one of the baby's godparents and she had rejected the idea out of hand? She had no better explanation than the fact that Harry was an unstable person who she didn't want having any responsibility for little Gert's upbringing. As if the role of godparent was anything but a gesture from the parents to a friend or relative. And she had hardly any relatives, and Harry was one of the few friends they had in common.

But Harry and Rakel had come to the christening as ordinary guests. And Harry had been the same as usual, had stood in a corner, talking without any enthusiasm to anyone who went over to him, glancing at the time and looking at regular intervals at Rakel, who was deep in conversation with different people, and every half an hour he signalled to Bjørn that he was going outside for a cigarette. It was Rakel who had reinforced Bjørn's suspicions. He had seen her face twitch when she saw the baby, heard the slight tremble in her voice when she dutifully told the parents what a miraculous child they had produced. And, not least, the pained look on her face when Katrine had passed the baby to her to hold while she sorted something out. He had seen Rakel turn her back on Harry so that he couldn't see her or the child's faces.

Three weeks later he had the answer.

He had used a cotton bud to take a sample of the child's saliva. He'd sent it to the Forensic Medical Institute, without specifying which case it related to, just that it was a DNA test subject to the usual oath of confidentiality covering paternity tests. He had been sitting in his office in the Criminal Forensics Unit in Bryn when he read the results that showed there was no way he could be Gert's father. But the woman he had spoken to, the new Romanian one, said they'd found a match with someone else in the database. The father was Harry Hole.

Rakel had known. Katrine knew, of course. Harry too. Maybe not Harry, actually. He wasn't a good actor. Just a betrayer. A false friend.

The three of them against him. Of those three, there was only one he couldn't live without. Katrine.

Could Katrine live without him?

Of course she could.

Because what was Bjørn? A plump, pale, harmless forensics expert who knew a bit too much about music and film, and who in a few years would be an overweight, pale, harmless forensics expert who knew even more about music and film. Who at some point had swapped his Rasta hat for a flat cap and had bought plenty of flannel shirts. Who had been convinced that these were personal choices, things that said something about personal development, about an awareness that only he had reached, because of course we're all special. Right up until he looked around at a Bon Iver concert and saw a thousand copies of himself, and realised that he belonged to a group, a group of people who more than any other—at least in theory—hate everything about belonging to a group. He was a hipster.

As a hipster he hated hipsters, and especially male hipsters. There was something insubstantial, unmanly, about that dreamy, idealistic striving for the natural, the original, the authentic; about a hipster trying to look like a lumberjack who lived in a log cabin and grew and shot his own food, but who was still an overprotected little boy who thought modern life, quite rightly, had stripped away all his masculinity, leaving him with a feeling of being helpless. Bjørn had this suspicion about himself confirmed during a Christmas party with his old schoolmates back home in Toten, when Endre, the cocky headmaster's son, who was studying sociology in Boston, had called Bjørn a typical "hipster loser." Endre had brushed his thick black fringe back with a smile and quoted Mark Greif, who had written an article in the *New York Times* saying that hipsters compensated for their lack of social and career achievements by trying to claim cultural superiority.

"And that's where we have you, Bjørn, an employee of the state in your mid-thirties, in the same job you were in ten years ago, thinking that as long as you have long hair and farmer's clothes that look like they were bought second-hand from the Salvation Army, you can still rise above the younger, short-haired, straighter colleagues who passed you by on the career ladder years ago."

Endre had said this in a single long sentence without pausing for breath, and Bjørn had listened and thought: Is this true, is this what defines me? Was this what he, a farmer's son, had fled the rolling fields of Toten to become? A feminised, militant conformist and loser? A failed, backward-looking police officer looking for an image to contradict that? Who used his roots—a quirky old car, Elvis and old country-music heroes, fifties hairstyles, snakeskin boots and his dialect—to trace a line back to something authentic, down to earth, but that was about as honest as the politician from west Oslo who takes off his tie, rolls up his shirtsleeves and says "gonna" and "gotta" as many times as he can when making election speeches in factories.

Maybe. Or, if that wasn't the whole truth, perhaps it was part of it. But did it define him? No. Just as little as the fact that he had red hair defined him. What defined him was that he was a damn good forensics officer. And one other thing.

"Maybe you're right," Bjørn had replied when Endre paused for breath. "Maybe I am a pathetic loser. But I'm nice to people. And you're not."

"What the hell, Bjørn, are you *upset*?" Endre had laughed, putting a comradely, sympathetic hand on his shoulder, and smiling conspiratorially at the onlookers, as if this were a game they were all playing, one where Bjørn hadn't understood the rules. OK, Bjørn may have drunk one glass too many of the moonshine they were serving for reasons of nostalgia rather than cost, but he had felt it then, just for a moment, had felt what he might be capable of. That he could have planted a fist in the middle of Endre's sociological smirk, broken his nose and seen the fear in his eyes. Bjørn had never got into fights when he was growing up. Not once. So he'd known nothing about fighting before he started at Police College, where he had learned a thing or two about close combat. Such as the fact that the surest way to win a fight is to strike first and with maximum aggression, which effectively brings nine out of ten fights to an immediate conclusion. He knew that, he *wanted* to do it, but could he? What was his threshold for resorting to violence? He didn't know, he had never been in a situation in which violence had looked like an adequate solution to the problem. Which it wasn't now either, of course. Endre posed no physical threat, and all a fight would accomplish was a scandal and possibly being reported to the police. So why had he wanted to do it so badly: to feel the other man's face under his knuckles, hear the dead sound of bone against flesh, see the blood spray from his nose, see the fear on Endre's face?

When Bjørn went to bed in his boyhood bedroom that night he hadn't been able to sleep. Why hadn't he done anything? Why had he merely muttered "No, 'course not, I'm not upset," waited for Endre to take his hand off his shoulder, mumbled something about needing another drink, then found some other people to talk to before leaving the party shortly afterwards? Those insults would have been the real cause. The moonshine could have been used as an excuse for getting into a fight at a party; that would have been acceptable in Toten. And it would have ended with one punch. Endre wasn't a fighter. And if he had hit back, everyone would have cheered for him, for Bjørn. Because Endre was a wanker, he always had been. And everyone loved Bjørn, they always had. Not that it had been much help to him growing up.

In Year 9, Bjørn had finally manned up and asked Brita if she wanted to go to the local cinema in Skreia. The manager of the cinema had taken the astonishing decision to show Led Zeppelin's filmed concert, *The Song Remains the Same*. Fifteen years after it was released, admittedly, but that didn't bother Bjørn. He had gone looking for Brita and eventually found her behind the girls' toilet. She was standing there crying, and sobbed to Bjørn that she had let Endre sleep with her at the weekend. Then, during break, her best friend had told her that she and Endre were now together. Bjørn had comforted Brita as best he could, then, without much preamble, asked if she'd like to go to the cinema with him. She had just stared at him and asked if he'd heard what she'd just said. Bjørn said he had, but that he liked both Brita and Led Zeppelin. At first she snorted "no," but then she seemed to have a moment of clarity and said she'd like to go. When they were sitting in the cinema it turned out that Brita had asked her best friend and Endre to go as well. Brita had kissed Bjørn during the film, first during "Dazed and Confused," then in the middle of Jimmy Page's guitar solo in "Stairway to Heaven," thereby sending Bjørn a fair way up those stairs. Nonetheless, when they were alone again and he had walked her home from the cinema, there hadn't been any more kissing, just a short "goodnight." One week later, Endre broke up with the best friend and got back together with Brita.

Bjørn had carried these things inside him, of course he had. The betrayal he should have seen coming, the punch that hadn't come. And that nonexistent punch had somehow confirmed what Endre had said about him, that the only thing that was worse than the shame of not being a man was the fear of being a man.

Was there a clear thread between then and now? Was there a causal connection, was this explosion of rage something that had built up and just needed a fresh humiliation to detonate it? Was the murder somehow the punch he hadn't managed to land on Endre?

The humiliation. It had been like a pendulum. The prouder he felt at being a father, the greater the humiliation when he had realised the child wasn't his. The pride when his parents and two sisters had visited mother, baby and father in hospital and Bjørn had seen the delight on their faces. His sisters who were now aunts, his parents now grandparents. Not that they weren't already, Bjørn was the youngest and the last to get started, but even so. He realised that they hadn't been sure it would ever happen for him. His mother hadn't thought that bachelor style of his had boded well. And they loved Katrine. There had been a slightly strained atmosphere during their first visits to Toten, when Katrine's direct, chatty Bergen attitude had come up against Toten's restrained, taciturn understatement. But Katrine and his parents had met each other halfway, and during the first Christmas lunch at the farm, when Katrine came downstairs after making a real effort to look nice, Bjørn's mother had nudged him in the side and looked at him with a mixture of admiration and astonishment, a look that seemed to ask: How did *you* manage to catch that?

Yes, he had been proud. Far too proud. Perhaps she had noticed too. And this pride, which was so hard to hide, may in the end have prompted her to ask herself the same question: How did *he* manage to catch me? And she had left him. Though that wasn't how he described it to himself—he thought of it as a pause, a temporary break in their relationship, caused by a bout of claustrophobia. Anything else was unthinkable. And eventually she had come back. It happened a few weeks later, maybe a couple of months, he didn't really remember, he had suppressed that whole period, but it was just after they thought they'd solved the vampirist case. Katrine had fallen pregnant at once. It was as if she had emerged from sexual hibernation, and Bjørn found himself thinking that perhaps the break hadn't been such a bad thing, that perhaps people needed a break from each other from time to time to realise what they had together. A child conceived in the joy of reconciliation. That was how he had seen it. And he had travelled around Toten with their child, showing him off to family, friends, ever more distant relatives, showing him off like a trophy, proof of his manhood to anyone who had doubted him. It had been stupid, but everyone's allowed to be stupid once or twice in their life.

And then the humiliation.

It had been unbearable. It was like sitting on a plane during takeoff or landing on the occasions when the narrow passageways inside his ear and nose didn't manage to even out the pressure and he was sure his head was going to explode, had *wanted* it to explode, anything to escape the pain that just kept getting worse, even when you thought it must have reached its apex. And sent you mad. Willing to jump out of the plane, shoot yourself in the head. An equation with only one variable: pain. And with death as the only liberating common denominator. Your death, other people's deaths. In his confusion he had thought that his pain—like the difference in pressure—could be evened out by the pain of others. Of Harry Hole.

He had been wrong.

Killing Rakel had been easier than he'd thought. Possibly because he had been planning it for so long, had worked out his game plan, as sportsmen would say. He had gone through it in his mind so many times that when he was actually there and it was about to happen in real life, it had felt almost as if he was still only in his thoughts, looking on from the outside. As Harry said, he had walked down Holmenkollveien, but not towards Sørkedalsveien. Instead he had turned left, into Stasjonsveien, then Bjørnveien, before weaving through smaller streets towards Vinderen, where a pedestrian would be less conspicuous. He had slept well the first night, didn't even wake up when Gert, according to Katrine, had cried hysterically from five o'clock in the morning. Exhaustion, presumably. The second night he didn't sleep as well. But it wasn't until Monday, when he saw Harry at the crime scene, that what he had done began to sink in. Seeing Harry had been like watching a church going up in flames. Bjørn thought back to the footage of Fantoft Stave Church burning in 1992, a fire started by a Satanist at six o'clock in the morning, on the sixth day of the sixth month. There was often an element of beauty to catastrophes, something that meant you couldn't take your eyes off them. As the walls and roof burned, the skeleton of the church, its true form and personality emerged, naked, unadorned. He had watched the same thing happen to Harry in the days that followed Rakel's death. And he couldn't take his eyes off it. Harry was stripped back to his true, pitiful self. He, Bjørn, had become a pyromaniac, fascinated by the spectacle of his destruction. But as he looked on, he suffered. He too was burning. Had he known that would happen from the start? Had he consciously poured the last remnants of the petrol over himself, and stood so close to Harry that he too would be consumed when the church burned? Or had he believed that Harry and Rakel would disappear, and that he would live on, move on with his family, make it his, become whole again?

Whole.

They had rebuilt Fantoft Church. It was possible. Bjørn took a deep, trembling breath.

"You know all this is just your imagination, Harry? A radio station and the adjustment of a car seat, that's all you've got. Anyone could have drugged you. With your history of substance abuse it isn't even implausible that you did it yourself. You have absolutely no evidence."

"Are you sure? What about the married couple who say they saw a large man walking down Holmenkollveien at quarter to midnight?"

Bjørn shook his head. "They weren't able to give a description. And seeing pictures of me wouldn't prompt their memory, because the man they saw was wearing a false black beard, glasses, and limped whenever anyone could see him."

"Mm. OK."

"OK?"

Harry nodded slowly. "If you're confident you haven't left any evidence, then OK."

"What the hell does that mean?"

"There aren't that many people who need to know."

Bjørn stared at Harry. There was nothing triumphant in his eyes.

No trace of hatred towards the man who had killed his beloved. All Bjørn could see in those blank eyes was vulnerability. Nakedness. Something approaching sympathy.

Bjørn looked down at the pistol Harry had given him. He had realised now.

They would know. Harry. Katrine. That was enough. Enough to make it impossible to go on. But if it stopped here, if Bjørn put a stop to it here, no one else would have to know. His colleagues. His family and friends in Toten. And, most important of all, the boy.

Bjørn swallowed. "You promise?"

"I promise," Harry said.

Bjørn nodded. He almost smiled at the thought that he would finally get what he had wanted. That his head would explode.

"I'm going now," Harry said.

Bjørn nodded towards the back seat. "Will you . . . will you take the lad with you? He's yours."

"He's yours and Katrine's," Harry said. "But yes, I know I'm his father. And that no one who isn't under an oath of confidentiality knows. And that's how it will stay."

Bjørn fixed his eyes ahead of him.

There was a nice place in Toten, a ridge from which the fields looked like a rolling yellow sea on a moonlit spring night. Where a young guy with a driving license could sit in a car and kiss a girl. Or sit alone with a sob in his throat and dream about one.

"If no one knows, how did you find out?" Bjørn asked, without any real interest in the answer, just to delay his departure for a few more seconds.

"Deduction," Harry Hole said.

Bjørn Holm smiled tiredly. "Of course."

Harry got out, unfastened the baby carrier from the back seat and lifted it out. He looked down at the sleeping child. Unsuspecting. All the things we don't know. All the things we will be spared. The simple sentence Alexandra had uttered that night when Harry declined the condom she offered him.

You don't want another kid, do you?

Another kid? Alexandra knew perfectly well that Oleg wasn't his biological son.

Another kid? She knew something, something he didn't know.

Another kid. A slip of the tongue, a simple mistake. In the eighties, psychologist Daniel Wegner claimed that the subconscious constantly makes sure we don't blurt out things we want to keep secret. But that when the secret pops up from the subconscious, it informs the conscious part of the brain and forces it to think about it. And from then on it's only a matter of time before the truth slips out by mistake.

Another kid. Alexandra had checked the cotton bud Bjørn had sent in against the database. Where the DNA profiles of all police officers who worked at crime scenes were stored, so that there would be no confusion if they messed up and left their own DNA at the scene. So not only did she have Bjørn's DNA and could rule out the possibility that he was the father—she had both parents' DNA, and could see that there were two matches: Katrine Bratt and Harry Hole. That was the secret that her oath of confidentiality prevented her from telling anyone except the person who had requested the analysis, Bjørn Holm.

The night Harry had sex, or at least some form of intercourse, with Katrine Bratt, he had been so drunk that he didn't remember anything. Or, more accurately, he remembered something, but thought it was something he'd dreamed. But then he started to suspect when he noticed that Katrine was avoiding him. And when Gunnar Hagen—rather than Harry—was asked to be the child's godfather, even though Harry was obviously a much closer friend of both Katrine and Bjørn. No, he hadn't been able to rule out the possibility that something had happened that night, something that had ruined things between him and Katrine. The way it had ruined things between him and Rakel when, after the christening, just before Christmas, she had turned his life upside down by asking him if he had had sex with Katrine in the past year. And he hadn't had the sense to deny it.

Harry remembered his own confusion after she had thrown him out and he was sitting on his hotel bed with a bag containing a few clothes and toiletries. He and Rakel were, after all, both adults with realistic expectations, they loved each other with all their faults and idiosyncrasies, they were *good* together. So why would she throw all that away because of a simple mistake, something that had happened and was over, which had no consequences for the future? He knew Rakel, and it didn't make sense.

That was when he figured out what Rakel had already figured out but hadn't told him. That that night *had* had consequences, that Katrine's child was Harry's, not Bjørn's. When had she first suspected? At the christening, maybe, when she saw the baby. But why hadn't Rakel told him, why had she kept it to herself? Simple. Because the truth would help no one, it would just ruin things for even more people than it had already: Rakel herself. But that wasn't something Rakel could live with. The fact that the man she shared her bed, her life with—but with whom she didn't have a child—had a child, one that was living among them, one they would have to see.

The sower. Svein Finne's words on the recording from outside the Catholic church had been echoing through Harry's head during the past day, like an echo that wouldn't fade. *Because I am the sower.* No. It was him, Harry, who was the sower.

He watched as Bjørn turned the key in the ignition and turned the radio on in the same automatic movement. The engine started, then settled into its rhythm, rumbling good-naturedly in neutral. And through the gap at the top of the passenger window, Rickie Lee Jones's voice floated above Lyle Lovett's on "North Dakota." The car slipped into gear and slowly drove away. Harry watched it go. Bjørn, who couldn't drive without listening to country music. Like gin and tonic. Not even when Harry was lying drugged in the seat beside him and they were on their way to Rakel's. Perhaps that wasn't so strange. Bjørn had probably wanted company. Because he could never have felt so alone as he did then. Not even now, Harry thought. Because he had seen it in Bjørn's eyes before the car drove off. Relief.

50

Johan Krohn opened his eyes. Looked at the time. Five past six. He thought his ears must be mistaken and rolled over to go back to sleep, but then he heard it again. The doorbell downstairs.

"Who's that?" Frida murmured sleepily beside him.

That, Johan Krohn thought, is the devil himself coming to claim his due. Finne had given him forty-eight hours to leave his response by the gravestone, and that didn't expire until that evening. But there was no one else who rang doorbells anymore. If there was a murder and they needed a defense lawyer straightaway, they phoned. If there was a crisis at work, they phoned. Even the neighbours phoned if they wanted something.

"It's probably to do with work," he said. "Go back to sleep, darling, I'll go and answer."

Krohn closed his eyes for a moment and tried to take deep, calm breaths. He hadn't slept well, had just stared into the darkness all night as his brain chewed over the same question: How on earth was he going to stop Svein Finne?

He, the master tactician of the courtroom, hadn't managed to come up with an answer.

If he arranged for Finne to get Alise to himself, he would be making himself an accomplice to a crime. Which was bad enough in itself, both for Alise and for him. And if he made himself an accomplice, that would only give Finne an even stronger hand when—and there was no question that it would be when—he showed up with more demands. Unless he could somehow persuade Alise to have sex with Finne, of course, so that it was voluntary. Was that a possibility? And what would he have to promise Alise in return? No, no, it was an impossible idea, as impossible as the one Frida had spontaneously suggested as a way of solving the problem in the fictitious case: hiring a hitman to get rid of Finne.

Should he confess his misdemeanour to Frida instead? A confession. The truth. Atonement. The thought was liberating. But it was no more than a brief, soothing puff of wind under the blazing sun in a desert with an unbroken horizon of hopelessness. She would leave him, he knew that. The firm, the courtroom victories, the newspaper articles, his reputation, the admiring glances, the parties, the women, the offers, to hell with all that. Frida and the children, they were all he had, they always had been. And when Frida was alone, when she was no longer his, hadn't Finne more or less said straight out that she would be open game, that he would take her? If you looked at it like that, didn't he have a moral obligation to bear his heavy secret alone and make sure that Frida didn't leave him, for her own safety's sake? Which in turn meant that he would have to let Finne have Alise, and the next time Finne . . . Oh, it was a fiendish Gordian knot! He needed a sword. But he had no sword, just a pen and a babbling mouth.

He swung his legs out of bed and put them into his slippers.

"I'll be back soon," he said. As much to himself as Frida.

He went downstairs and through the hall towards the oak door.

And knew that when he opened it, he needed to have his answer ready for Finne.

I'll say no, Johan Krohn thought. And then he'll shoot me. Fine.

Then he remembered that Finne used a knife and changed his mind.

A knife.

He cut his victims open.

And he didn't kill them, he just wounded them. Like a landmine. Mutilated them for the rest of their life, a life they had to live even when death would be preferable. On the terrace Finne had claimed to have raped a young girl from Huseby. The bishop's daughter. Had that been a subtle threat against his own children? Finne hadn't been risking anything by admitting the rape. Not only because Krohn was his lawyer, but because the case must have passed the statute of limitations. Krohn couldn't remember any rape case, but he did remember Bishop Bohr, who people said died of grief because his daughter had drowned herself in a river. Was he going to let himself be terrorised by someone who had made it his life's work to ruin other people's? Johan Krohn had always managed to find a socially defensible, professional and occasionally also an emotional justification to fight tooth and nail for his clients. But now he gave up. He detested the man standing on the other side of the door. He wished with all his heart, as well as all his brain, that the pestilential, ruinous Svein Finne might die a soon and not necessarily painless death. Even if it meant that he got dragged down with him.

"No," Krohn muttered to himself. "I'm saying no, you fucking bastard."

He was still wondering about whether or not to swear as he opened the door.

He stared speechless at the man in front of him, who was looking him up and down. He felt the biting morning chill against his naked, scrawny body and realised that he hadn't put his dressing gown on, and was standing there wearing nothing but the boxer shorts Frida gave him every Christmas, and the slippers the children had given him. Krohn had to clear his throat before he could make a sound: "Harry Hole? But aren't you . . ."

The policeman, if it was him, shook his head and gave him a wry smile. "Dead? Not quite. But I need a bloody good lawyer. And I've heard that you could do with some help too."

Part 4

51

It was lunchtime at the Statholdergaarden restaurant. On the street outside, a young busker blew on his fingers before he started to play. A lonely job, Sung-min Larsen thought as he watched him. He couldn't hear what he was playing, or if he was any good. Alone and invisible. Perhaps the older buskers who ruled Karl Johans gate had exiled the poor kid out here, to the presumably less lucrative Kirkegata.

He looked up when the waiter snapped the napkin open like a flag in the wind before letting the white damask settle on Alexandra Sturdza's lap.

"I should have made an effort," she laughed.

"You look like you did." Sung-min smiled, and leaned back as the waiter repeated the same gesture with his napkin.

"This?" she said, pointing at her tight skirt with both hands. "These are my work clothes. I just don't dress as informally as my colleagues. And *you've* made an effort. You look like you're going to a wedding."

"I've just come from a funeral," Sung-min said, and saw Alexandra flinch as if he'd slapped her.

"Of course," she said quietly. "I'm sorry. Bjørn Holm?"

"Yes. Did you know him?"

"Yes and no. He worked in forensics, so obviously we spoke to each other over the phone from time to time. They're saying he killed himself?"

"Yes," Sung-min said. He replied "yes" rather than "it looks like it" because there really wasn't any doubt. His car had been found parked at the side of a grit track at the top of a ridge with a view over the farmland of Toten, not far from his childhood home. The doors were locked, the key was in the ignition. A few people had been confused that Bjørn Holm had been sitting in the back seat, and that he had shot himself in the temple with a pistol whose serial number couldn't be traced back to anyone. But his widow, Katrine Bratt, had explained that Holm's idol, Something-or-other Williams, had died in the back seat of his car. And it wasn't particularly unlikely that a forensics officer had access to a weapon with no registered owner. The church had been full of family and colleagues, from both Police Headquarters and Kripos, because Bjørn Holm had worked for both. Katrine Bratt had seemed composed—more composed, in fact, than when they had met at Norafossen.

After she had efficiently worked her way through the queue of people offering condolences, she had come over to him and said there were rumours that he wasn't happy where he was. That was the word she had used, pronounced in her distinct Bergen accent. *Happy.* And said they should have a chat. She had an empty position that needed to be filled. It had taken him a moment to realise that she was talking about Harry Hole's job. And he wondered if it was doubly inappropriate for her to be talking shop after her own husband's funeral, and to offer Sung-min the job of a man who was still only missing. But presumably she needed whatever distractions she could find to take her mind off the pair of them. Sung-min said he'd think about it.

"I hope Kripos's budget can handle this," Alexandra had said when the waiter brought the first course and told them it was raw scallop, black pepper mayonnaise, Ghoa cress and a soy-butter sauce. "Because Forensic Medicine can't."

"Oh, I think I'll be able to justify the expense, if you can keep the promise you made over the phone."

Alexandra Sturdza had called him the previous evening. Without beating around the bush, she had told him that she had information regarding the Rakel Fauke case. That she was calling him because the implications were sensitive, and that she had decided she trusted him after their first encounter. But that she would prefer not to discuss it over the phone.

Sung-min had suggested lunch. And booked a table somewhere she had rightly guessed wasn't within the price range covered by Kripos. He would have to pay for it himself, but he had told himself it was a wise investment, a way of nurturing a professional contact in the Forensic Medicine Institute that could turn out to be useful if and when he needed a favour. A DNA analysis that needed to be prioritised. Something like that. Probably. Somewhere at the back of his mind he had an idea that there was more to it than that. What? He hadn't had time to give the matter too much thought. Sung-min glanced at the busker, who was in full flow now. People were rushing past, paying him no attention. Hank. That was what his colleague had said. Hank Williams. He would have to google him when he got home.

"I've analysed Harry Hole's blood from the trousers he was wearing on the night of the murder," she said. "It contains Rohypnol."

Sung-min looked back from the street and focused on her.

"Enough to knock a man out for four or five hours," she said. "That got me thinking about the time of the murder. Our medical officer narrowed it down to between 22:00 and 02:00, of course. But that was based on body temperature. There were other indications, such as the discolouration around the wounds, which suggest that it could"—she held up a long forefinger, which looked even longer because of the vivid pink of her fingernail—"and I repeat *could*, have happened earlier."

Sung-min remembered that she hadn't been wearing nail polish last time. Had she painted them specially?

"So I checked with the company that supplies electricity to Rakel Fauke's home. It turns out that consumption went up by seventy kilowatts between 20:00 and 24:00. All that electricity suggests an increase in temperature, and if that happened in the living room, it would mean a rise in temperature of five degrees. My medical officer says that if that was the case, she would have given the time of death as between 18:00 and 22:00."

Sung-min blinked. He had read somewhere that the human brain can only process sixty kilobits per second. And that that makes the brain a very weak computer. But the fact that it can work as fast as that depends on how data already stored there is organised. That most of our conclusions rely on recalling memories and patterns and using them rather than thinking new thoughts. Perhaps that was why it was taking him so long. He was having to think new thoughts. Completely new. He heard Alexandra's voice as if it were coming from far away:

"From what Ole Winter has said in the papers, Harry Hole was in a bar with witnesses until 22:30. Is that correct?"

Sung-min stared down at his crayfish. It stared back disinterestedly.

"So the question now has to be whether you have ever had anyone else in your sights? Someone you might have ignored because they had an alibi for the time it was assumed Rakel was murdered. But who may not have had an alibi between 18:00 and 22:00."

"You'll have to excuse me, Alexandra." Sung-min stood up, then realised he'd forgotten his napkin, which fell to the floor. "Please, finish your lunch. I need . . . I've got some things I need to get on with. Another day we can . . . you and I can . . ."

He saw from her smile that they could.

He walked away, gave the maître d' his card and asked him to send him the bill, then hurried out into the street. The busker was playing a song Sung-min had heard, something about a car crash, an ambulance and Riverside, but he wasn't interested in music. Songs, lyrics, names, for some reason none of them stuck. But he remembered every word, every moment of the transcription of the interview with Svein Finne. He had arrived at the maternity ward at 21:30. In other words, Svein Finne had had three and a half hours in which to murder Rakel Fauke. The problem was that no one knew where Finne was.

So why was Sung-min running?

He was running because it was quicker.

What difference did it make if he was quicker, if everyone was already trying to find Svein Finne?

Sung-min wanted to try harder. And he was better. And extremely motivated.

Ole Winter, the useless scavenger, would soon be choking on his big fat team victory.

Dagny Jensen got off the metro at Borgen. She stood there for a moment, looking out across Western Cemetery. But that wasn't where she was going; she didn't know if she would ever go into a cemetery again. Instead she walked down Skøyenveien to Monolitveien, where she turned right. She walked past the white wooden houses behind picket fences. They looked so empty. Afternoon, a weekday. People were are work, at school, doing things, being active. She was static. On sick leave. Dagny hadn't asked for it, but her psychologist and the head teacher had told her to take a few days off to compose herself, and see how she *really* felt after the attack in the women's toilet. As if *anyone* wanted to think about how they really felt!

Well, at least now she knew how bloody awful she felt.

She heard her phone buzz in her bag. She took it out and saw that it was Kari Beal, her bodyguard, again. They would be looking for her now. She pressed Reject and tapped out a message: *Sorry. No danger. Just need some time alone. Will be in touch when I'm done.*

Twenty minutes earlier Dagny and Kari Beal had been in the city centre when Dagny said she wanted to buy some tulips. She had insisted that the police officer wait outside while she went into the florist's, which she knew had another door in the next street. From there, Dagny had made her way to the metro station behind Stortinget and took the first train heading west.

She looked at the time. He had told her to be there by two o'clock. Which bench she should sit on. That she should wear something different from what she usually wore, to make her harder to recognise. What direction she should be looking in.

It was madness.

It was what it was. He had called her from an unknown number. She had answered and not been able to hang up. And now, as if she had been hypnotised and had no will of her own, she was doing as he had instructed, the man who had used and deceived her. How was that possible? She had no answer to that. Just that she must have had something in her that she didn't know was there. A cruel, animalistic urge. Well, it was what it was. She was a bad person, as bad as him, and now she was letting him drag her down with him. She felt her heart beat faster. Oh, she was already longing to be down there, where she would be cleansed by fire. But would he come? He *had* to come! Dagny heard her own shoes hitting the pavement, harder and harder.

Six minutes later she was in position, on the bench she had been told about.

It was five minutes to two. She had a view of Smestaddammen. A white swan was gliding over the water. Its head and neck formed a question mark. Why was she having to do this?

Svein Finne was walking. Long, calm, terrain-conquering strides. Walking like that, in the same direction, for hour after hour, was what he had missed most during his years in prison. Oh well. Spilled milk.

It took him just under two hours to walk from the cabin he had found in Sørkedalen into the centre of Oslo, but he guessed it would have taken most people three.

The cabin lay at the top of a vertical rock face. Because there were bolts drilled into the cliff and he had found rope and carabiners in the cabin, he guessed it had been used by climbers. But there was still snow on the ground, and meltwater was trickling down the red and grey-black granite when the sun was shining, and he hadn't seen any climbers.

But he had seen evidence of the bear. So close to the cabin that he had bought what he needed and set a trap with a tripwire and some explosives. When the last of the snow melted and the climbers began to appear, he would find himself a place deeper in the forest, build himself a teepee. Hunt. Go fishing in the lakes. Only as much as he needed. Killing anything you weren't going to eat was murder, and he wasn't a murderer. He was already looking forward to it.

He walked through the grey, urine-stinking pedestrian tunnel beneath the Smestad junction, emerged into the daylight and carried on towards the lake.

He saw her as soon as he entered the park. Not that he—even with his sharp eyesight—could recognise her from this distance, but he could tell by her posture. The way she was sitting. Waiting. A little scared, probably, but mostly excited.

He didn't walk directly towards the bench, but took a detour to check that there were no police around. That was what he did when he visited Valentin's grave. He quickly concluded that he was alone on this side of the lake. There was someone sitting on a bench on the other side, but they were too far away to see or hear much of what was about to happen, and they wouldn't have time to intervene. Because this was going to happen quickly. Everything was ready, the scene was set and he was ready to burst.

"Hello," he said as he approached the bench.

"Hello," she said, and smiled. She seemed less frightened than he had expected. But of course she didn't know what was about to happen. He glanced around once more to make sure they were alone.

"He's running a bit late," Alise said. "That sometimes happens. You know, being a successful lawyer."

Svein Finne smiled. The girl was relaxed because she thought Johan Krohn was going to be joining them. That must be the explanation Krohn had given her for why she should be sitting on a bench beside Smestaddammen at two o'clock. That she and Krohn were going to be meeting Svein Finne, but because their client was currently being sought by the police, the meeting couldn't take place in the office. All of this had been in the note Finne had found pinned to the ground with a knife in front of Valentin's grave, signed by Johan Krohn. Krohn had also used a splendid knife, and Finne had put it in his pocket to add to his collection. It would come in useful in the cabin. Then he had opened the letter. It looked like Krohn had thought of pretty much everything to let both Finne and Krohn himself walk free afterwards. Apart from the consequences of having given his mistress to Finne, of course. Krohn didn't know it yet, but he would never again be able to love Alise the way he had before. And he would never be free. Krohn had, after all, entered into a pact with the devil, and, as everyone knows, the devil is in the detail. Finne was never going to have to worry about getting hold of anything he needed again, whether it be money or pleasure.

Johan Krohn was still sitting in his car in the visitors' car park at Hegnar Media. He had arrived early, he mustn't be at the lake in the park on the other side of the road before five past two. He took out the new packet of Marlboro, got out of the car—because Frida didn't like the smell of smoke in the car—and tried to light a cigarette. But his hands were shaking too much and he gave up. Just as well, he'd decided to stop anyway. He looked at his watch again. The plan was for him to get two minutes. They hadn't been in direct contact, it was safest that way, but his message had said that two minutes were all he needed.

He followed the second hand with his eyes. There. Two o'clock.

Johan Krohn closed his eyes. Naturally it was terrible, something he would have to live with for the rest of his life, but when it came down to it, it was the only solution.

He thought about Alise. What she was having to go through right now. She would survive, but the nightmares would obviously haunt her. All because of the decision he had taken, without saying a word to her. He had deceived her. It was him, not Finne, who had done this to Alise.

He looked at his watch again. In one and a half minutes he would walk into the park, making out that he was just a bit late, comfort her as well as he could, call the police, act appalled. Correction: he would hardly have to act. He would give the police an explanation that was 90 percent true. And Alise an explanation that was 100 percent lie.

Johan Krohn caught sight of his own reflection in the car window.

He hated what he saw. The only thing he hated more was Svein Finne.

Alise looked at Svein Finne, who had sat down on the bench beside her.

"Do you know why we're here, Alise?" he asked.

He had a red bandana tied around his black hair, with just a few strands of grey.

"Only in general terms," she said. All Johan had told her was that it was to do with the Rakel Fauke case. Her first thought had been that they were going to press charges against the police for the physical injuries inflicted on their client by Harry Hole in the bunker in Nordstrand. But when she asked, Johan had simply replied curtly that it was to do with a confession, and that he didn't have time to explain. He had been like that for the past few days. Cold. Dismissive. If she didn't know better, she would have thought he was starting to lose interest. But she did know better. She had seen him like this before, during the brief periods when his conscience was getting at him and he suggested taking a break, saying he needed to focus on his family, the firm. Yes, he had tried. And she had stopped him. Dear Lord, it didn't take much. Men. Or, to be more accurate: boys. Because every so often she got the feeling that she was the older of the pair of them, that he was just an overgrown Boy Scout equipped with a razor-sharp legal brain but not much else. Even if Johan liked to play the role of master to her slave, they both knew it was the other way around. But she let him play that role, the way a mother plays a frightened princess when her child wants to pretend to be a troll.

Not that Johan didn't have his good qualities. He did. He was kind. Considerate. Loyal. He *was*. Alise had known men who had far fewer scruples about deceiving their wives than Johan Krohn. The question that *had* begun to worry Alise, though, wasn't Johan's loyalty to his family, but what she herself was getting out of it. No, she hadn't had a carefully thought-out plan when she embarked upon the affair with Johan, it wasn't that calculated. As a newly qualified lawyer she had obviously been star-struck by the hotshot lawyer who had been permitted to practise in the Supreme Court when he had barely started shaving, and was a partner in one of the best law firms in the city. But Alise was also fully aware of what she, with her average grades, had to offer a law firm, and what with her youth and appearance she had to offer a man. At the end of the day (Johan had stopped correcting her Anglicisms and had instead started to copy them), the reasons why you choose to have an affair with someone were a combination of rational and apparently irrational factors. (Johan would have pointed out that factors lead to a *product*, not a *combination*.) It was hard to know what was what, and perhaps it wasn't that useful to know anyway. What was more important was that she was no longer sure if the combination was positive. She may have got a slightly larger office than the others on the same level as her, and perhaps *slightly* more interesting cases as a result of working for Johan. But her annual bonus was the same, symbolic amount that the other non-partners got. And there hadn't been any indication that she could expect anything more. And even if Alise knew how much married men's promises to leave their wives and families were worth, Johan hadn't even bothered to make any of those.

"In general terms," Svein Finne said, and smiled.

Brown teeth, she noted. But also that he didn't smoke, seeing as he was sitting so close to her that she could feel his breath on her face.

"Twenty-five," he said. "You kn-know you're heading past the most fruitful time for having children?"

Alise stared at Finne. How did he know how old she was?

"The best age is your late t-teens, up to twenty-four," Finne said, as his eyes slid over her. Yes, slid, Alise thought. Like a physical thing, like a snail leaving a trail of slime behind it.

"From then on, the health risks increase, and also the chances of spontaneous miscarriage," he said, tugging up one cuff of his flannel shirt. He pressed a button on the side of his digital watch. "While the quality of men's semen remains the same throughout their lives."

That isn't true, she thought. She had read that compared to a man her age, the risk of a man over the age of forty-one getting you pregnant was five times lower. And he was five times as likely to give you a child suffering from some sort of autism. She'd googled it. She had been invited by Frank to join him and a couple of fellow students on a trip to the mountains. When she and Frank were together he had been rather too fond of partying, without any clear goal or good grades, and she had written him off as a daddy's boy with no motivation of his own. That turned out to be wrong, Frank had done surprisingly well in his father's law firm. But she still hadn't replied to the invitation.

"So look upon this as my and Johan Krohn's gift to you," Finne said, undoing his jacket.

Alise looked at him intently. A thought flew through her head, that he was going to attack her, but she dismissed it. Johan would be here any minute, and they were in a very public place. OK, there was nobody in their immediate vicinity, but she could see someone on the other side of the lake, maybe two hundred metres away, sitting on another bench.

"What . . ." Alise began, but got no further. Svein Finne's left hand had locked around her throat, and his right hand was shoving his jacket aside. She tried to breathe but couldn't. His erect penis had a curve, like a swan's neck.

"Don't be scared, I'm not like the others," Finne said. "I don't kill."

Alise tried to get up from the bench, tried to push his arm away, but his hand was like a claw that had locked around her throat.

"Not if you do as I say," Finne said. "First, *look*."

He was still holding her with just one hand, and sat there, legs apart, exposed, as if he wanted her to look at it, see what she had coming. And Alise looked. Saw the white swan's neck with its veins and a dancing red dot that was moving up the shaft.

What was that? What *was* that?

Then the head of his penis exploded as she heard a muffled sound, like when she tenderised a steak extra hard with the meat hammer. She felt a warm rain on her face and got something in her eye, and closed them as she heard thunder roll over them.

For a moment Alise thought it was her screaming, but when she opened her eyes again she saw that it was Svein Finne. He was holding both hands to his groin, blood was pumping between his fingers, and he was staring at her with big, shocked, accusing eyes as if she was the person who had done this to him.

Then the red dot was there again, on his face this time. It slid over his furrowed cheek, up to his eye. She could see the red dot on the white of his eye. And perhaps Finne saw it too. Either way, he whispered something that she didn't hear until he repeated it.

"Help."

Alise knew what was coming, closed her eyes and managed to put one protective hand in front of her face before she heard the sound again, more like a whip crack this time. And then, with a long delay, as if the shot had been fired from a long way away, the same rolling thunder.

Roar Bohr looked through the sniper sight.

The last headshot had thrown the target backwards, then he had slid sideways off the bench and was now lying on the gravel path.

He moved the sight. Saw the young woman running along the path towards Hegnar Media, saw her throw her arms around a man who was hurrying towards her. Then the man took out a phone and started tapping at it, as if he knew exactly what he should do. Which he probably did, but what did Bohr know?

No more than he wanted to know.

No more than Harry Hole had told him twenty-four hours ago.

That he had found the man Bohr had been looking for all these years.

In a conversation with what Harry said was an extremely reliable source, Svein Finne had claimed to have raped Bishop Bohr's daughter many years ago in Mærradalen.

The case had long since passed the statute of limitations, of course.

But Harry had what he called a "solution."

And he had told Bohr all he needed to know, and no more. Just like when he was in E14. Two o'clock by Smestaddammen, on the same bench that Harry and Pia had sat on.

Roar Bohr moved the sight, and from the other side of the lake he saw a woman walking away quickly. As far as he could tell, she seemed to be the only other witness. He closed the basement window and put the rifle down. Looked at the time. He had promised Harry Hole that it would be done within two minutes of the target arriving, and he had stuck to that, even if he had given in to the temptation of letting Svein Finne have a little foretaste of his impending death when he exposed himself. But he had used so-called frangible bullets, bullets with no lead that disintegrate and stay inside the body of the target. Not because he needed them to in order to be fatal, but because the police's ballistics experts wouldn't have a projectile that could be matched to a weapon, or any point of impact in the ground that would enable them to work out where the shots had been fired from. In short, they would be left standing there, looking up help-lessly at a hillside covered with something like a thousand houses, and with absolutely no idea where they should start looking.

It was done. He had shot the mink. He had finally avenged Bianca.

Roar felt ecstatic. Yes, that was the only way he could describe it. He locked the rifle away in the gun cabinet, then went and had a shower. On the way he stopped and pulled his phone from his pocket. Called a number. Pia answered on the second ring.

"Is anything wrong?"

"No." Roar Bohr smiled. "I just wondered if you'd like to go out for dinner this evening?"

"Out for dinner?"

"It's been ages since we last did that. I've heard good things about Lofoten, that fish restaurant on Tjuvholmen."

He heard her hesitation. Suspicion. He followed her train of thought on towards the same *why not?* that he had thought.

"OK," she said. "Are you going—"

"Yes, I'll book a table. How does eight o'clock sound?"

"Great," Pia said. "That all sounds great."

They hung up, and Roar Bohr undressed, got in the shower and turned the water on. Warm water. He wanted to have a warm shower.

Dagny Jensen left the park the same way she had come. She thought about how she *really* felt. She had been sitting too far away to see any of the details on the other side of the lake, but she had seen enough. Yes, she had let herself be persuaded by Harry Hole's almost hypnotic request, but this time he hadn't deceived her, he had kept his promise. Svein Finne was out of her life. Dagny thought about Hole's deep, hoarse voice on the phone, when he had told her what was going to happen, and why she must never, ever tell anyone. And even if she had already felt a peculiar excitement, and knew she wasn't going to be able to resist, she had asked why, and if he thought she was the sort of person who would allow themselves to be entertained by a public execution.

"I don't know what entertains you," he had replied. "But you said it wasn't enough for you to see him *dead* for him not to haunt you. You needed to see him *die*. I owe you that much, after everything I've put you through. Take it or leave it."

Dagny thought about her mother's funeral, the young female priest who had said that no one knew for certain what lay beyond the threshold of death, just that those who crossed it never came back.

But Dagny Jensen knew now. She knew that Finne was dead. And how she *really* felt.

She didn't feel brilliant.

But she did feel better.

Katrine Bratt was sitting behind the desk, looking around.

She had packed the last of the things she wanted to take home. Bjørn's parents were in the flat looking after Gert, and she knew that any good mother would probably have wanted to get home as quickly as she could. But Katrine wanted to wait a little longer. Catch her breath. Stretch this pause from the suffocating grief, the unanswered questions, the nagging suspicions.

The grief was easier to deal with when she was alone. When she didn't feel she was being watched, didn't have to stop herself from laughing at something Gert did, or from saying something wrong, like she was looking forward to spring or something. Not that Bjørn's parents reacted—they were sensible, they understood. They were wonderful people, actually. But she clearly wasn't. The grief was there, but she was able to chase it away when no one else was there to remind her constantly that Bjørn was dead. That Harry was dead.

The unspoken suspicion she knew they must be feeling, but didn't show. That she, one way or another, must be the reason why Bjørn had taken his own life. But she knew she wasn't. On the other hand, though: Should she have realised something was wrong with Bjørn when he had gone completely to pieces when he heard that Harry was dead? Should she have known that it was more than that, that Bjørn was struggling with something bigger, a deep depression he had managed to fend off and keep hidden until Harry's death came along. Not just the drop that made his cup overflow, but burst the entire dam. What do we really know about the people we share our beds, our lives with? Even less than we know about ourselves. Katrine found it an unpalatable idea, but the impressions we have of the people around us are precisely that: impressions.

She had raised the alarm when Bjørn handed Gert over without wanting to talk to her.

Katrine had just got home from the terrible press conference with Ole Winter, to an empty flat and no message saying where Bjørn and Gert were, when someone rang the front doorbell. She had picked up the entryphone and heard Gert crying, and opened the door to the flat in case Bjørn had forgotten his keys, then pressed the button to open the door down on the street. But she hadn't heard the whirr of the lock, just the baby crying close to the microphone. After saying Bjørn's name several times without getting any response, she had gone downstairs.

The Maxi-Cosi baby carrier with Gert in it was sitting on the pavement right outside the door.

Katrine had looked up and down Nordahl Bruns gate, but couldn't see any sign of Bjørn. Nor had she seen anyone in any of the darkened

doorways on the other side of the street, although that didn't necessarily mean there was no one there, of course. And then a random
thought occurred to her: that it hadn't been Bjørn who rang the bell.

She had taken Gert up to the flat and called Bjørn's number, only
to be told that his phone was switched off or out of reach of the network. She realised something was wrong and called Bjørn's parents.
And it was the fact that she had instinctively called them rather than
any of Bjørn's friends or workmates, who, after all, lived in the city,
that made her realise that she was worried.

His parents had reassured her, saying that he was bound to get in
touch with a good explanation, but Katrine could hear from Bjørn's
mother's voice that she too was concerned. Perhaps she too had
noticed that Bjørn didn't seem to have been himself recently.

You might think that a murder detective would eventually come to
accept that there are some things, some questions you will never get
an answer to, and you just have to move on. But some of them never
managed that. Like Harry. Like her. Katrine didn't know if this was
an advantage or a hindrance from a professional perspective, but one
thing was certain: for life outside of work it was nothing but a disadvantage. She was already dreading the weeks and months of sleepless
nights that lay ahead of her. Not because of Gert. You could set your
watch by when he slept and woke up. It was the restless, compulsive
activity of her brain in the darkness that would stop her sleeping.

Katrine zipped up the bag containing the case files and papers she
needed to take home, walked towards the door, turned out the light
and was about to leave her office when the phone on her desk started
to ring.

She picked it up.

"It's Sung-min Larsen."

"Great," Katrine said, in a toneless voice. Not that she meant that
it wasn't great, but if this phone call meant he had decided to accept
her offer of a job in Crime Squad, the timing wasn't exactly good.

"I'm calling because . . . Is now a good time, by the way?"

Katrine looked out of the window, towards Botsparken. Bare
trees, brown, withered grass. It wouldn't be long before the trees
grew leaves and blossoms, before the grass turned green. And then,
after that, it would be summer. Or so they said.

"Yes," she said, and heard that she still wasn't managing to sound
enthusiastic.

"I've just experienced a remarkable coincidence," Larsen said.
"Earlier today I received information that sheds new light on the

Rakel Fauke case. And I've just had a phone call from Johan Krohn, Sv—"

"I know who Krohn is."

"He says he's at Smestaddammen, where he and his assistant had arranged to meet his client, Svein Finne. And that Svein Finne has just been shot and killed."

"What?"

"I don't know why Krohn called me in particular, he says he'll explain that later. Either way, this is primarily a case for Oslo Police District, which is why I'm calling you."

"I'll pass it on to the uniforms," Katrine said. She saw a deer creep across the brown lawn in front of Police Headquarters, heading towards the old prison block, Botsfengselet. She waited. Noted that Larsen was also waiting. "What did you mean when you said it was a coincidence, Larsen?"

"It seems odd that Svein Finne has been shot just an hour after I received information that means Finne is back as a suspect in the Fauke case."

Katrine let go of her bag and sank down on the chair behind the desk. "You're saying . . ."

"Yes, I'm saying I'm in possession of information that indicates that Harry Hole is innocent."

Katrine felt her heart start to beat. Blood was coursing through her body, pricking her skin. And something else, something that had been lying dormant, woke up.

"When you say 'in possession of,' Larsen . . ."

"Yes?"

"It sounds as if you haven't shared this information with your colleagues yet. Is that correct?"

"Not entirely. I've shared it with you."

"All you've shared with me is your own conclusion that Harry's innocent."

"You'll end up reaching the same conclusion, Bratt."

"Really?"

"I've got a suggestion."

"I thought you might have."

"That you and I meet at the crime scene, and we'll take it from there."

"OK. I'll come over with the uniforms."

Katrine called the duty officer, then let her parents-in-law know she was going to be late. While she was waiting for them to answer she looked down at Botsparken again. The deer was gone. Her late father, Gert, had told her that badgers hunt everything. Anytime, anywhere. They'll eat anything, and fight anything. And that some detectives had the badger in them, and some didn't. And what Katrine could feel right now was the badger waking from hibernation.

52

Sung-min Larsen was already there when Katrine arrived at Smestad-dammen. Between his legs stood a quivering, trembling dog, as if it was trying to hide. There was a thin but insistent bleeping sound, like an alarm clock, coming from somewhere.

They walked over to the body, which was lying on the ground beside the bench. Katrine realised that the bleeping was coming from the dead body. And that the body was Svein Finne. That the deceased had been shot in the groin and through one eye, but that there were no exit wounds in his back or head. Special ammunition, perhaps. Even if Katrine knew it couldn't be the case, it felt like the monotonous electronic bleeping from the dead man's watch was gradually getting louder.

"Why hasn't anyone . . ." she began.

"Fingerprints," Sung-min said. "I have a preliminary witness statement, but it would be good to be able to know for certain that no one else has touched his watch."

Katrine nodded. Then gestured that they should move away.

The officers were setting up cordon tape as Sung-min told Katrine what he had found out about the sequence of events from Alise Krogh Reinertsen and her boss, Johan Krohn, who were standing on the other side of the lake with a small crowd of curious onlookers. Sung-min told Katrine that he had ushered them all over there to get them out of the line of fire, seeing as it couldn't be ruled out entirely that Svein Finne was merely a random victim, and that the perpetrator was looking for others.

"Hmm," Katrine said, squinting up at the hillside. "You and I must be right in the line of fire right now, so we don't really believe that, do we?"

"No," Sung-min said.

"So what do you think?" Katrine said, crouching down to pat the dog.

"I don't think anything, but Krohn has a theory."

Katrine nodded. "Is it the body that's upset your dog?"

"No. He got attacked by a swan when we arrived."

"Poor thing," Katrine said, scratching the dog behind one ear. She got a lump in her throat, as if there was something familiar about the trusting look in the dog's eyes as it gazed up at her.

"Has Krohn explained why he called you specifically?"

"Yes."

"And?"

"I think you should talk to him yourself."

"OK."

"Bratt?"

"Yes?"

"Like I said before, Kasparov used to be a police dog. Is it OK if he and I start to look into which direction Finne came from?"

Katrine looked at the trembling dog. "I can have the dog unit here within half an hour. I presume that's one of the reasons why Kasparov was retired."

"His hips are worn out," Larsen said. "But I can carry him if it turns out to be a long way."

"Really? But don't dogs' sense of smell get weaker as they get older?"

"A little," Larsen said. "Same as human beings."

Katrine looked at Sung-min Larsen. Was he referring to Ole Winter?

"Get going," she said, patting Kasparov's head. "Good hunting."

And, as if the old dog recognised what she said, its tail, which had been drooping down, started to wag.

Katrine walked around the lake.

Krohn and his assistant both looked pale and cold. A slight but chill north wind had started to blow, the sort that puts a temporary stop to Oslo's inhabitants' thoughts of spring.

"I'm afraid you're going to have to go through everything again, from the start," Katrine said, taking out her notebook.

Krohn nodded. "It started when Finne came to see me a few days ago. All of a sudden he was just standing there on my terrace. He wanted to tell me he'd killed Rakel Fauke, so I could help him if and when you started to close in on him."

"And Harry Hole?"

"After the murder he drugged Harry Hole and left him at the scene. He fiddled with the thermostat to make it look like Rakel was killed after Hole arrived there. Finne's motive was that Harry Hole had shot his son when he was trying to arrest him."

"Really?" Katrine didn't know why she didn't instantly buy this story. "Did Finne tell you how he got inside Rakel Fauke's house? Seeing as the door was locked from the inside, I mean."

Krohn shook his head. "The chimney? I have no idea. I've seen that man arrive and leave in the most inexplicable ways. I agreed to meet him here because I wanted him to hand himself in to the police."

Katrine stamped her feet on the ground. "Who do you think shot Finne? And why?"

Krohn shrugged. "A man like Svein Finne, who assaulted children, gets plenty of enemies in prison. He managed to stay alive in there, but I know that several of them who'd been released were just waiting for Finne to get out. Men like that often have access to firearms, sadly, and some of them know how to use them as well."

"So we've got loads of potential suspects, all of whom have served time for serious offences, some of them for murder, is that what you're saying?"

"That's what I'm saying, Bratt."

Krohn was a persuasive storyteller, there was no doubt about that. Maybe Katrine's skepticism was based on the fact that she had heard too many of the stories he had told in court. She looked at Alise. "I've got a few questions, if that's OK?"

"Not yet," Alise said, folding her arms over her chest. "Not until six hours have passed. New research shows that dwelling on dramatic experiences before that increases the risk of long-term trauma."

"And we've got a killer who's getting a bit harder to catch with each minute that passes," Katrine said.

"Not my responsibility, I'm a defense lawyer," the woman said, with a defiant look in her eyes but in a shaky voice.

Katrine felt sorry for her, but this wasn't the time for kid gloves.

"In that case you've done a terrible job, because your client's dead," she said. "And you're not a defense lawyer, you're a young woman with a law degree and a boss you're fucking because you think it'll help you climb the ladder. It won't. And it won't help you to try and play tough with me, OK?"

Alise Krogh Reinertsen stared at Katrine. Blinked. A first tear began to make its way through the powder on the young woman's cheek.

Six minutes later, Katrine had all the details. She had asked Alise to close her eyes, relive the first shot, and say "now" when the bullet hit, and "now" when she heard the rumble. There was over a second between them, so the shot had come from at least four hundred metres away. Katrine thought about the points of impact. The man's genitals, then one of his eyes. That wasn't an accident. The killer had to be either a competitive marksman or have specialist military training. There couldn't be many people like that who had served time at the same time as Svein Finne. Probably none, at a guess.

And a suspicion, almost a hope—no, not even that, just a vain wish—ran through her. Then disappeared. But that glimpse of an alternative truth left something warm and soothing behind it, like the faith religious people cling to even though their intellect rejects it. And for a few moments Katrine couldn't feel the northerly wind as she looked at the park in front of her and imagined it in the summer, the island with the willow tree, the flowers, insects buzzing, birds singing. All the things she would soon be able to show Gert. Then another thought struck her.

The stories she was going to tell Gert about his father.

The older he got, the more he would want to know about that part of him, the man he had come from.

Something that would make him either proud or ashamed.

It was true that the badger in her had woken up. And that a badger, in theory, could dig right through the planet in the course of its lifetime. But how deeply did she want to dig? Maybe she'd found out all she wanted to know.

She heard a sound. No, it wasn't a sound. Silence.

The watch on the other side of the lake. It had stopped bleeping.

A dog's sense of smell is, roughly speaking, a hundred thousand times more sensitive than a human's. And, according to recent research that Sung-min had read, dogs can do more than just smell. A dog's Jacobson's organ, located in its palate, also allows it to detect and interpret scentless pheromones and other information without any smell. This means that a dog—in perfect conditions—can follow the trail left by a human being up to a month later.

The conditions weren't perfect.

The worst of it was that the trail they were following ran along a sidewalk, which meant that other people and animals had confused the scent. And there wasn't much vegetation for scent particles to cling to.

On the other hand, both Sørkedalsveien and the sidewalk—which ran through a residential area—weren't as heavily trafficked as the city centre. And it was cold, which helped preserve scent. But, more important, even if there were large clouds blowing in from the northwest, it hadn't rained since Svein Finne had been there.

Sung-min felt tense each time they approached a bus stop, sure that the trail was about to end, that that was where Finne had got off a bus. But Kasparov just kept going, straining at his leash—he seemed to have forgotten all about his aching hips—and on the slopes heading up towards Røa, Sung-min began to regret not changing out of his suit into jogging gear.

But as he sweated he was getting more and more excited. They had been going for almost half an hour, and it seemed unlikely that Finne would have used public transport at all, only to walk such an unnecessarily long way after he got off.

Harry stared out across Porsanger Fjord, towards the sea, towards the North Pole, towards the end and the beginning, towards where there was probably a horizon on clearer days. But today, the sea, sky and land all blurred together. It was like sitting under a huge, grey-white dome, and it was as quiet as a church, the only sounds the occasional plaintive cry of a gull and the sea lapping gently against the rowing boat the man and boy were sitting in. And Oleg's voice:

". . . and when I got home and told Mum that I put my hand up in class and said that Old Tjikko isn't the oldest tree in the world, but the oldest roots, she laughed so much I thought she was going to start crying. And then she said that the three of us had roots like that. I didn't tell her, but I thought that couldn't be right, because you're not my father the way the roots are Old Tjikko's father and mother. But as the years passed, I realised what she meant. That roots are something that grow. That when we used to sit there talking about . . . I don't know, what did we talk about? Tetris. Skating. Bands we both like . . ."

"Mm. And both . . ."

". . . hate." Oleg grinned. "That's when we grew roots. That was how you became my father."

"Mm. A bad father."

"Rubbish."

"You think I was an average father?"

"An *unusual* father. Lousy grades in some subjects, world's best in others. You saved me when you came back from Hong Kong. But it's funny, I remember the little things best. Like the time you tricked me."

"I *tricked* you?"

"When I finally managed to beat your Tetris record, you boasted that you knew all the countries in the world atlas in the bookcase. And you knew exactly what was going to happen after that."

"Well . . ."

"It took me a couple of months, but by the time my classmates looked at me weirdly when I mentioned Djibouti, I knew the names, flags and capital cities of every country in the world."

"Almost all."

"All."

"Nope. You thought San Salvador was the country and El Salvador—"

"Don't even try."

Harry smiled. And realised that was exactly what it was. A smile. Like the first glimpse of sun after months of darkness. Even if a new period of darkness lay ahead of him, now that he had finally woken up, but it couldn't be worse than the one that lay behind him.

"She liked that," Harry said. "Listening to us talk."

"Did she?" Oleg looked off to the north.

"She used to bring the book she was reading, or her knitting, and sit down near us. She didn't bother to interrupt or join in the conversation, she didn't even bother to listen to what we were talking about. She said she just liked the sound. She said it was the sound of the men in her life."

"I liked that sound too," Oleg said, pulling the fishing rod towards him so that the tip bowed respectfully towards the surface of the water. "You and Mum. After I'd gone to bed I used to open the door just so I could listen to you. You used to talk quietly, and it sounded like you'd already said pretty much everything, understood each other. That all that needed adding was the occasional key word here or there. Even so, you used to make her laugh. It was such a safe sound, the best sound to fall asleep to."

Harry chuckled. Coughed. Thought that sound carried a long way in this weather, possibly all the way to land. He tugged dutifully at his own fishing rod.

"Helga says she's never seen two grown-ups as in love with each other as you and Mum. That she hopes we can be like you."

"Mm. Maybe she ought to hope for more than that."

"More than what?"

Harry shrugged. "Here comes a line I've heard too many men say. Your mother deserved better than me."

Oleg smiled briefly. "Mum knew what she was getting, and it was you she wanted. She just needed that break to remember that. For the pair of you to remember Old Tjikko's roots."

Harry cleared his throat. "Listen, maybe it's time for me to tell—"

"No," Oleg interrupted. "I don't want to know anything about why she threw you out. If that's OK with you? And nothing about the rest of it either."

"OK," Harry said. "It's up to you how much you want to know." That was what he used to say to Rakel. She had made a habit of asking for less rather than more information.

Oleg ran his hand along the side of the boat. "Because the rest of the truth is bad, isn't it?"

"Yes."

"I heard you in the spare room last night. Did you get any sleep?"

"Mm."

"Mum's dead, nothing can change that, and for the time being it's enough for me to know that someone other than you was guilty. If I discover that I do need to know, maybe you can tell me later on."

"You're very wise, Oleg. Just like your mother."

Oleg gave him a sardonic smile and looked at the time. "Helga will be waiting for us. She's bought some cod."

Harry looked down at the empty bucket in front of him. "Smart woman."

They reeled their lines in. Harry looked at his watch. He had a ticket for an afternoon flight back to Oslo. He didn't know what was going to happen after that; the plan he had worked out with Johan Krohn went no further than this.

Oleg put the oars in the rowlocks and started to row.

Harry watched him. Thought back to the time he used to row

while his grandfather sat in front of him, smiling and giving Harry little bits of advice. How he should use his upper body and straighten his arms, row with his stomach, not his biceps. That he should take it gently, never stress, find a rhythm, that a boat gliding evenly through the water moves faster even with less energy. That he should feel with his buttocks to make sure he was sitting in the middle of the bench. That it was all about balance. That he shouldn't look at the oars, but keep his eyes on the wake, that the signs of what had already happened showed you where you were heading. But, his grandfather had said, they told you surprisingly little about what was going to happen. That was determined by the next stroke of the oars. His grandfather took out his pocket watch and said that when we get back on shore, we look back on our journey as a continuous line from the point of departure to the point of arrival. A story, with a purpose and a direction. We remember it as if it were here, and nowhere but here, that we intended the boat to meet the shoreline, he said. But the point of arrival and the intended destination were two different things. Not that one was necessarily better than the other. We get to where we get to, and it can be a consolation to believe that was where we wanted to get to, or at least were on our way towards the whole time. But our fallible memories are like a kind mother telling us how clever we are, that our strokes with the oar were clean and fitted into the story as a logical, intentional part. The idea that we may have gone off course, that we no longer know where we are or where we are going, that life is a chaotic mess of clumsy, fumbled oar strokes, is so unappealing that we prefer to rewrite the story in hindsight. That's why people who appear to have been successful and are asked to talk about it often say it was the dream—the only one—they'd had since they were little, to succeed in whatever it was that they had been successful in. It is probably honestly meant. They have probably just forgotten about all the other dreams, the ones that weren't nurtured, that faded and disappeared. Who knows, perhaps we would acknowledge the meaningless chaos of coincidences that make up our lives if—instead of writing autobiographies—we had written down our predictions for life, how we thought our lives would turn out. We could forget all about them, then take them out later on to see what we had *really* dreamed about.

Around now his grandfather would have taken a long swig from his hip flask, then looked at the boy, at Harry. And Harry would have looked at the old man's heavy eyes, so heavy that they looked like they were going to fall out of his head, as if he were going to cry egg white and iris. Harry hadn't thought about it at the time, but he thought about it now—that his grandfather had sat there hoping his grandson would have a better life than him. Would avoid the mistakes he had made. But perhaps also that one day, when the boy was grown up, he would sit like this, watching his son, daughter, grandchild row. And give them some advice. See some of it help, some get forgotten or ignored. And feel his chest swell, his throat tighten, in a strange mixture of pride and sympathy. Pride because the child was a better version of himself. Sympathy because they still had more pain ahead of them than behind them, and were rowing with the conviction that someone, they themselves perhaps, or at least their grandfather, knew where they were going.

"We've got a case," Oleg said. "Two neighbours, childhood friends, who fell out at a party. There'd never been any trouble between them before, solid types. They each went home, then the next morning one of them, a maths teacher, showed up at the other's door with a jack in his hand. Afterwards the neighbour accused the maths teacher of attempted murder, said he'd hit out at his head before he managed to close the door. I questioned the maths teacher. And I'm sitting there thinking: no, if he's capable of murder, then we all are. And we aren't. Are we?"

Harry didn't answer.

Oleg stopped rowing for a moment. "I thought the same thing when they told me that Kripos had evidence against you. That it just couldn't be true. I know you've had to kill in the course of duty, to save your own or someone else's life. But a premeditated, planned murder, the sort of murder where you clean up all the evidence afterwards . . . You couldn't have done that, could you?"

Harry looked at Oleg, sitting there waiting for him to answer. The boy, almost a man, with his journey still ahead of him, with the possibility of becoming a better man than him. Rakel had always had a note of concern in her voice when she told him how much Oleg looked up to him, tried to copy him down to the smallest details, the way he walked, with his feet turned out slightly, a bit like Charlie Chaplin. That he used Harry's special words and expressions, such as the archaic "indubitably." He copied the way Harry rubbed the back of his neck when he was thinking hard. Repeated Harry's arguments about the rights and limitations of the state.

"Of course I couldn't have done it," Harry said, pulling his cigarettes from his pocket. "It takes a particular type of person to plan a cold-blooded murder, and you and I, we're not like that."

Oleg smiled. Looked almost relieved. "Can I bum a—"

"No, you don't smoke. Keep rowing."

Harry lit a cigarette. The smoke rose straight up, then drifted off towards the east. He squinted towards the horizon that wasn't there.

Krohn had looked utterly confused, standing there in the doorway in just his boxer shorts and slippers. He had hesitated for a moment before asking Harry in. They had sat down in the kitchen, where Krohn had served tasteless espresso from a black machine while Harry briefly checked that everything he said was in confidence, then he served up the whole story.

When he had finished, Krohn's coffee cup was still standing untouched.

"So what you want is to clear your name," Krohn said. "But without identifying your colleague, Bjørn Holm."

"Yes," Harry said. "Can you help me?"

Johan Krohn had scratched his chin. "That's going to be difficult. As you know, the police don't like to let go of one suspect unless they've got another one. And what we've got, the analysis of some blood on a pair of trousers that shows you were drugged with Rohypnol, and the electricity usage that shows the thermostat had been turned up and then down again, those are just corroborating factors. The blood could have come from another occasion, the electricity could have been used in another room, it doesn't prove anything at all. What we need . . . is a scapegoat. Someone who hasn't got an alibi. Someone with a motive. Someone everyone would accept."

Harry had noted that Krohn said "we," as if they were already a team. And something else had changed in Krohn. His face had a bit of colour in it again, he was breathing deeper, his pupils had dilated. Like a carnivore that's caught sight of some prey, Harry thought. The same prey as me.

"There's a widespread misconception that a scapegoat has to be innocent," Krohn said. "But the purpose of the scapegoat isn't to be innocent, but to take the blame, regardless of what he has or hasn't done. Even under the current rule of law, we see that offenders who arouse public disgust but who are only tangentially guilty receive disproportionately severe sentences."

"Shall we get to the point?" Harry said.

"The point?"

"Svein Finne."

Krohn looked at Harry. Then gave a brief nod to indicate that they understood each other.

"With this new information," Krohn said, "Finne no longer has an alibi for the time of the murder, he hadn't arrived at the maternity ward by then. And he has a motive: he hates you. You and I can ensure that an active rapist ends up behind bars. And he isn't an innocent scapegoat. Think about all the suffering he's caused people. Do you know, Finne admitted . . . no, he *boasted* about assaulting the daughter of Bishop Bohr, who lived just a couple of hundred metres away from here."

Harry took his cigarette packet from his pocket. He tapped out a bent cigarette. "Tell me what Finne's got on you."

Krohn laughed. Raised his cup to his lips to camouflage the fake laughter.

"I haven't got time for games, Krohn. Come on, all the details."

Krohn swallowed. "Of course. I'm sorry, I haven't slept. Let's go and have coffee in the library."

"What for?"

"My wife . . . Sound doesn't carry as far there."

The acoustics were dry and muffled among the books that lined the walls from floor to ceiling. Harry listened as he sat slumped in a deep leather armchair. This time it was his turn not to touch his coffee.

"Mm," he said when Krohn had finished. "Shall we skip the bit where we beat around the bush?"

"Of course," said Krohn, who had put a raincoat on and reminded Harry of a flasher who used to hang around in a patch of woodland in Oppsal when Harry was a boy. Øystein and Harry had snuck up on the flasher and shot at him with water pistols. But what Harry remembered most was the look of sorrow in the wet, passive flasher's eyes before they ran off, and that he regretted it afterwards without really knowing why.

"You don't want Finne behind bars," Harry said. "That wouldn't stop him telling your wife what he knows. You want Finne out of the way. For good."

"So . . ." Krohn began.

"That's your problem with taking Finne alive," Harry continued. "Mine is that if we manage to find him at all, he may still have an alibi for between 18:00 and 22:00 that we don't know about. It may be that he was with the pregnant woman during the hours before they went to the maternity ward. Not that I imagine that she'd come forward if Finne was killed, of course."

"Killed?"

"Liquidated, terminated, annulled." Harry took a drag on the cigarette, which he had lit without asking permission. "I prefer 'killed.' Bad things deserve bad names."

Krohn let out a short, bemused laugh. "You're talking about cold-blooded murder, Harry."

Harry shrugged. "Murder, yes. Cold-blooded, no. But if we're going to manage this, we need to lower the temperature. If you understand me?"

Krohn nodded.

"Good," Harry said. "Let me think for a minute."

"Can I have one of your cigarettes?"

Harry handed him the packet.

The two men sat in silence, watching the smoke rise towards the ceiling.

"If—" Krohn began.

"Shhh."

Krohn sighed.

His cigarette had almost burned down to the filter when Harry spoke again.

"What I need from you, Krohn, is a lie."

"OK?"

"You need to say that Finne confessed to killing Rakel. And I'll be inviting two more people to participate in this. One works at the Forensic Medicine Institute. The other is a sniper. None of you will know the names of the others. OK?"

Krohn had nodded.

"Good. We need to write an invitation to Finne, telling him when and where to meet your assistant, then you need to attach it to the grave with something I'm going to give you."

"What?"

Harry took one last drag on his cigarette, then stubbed it out in his coffee cup. "A Trojan horse. Finne collects knives. If we're lucky, it'll be enough to kill any other speculation stone dead."

Sung-min heard a crow somewhere among the trees as he looked up at the sheer rock face in front of him. The meltwater was painting black stripes down the grey granite, which rose up some thirty metres above him. He and Kasparov had been walking for almost three hours, and it was obvious that Kasparov was in pain now. Sung-min didn't know if it was loyalty or the hunting instinct that was driving him on, but even when they had been standing at the end of the muddy forest track looking at the fragile rope-bridge across the river, with snow and pathless forest on the other side, he had been straining at the leash to keep going. Sung-min had seen footsteps in the snow on the other side, but he would have to carry Kasparov over the bridge while at the same time holding on with at least one hand. He found himself wondering: Then what? Sung-min's hand-sewn Loake shoes were long since soaked through and ruined, but the question now was how far he would get on the slippery leather soles on the rugged, snow-covered terrain on the other side of the river.

Sung-min had crouched down in front of Kasparov, rubbed both hands together and looked into the old dog's tired eyes.

"If you can, then so can I," he had said.

Kasparov had whimpered and squirmed as Sung-min picked him up and carried him towards their wet fate, but somehow or other they had managed to get across.

And now, after twenty minutes of sliding about, their path was blocked by this rock face. Or was it? He followed the tracks that led to the side of the cliff, and there he saw a worn, slippery rope that was tied to a tree trunk farther up the almost vertical surface. Then he spotted that the rope carried on through the trees, and that there were some steps cut into the ground to make a path. But he wouldn't be able to climb the rope and carry Kasparov at the same time.

"Sorry, my friend, this is bound to hurt," Sung-min said, then knelt down, put Kasparov's front legs around his neck, turned and strapped the dog's legs around him tightly with his belt.

"If we don't see anything up there, we'll go back," he said. "I promise."

Sung-min grabbed the rope and braced his feet. Kasparov howled as he hung helplessly round his owner's neck like a rucksack, his back legs scratching and scrabbling at the jacket of Sung-min's suit.

It went quicker than Sung-min expected, and suddenly they were standing at the top of the cliff, where the forest carried on in front of them.

There was a red cabin twenty metres away.

Sung-min freed Kasparov, but instead of following the trail that led straight to the cabin, the dog shrank between his owner's legs, whimpering and whining.

"There now, there's nothing to be scared of," Sung-min said. "Finne's dead."

Sung-min spotted animal tracks—large tracks, at that. Could

that be what Kasparov was reacting to? He took a step towards the cabin. He felt the wire against his leg, but it was too late, and he knew he'd walked into a trap. There was a hissing sound, and he had time to see a flash of light from the object filled with explosive that flew up in front of him. He closed his eyes instinctively. When he opened them again, he had to lean his head back to see the object as it rose up into the sky, leaving a thin trail of smoke behind it. Then there was a damp *kerblam* as the rocket exploded, and even though it was daylight he saw the shower of yellow, blue and red, like a miniature Big Bang.

Someone had evidently wanted to be warned if anything was approaching. Possibly also to scare something off. He could feel Kasparov trembling against his leg.

"It's only a firework," he said, patting the dog. "But thanks for the warning, my friend."

Sung-min walked over to the wooden terrace in front of the cabin.

Kasparov had plucked up courage again and ran past him, up to the door.

Sung-min saw from the splintered door frame beside the lock that he wasn't going to have to break in, that job had already been done for him.

He pushed the door open and stepped inside.

He noted at once that the cabin had no electricity or water. There were ropes hanging from hooks on the walls, possibly strung up there to stop mice eating them.

But there was food on the bench by the west-facing window.

Bread. Cheese. And a knife.

Not like the short, all-purpose blade with the brown handle he had found when they searched Finne's body. This one had a blade that he estimated to be just under fifteen centimetres long. Sung-min's heart started to beat harder, more happily, almost like when he had seen Alexandra Sturdza walk into Statholdergaarden.

"You know what, Kasparov?" he whispered as he looked along the oak handle and horn collar. "I think winter really is almost over."

Because there was no doubt. This was a Tojiro kitchen knife. This was the knife.

53

"What can I get you?" the white-clad bartender asked.

Harry let his eyes roam along the bottles of aquavit and whisky on the shelves behind him before settling once again on the silent television screen. He was the only person in the bar, and it was oddly quiet. Quiet for Gardermoen Airport, anyway. A sleep-inducing voice was making an announcement at one of the gates in the distance, and a pair of hard shoes was clicking on the floor. It was the sound of an airport that would soon be closing down for the night. But there were still several options. He had arrived on the flight from Lakselv, via Tromsø, an hour ago, and with only his hand luggage he had walked to the transit area instead of the arrivals hall. Harry squinted at the large screen of departures hanging next to the bar. The options were Berlin, Paris, Bangkok, Milan, Barcelona or Lisbon. There was enough time, and the SAS ticket desk was still open.

He looked back at the bartender, who was waiting for his order.

"Since you ask, I'd quite like some volume," Harry said, pointing towards the television, where Katrine Bratt and the Head of Information, Kedzierski, a man with a head of thick, curly hair, were sitting behind the desk in the Parole Hall, the usual venue for press conferences, on the fourth floor of Police Headquarters. Below them ran the single, repeated line of text: *Murder suspect Svein Finne shot by unknown sniper in Smestad.*

"Sorry," the bartender said. "All televisions in the airport have to be silent."

"There's nobody here except us."

"Those are the rules."

"Five minutes, just this item. I'll give you a hundred kroner."

"And I can't accept bribes."

"Mm. It wouldn't be a bribe if I ordered a Jim Beam, then gave you a tip if I thought I'd received particularly good service?"

The bartender smiled briefly. Looked at Harry more closely. "Aren't you that author?"

Harry shook his head.

"I don't read, but my mum likes you. Can I have a selfie?"

Harry nodded towards the screen.

"OK," the bartender said, leaning over the counter with his phone in his hand and snapping a selfie of the pair of them before pressing the remote. The television rose a few cautious decibels and Harry leaned forward to hear better.

Katrine Bratt's face seemed to glow every time a flash went off. She was listening intently to a question from the floor that the microphone couldn't pick up. Her voice was clear and firm when she answered the reporter.

"I can't go into detail, only repeat that in the process of investigating the murder of Svein Finne earlier today, Oslo Police District has found compelling evidence that Finne was responsible for the murder of Rakel Fauke. The murder weapon has been found in Svein Finne's hideout. And Finne's lawyer has told the police that Finne told him he killed Rakel Fauke and afterwards planted evidence to frame Harry Hole. Yes?" Katrine pointed to someone in the room.

Harry recognised the voice of Mona Daa, *VG*'s crime reporter. "Shouldn't Winter be here to explain how he and Kripos were so thoroughly taken in by Finne?"

Katrine leaned towards the forest of microphones. "Winter will have to answer that when Kripos hold their own press conference. We at Oslo Police District will be sending what we know about Finne's connection to the Rakel Fauke case to Winter, and we're here primarily to account for Finne's murder, seeing as that case is solely our responsibility."

"Do you have any comment on Winter's handling of the case?" Daa went on. "He and Kripos have gone public with allegations of murder against an innocent and deceased police officer who worked here in the Crime Squad Unit."

Harry could see Katrine stop herself just as she was about to speak. Swallow. Compose herself. Then she said: "I and Oslo Police District aren't here to criticise Kripos. On the contrary, one of Kripos's detectives, Sung-min Larsen, has been instrumental in what appears to be our successful identification of Rakel Fauke's killer. One last question. Yes?"

"*Dagbladet.* You say you haven't identified a suspect for Finne's murder. We have sources who've told us he had been threatened by men he was in prison with who have since been released. Is that something the police are looking into?"

"Yes," Katrine said, and looked at the Head of Information.

"Well, thanks very much for coming," Kedzierski said. "We don't have another press conference planned, but we'll . . ."

Harry signalled to the bartender that he'd heard enough.

He saw Katrine stand up. Presumably she would be going home now. Someone would have been watching Gert for her. The child who had lain there in the baby carrier, smiling, just awake, peering up at Harry as he carried him through the city streets. He had rung the buzzer for Katrine's flat, felt something around his forefinger and looked down. The tiny, pale baby fingers looked like they were clutching a baseball bat. Those intense blue eyes looked like they were commanding him not to go, not to leave him like this, not here. Telling Harry that he owed him a father now. And when Harry had stood in the darkness of one of the doorways on the other side of the street and watched Katrine come out, he had been on the verge of stepping forward into the light. And telling her everything. Letting her make the decision for herself, for them both. For all three of them.

Harry straightened up again on the bar stool.

He saw that the bartender had placed a glass containing something brown next to him on the bar. Harry studied it. *Just one glass.* He knew it was the voice he mustn't listen to talking. Saying: *Come on, you deserve a little celebration!*

No.

No? OK, not to celebrate, but to show respect to the dead, to drink a toast in their memory, you heartless, dishonourable bastard.

Harry knew that if he entered into a discussion with that voice, he would lose.

He looked at the departure board. At the glass. Katrine was on her way home. He could walk out of here, get in a taxi. Ring her doorbell again. Wait in the light this time. Rise from the dead. Why not? He could hardly hide forever. And now that he was no longer a suspect, why should he? A thought struck him. In the car, under the ice in the river, there had been something there. But it had slipped away from him. The question was: What did he have to offer Katrine and Gert? Would the truth and his presence do them more damage than good? God knows. God knows if he had invented these dilemmas to give himself an excuse to leave. He thought of those small fingers wrapped around his. That commanding stare. His thoughts were interrupted when he felt his phone ring. He took it out and looked at it.

"It's Kaja." Her voice still sounded close. Perhaps the Pacific wasn't so far away after all.

"Hi. How are you getting on?"

"It's been crazy. I've only just woken up, I slept for fourteen hours solid. I'm standing outside the tent, on the beach. The sun's just coming up. It looks like a red balloon being slowly inflated, and sometime soon it might just pull free of the horizon and take off."

"Mm." Harry looked at the glass.

"How about you? How are you coping with waking up?"

"Being asleep was easier."

"It's going to be tough, the grieving process you're setting out on. And now that you've lost Bjørn too. Have you got people around you who can . . ."

"God, yes."

"No, you haven't, Harry."

He didn't know if she could sense him smiling. "I just need someone to make some decisions," he said.

"Is that why you called?"

"No. I called to say I'd put your key back. Thanks for letting me stay."

"Letting you stay . . ." she repeated. Then sighed. "The earthquake's wrecked a lot of what few buildings there were, but it's incredibly beautiful here, Harry. Beautiful and wrecked. Beautiful and wrecked, get it?"

"Get what?"

"I like beautiful and wrecked. Like you. And I'm a bit wrecked myself."

Harry guessed where this was going.

"Can't you get a flight out here, Harry?"

"To a Pacific island that's just been wiped out by an earthquake?"

"To Auckland in New Zealand. We'll be coordinating the international effort from there, and they've put me in charge of security. I'm setting off on a transport plane this afternoon."

Harry looked at the departure board. Bangkok. Maybe there were still direct flights from there to Auckland.

"Let me think about it, Kaja."

"Great. How long do you think—"

"One minute. Then I'll call you back, OK?"

"*One* minute?" She sounded happy. "OK, I can just about cope with that."

They ended the call.

He still hadn't touched the glass in front of him.

He could disappear. Sink down into the darkness. And then he caught it again, the thought that kept escaping him, from when he was in the car under the ice. It had been cold. Frightening. And lonely. But something else too. It had been quiet. So incredibly peaceful.

He looked at the departure board again.

Places a man could disappear.

From Bangkok he could go to Hong Kong. He still had connections there, he could probably get a job without too much difficulty, maybe even something legitimate. Or he could head off in the other direction. South America. Mexico City. Caracas. Really disappear.

Harry rubbed the back of his neck. The ticket desk closed in six minutes.

Katrine and Gert. Or Kaja and Auckland. Jim Beam and Oslo. Sober in Hong Kong. Or Caracas.

Harry felt in his pocket and pulled out the small, blue-grey lump of metal. Looked at the dots on its sides. Took a deep breath, cupped his hands, shook the dice. Rolled it along the counter.

A NOTE ABOUT THE AUTHOR

Jo Nesbø is a musician, songwriter, economist, as well as a writer. His Harry Hole novels include *The Redeemer, The Snowman, The Leopard* and *Phantom,* and he is also the author of several stand-alone novels and the Doctor Proctor series of children's books. He is the recipient of numerous awards including the Glass Key for best Nordic crime novel.

A NOTE ON THE TYPE

This book was set in Janson, a typeface long thought to have been made by the Dutchman Anton Janson. However, it has been conclusively demonstrated that these types are actually the work of Nicholas Kis (1650–1702), a Hungarian, who most probably learned his trade from the master Dutch typefounder Dirk Voskens.

Typeset by North Market Street Graphics,
Lancaster, Pennsylvania

Printed and bound by Berryville Graphics,
Berryville, Virginia